Cleopatra Victorious

Helen R. Davis

Savant Books and Publications
Honolulu, HI, USA
2019

Published in the USA by Savant Books and Publications
2630 Kapiolani Blvd #1601
Honolulu, HI 96826
http://www.savantbooksandpublications.com

Printed in the USA

Edited by Daniel S. Janik
Cover by Daniel S. Janik

Copyright 2018 Helen R. Davis. All rights reserved. No part of this work
may be reproduced without the prior written permission of the author.

13 digit ISBN: 9780999463338

All names, characters, places and incidents are fictitious or used
fictitiously. Any resemblance to actual persons, living or dead, and any
places or events is purely coincidental.

First Edition: January 2019
Library of Congress Control Number: 2018967940

Dedication

To Frederic, my harbinger.

Acknowledgements

I wish to acknowledge Thomas Legeberger, my guide on an amazing 14-day tour of Israel taken to field research this book. Although we did not enter Egypt, it was a spectacular feeling to look to my left and know Cleopatra's Egypt was just beyond the horizon from the Taba border crossing. Israel was exactly as I imagined. I plan to return to do further field research for the third book in my Cleopatra series, tentatively entitled "Cleopatra Magnifica." I also wish to thank my tour guides for organizing a tour that was fun, educational, and spiritual all in one. Finally, both last and first but in no way least, I wish to thank the King of Kings, who, but for reasons of His own, this alternative history might have been history.

Foreword

It is my honor and privilege to serve as editor for Helen R. Davis' alternative history of the life of Cleopatra, following the impact she and Marc Antony, had they lived and the power-mad Octavian died, might have had on an otherwise largely Roman world. This second book in the series takes up immediately after their victory rather than defeat at Actium and follows what might have been the couple's life as they plotted and strived to create a single Egyptian-Roman Empire. In the richly detailed discourse, one gets to further know both the actual and potential Cleopatra of history. Antony, sometimes portrayed historically as a roguish, alcoholic, devil-may-care, has the opportunity to develop further as a husband, father and world leader, revealing another side that might actually have been, to some extent, also historically accurate.

Much of the work explores the fictional, future relationship between Cleopatra and Antony's youngest son, Philadelphos, once again, in the process, revealing aspects of the Egyptian Pharaoh Queen and Roman Imperator lost over time. History, it is said, is written by the victor. Making Antony and Cleopatra victorious against Octavian allows one to explore more fully the characters of the historically tragic couple.

In this second book in Davis' Cleopatra series, the stage is set for the third book in which Antony and Cleopatra's next generation experience the coming of the Messiah and Christianity, posing the intriguing question, "What would Christianity have been like had it developed in a decidedly different cultural mileau, namely an Egyptian-Roman Empire?

- Daniel S. Janik

Prologue

It is with aged fingers but clarity of mind that I continue this, my memoirs. Whether future generations will read it, or even remember my name is known only to the great Goddess, Isis, who in her infinite wisdom refrains from sharing with us the whole of the results of our accomplishments during our mortal lifetime. But this I do know: The Goddess, having appeared to me in her many guises repeatedly throughout my life, whatever my fate, another even more glorious life awaits me when, at last, my spirit returns to her outstretched arms.

This memoir, then, is not so much about my life or Antony's, but of the fate of the world after our victory at Actium.

- Cleopatra VII Philopater, Queen of Egypt

Helen R. Davis

Chapter One

The Fate of Octavian, Who Thought to Call Himself Caesar Augustus
37 B.C.
Year 15 of Cleopatra's Reign
The Underworld

Octavian stumbled out of a small grey tent in the center of a seemingly limitless, dry, gray land. Bruised and aching, he rubbed his tired eyes, thanking the gods that he had somehow survived the sinking of his flagship and was, at least, alive. The air was still and cold—the kind of cold that penetrated the marrow of the bones. Shaking the blood and salt water off his golden armor and soiled purple cape, he knelt and began searching the hard dirt for his sword. He felt naked without it.

Fumbling about as if he were blind—which he was definitely not—his hand touched what appeared to be a rectangular shield, it's design unfamiliar. On closer examination, the shield bore two circular devices that blazed like gems in the afternoon sun: One was blue, like a Mediterranean-blue sapphire, the other deep red, like a blood ruby. Curious, Octavian touched the nearer blue one and a mirage-like image appeared before him from out of the shimmering desert air. It was that of his rival, Marcus Antonius, in silver dress armor, white tunic and royal cape—a scarlet *paludamentum*—draped over his shoulders, billowing behind him, riding along the *Via Sacra*, the main street of Rome, in a triumphal chariot.

"IO TRIUMPHE!" thousands of Romans were shouting on either side of the street, tossing flowers high in the air before him. "Hail, Triumphant God!" Immediately behind his chariot was a second chariot, carrying Cleopatra, looking to Octavian like the Egyptian harlot he had always regarded her. Next to her, in the place of honor, stood her and Caesar's bastard son, Caesarion, dressed in gold as the boy pharaoh, Tutankhamen. Slightly behind and to either side of mother and child were Cleopatra's two maids and the twins she had borne Antony. Octavian shook his head trying to clear his fuzzy mind, but couldn't recall their names. Instead, Octavian stood, fists clenched at his sides and seethed. This victory procession should have been his! What cruel trick of fate...?

Octavian slammed his fist against the red circle next to the blue one on the shield and the apparition disappeared, replaced by what appeared to be his own rightful triumph seven or eight years later. This time there was no trace of the usurpers. Instead, a wooden statue of the Egyptian witch, Cleopatra, with real serpents coiling and hissing around her arms was being paraded through the backstreets of Rome, where commoners were tossing rotted vegetables and hurtling expletives at the statue.

Now this is more like it, Octavian snickered with joy, watching the twins weighted in golden chains being dragged behind the statue, followed by a small boy, dirty and barely clothed, in a golden cage. While Octavian gloated, the mirage abruptly switched back to that of Antony and Cleopatra, and Octavian realized to his horror that the "twins" were, in fact, his own stepson, Tiberius, and his wife, Livia, with his sweet, proud sister Octavia following in the cage. Octavian gritted his teeth and raised a fist to strike the shield, and, as he did, he heard the voice of a woman:

"If you do that, you will never see that scene again," the voice warned.

"Who's there?" Octavian demanded, seeing no one anywhere about him.

"I am Proserpina, queen of Pluto and the Underworld. I bring you greetings from my husband," said the woman, forming out of mist. She was pale as death and had black roses braided into her snow-white hair. She wore a black tunic that touched the ground. Octavian, looking at the endless bleakness surrounding him, suddenly realized he was in Tartarus, the Underworld, and it was winter, for Proserpina joined her husband as his bride only during wintertime. Octavian shuddered, unable to discern whether it was from the cold of winter, the vision of the queen of the dead standing before him, or at the realization of his own death.

"Why does Pluto not speak directly to me?" Octavian demanded.

Proserpina laughed coldly. "Your punishment here is two-fold: First and foremost, you are to bear witness to Antony's triumph and the reign of Antony and Cleopatra for the rest of eternity. Second, you are to constantly prostrate yourself not before the god, my husband, Pluto, but before me, again for eternity."

"But you're a woman!" Octavian yelled angrily.

Proserpina laughed at the delicious irony. "And a goddess. You were fool enough to imagine yourself above the gods. Do not think for a moment that we don't notice such perversion," Proserpina stated, handing Octavian a withered, black pomegranate.

"What is this?" Octavian demanded, shaking with disgust.

"This is the food of the underworld. You must be famished. Dying makes one so very…hungry," Proserpina purred.

Octavian, suddenly noticing his belly was ravishing with hunger, accepted the black pomegranate and cut it with a knife—the only weapon he was apparently permitted here, and indulged, gulping down the entire retched-appearing fruit greedily. As he finished, he heard the voice of Pluto, Proserpina's husband, resonate about him.

"Well done, wife. Now that excuse for man can never leave Tartarus."

"Show yourself!" Octavian demanded, angrier than ever. But the god of the dead did not.

Instead, Proserpina laughed again. "And one final punishment: The goddesses can speak to you and show you their beauty at your command, but never again will you be permitted to touch any female—goddess or mortal! Come now, Pluto. I believe it will soon be time for us to welcome Octavian's family to this abode."

With her final pronouncement, Proserpina vanished and Octavian was once again alone.

Chapter Two

Cleopatra Victorious
37 B.C.
Year 15 of Cleopatra's Reign
The Beach at Actium

I awoke in my military headquarters' tent in on the beach in Actium. I was by myself, although guarded by men loyal to Antony and me outside. Antony had shared my bed in the night, but now he was nowhere to be found. Still, his cape lay at the bedside. I reached for and held the cape of my beloved close to me, inhaling his scent. Antony had been injured in battle. He had suffered a cut to his knee—painful, but not lethal. I had been deeply frightened when I heard the first reports of the battle, just as I had when I had seen my former husband, Gaius Julius Caesar, swimming for his life in a flaming sea ten years ago. Both Antony and I were, in fact, blessed by the gods to be alive.

Antony and I had won the Battle of Actium; Octavian was dead.

We had promised each other to celebrate together that night with the same wine he had given me at the Battle of Philippi five years ago. We had shared the wine back then in celebration of our love; this time, though barely enough remained for a half-glass each, we celebrated our victory and the thrill of being alive to celebrate it together.

"Octavian is dead," I said in disbelief to Antony as he and I reclined on indigo cushions in the dimly lit tent, the burning oil lamps the only source of warmth this winter night. Antony had looked exhausted.

"Yes," Antony said as he poured the last drops of the wine into our goblets. He did not sound as joyous as I felt.

"What's wrong?" I asked.

"He *is* dead. I saw his ship sink. But his body has not yet been found," Antony said glumly, staring into the distance.

I pursed my lips in concern. I had faced a similar situation ten years ago when my first co-ruler, my younger half-brother, Pharaoh Ptolemy XIII Theos Philopator, had drowned in the Nile, weighted down by his golden armor after attempting to assassinate me. He had been the son of the Syrian Princess, Roxane, who my father, Pharaoh Ptolemy XII Neos Dionysos, had married after the death of my mother, whom he had continued to love. Roxane had done nothing to dispel the disrespect towards my father shown by the Egyptian people, his few admirers calling him Auletes, the flute player, his many detractors calling him Nothos, the bastard, and a narcissistic, self-indulgent drunk. Such are the vicissitudes of power, particularly among the Ptolemies.

My then husband, Julius Caesar, had quickly retrieved the lad's body and showed it to the Egyptian people along with his toy soldier army, to prove to them that, unlike Osiris, the consort of Isis, my brother had not risen from the dead. My youngest brother, Ptolemy XIV Theos Philopater, later faced a similar fate when he secretly allied himself with Arsinoë, my sister, to wrest control of Egypt from my hands. Julius Caesar's death, on the other hand, had been witnessed only by me and those in my inner circle, and this proved problematic. People demand to know the status and nature of those by whom they are being governed; otherwise, rumors can prove more powerful than legions of soldiers.

"What exactly happened?" I asked. Isis had granted me a vision of Octavian drowning, and one of Antony's commanders had recounted the tidal wave that had engulfed Octavian's ship after Octavian had prematurely claimed victory. Antony finished the story: Mars, he said, being my current husband's patron god, could not ignore Octavian's boast, and Isis, my patron goddess, could not ignore Octavian's subsequent oath to "wipe the abomination Cleopatra" from human memory.

The mast of Octavian's ship had been shattered in a flash of thunderous lightening, the pieces being directed at the surprised young man. Octavian, seeing his death, turned to run, but too late. Afterward, Octavian's flagship and all aboard were sucked beneath the turbulent waves, leaving no claimant other than my son, Caesarion, to the dictatorship of Rome.

There was a loud kick on the door. Antony's slave, Eros entered. With him came Cicero Minor, a close friend of Antony and mine. The son of Cicero Major, who, though a rival of Caesar's, being an honorable soldier, had become a strong supporter of Antony and myself following Caesar's untimely assassination. Cicero Minor's father was eventually beheaded in the purge after Julius Caesar's death. It was rumored that Fulvia, Antony's third wife, had stuck a silver pin through his lifeless tongue for the damage he had done to Caesar through his speeches. Cicero Minor had inherited his father's ability with words. When he spoke publicly, they seemed to fly from him like darts directly at the heart of their target. He had also inherited his father's genteel handsomeness.

"Greetings, Antony. Greetings, Queen Cleopatra," Cicero Minor said, bowing slightly. Antony welcomed his friend warmly while Eros procured a chair for him to sit and join us in our celebration.

11

"I bear both good and bad news," Cicero Minor began as he partook of some honey cakes I offered him. They were a Jewish delicacy I had come to particularly enjoy.

"The bad news first," Antony demanded.

"Actually, two items of bad news: The first, Antony, is that your sons by your third wife, Fulvia, are both dead. The more bad news is that there were survivors from Octavian's ship." Cicero Minor paused a moment to let the two news items fully sink in. "The good news is singular: Octavian was not among the survivors. We later found his body, mutilated, floating among the flotsam and jetsam."

"Show us the body!" Antony commanded. "I must see it, as must the people of Egypt and Rome." Cicero Minor signaled with a finger and a Roman and an Egyptian soldier together carried in Octavian's body in a sling. Upon seeing the shape of a body wrapped in linen, my mind raced back to the day of the assassination of my first husband, Julius Caesar, seven years ago. He had been brought to me wrapped in a blood-stained linen garment on a blood-drenched cot. I instantly remembered his feeble voice calling out my name and that of his legal Roman wife, Calpurnia, and I found myself reliving that day again. Thankfully, Octavian could call for no one. Laying the bloated body on the floor before us I could see it had been crushed almost beyond recognition. Even so, Antony and I agreed with sighs of relief that the body was Octavian's.

"Display his body to the soldiers and people, then create for him a funeral pyre, for he was the nephew of Caesar," Antony said quietly. I understood exactly what my Antony was doing: He was honoring his opponent as Julius Caesar's *legal* but not direct blood relative. In doing so, Antony was displaying magnanimity, strength and mercy, the very attributes that had attracted me to him after Caesar's death. The very attributes of a Caesar. The Roman soldier saluted Antony, but the Egyptian soldier remained at attention.

"Do it," I iterated in agreement.

The Egyptian soldier saluted, and the two turned to carry out the body and their orders.

"It will be done, *Domino*," Eros reassured both Antony and me. Eros was a young boy, very handsome, with a head of curls like his master. Before going into battle, Antony told me that Eros had declared he would fall on a sword should his master lose. Happily, neither Eros nor I would have to honor that vow.

After reciting additional, less important post-battle news, Cicero Minor asked to speak to me in private.

"But let me stay," Antony replied in earnest. "This is *our* victory celebration!"

"With all due respect, Great Antony, it is urgent I speak to the Queen of Egypt alone," Cicero Minor said with careful deference, awaiting Antony's approval.

Antony locked eyes with me, then reluctantly nodded his approval, knowing that Cicero Minor, having addressed me "Queen of Egypt," was carrying important information about Egypt.

Cicero Minor and I rose, walking outside the tent together, where a full moon bathed us in iridescence.

"Speak," I said.

"Queen Cleopatra, although Antony has won over Octavian, should you return with him to Rome as I suspect you will be inclined to do, you will not be welcomed." From his tone, I knew this was an understatement.

"I was afraid of that," I answered honestly. "Your speeches have done much there to improve my reputation, but more yet remains to be

13

done." Prior to Antony's victory, Cicero Minor had made it a point to speak publicly in Antony's favor. Many had been won over to my husband's side, but that did not necessarily mean that they had become any more a supporter of Cleopatra than before. Not yet.

"As is always the case," replied Cicero Minor. "Also, there is the problem of that troublesome King Herod of Judea, a province arguably Roman or Egyptian depending on your point of view these days, whose allegiance continues to change with the wind. Before the battle, he publicly allied himself with Octavian. Now that you and Antony are victorious, he allies himself with you. Where his allegiance will ultimately, if ever settle remains to be seen. But whether it be with Antony and Rome, you and Egypt, or both, he will be trouble," Cicero Minor declared.

"I have had reservations about him since first he and I met."

"Oh?" Cicero Minor asked.

"I first met him at Philippi, where he was forthright to rude. He insulted me in Hebrew," I said.

"You know Hebrew?" Cicero Minor asked in surprise.

"I do. Perhaps better than he," I replied sarcastically.

Cicero Minor smiled. "I'm impressed but not surprised. Your gift of tongues is well known. In any case, having identified Herod as a problem, let us put him aside for the moment and return to the matter of improving your reputation in Rome. Now that the war is ended, I can begin speaking specifically on your behalf. However, there is something crucial I need suggest. Octavian may be dead, but his wife, Livia, still lives. She is a poisoner of minds and bodies, and a master of disguise. You must persuade Antony to put her to death immediately. If you do not, she will seek to destroy you."

"I understand," I said, with more calmness then I felt, as I despised

Livia with every fiber of my being. She had attempted to assassinate me with a poisoned dagger on my way to the Temple of Venus after Caesar's death, and also attempted to poison Marcus Aurelius Lepidus, who commanded Rome's City legions, in both instances to help Octavian consolidate power. This was a woman condemned, whose vengeance while alive would know no bounds.

Pondering, an idea occurred to me.

"Would justice not best be served if Livia died by drinking one of her own poisons after being marched through the triumph?" I suggested.

"Indeed. I can think of no better punishment for her," Cicero Minor agreed, and our private discussion that evening ended.

Chapter Three

Future World
Winter 37 B.C.
Year 15 of Cleopatra's Reign
Cleopatra's Palace in Alexandria

Although Antony and I were the victors at Actium, much had to be done to restabilize our empires. At Cicero Minor's insistence, Antony agreed I should sail to Egypt for now, and rejoin him in Rome for a spring triumph.

"Why must we part so soon after our victory?" I teased Antony, playing as if Cicero Minor and I had never broached the subject, as, the next morning Antony and I feasted on honey cakes and wine.

"Because, my love, Egypt is *your* country. You have fought long and hard to preserve it and the Ptolemaic Dynasty. Now, with Octavian gone, your goal is in sight. As long as I live, Rome and Egypt shall remain allies. But you need to return to Egypt to re-secure your position so that we can proceed with our alliance."

Antony was playing gentleman to my coquette and spared me mention of my current reputation in Rome.

"But I don't want to leave you. I *love* you," I said, pouting like a child at his lecturing.

"More than you did Caesar?" Antony asked.

My ears perked, hearing both playfulness and, I thought, a thread of jealousy in his voice. "Well...I greatly love and appreciate what I have with you, but I still cherish the past," I replied, suddenly wanting to end the *tête à tête* I'd begun in jest.

"Good," Antony replied. "It's important to cherish and remember the past, Cleopatra, but we cannot afford to live in it. On a more practical note, you are not my wife by Roman law. As such, it would be improper for us to appear together in Rome just now."

"True," I replied. "But..."

"When I have solidified my power, I will marry you in Rome," Antony said.

"By all the Gods, I have waited long to hear those words! Embrace me!" I cried in earnest.

Antony held me close and, thus entwined, we kissed long and deep.

"Now go back to Egypt as the Queen I adore!" Antony said with a wink when we finally disengaged.

Over the next week, I gathered my naval forces and prepared for the trip. I had all the exterior wood of my flagship refurbished and covered with gold leaf to show me victorious and had several translucent scarlet chitons as well as gold hair and neck jewelry inlaid with lapis and precious diamonds made for my return. Before I left, Antony gave me a gift of two snake bracelets, one of pure white pearls the other of mixed green emeralds, both with ruby eyes. After a lengthy but uneventful sea voyage, my fleet entered the harbor at Alexandria.

As I stepped in my victory regalia from my flagship onto the gangway, I was greeted by a shower of flowers accompanied by hails and cheers which continued all the way through the city to my open-air, multistoried seaside palace, filled with centuries of the accumulated wealth of the Ptolemies. I walked up the marble steps, passed quickly through the rows of rose-colored Greek columns, and entered the receiving room replete with lapis mosaics depicting the myths and legends of Macedonia. As custom dictated, I knelt briefly before the many flaming torches lit to Nike, the goddess of victory, then walked humbly past the massive statue of Isis that dominated the far wall, passing into the throne room to the dais where my gold-inlaid throne with its purple seat awaited. Seating myself on the throne of Egypt, it felt good to be back.

After addressing only the most urgent matters of state, I rose and entered my adjoining private chambers, where my great bed awaited. Covered in crisp, white Egyptian linen decorated with purple silk pillows and oversheets from Persia, it was like balm for my body after the rigors of my long sea voyage. Alexandria, being by the sea, experienced mild weather, in contrast to the oppressively hot summers and the bone-chilling cold of winters in Rome. In each corner a lamp burned brightly over an open-flamed heating tripod.

The marble floors felt cool and refreshing against my tired feet, after the weeks I'd spent in a military tent. As I made my way to my bed, I walked over mosaics depicting the gods of Egypt, the glories of Greece and, since my marriage to Julius Caesar, the splendors of Rome. Halfway across the bedchamber, my longstanding Egyptian servant, Charmion, and my personal attendant and friend, Iras, ran to greet me.

Charmion was a Nubian who had served me since birth. A devoted servant to my mother, Cleopatra V, she had been dismissed by my father in Ephesus after a misunderstanding, only to be reunited with me and forgiven. While she was gone, the buxom blonde, Iras, had acted as her replacement. Formerly a slave, I had freed Iras in repayment for her services, but she remained in my service. The two greeted me as if we were all childhood friends, then immediately set to catching me up on palace gossip and intrigue.

"Cleopatra, have you heard about Panhesy and his lover Pawaro?" Charmion asked while hugging me excitedly. Iras, unable to hold back her curiosity, ventured, "What did you do at Actium? Did you, as they are saying, ride into battle like the goddess Artemis?"

"Charmion. Iras. I am delighted to be home, but I am too tired to hear or talk about anything at this time," I replied, sighing with fatigue.

My two ladies looked at each other, disappointed, but hushed.

Seeing their disappointment, I offered, "I really am tired. Let us talk first thing tomorrow," and loosed myself from their hugs, then flung myself onto my bed—my own familiar bed—falling asleep the moment my head touched the pillow.

Next morning, I was awakened not by Charmion or Iras, but by my three wonderful children. The first, Selene, ran without reserve to my bed and grasped me in her arms. She was now two years old. When I stood, she clutched at my legs, and I wrapped the two of us in a warm, red, woolen chiton. Red was the color of victory in Egypt—I had not chosen this color in which to be seen by accident.

Scooping Selene into my arms, she immediately clutched my neck and squealed with delight. Her hair was midnight black, woven into plaits on either side of her face. She was wearing a thin, sky-blue chiton covered by a green woolen cloak.

"Selene, guess what? We will be going to Rome soon!" I exclaimed.

In the meantime, Charmion entered, stating obsequiously, "My lady, I can't help but notice that you are dressed in red. You must tell us about the victory the gods granted you."

"Of course. And a glorious victory it was," I replied, smiling, ready to recount my, and by my participation, Egypt's part in the battle.

Iras followed on Charmion's heels. "Thank Isis! Last night, when you fell like a stone onto your bed, I feared something untoward had happened!" Iras said. It was then, I looked just past her and saw Caesarion. He was my eldest, my son by my first husband, Julius Caesar.

"Mother," he said shyly from the entrance to my bedroom. "I heard that you rode in armor at Antony's side to face Octavian, and that you single handedly slew Octavian! Is it true?" His eyes were wide with eagerness and wonder. Clearly he was imagining in his mind's eye what he was recounting. Without waiting for my reply, he continued, "The people are calling you the Royal Egyptian Amazon."

I laughed at his grossly exaggerated statements, knowing that the commoners of Egypt, being who and what they were, would even now likely be telling the same or even greater embellished stories among themselves, stories that, if I didn't intervene, would eventually become history.

"Well, I did wear armor. That is true," I conceded. "But I didn't ride at Antony's side or slay Octavian. And I am certainly no Amazon!" I said, although I allowed myself the enjoyment of being hailed as the one who had rid the world of Octavian.

"Mother. Is all the rest of what's being said true?" Caesarion asked, struggling to get me to sit and allow him up onto my lap.

"I don't doubt that some, at least, is true. Egypt is safe and Octavian dead," I said. While I talked, Helios entered the room and ran up to me, cuddling against my legs, bursting into tears as he did so. Caesarion smiled.

"Mother, I want to be Pharaoh instead of Helios," Caesarion stated. "Selene is already acting like a queen, but Helios still acts like a big baby."

"Caesarion, Helios *is* a baby," I said. At barely two years of age, I still considered him my baby.

"And I'm your oldest!" Caesarion said, revisiting his claim. "Doesn't that mean I get to be King-Pharaoh of Egypt?"

I hesitated at that. I had wanted Caesarion to be my successor, yes, but with the rapid shifts in politics that were going on, this was in question. I had two sons now, and a daughter. If I wanted to solidify my position in Egypt and at the same time my link with Rome, Caesarion, being my son with Julius Caesar, would, indeed, be a perfect choice. Helios, however, was my son by Antony and as Antony and I weren't formally married by either Egyptian or Roman custom, he would be severely disadvantaged in Rome. Even being the victor of Actium, Antony was still not as well thought of as Caesar.

"Caesarion," I concluded. "You are indeed the heir of Cleopatra. That will not change. But whether you will rule Egypt or Rome remains to be seen," I stated, and with that, began to turn my thoughts to the upcoming morning's meeting about the governing of Egypt now that I was back.

"Caesarion, can you please watch over your brother and sister while I attend an important meeting? I'm sorry, but you cannot come with me to this particular meeting."

Caesarion looked disappointed. He was in that awkward place between boy and man. He still enjoyed playing, yet more and more wanted to be treated as an adult.

"Fine," he said with a pout.

"Men don't pout," I told him, and Caesarion changed his expression.

"I understand, Mother. But they still act like babies and babies are boring," Caesarion stated with finality.

"Surely you can find something to play with them," I suggested. "Why don't you come up with a clever game using Helios' animals and Selene's dolls? Are you not the bright son of the Great Caesar?"

"All right. I can do that. I like Helios' toy lion the best," Caesarion acceded.

Having for the moment solved my maternal problems, I felt free to turn my attentions to governing the land.

I began my governing duties by discussing with my advisors how best to restabilize Egypt, updating my orders as I received word from Antony on his evolving situation in Rome.

Things there were going well. Lepidus, a supporter since the time of the Second Triumvirate and a close ally of my first husband, Julius Caesar, had recovered from a poisoning attempt by Livia. He was a handsome man with high cheekbones, a dignified nose and big ears. Following Cicero Minor's lead, he was speaking boldly in my favor, arguing that the gods were obviously smiling on Antony and my, and thereby Rome and Egypt's developing relationship. I received a copy of one of the speeches made on my behalf, in which Lepidus stated that "although a foreigner to many Romans, Cleopatra is an Egyptian Queen of Greek descent. As Helen of Troy, the wife of Virgil, who founded Rome, Cleopatra shall, as the wife of Antony, be the mother of a new and glorious Empire—one that will elevate, consummate and perfect the best of Rome, Egypt and Greece."

I smiled. Helen had been a brave woman and a competent queen, one I hoped to emulate, although I could never betray Antony as she had Melaneus.

Antony also wrote for me to bring the twins when I returned to Rome, since he had not yet met his offspring by me, and I was now being heralded by Cicero Minor as the future of the Roman Empire!

Finally, he wrote that Octavian's family had been imprisoned, and were being watched to prevent them from committing suicide. Livia's poisons had been taken from her so she could not directly commit any further surprises before she was formally put to death.

Good riddance, I thought. I was so excited by the thought of her joining her evil husband in the underworld that, without thinking, I hugged myself with joy.

"Mother, you are overjoyed?" Caesarion asked, having read Antony's letters with my assist in order to better his understanding of rulership, and to know where to edit the letters before they were read to my two younger children.

"Of course," I said. "We have just won a war, my son. One that has directed Fate in our favor."

"Yes!" Caesarion screeched, jumping about. Eventually, he calmed and to my surprise took on Caesar's demeanor. "And what now?" he asked solemnly in his father's voice.

"After settling things here, we go to Rome, of course," I replied. Standing next to me, Mardian, the Greek soldier who headed my Army and had proved time and again to be one of my most trusted friends and servants, completed my statement, adding, "To celebrate our victory and execute Octavian's family. Then the real work begins: Conquering the world!"

"I must first announce my return to Rome to my people," I said, in reply to Caesarion's wise question. "Please announce that I would speak to them."

"No need, Mother," Caesarion replied. "They await you."

It was then I noticed the growing clamor coming from outside. "Long live our great Queen, Cleopatra Soter, savior of Egypt, defeater of Octavian!" cried the large gathering of exuberant men and women. The cheers of my people have always been like honey to me. I adore ruling over subjects who love me, rather than ones who fear me, though, in truth, both were essential faces of Janus necessary to rule as large and cosmopolitan a nation as Egypt. I exchanged my red woolen cape for a translucent red silk one which I draped over a red over chiton. I added a gold and lapis sun necklace and Antony's bracelets for it was Antony's victory that meant Egypt's rebirth.

Walking regally out onto the porch, I waved and shouted, "My people! We have triumphed over Octavian, the man-child tyrant who sought Egypt as a Roman breadbasket! Egypt is free! Antony and I have won the Battle of Actium, and he and I will rule supreme, he over the Northeast and I over the Southwest! It is time to rebuild our nation, regain Egypt's lost territories and celebrate a new time of economic prosperity for all!"

I made many such promises over the next few days, pondering only much later how I would keep them.

Helen R. Davis

Chapter Four

Triumph

Spring 36 B.C.

Year 16 of Cleopatra's Reign

Rome

Winter passed slowly in an endless stream of administrative meetings, until in early spring I received the long-awaited missive from Antony summoning me back to Rome for our triumph. In the overtly officious letter, he said he had proclaimed our triumph to be held on the Ides of Martius, but I quickly replied in an equally officious letter accepting his invitation, that the month must be to Aprilus. My former husband, Julius Caesar, had been assassinated on the Ides of Maritus, and I wanted Antony and my triumph as well as our future plans to be free of past dark associations. In anticipation of my leaving, I appointed Rufio as Regent. He had been left in Egypt by Julius Caesar many years ago when Caesar had had to return to Rome. Rufio, he'd assured me, was trustworthy and would guide and protect me in his absence. Over the years, Rufio proved to be that and more. An experienced Roman military officer, he crushed several rebellions while I was away on business, always portraying me as a beloved Queen Pharaoh and, more importantly a friend of Rome, for in Rome's eyes, I was still a scheming Egyptian, and in many Egyptians' eyes, a Roman-lover.

With Egypt at peace, my journey by boat back to Rome proved as pleasant as my return from Rome to Egypt—as pleasant, at least, as a month-long sea voyage across Mare Nostrum in the spring could be. I had decked out my royal boat for this important voyage, re-inlaying it with with gold leaf, adding panels of ocean-blue lapis studded with Libyan gems, adding many bright flags so my ship, when seen pulling into Ostia, would ostentatiously display Egypt's wealth. With me I took Charmion, Iras, Mardian, Caesarion, the twins and my children's teacher, Olympos. When we arrived at the Imperial Port at Ostia – built by my former husband, Julius Caesar, to receive Egyptian grain necessary to feed the burgeoning city-state—I was greeted as close to that of an Imperial Queen as Antony could get the Romans to tolerate without inciting riots. The port was, after all, the handiwork of Rome's former Dictator, both beloved and reviled, and I was his widow, bearing with me his surviving son, Caesarion, as well as Antony and my twin sons.

"Why?" was Antony's first utterance after greeting me warmly before the crowds. "Why are you insisting on having me change the date of our triumph? To delay it just to avoid superstition, seems unlike you."

"It is not just unwise to tempt the gods, Antony," I replied. "I am thinking also from a practical viewpoint: I believed the earlier date to be *politically* unwise. Remember that in some Romans' eyes, I am still Caesar's harlot and to a few, the reason for the Senate's need to 'remove' him…"

Antony thought for a moment then acquiesced. "Unfortunately, you are correct. I shall officially announce that the triumph will be held on the Ides of Aprilus and we shall intensify our program to encourage Romans to see you differently."

I must admit that as we walked together from the royal receiving area at Ostia to our land transportation, I was surprised at both how quickly he acknowledged the urgency of the issue and the ease at which he conceded. It left me wondering if this was a lover's gift or a portent of things to come when we truly ruled the world together.

"Where should I stay?" I asked Antony, wishing I could stay with him, but knowing from our conversation that it was too soon.

"I have prepared some choices. The first is your old lodging where Caesar kept you," Antony said.

I shook my head in the negative without thinking. I didn't want to take any chance that the past might interfere with the present.

"Very well then. A country villa? I have provisioned one for you," Antony stated.

"Hmmm," I said, considering.

"Or perhaps a private villa I keep for visiting dignitaries?" Antony asked, seemingly annoyed that I hadn't immediately accepted the country alternative.

"I wish to stay in the private villa for dignitaries. We cannot make things too public," I said.

"Ah. You are right, of course," Antony replied.

I smiled and the Roman guards accompanying us smiled, though they didn't know of what Antony and I were speaking.

The dignitaries' villa was pleasant enough. I enjoyed being near water, and this one boasted many beautiful fountains and pools. It also had intricately inlaid marble floors and a decent library. After unpacking, I began preparing for the triumph by seeking out Cicero Minor and Lepidus to gauge the current mood in Rome. As always, both men were forthright, more so than either of the Romans I loved.

"I was flattered by your comparison of me to Helen of Troy, although I worry that could send the wrong connotations," I said to Lepidus.

"Helen was a survivor and one who could rebuild from nothing," Lepidus reminded me. "Trust me, it was a useful comparison and was well-received."

"I understand," I said. The Romans would not have seen Helen the way I, with my Macedonian Greek and Egyptian background, do.

"Are the streets safe for me to walk?" I asked Cicero Minor.

"No," he said bluntly. "But then, are they ever really 'safe' for anyone in Rome? In fact, you took great risk in coming here, although I would expect no less from you. The Roman people support Antony and through him they will eventually support you because we Romans always support the victor," Cicero Minor said.

I smiled to myself. For all their claims of worshiping all the gods equally, their only real god was victory. I recalled Octavian's supporters loudly expressing their undying loyalty, and how quickly that had changed when it was announced he was dead.

"More like rats always ready to abandon a sinking ship," I said, crossing my arms.

"Not a flattering allusion, but an apt one," offered Lepidus.

"Exactly, great queen," Cicero Minor said. "The rats need to be constantly reminded that their ship is not only stable, but that the captain and navigator are blessed by the gods. I would advise you not to show yourself until the triumph."

"Indeed," agreed Lepidus. "Antony had me assign a guard to you while you are here, and Cicero Minor and I will be watching for any attempts on your life at the triumph," Lepidus said, unconsciously moving his right hand to where the hilt of his short sword would be.

"I understand." I said grimly. "I will take my leave, then, and allow you two to return to your labors on my and Antony's behalves."

Martius passed, it's latter days in ever increasing preparation for the triumph. Though it had been a cold winter and a decidedly cool spring, the day of the triumph felt more like summer. I was led under heavy guard to the Via Sacra along with my children. We were dressed in simple white linen togas to emphasize before the public our purity and thereby contradict Octavian and his few remaining supporters' propaganda in which I was being portrayed as an Eastern sorceress. Ah, that. Before the Battle of Actium, Octavian had had images of me circulated throughout Rome with the head of Medusa, casting spells on Caesar, Antony and him. This was, of course, a complete fabrication. If anything, it was them who were attempting to cast their spells on me!

In the royal box, sided by Cicero Minor and Lepidus with a line of armed Roman and Egyptian soldiers standing at attention behind us, our final dress was completed in sight of the public for the triumph. Cicero Minor came up with the idea to help influence the expectant mob's opinion of me and my offspring. Cicero Minor was careful to never miss an opportunity to further us in the eyes of Romans.

My children were dressed in Roman regalia, Selene the *stola* and *palla* of an adult woman with a golden crown on her head to present her as a future queen. Caesarion was dressed to look like a virile, young, boy-Pharaoh, and Helios, a miniature Roman General compete with red cape and golden short sword. As for myself, a purple *palla* was draped over my shoulders to indicate my royal status, my head bearing the triple uraeus crown of Egypt with the three cobras to present me before the public as Queen-Pharaoh of Egypt. An ankh, symbol of the source of life, was placed around my neck, and about my wrists were placed golden bracelets depicting the image of goddess Isis.

Thus prepared, we waited to view the triumph and be viewed by the Roman mob. I had originally planned to travel aside Antony in the triumph, but Antony, Lepidus and Cicero Minor all said that would have been too dangerous. As such, I focused on the spectacle below that was about to begin while the growing crowds focused on us in the elevated royal box.

When the sun finally rose overhead, the spectacle began with Octavian's surviving men being marched in iron chains through the streets to the jeers of the crowds. As they shuffled past, they looked up at me in anger. One shouted, "There's Antony's whore!" but I ignored the insult and was secretly pleased when the mob decried the outburst and pummeled the man with stones they picked up from the street. Caesar's whore, Antony's whore, what did it matter? I was twice the consort of a Roman victor!

Next came Antony's men, resplendent in their burnished armor and red flowing capes marching together in a palpable thrump, thrump, thrump, in columns of abbreviated centuries, each century lead by brightly decorated standards topped with gilt Roman eagles! They were followed by women in white *stolas* and *pallas*, throwing rose petals in the streets. Behind these, came Livia, widow of Octavian, and Tiberius, her young stepson. As they passed below me, I thought of Tiberius, barely a boy, who would soon be dead. Everyone agreed it was not possible to let the boy live, for the seeds of revenge could not be left to sprout in the future. Yet, still, Tiberius was a child and his execution I could only understand in principle, and I held my own son, Helios, closer. What if the reverse had happened? Would my sons have been allowed to live? I needn't ask for I could see the answer in Livia's eyes.

Antony had graciously allowed Livia, though she would be publicly humiliated, to choose her garments. As such, she had dressed to diminish or at least equal me in the eyes of the mob by wearing the dark purple *palla* and *stola* of a Patrician. She even wore golden serpents twisted around her arms, the sacred symbol of Egypt. As she passed, she glared venomously up at me in spite of the heavy golden chains wrapped about her body. She seemed impervious to the physical and psychic pain the chains were meant to cause her, and lifted her head proudly, as though she, not I, were the victor. And her tactic worked. I noticed the people of Rome look upon Octavian's widow for a moment with quiet sympathy. But only for a moment. Their jeering quickly resumed. At least they were not jeering *me.*

Octavia and her husband followed, also weighted down in golden chains. I felt a bit of pity for this young woman. She was a pretty little thing, not yet out of her teens. Her dark curls perfectly framed her alabaster skin, betraying a pampered existence as well as intense emotion. I could not bear to look at her, and turned my face away, awaiting the triumphal entrance of my beloved Antony.

When he at last appeared, he was dressed as Mars, the god of war, riding in the Triumphal Chariot. My heart skipped a beat when he pulled up next to where I was and exited the Chariot shouting for all to hear, "*IO TRIUMPHE*—Hail the God of Triumph!" smiling in my direction, one arm outstretched and gave me a lover's glimpse, yet one all too brief for me. This was the man who had proven to be Julius Caesar's truest friend and now commanded Rome's heart as well as mine.

Antony returned to his chariot to resume the triumph, to have a particularly endearing scene ensue where a young boy and girl, not much older than Selene and Helios, our twins, ran up to his chariot, stepping in front of his horses. Antony reigned the skittish horses in and scooped down to accept something from the two. It was a laurel wreath, much like the one given to Caesar seven years ago when he had declared himself Caesar. The children however had woven into the wreath some early spring flowers. The triumph halted as Antony admired the gift, and, to the crowd's delight, did not punish the children for the disruption, but instead accepted their gift and placed it on his brow, stating loudly for all to hear, that the gift was a sign of the gods' approval, heralding a new era for Rome and, as Ceres, goddess of the earth had been pleased with Proserpina's return from the land of the dead, the gods were smiling upon his, and by implication, my victory and our shared future. The crowds went wild, and their joyous adulation continued throughout the rest of the triumph.

That evening, at the triumphal dinner, Antony was obligated by tradition to order the death of his living rivals, beginning with Livia Drusilla, the most recent wife of Octavian. Livia, prepared to make a dramatic exit, sat at Antony's guest table as guest of honor, although the meal placed before her containing poison mushrooms was meant to kill her. Her arms had been left free though her legs were chained to the table to prevent escape. Livia, however, avoided touching the food. Dolabella, Antony's favorite general, watched with annoyance as Livia refused to accept her fate. Finally, Dolabella spoke on behalf of Antony, who for customs sake, needed to remain distanced from the act.

"Eat," Dolabella ordered.

"Never!" Livia hissed.

"Eat!" Dolabella said again, this time with deadly finality.

Livia gave Dolabella a sardonic smile and spoke for all to hear: "I shall not eat the meal you have prepared to kill me, for your victory is invalid. You and your generals, Antony, won not by legitimate military means. My 'Tavius did not die by your hand! He died as the result of this woman's dark sorcery! My 'Tavius is the true victor of Actium!"—'Tavius was her nickname for Octavian, and Livia spoke as though he were still alive, and she was the wife of a victor, not the humiliated widow of a pathetic, dead ingrate.

Antony flushed livid and interrupted. "Fine. If you will not eat, then drink this poisoned wine I present you and toast your dead! I have tried to show you mercy, Livia, but if you remain too proud to accept your fate, I can arrange instead to crucify you and your family. Your husband is already dead and awaits you. What have you left to live for?"

I gasped. Crucifixion! Surely Antony was bluffing! I hated Livia, but I would not wish that punishment on my worst enemy, though, in fact, she was and always had been exactly that.

"You wouldn't dare!" Livia snarled, staring Antony straight in the eyes. "I may be the widow of Octavian, but at least I am the wife of a Roman citizen!" Frightened by Antony's hard, emotionless stare, she added, "Besides, women are not crucified. It is not done."

"Eat, drink, or by the gods, be crucified, for those are your options, and I'll personally attend to the latter if that is your choice," Dolabella stated grimly, his voice now menacing. "This is your last chance. Great Antony may not crucify you and may even prevent me from doing so, but there are other ways of ending a defiant prisoner's life which are only slightly less unpleasant. Would you, for instance, prefer to be fed to the lions in the arena for public entertainment?"

Livia blanched at the thought. "Very well. I shall go to meet my husband in the Underworld. But each of you will regret this day," Livia cursed, seizing the goblet, toasting the hushed crowd and drinking deeply, as if celebrating her and Octavian's victory. Finished, she seized her belly and gasped, struggled for more than a few horrible minutes and died a most wretched death.

"And now you," Dolabella said to Tiberius, Octavian's young stepson. Octavia, Octavian's sister, sitting beside the boy, tried to shield her eyes from what would be a more violent "man's" death, but one of Antony's men grabbed her chained hands and held them behind her back, requiring her to watch as Dolabella wrung the boy's neck. Tiberius died instantly, and with his death the long and destructive civil war between Octavian and Antony ended.

"And Octavia? What is to happen to her?" I asked Dolabella.

"I've no wish to live in a world that no longer contains any of my family," Octavia stated with a whimper. I looked at the face of this once proud, now pathetic woman. She had been a rival for Antony's affections. Antony had not married her, but I never forgot. As Octavian's sister and as a once rival for Antony, I couldn't object to her death. Still, the death of someone who had once loved Antony as I now did? My mind withdrew abhorrent from that thought.

"She proclaims she has no wish to live," Antony insisted, but I could tell from the tone of his voice that he still carried some distant affection for her. Indeed, he did not threaten her as he had Livia or Tiberius. "A quick death would therefore be kindest." Pointing at the goblet of poisoned wine presented to Lydia, he said, "There is still some wine left."

"Then I will drink it," Octavia stated, tears appearing, adding in a former lover's postscript, "gladly." Antony, moved by her words, signaled for Dolabella to remove Octavia's chains, which he did, and she drank the bitter dregs of the wine that moments ago had taken her sister-in-law. She, too, struggled, then gasped, but she breathed her last more as a sigh and release from this world. With this, all of Octavian's family was gone. Now the true banquet and celebrations could begin.

Chapter Five
Dividing the World
Spring 36 B.C
Year 16 of Cleopatra's Reign
Rome

Late the next evening, I was interrupted by a kick at the door. It was Cicero Minor.

"Queen Cleopatra? Are you ready to attend the *imperativa*? Antony awaits!"

"I am," I replied. Charmion was just finishing dressing me in a heavy, pure-spun-gold chiton. Even my jewelry was pure gold without colored gems. Though normally I wore no cosmetics in Rome, I had lined my eyes with kohl. Today, I wanted to flaunt Egypt and its wealth as ostentatiously as possible.

Cicero Minor wrapped a woolen cape about me and led me to a waiting palanquin. After a half hour ride through the hills and streets of Rome, it stopped in front of a private banquet building where I was escorted by Cicero Minor up a short flight of white marble stairs, then down a winding hallway to the banquet hall. As we approached the vast chamber, loud music and the strong smell of Roman food engulfed me. The interior was filled with a boisterous crowd of generals and officers, most in dress armor, others in dress togas, all seeming ready to party all night. Interspersed among them were wives, escorts and concubines dressed in beautiful *pallas* and *stolas* in various muted shades. One among them, however, was dressed in bold lapis blue with glittering gold trim. I smiled to myself At least in fashion I was influencing some of the Roman women!

The woman, Cicero Minor's wife, looked at me and sent a friendly smile. I waved back, but we could not speak to each other for the crowd between us. Catching sight of Antony reclining next to Dolabella on a slightly raised central dais, I spotted the empty seat on Antony's other side, and began to advance toward it when Cicero Minor stopped me and explained. "That is where I must sit."

"Where is Caesarion?" I asked partly to hide the slight, partly from anger at Cicero Minor's outspokenness, and partly out of a mother's concern and curiosity.

"He is reclining with the soldiers," Cicero Minor informed me.

"Then am I to sit with the women?" I asked brusquely, my anger now visible.

Cicero Minor flinched, but kept his face carefully devoid of expression, replying, "Antony and I conversed about that. You are a woman and neither Roman nor a soldier's wife, concubine or escort. Still, you *are* a Queen and honored Roman ally, and you commanded your navy which helped us win; therefore, we are obliged to seat you near us. It is, however, an honor never before bestowed upon any woman, least of all a foreigner."

I knew well this honor was not being bestowed lightly, and that in granting it, Antony was taking great risk. As such, I relaxed, smiled and accepted Cicero Minor's explanation.

Cicero Minor sighed with relief. "My Queen," he continued. "Allow me to present you." Although the music, feasting, talking and debauchery did not die down, at the flick of his wrist one musician rattled a *tympanum,* and another followed with a loud blast on his curved brass *buccina*, an opening typically reserved for the highest-ranking generals. The same moment, he loosened my cape, letting it fall freely. There was a sudden hush, followed by myriad gasps. Even so, Cicero Minor announced me in a loud voice.

To my surprise, there was no cheering, just a general mumble of approval. The women continued to stare at me, then slowly returned to chattering and gossiping among themselves. Some of the officers rolled their eyes. Cicero Minor had spoken truthfully. In the minds of those attending this *imperativa*, it was Antony who had triumphed at Actium, with or perhaps even in spite of my diminutive assistance. My work was clearly far from over; it was just beginning.

Cicero Minor led me through the partying crowds to the dais where Antony and Dolabella, the official witness for Rome, along with several other military dignitaries were reclining head-to-head.

"Welcome to Rome, Queen Cleopatra," Antony shouted for all to hear. A brief cheer arose from the crowd, then quickly faded back into the din.

"An exceptional welcome, made even better now that Octavian, his wife and step-son have been dealt with," I said, having to force a smile, given the lukewarm reception. "It is time, it appears, for Rome and Egypt to take their deserved places and rule the world—North, South, East and West."

Dolabella laughed softly. I could tell from his tone that he would be a lifelong friend. "I hear they are calling you Cleopatra the Great in Egypt, likening you to Penthesilea, Queen of the Amazons who led her army in the Trojan War, even to Alexander himself! Well, Cleopatra the Great, you may have won the battle in Egypt, but tonight, here, the fight has just begun. This is a night not just for celebration, but, as you've so astutely noted, for politics. Sit." At his signal, breaking even more tradition, slaves placed a fourth couch nearest the edge of the dais, closing the usually U-shaped constellation of a common table and two *triclinia*, the nearest *triclinia* seating Cicero Minor, Antony and Dolabella.

I nodded proudly and took this place of honor.

"Do you really mean to share the Empire with her?" Dolabella asked Antony, sounding both bemused and skeptical at once.

Antony nodded affirmatively. "Of course. The new empire will be far too big for any one person to rule alone." Turning towards me, he added, "But she cannot have Rome, of course."

"Of course," echoed Dolabella obediently, then Cicero Minor. "Of course!"

"But I do not want it," I said, laughing diplomatically. Me, a Consul of Rome? Queen of such ruffians? The very idea…!

Dolabella chuckled and the mood further lightened.

"Egypt you may forever keep and rule," Antony said, adding adroitly, "under two conditions."

I raised my eyebrows, keeping my irritation in check. "And those conditions are?" It had never occurred to me that Antony would even *think* of taking Egypt from me and I had to quickly resume my composure. I had to remember this was Antony Triumphant speaking: Roman men's politics, clearly necessary to pave the way for our joint rule.

"First, that you give half your grain to Rome, and second, that you provide your navy when needed."

This was more than the expected acknowledgement of the role Egypt and I had played in the Battle at Actium, and I suddenly saw what

Antony was doing: He was reassuring Rome that, despite its current limitations, he would not let it fall hegemony to a new, stronger, dynastic Egypt. A soft hush fell about us.

"I accept," I graciously replied. The hush was broken by the three men's sighs.

"But I must bargain with those terms," I added, the hush returning in earnest. "I will guarantee Rome a quarter of Egypt's yearly grain. And, while Egypt will need her navy to police our shared sea, the Mare Nostrum, and protect us both from invasion, I will provide my navy when asked, in times of Roman crisis. That is fair, don't you think?"

Antony glanced at Dolabella, who was frowning and rubbing his chin. "I can agree to the second, but must bargain further with the first. Three-eighths," Antony replied off-handedly.

I was shocked silent for a moment. What was Antony doing? Then I realized he was demonstrating not only his command in front of his fellow Romans, but acknowledging through negotiation that Egypt and I were, if not fully Rome's equal, then at least equal enough in authority in this new partnership to bargain. Antony was placing me in the enviable position of being key to Rome's future success, a future where I would co-rule the world with the leader of the Roman Empire. It was the negotiation, not its outcome that was important here. There was no need to firmly negotiate everything I wanted and needed this moment at this table. I would have many opportunities in the future alone with Antony as my co-ruler."

"Agreed," I acquiesced. "Three eighths."

Antony surprised me by nodding his agreement and stating further, "Now, as for dividing up the empire…"

"For our sake, we must always represent it as a republic," Cicero Minor interrupted.

"...the 'broader Republic', then," Antony stated. "We can figure out *exactly* how to do this as things progress, Cicero Minor, but for now, I am thinking more of how to divide and rule our combined territories. In particular, what to do with the provinces."

"I want Judea," I said, instantly regretting my boldness.

"Cleopatra, you well know that Judea is already part of Rome. Pompey the Great paid his life to conquer it and at the same time save Egypt. That is too high a price for me to simply hand it over to Egypt. Also, for the time being, Rome needs Herod as an ally to control the rebellious Hebrews. I have warned you to be cautious of him," Antony said to me firmly yet with obvious concern.

I frowned.

"I can, however, give you the territories around Jericho, the lands that contain the shrubs known as the Balm of Gilead, which are precious to Egypt and the world."

This was better than I hoped. While I desired the entire province—with it being located on one of Egypt's borders, it would have been better if I could have controlled all of it—the income from the lands around Jericho that produced the Balm of Gilead would alone be sufficient to finance the rebuilding Egypt's lost glory and at the same time position it to eventually expand into Judea. This was no small prize, and by accepting Antony's proposal, I realized from the look in his eyes that I would also advance him in the eyes of the Romans.

"So be it," I replied, casting my kohl-lined eyes down to further accent what would appear to those present as Antony's second victory.

Antony, satisfied, continued speaking. "We must expand Egypt with provinces that will increase Egypt's maritime strength. Provinces that Romans won't contest, like parts of Africa and islands like Crete and Cyprus. And Rome will help you recover any territories previously lost which you will rule over," he said.

I paused. In fact, I was so shocked by his generosity, I had no words.

Antony, however, must have taken my silence as grudging acquiescence, for he continued. "Resolved, Cleopatra, you shall receive all territories formerly presided over by your dynasty. I will also order the Arabs of Nabataea, from whom our supposed ally Herod hails, to hand over to you their Kingdom including their capital, Petra and their Dead Sea trade."

The Dead Sea! Of the many treasures to be found in that part of the world, Petra, the very center of East-West trade, was by far the greatest. I had bathed in Dead Sea salt, which kept my skin looking youthful and young, and had my daughter washed in it, too. I might not get all of Judea, but Jericho, Petra and the Dead Sea were, for the time being, more than enough. Still, however, there still remained a singular problem. "Antony! What of Octavian's extended family, their distant cousins, for example? We can't kill them *all*. How will we keep them in check?" I asked.

It was Cicero Minor who offered the solution. "Easy," he interrupted. "We'll give them lucrative but non-vital, easily controlled outposts, for example, positions as provincial tax collectors or minor governors."

Antony nodded his agreement. "We can't allow weeds to grow in our beautiful Roman-Egyptian garden!"

With that, the conversation ended, and the three men turned their attention to the food and entertainment. Unsure of what to do, I was startled when Antony whispered in my ear, "I have an idea I'm certain will further please you."

"And what is that?" I asked, my curiosity piqued.

Antony spoke quietly, using the din of the banquet to mask his words. "I've discovered a separate will declaring Caesarion to be Julius Caesar's heir. When the time is right, I will reveal it publicly and announce that, according to Caesar, Octavian's claim was never valid. When the time is right, I will have this knowledge spread throughout Rome."

"Caesar once showed it to me, but I thought it better to be silent about it for the time," I said.

"Indeed," Antony agreed. " The time is still not *quite* right, but the moment is fast approaching. Now let us enjoy our evening of military triumph, dear Cleopatra. We've many more nights ahead to plan and plot together."

During the evening and night, groups of soldiers, most sated, some raucous and unruly, departed to return to their duties and families. Just before sunrise, Dolabella and Cicero Minor departed, and Caesarion joined Antony and me.

"Cleopatra," Antony said, taking my hands in his. "I've missed you so," he sighed.

He does truly love me! How could I be happier? I thought. All during the banquet, I'd felt Antony's presence. By now I ached for the man, strong in battle and politics, yet gentle enough to express his feelings toward me, a woman and not just the Queen. I felt at this moment the most blessed woman alive. And yet, I had one more overarching concern. So, instead of simply joining him on his softly pillowed pallet, I spoke thus: "Antony, what is to become of our children?"

Antony cocked his head. "What?"

"Our children, Antony. What is to become of Caesarion and the twins. They are our legacy. What shall we do? Where...? How...?" I grabbed his shoulders and stared into his eyes.

From Antony's look, I knew he understood me and I fell yet again in love, this time, if possible, even more deeply. Antony loved me for my mothering as much as he did for my military and political expertise.

"Caesarion, of course, must remain with me in Rome," he replied with thoughtful reserve.

Caesarion smiled proudly.

"I'm not sure about Helios," Antony continued, "and as for our daughter, I leave that to you. Perhaps an Armenian, Parthian or Arabian prince for her?"

My mother's mind at first agreed. Now that I had control over the Dead Sea Kingdom, it would be easy to assert my dominance and protect her and our grandchildren. But then I pictured Selene in the Arabian desert and remembered the nights I had spent in fear of my life in Gaza, hiding in tents against the scalding sun and abrasive sand. I could not do that to Selene, my daughter.

"The deserts of Arabia are no place for a princess of Egypt. Helios is named for the sun, he can handle the scorching desert," I said to Antony.

"Yes, yes, good thinking, my Cleopatra. So, what of little Selene?" Antony asked.

Caesarion moved to the edge of his, formerly Cicero Minor's, couch, and listened eagerly.

I smiled. Antony had called me "my Cleopatra," and it made me remember my time with Julius Caesar. Though he had been a good husband, he had never been tender like Antony. Shaking away the memories, I returned to the present. I had no time to think on the past, with Selene's future about to be decided. With Caesarion in Rome and Helios in Arabia, that left her to…rule Egypt after me! "Selene will rule

Egypt," I stated emphatically, pulling my hands abruptly out from Antony's, the idea of her as Queen of Egypt after me both delighting and scaring me.

"Mother?" Caesarion said in shock. "I thought *I* was to rule Egypt."

For a moment, I feared a tantrum of Ptolemaic proportions, knowing how my brothers had acted whenever their expectations were thwarted. But Caesarion was Caesar's son as much as he was a Ptolemy, and his words, voice and demeanor were indicative more of his dignified father than the immature actions of the males on my side of the family. Then the political implications hit me. It seemed, at the same time, to hit Antony, as well as Caesarion.

"I see," Caesarion said. "If I am declared Caesar's true heir, then I must remain in Rome. But Mother, Selene is a woman and will need to be paired with a male Pharaoh. Look how much trouble came from the men with whom you were paired... "

"Indeed," Antony said knowingly to Caesarion. Antony then turned and addressed me. "Could your people be content being ruled by a singular queen-pharaoh?"

"In Egypt, women have always had a different place in politics than their Roman counterparts, My Love," I replied. "Women have before been Queen-Pharaoh. In three thousand years, however, only Hatshepsut, Nefertiti and I have been bold enough to invoke this custom for ourself, and Hatshepsut and Nefertiti both paid dearly for the privilege—Hatshepsut's son was later forced to erase her from all monuments, and Nefertiti died at the hands of assassins," I explained.

"Yet, your people seem to greatly love you, and you do not appear to fear for your life though you are acting even now as Queen-Pharaoh. If you are special, why would the daughter of Antony and Cleopatra not be so?" Antony asked.

"Well..." I replied, lost in thought. Antony was right. If Egypt had not always welcomed my father, sisters and brothers, it had always welcomed me and my children.

"Egypt loves you, Mother," Caesarion affirmed.

"Tell me if this is not so," Antony insisted.

"Yes, they do," I replied. "I did not become Queen-Pharaoh out of a desire to pervert Ma'at's will or raise myself before the gods. I became such because my sisters and brothers were all incompetent."

"These other Queen-Pharaohs you mentioned: They weren't like you, so why then judge you and your children's future by their lives?" Antony asked.

"I..." I mouthed, realizing Antony and my son by Caesar were correct. Hatshepsut and Nefertiti were not me. Their lives were not like mine. Who could say whether or not I would have done the same things they had done had I been in their place? The important thing was that *I am not them*. I am myself, bestowed by my people with the attribution, "Cleopatra the Great." I breathed a silent prayer to Ma'at in apology for my momentary doubts, and to Isis, my personal goddess, for her continued guidance.

"You're right, of course. This isn't about the past," I said. "Selene may be a little girl, but she *is* Egypt's future."

Antony and Caesarion laughed. They apparently had more confidence in me and my daughter than I did.

"A woman could never rule Rome, but Egypt, why not?" Antony said. Seeming to sense a lingering uncertainty within me, Antony continued speaking: "My Love, together we've challenged many customs and broken many traditions. What, then, is one more?"

"A dynasty of women pharaohs..." I said in wonder.

"Not yet done, but not unheard of," Antony said with a smile. "And that is a challenge worthy of Cleopatra the Great," he said, pressing me further.

"Indeed," I agreed, still overwhelmed by the thought of a line of women determining the future of the world. Yet, the queens in my family line had already begun so. The cults of Arsinoë II, Cleopatra I, Cleopatra II and Cleopatra III still continued in Egypt. Inspired especially by Arsinoë II and Cleopatra III, I had already dared and gone beyond these four women in challenging many of the long-held customs of the Ptolemies. Antony was right—what was breaking yet another tradition? With this in mind, I continued speaking. "This brings to mind a custom I've twice rejected—royal incest. I assumed Caesarion and Selene would marry, or, according to Egyptian custom, perhaps she would marry Helios, but I chose you, Antony, and Julius Caesar. So, Selene, too, should choose her husband, be he Egyptian or from another nation, but not from her own nursery," I said. "Unmarried she can remain unchallenged Queen-Pharaoh. Married, she can remain such, keeping her consort as a helpmate." A world where women ruled? The thought made my head swim, but not at all unpleasantly.

Antony laughed aloud. "There's the woman I love!" he said and, standing, picked me up and twirled me like a little girl. I smiled, shrieking with laughter. Caesar had *never* been so free with his affections. I was not just freer with Antony, I was experiencing in my own small way my dream of a female dynasty.

At last, both of us breathless, he sat back on his couch and pulled me onto his lap. Caesarion watched us throughout our brief whimsy, as if considering whether to do the same with his mate someday.

"You told me that Selene, our daughter, is named after the great Ptolemaic Egyptian Queen, Cleopatra Selene I, who later ruled Syria,"

Antony said more seriously, "Our Selene is worthy of this name-honor. Now, let's bed. I have waited too patiently to make love to you."

Caesarion bowed slightly, rose, turned and left.

"Antony, I'm pregnant," I whispered, hoping the spinning had not hurt the baby.

Antony, momentarily taken aback, frowned, then asked if I was certain.

"As certain as a woman can be. I've suspected for over a month and a half now," I replied. "But that doesn't stop us from making love," I said with an inviting smile.

Chapter Six

Creating an Empire

Spring 36 B.C

Year 16 of Cleopatra's Reign

Rome

The next morning, in bed, in each other's arms, we continued building our empire.

"I must spend the winters in Rome consolidating power. I'll spend springs and summers with you in Alexandria. Caesarion, however, will have to remain in Rome. I need to Romanize him," Antony stated.

Initially, I thought to protest, but Antony stopped me with a further explanation: "He's Caesar's son, and when later I reveal Caesar's true last will and announce Caesarion as his legitimate heir, he must appear completely Roman in order to inherit and assume his immediate and future responsibilities."

I liked what I was hearing. Caesar had assured me of having created this second will, but despite what I'd told Antony yesterday at the *imperativa*, I'd never *actually* seen it. "Where did you find the will?" It was one thing to hear of this will, but without a physical copy, rumor was useless.

"Cicero Minor found it, actually," Antony said. "Caesar left it for safekeeping in the Temple of Venus. One of the priests sought out Cicero

Minor and revealed its existence after our Triumph."

This was entirely plausible. Caesar's personal goddess was Venus, and he'd created the Temple of Venus after our Egyptian marriage, having the goddess' statues carved in my image. "Could I see it?" I asked, explaining, "Caesar respected Rome and its laws. Doesn't Roman law forbid any bequeaths to foreigners?"

Antony sighed in a frustrated manner but answered both my questions. "Nonetheless, the will exists, and he bequeathed all his possessions to Caesarion. I can take you to the temple this afternoon to view it, if you wish." After a pause, he spoke again. "Cleopatra, I, too, respect Rome and Roman law. My admiration for Greece and love for your Egypt does not mean I in any way disrespect *Roma Dea*. But as I've said, you and I are laying the foundations for a new world, one that will bring with it new customs and traditions. Come, let us arise, dress and I will escort you to the temple to read the will for yourself."

My head was spinning as I dressed. *Had Caesar actually left his entire estate to Caesarion? Caesarion ruler of Rome after Antony?* I dare not speak my thoughts, lest the gods take offense at my hubris. Donning simple Roman attire, I let Antony lead me through the streets to the Temple of Venus, recalling again the time when, visiting this same temple, Livia had tried to assassinate me with a poisoned dagger. I shuddered as we passed the side street where it had happened.

I knew we'd arrived at the Temple of Venus when, between the white pillars, naked statues of the goddess of love, all in my image, greeted us. I stopped to touch one. The marble was cool, indifferent. Antony waited, smiling at the goddess carved in my likeness, until the tapping of sandals interrupted the moment.

Several priests approached. The shorter, stockier, older one stopped immediately before us, staring first at Antony, then at me and the statue next to me.

"Hail, Antony!" he cried. "Is this Cleopatra?" he asked, referring obliquely to me and the statue.

"We are," I assured him.

"They are," Antony expanded.

"Antony's lover! Queen of the East!" the taller, leaner, younger priest cried in awe, bowing low before me.

"What brings you to the Temple of Venus? To honor Caesar or his ancestress?" the first asked.

I took several steps forward and searched the interior for others before answering. Noting the central statue of me as Venus Genetrix Caesar had dedicated seven years ago still undamaged, I breathed a silent prayer of thanks.

"I heard Caesar left a second will here," I said, adding, "naming my son as his sole heir. I didn't feel it right to believe it until I saw it myself."

Both priests laughed conspiratorially.

"We had heard," the older said, his eyes sparkling as he visibly compared me to the life-sized figure of Venus Genetrix, "that you were an extraordinary woman. This is to be expected of a friend and ally of Rome, a Queen descended from the goddess Isis, and the wife of Julius Caesar who was himself declared a God. The will is here under our protection." The older priest turned and left, his tap-tap-tapping sandals creating echoes of echoes throughout the great hall.

I waited, apprehensive but intrigued. Some Romans seemed to be accepting me as an ally, though some, I knew, still reviled, even hated me. In this time of change, I was never certain of anything Roman except what Antony said directly to me.

"Cleopatra?" Antony asked, interrupting my thoughts.

"I can't help but feel that while your people, Antony, are beginning to accept me, it might be as some sort of farce. It hasn't ever been enough that I helped you win, and I'm wondering if they won't hate me again later."

Before we could discuss this further, we were distracted by the voice of the returning priest. "The will, Your Egyptian Majesty," he said. The two priests bowed as one before me, though whether in true sincerity or to mock me, I couldn't tell. I chose the former interpretation and stood taller, pleased to see the two Roman priests wait for an acknowledging nod.

"Ah, yes," I said, relieving the scroll from his outstretched hand and reading it to myself:

"Resolved: That Caesarion is my only heir..." It was indeed written and signed in my former husband's hand. I smiled as I continued reading.

"Have you destroyed the other will?" I asked the three men after completing the read. "Caesar's previous will identified Octavian as his heir and will undoubtedly be used to contest this newer one."

Antony nodded affirmatively. "Yes, we have. Cicero Minor is planning to present this one to the Senate."

"But the other will..." I asked, knowing that others who had known of the first will would likely challenge this one.

"When Cicero Minor announces this will, he will also state that, upon examination by several senators, Caesar's previous will naming Octavian his heir was determined to be a forgery. But we'd best leave that job to Cicero Minor."

"Of course," I agreed. Then I thought, *I am in the Temple of Venus, the goddess of love, and I love Antony.* "Antony," I asked, "I am wondering if you and I shouldn't officially marry."

Antony laughed at my bold proposal. Women didn't ask men to marry them, even in Egypt, the country of queens, but especially in Rome! He stopped laughing the next instant, realizing it wasn't meant as a marriage proposal, it was an invitation for *him* to propose to *me*, and in doing so, address yet another issue that needed to be resolved before we could openly progress to talking Empire. It was about the budding relationship between our two nations, our two cultures with their own gods and goddesses, and ourselves being the physical manifestation of what was yet to come.

"In Egypt, then. This summer. By Egyptian, not Roman rites. So, Cleopatra, will you be my Egyptian wife?" he asked in all sincerity before the priests of Venus.

"It would be my great honor," I answered. We immediately embraced, our arms encircling each other's neck, exchanging kisses that to me were better than figs or honey. The two priests looked on beneficently, as was only proper in the Temple of the Goddess of Love, the goddess whose images were all of me.

Helen R. Davis

Chapter Seven

Goddesses Reflect

Aprilus 36 B.C

Year 16 of Cleopatra's Reign

The Temple of Venus in Rome from The Vault of Nut

Isis, Venus and Athena leaned over the heavenly balustrade of the Vault of Nut and viewed the two lovers embracing in Venus' temple. Venus smiled, enjoying the scene as she combed her long blonde hair, with each stroke, showering the couple with translucent, barely visible rose petals.

"So, you approve of their union?" Athena asked Venus icily. In Athena's heart of hearts, she respected Antony and Cleopatra for being fierce warriors. In fact, she liked Antony better than Caesar for, though Roman, Antony admired all things Greek. *Antony*, Athena thought, *will prove a better match for Cleopatra*. Athena worried, however, whenever Antony or Cleopatra displayed the slightest hint of Caesar's hubris. Cleopatra deserved better than a tyrant, and to be better than one herself.

"Why do you ask?" Venus asked cautiously, knowing Athena liked to test mortals and gods alike. Everyone knew of the fates of Paris of Troy and Arachne, both of whom had angered Athena and met horrible fates—Paris losing his kingdom and Arachne being turned into a spider.

"I would know your thoughts first," Athena, goddess of wisdom as well as war, stated, adding even more icily, "if you have any."

"Ladies! Why this arguing?" Isis intervened. "Venus approves of the union, and I, too. Athena! For once, have a heart! When you taunt Venus about her thoughts, you make me wonder if you have any feelings at all."

Athena, realizing she had just been both outsmarted and out felt, chose to consent to the union, at least for now. A protector, primarily of bold young men, Athena, while feeling no desire for any man at the moment, felt protective and perhaps even desirous of Cleopatra.

Isis opened her cape, and, in addition to the rose petals that Venus was showering on the couple, made a waterfall of sunlight appear above and behind Antony and Cleopatra, a gift that came ultimately from Ra, the Egyptian Sun God.

"*My* thoughts, Athena, are the same as my *feelings*: that these two truly love each other, and therefore I them," Venus stated.

Athena pondered Venus' words and finally acquiesced. Her differences with Venus were not a battle that needed fighting, certainly not at this time and in this place, and she offered Venus the closest thing she knew to an apology: "My intention was never to argue, Venus. It was to say that I approve of their union in a practical sense. They are warriors and leaders of their respective peoples. Both deserve the others' devotion. Yet as goddess of wisdom, I know the rational fate of all, and in that knowing, that Antony will not be completely faithful."

"Men never are," Venus scoffed sadly.

"So, we agree also about the perfidy of men," Athena said, extending a hand to Venus in friendship. Venus accepted, although in her heart, she knew their friendship would be prove short-lived.

"Not *all* men," Isis said, thinking of the fidelity of her beloved Osiris.

"Most," Venus and Athena agreed in unison.

Isis smiled. Perhaps she was proving to be a good influence on her two fellow goddesses.

"All three of us are in agreement regarding Cleopatra, if not on men," Isis said. "I saved her and her dynasty from defeat by creating the storm that swallowed Octavian. But now she must finish what I've helped start. Athena, goddess of battle, I call on you to assist her!"

"I will, but first she must actually *marry* Antony," Athena stated in deference to her new friendship with Venus.

"Are Egyptian rites enough to satisfy you?" Venus asked.

"I'll accept *any* rites, as long as she *marries*," Athena restated. "Until then, I cannot grant her my full blessing. But I know Cleopatra well. She will find a way to make him her true husband, if necessary, first in Egypt, then in Rome. Cleopatra is a woman who may not always do the right thing at first, but she does it eventually."

"Then let us hasten her trip to Egypt and assist with her plans to become Antony's wife," Isis summarized, using her magical power to plant the idea of a hasty return and a glorious Egyptian wedding firmly in Cleopatra's mind.

Helen R. Davis

Chapter Eight

Cleopatra Betrothed
Spring-Summer, 36. B.C.
Year 16 of Cleopatra's Reign
Rome

I remained in Rome until Maia, the last month of spring, for many things remained to be decided. Antony and I continued discussing the future of my three children. When the baby growing within me was born, we would see its sex and decide its future.

"The soothsayers say it is a son," I offered.

"Soothsayers will always say it is a son," Antony retorted.

"I believe it to be a son, but I could be wrong," I stated carefully. Antony was right. Very rarely, if ever, did soothsayers deliver bad news to the leader of a nation, let alone the future leaders of the world. If a soothsayer predicted a daughter, many leaders would have had them killed. I would not, but I was an extraordinary woman and queen, and Egypt an extraordinary country. For example, in Egypt a woman could inherit.

In any case, Antony had decided that Caesarion, Caesar's son and now declared heir, would stay in Rome with him. This decision was made after much anguish on my part, as, being my first and oldest, he was admittedly my favorite. Declaring him Julius Caesar's heir would put him in mortal danger. I realized that either way, it was necessary, though he was but ten years of age, to begin training for his future as not only as Antony's but also Caesar's Roman heir.

"I thought I was to be Pharaoh of Egypt," Caesarion yet again repeated when he learned of his fate, pouting and looking at me for assurance. He had already acquiesced to eventually becoming the leader of Rome in every sense of the word, but was having second thoughts, as would anyone when their future was constantly being rewritten.

"We have decided upon a *better* future for you," Antony reaffirmed. "When all is complete, you shall inherit Rome after me."

"But, you are Roman! You can't marry Mother. She may be Queen-Pharaoh of Egypt, but she's not a Roman!" Caesarion argued, demonstrating his amazingly early and sound understanding of politics. This was no surprise to me, his father being Julius Caesar, but it never ceased to delight Antony, who had already begun to include the child in our confidence, a move both of us knew Caesarion could handle.

"Have you forgotten about your father's will? That you are his heir, and that eventually, Caesarion, I will adopt you," Antony said, smiling condescendingly. Antony had always been accepting of Caesarion, even more so since the last of his sons by his Roman wife, Fulvia, had died. In spite of the fact we had been rivals for Antony, I felt for Fulvia, and wondered if her children with Antony had truly met their deaths as naturally as everyone in Rome seemed to think. I also wondered if Caesar would have been as accepting of Antony's child would the reverse have occurred. Likely not. In fact, in my heart, I knew not.

Caesarion's eyes widened. "So, I shall be Dictator of Rome, like my first father?" he asked.

"Dictator?" I repeated questioningly. "Ah, Antony. He brings up a good point. What shall we call you now and Caesarion later? Consul? Principal Citizen? Dictator-for-Life? King? Emperor?"

Antony rubbed his chin, a gesture he did when deep in thought. "We must leave that to Cicero Minor. Some vestiges of the Republic must remain in place while we rule Rome as an Empire. Watch me closely in the days ahead, Caesarion. Watch and learn."

"Antony," I said when Caesarion at last left to take a swim in the Tiber. It was hot for Maia. I enjoyed swimming on hot days in Alexandria, but in Rome, I could not do that for a variety of reasons. Antony and I walked outside and sat together in Caesar's house on the rim of the fountain in the center of which stood a statue of me as naked Venus Genetrix, beckoning to any who passed to rest at my feet. Clinging to his arm, I spoke his name softly.

"Yes, Cleopatra?" he asked, mildly annoyed.

I wondered if I should push him, but I desperately wanted to discuss plans for our upcoming Egyptian wedding, so I quieted the warning voice inside and decided to broach the subject. "When we were in the Temple of Venus, I felt the goddess' blessing." I said, adding when he looked puzzled, "on our union." In the water, a few frogs peaked their eyes above the water's surface. One looked exactly like Heket, the Egyptian goddess who formed babies in the womb, and I breathed a prayer to her to make the child growing within me a boy. While I would accept a girl, I knew Antony needed a son. The loss of his sons by Fulvia wore on him, though he would not speak of it.

"While we have discussed it, I am not yet your wife, either Egyptian or Roman."

"That is true," Antony mused. "Is it really true that Caesar married you by Egyptian rites in your country?" Antony asked, as if needing my reassurance.

"It is," I said.

"Then, to show I am indeed Caesar's true friend, I will honor him by marrying the mother of his heir in Egypt."

I knew Antony loved me as I loved him, but this was the kind of political reasoning I needed to hear from him so that I could continue to advance our eventual co-rulership with assurance.

"You spoke before of wedding in summer. Summer will soon be upon us. A royal wedding takes preparation, and to be wed in Egypt, I must return to make preparations and you must leave Rome to join me…" I was leading him delicately to annotate his proposal. There was a Temple of Isis in Rome, Isis being a popular goddess not just in Egypt but also around the world. "In fact, there is no need for either of us to return to Egypt just now," I said. "Is there not a Temple of Isis here in Rome?"

"There is," he acknowledged thoughtfully, then said with an amused smile, "But I am a Roman and a man. Would the priests and priestesses of Isis' temple allow me entry into their sacred temple?" he teased. I knew he was making a play on what some Romans were still saying about me, and I loved it.

"Of course, Antony," I replied with sham irritation. "Isis welcomes all who enter her temple, whether they are from Rome or Egypt, man or woman." Antony had taken my hint. Now I wanted him to take another. I remembered back to the day when Caesar and I had married. "Let us marry on the next full moon," I suggested.

"Why then?" Antony asked.

"That's when Caesar and I married. And our daughter, Cleopatra Selene, is named for the Moon. She will be the next incarnation of Isis. Our newest son can then be the next incarnation of Osiris."

"On the next full moon, then," Antony agreed, in a voice that reminded me surprisingly of Caesar's.

The next full moon was only two weeks away. Antony did not announce to the Romans that he was going to marry me in their city by the rites of Egypt. This was, for now, to be our secret. Instead, he presented me to the Roman populace as his most trusted Roman ally, the one who had aided him against Octavian. He announced that, in gratitude, he would adopt Helios and Selene as his legal wards, shocking some, though to most, their resemblance to their father was undeniably more so than to me. Selene especially resembled Antony and I often noticed him doting on her.

The night before the wedding, I came across Selene in the latrine, vomiting.

"She has been poisoned!" I cried, calling for Iras and Charmion, my eyes wide with anger. How could they have been so careless?

The two were instantly at Selene's side.

"No, my queen," Iras said with a concerned but calm smile. My dearest companion, Iras had aged since purchased by my father nearly twenty years ago. She still retained her blonde hair, although her face was beginning to wrinkle. Pointing to a sweet in her hand, she said, "She's merely eaten too many *dulcis coccora*. She loves them, you know, and Antony cannot deny her."

I breathed a sigh of relief and apologized. "I am sorry to accuse you of neglect, even in thought, Iras." I said. She smiled, and I took her hand to let her know all was forgiven.

Dulcis coccora, little balls of flour, walnuts and figs or dates cooked, then caramelized in boiled honey and dusted with *coccora* – ground pomegranate seeds—were my favorite dessert, and Selene of my children, was the most like me even in her food preferences.

Charmion breathlessly reconfirmed Iras' statement: "Antony brings Selene sweets...every night." Charmion, too, was growing old. Her ebony hair was streaked with grey, and her skin wrinkled about the corners of her eyes when she smiled. Her creams, however, made the rest of her skin look ten years younger. She had always tended my cosmetics, having worked selling cosmetics and perfumes after my father had dismissed her in Ephesus until we had reunited before my fateful flight to Gaza. We were becoming known throughout Rome for the quality of our constantly invented creams and perfumes.

"How many nights?" I asked, my anxiety melting into relief, albeit mixed with mild annoyance at Antony.

"The last three nights at least, including tonight," Iras detailed.

"Well, no more sweets for now, Selene," I said to the poor girl. Selene wiped her mouth, stood, stamped her foot and begged for more.

"Aren't you sick?" Charmion asked of Selene.

"Selene want more!" she said forcefully, guiltily gulping back another urge to vomit.

"Well, not tonight!" Iras, Charmion and I all said simultaneously. Thankfully, Selene quit begging, unlike her spoiled aunt, Arsinoë, who had thought "no" meant "yes" ever since we had grown up in the nursery. Arsinoë's argumentative attitude eventually led to her death.

Charmion stayed with Selene, while Iras and I retired together to my chamber. We were soon rejoined by Charmion who assured me that Selene was lying quietly in her chamber. When Antony was not present, I sometimes invited Iras and Charmion to share my bed, knowing that, at times, Antony and Eros, his manservant, sometimes similarly shared his.

The next morning, Iras woke me at first light, for she was to spend the day preparing me for my wedding. Charmion procured for me a hot milk bath scented with rose and lavender to soften my skin. I had ylang

ylang petals, which I imported from India, added to the bath, for, being an expert on scents and their biological properties and having heard that it was used for new beginnings. When bathed in immediately prior to marriage, it blessed the union. For scent, I no longer used jasmine, which had been favored by Caesar. It brought back memories both sweet and painful, for it had been the scent I'd also worn on the day of his death. Antony favored rose and Egyptian *neroli*—from the blossom of the bitter orange tree—so I scented the bath with them, adding the tiniest amount of sandalwood and myrrh to invoke the blessing of Hathor, goddess of sexuality, motherhood and healing. Afterwards, I rinsed my hair with a touch of orange and lemon oil. Although I was marrying Antony by Egyptian rites, I thought it wise to include some Roman customs, so, when finished, I donned a traditional white Roman *stola* and *palla*; about my waist, Charmion tied the Knot of Hercules, which would be untied later by Antony. Antony was, it was claimed, a direct descendant of the great hero.

I applied only minimal Egyptian kohl about my eyes—just enough to create an air of mystery.

"Pearls?" Iras asked.

"No. They are considered a display of vanity here," I replied. "Fetch instead my gold and emerald necklace. And my golden amethyst bracelet and lapis ring, also."

"Pearls are vain, but a gold and emerald choker, amethyst bracelet and lapis lazuli ring are not? What strange creatures, these Romans are," Charmion exclaimed, refusing to make the transition from Egyptian to Roman life even while living in Rome.

I nodded, not verbalizing my agreement. I put on the bracelet and ring while Iras fastened my necklace. "All that remains is to style my hair with spears, as Roman brides do," I said to Iras.

That night at the Temple of Isis, Antony and I were married in Rome by Egyptian rites. Antony awkwardly repeated the necessary words in Egyptian, the irony not being lost on me. Caesar, the most Roman of Romans, had married me in Egypt. Antony, Triumvir of the East, was marrying me in Rome. To Caesar, the marriage had been a formality. To Antony I sensed this wedding was, if not as binding as a Roman ceremony, then at least an acknowledgement of the formation of a marriage relationship, as a result of which he was seeing me as his wife in truth. I had never been Caesar's wife, but henceforth I *was* Antony's. I briefly imagined Caesar watching the ceremony from above, and wondered of his thoughts.

I asked Antony that night.

"Caesar would have wanted us to be happy. And he would have wanted the best for Rome. I think we are the answer to both," Antony stated. I knew from his statement that he wished to discuss Caesar no further that night.

"I will return to Egypt after the summer solstice," I said, wisely changing the subject.

"Indeed. But before you return, we need to spend time together as newlyweds," Antony stated, smiling as he encircled me in his muscled arms.

Marrying proved a pleasant and wise decision. Getting to know Antony as a husband proved delightful. Getting Rome to know and accept me as his Egyptian wife, and our children as his own proved more challenging. My presence in the city that summer led the Roman people to, if not accept me entirely, then at least understand that, like it or not, my children and I were a singular part of Antony's and by that fact, Rome's life. I still did not wander Rome unguarded, and Olympos, my former teacher, and Mardian, the head of my armies and, when traveling with me, the head of my personal guard, remained always at my side when in public, not infrequently with their hands constantly on each's weapon hilt. Mardian's sword kept anyone dangerous at length. Should anyone escape his attention, Olympos had a slender dagger, and he'd been taught by Mardian to use it most efficiently. When traveling in public with them at either side, I felt safe.

The day before I was to return to Egypt, a Roman senator approached me in the forum and greeted me warmly. "Hail, Cleopatra, friend of Antony and ally of Rome!"

Mardian and Olympos tensed their hands already on their weapon hilts. I signaled for them to be at ease. I recognized this man, and, though I couldn't place his name, I could recall that he was not someone who was a danger to me.

"Hail, good sir," I replied.

The man approached closer and introduced himself. "Most revered Queen of Egypt and wife of Marc Antony, I am the poet, Virgil."

"*Ave*, Virgil," I replied in the familiar, giving him a warm smile. My two guardians removed their hands from their weapons but continued scanning the area about us while keeping a keen eye on the man.

"These are your bodyguards, I presume," Virgil stated, nonplussed.

"They are Olympos and Mardian, loyal servants of mine. Mardian is my personal bodyguard in Rome, and Olympos, my former tutor and guest." It was never wise to reveal the full extent of one's defense.

"I see," Virgil stated. "Well, noble queen, it appears you have learned much about Rome and her ways since the death of Caesar. Defeating Octavian, the abomination, has proven fruitful. Still, if I may be so bold, what you and Antony wish to *make* of your victory will require further battles, further alliances, perhaps further wars. Like

Helen of Troy, wife of our founder, Romulus, you must now prove your ongoing loyalty and fidelity to the country of your husband. Not a small task, I perceive, given Rome's traditional reluctance to embrace foreigners, especially as family."

"I have every intention of being loyal to the country of my husband, good Virgil. I also have every intention of defending my own people and preserving Egypt," I stated, wondering where this conversation was going. "I am a wife, but also a queen. My path may be difficult, but not impossible."

"Indeed. It is not an easy path you have chosen, Great One. But those the gods call to greatness are rarely given easy tasks," he replied.

"You flatter me, but in the flattery, speak the truth. You seem an honest flatterer," I mused.

"In truth," Virgil continued, "Octavian is dead, but your troubles are not over. You are undisputed Queen of the East and wife of Rome's principal Consul, but both East and West hold challenges," Virgil stated.

"Indeed," I replied. "Among them, that troublesome king of Judea, Herod."

"Herod—what is to be said of him?" Virgil half-asked, half-stated. "He *appears* a good, strong ruler. But appearances can be deceiving and often change. What if Herod, in time, were to make Octavian seem the better?"

"As might be expected of a poet, you talk too much," I said, offput by his insolence. I would wish later I had heeded his warning. Herod would indeed become my living nightmare and a worse enemy than Octavian had ever been.

After stilted farewells, Virgil departed and I mused over what he'd said while completing preparations for my return to Egypt. The parting that hot summer morning was bittersweet. I was happy that my oldest was going to grow to manhood in Rome at the side of a man I completely trusted and who had chosen to replace his father. But I would miss Caesarion dearly. That night before leaving, I saw Caesarion dressed formally as a Roman. He was not yet old enough to wear a toga—the Roman sign of manhood—but he wore a man's *bulla*—a masculine protective charm—around his neck. It held a likeness of Mars, the Roman god of war. Antony worshipped both Bacchus and Mars.

"I will fight for our future, Mother," Caesarion promised, sounding too much for me like a man. His voice was deepening. In this and other ways, especially in gesture and walk, he bore a strong resemblance to Caesar.

"I have faith in you, my son," I said warmly, tears forming in the corners of my eyes. It is said that Isis' tears created the Nile. Mine created but awkwardness, causing Caesarion to command, "Do not cry, Mother! I do not like to see you cry." Caesar had said the same to me once, and the memory caused more tears. Once again, I was forced to let go of Caesar, this time by way of our son. When I stopped weeping, Antony joined us and together with an escort of centurions, accompanied me to the harbor at Ostia to see me off.

In the water before me, awaiting me and my signal to depart, was my grand Egyptian fleet, reassembled ostentatiously for a triumphant return to Egypt. I would sail in the flagship with its red painted mast and white sails, decked with purple and red victory streamers. My men, well-muscled Egyptians and Nubian Africans, were loading the last of my personal luggage and gifts for the trip home.

"*Vale en pace*, Cleopatra," Antony said, embracing and kissing me, as the moon beamed down, illuminating us as if we were god and goddess.

"*Vale*," I said in return, when I finally climbed the gangplank of my flagship. Once aboard, I ran to the side of the ship and called, "When will I see you again, Antony?"

"When the gods will it," Antony called back with a wave.

Caesarion stood beside Antony, tall and proud, and gave me a firm smile. "*Vale en pace*, Mother! It is Egypt who now needs you. May the gods of Egypt and Rome smile upon you!"

Despite of the sorrow of parting, I could not have been happier or prouder as I set sail toward my Egyptian home and the future awaiting me.

Chapter Nine

David and Cleopatra
36. B.C.
Year 16 of Cleopatra's Reign
Alexandria, Egypt

Caesarion was now firmly under the tutelage of Antony. Before I departed Rome, Antony had assured me that he would formally adopt Caesarion, though not right away. As a mother, I remained concerned for my eldest son, but wisdom demanded I redirect my concerns to the other children still in my care.

My father had played favorites, and although I had always been his and felt pleased to be so, this had caused fighting and strife between me and my siblings, eventually leading to tragedy. This I wanted to avoid for my three remaining children. In addition, my plans had changed several times while in Rome. All the work I had done to ensure that Caesarion would be Pharaoh would now have to be transferred to Selene, my three-year old daughter. Her ascension would be a daunting task, as she was still in the nursery.

My first action was to give her the Isis doll that my mother had given me. It had inspired me and opened a door directly to the goddess. It was my hope that it would do the same for her, and, one day after Selene was Queen Pharaoh, she would have a daughter and heir to whom she could pass on the doll. As for her brother, I did not yet know what to do. It seemed to me that these twins should not be separated. I took their birth and my survival three years ago as a sign that Isis was smiling upon my future plans, since not only were twins of different sexes rare, a mother surviving the birth of twins was even more so.

I insisted that Olympos give both of them a rigorous education. "Olympos, treat them as you would non-royal children," I instructed. "If they miss an answer, correct them. Especially so in geography. Egypt cannot border Gaul, for example, simply because either hasn't studied sufficiently."

"My queen...?" Olympos began, appearing perplexed. "In your example, was there a reason to choose Egypt bordering Gaul?"

I smiled, the memory of Arsinoë's sloth in her studies and eventual idiocy in action returning to me. Of course, Olympos would have had no knowledge of this, so I took the time to explain.

"When I was very young, Ganymede, Arsinoë's tutor, taught both of us geography. Arsinoë said Gaul bordered Egypt. I stated this was not the case, but Ganymede, at our step-mother Roxane's orders, had had my ears boxed and gave Arsinoë a plate of sweets."

Being Olympos, he responded with a question: "Do I box their ears then for incorrect answers?"

"No. Just inform them sternly when they are wrong and give them the correct answer. No need to *punish* wrong answers, but never allow ignorance to continue," I explained.

"Egypt bordering Gaul..." Olympos mused. "An intriguing idea, actually. But...I worry that you expect too much from an old teacher." Olympos had been my tutor, but I could see that for some reason he was apprehensive about tutoring my children. "Cleopatra, I fear I cannot do it."

"Then I shall have to find a new tutor," I said, fully expecting him to relent.

Instead, he asked, "Am I dismissed then?" There was an edge of anxiety in his voice. I couldn't tell if he didn't actually want to leave my service or not.

"No, Olympos, you are not! Over the years, you have proven far more than a teacher to me. You have become perhaps my most trusted counselor. I often rely on your opinion with your Greek perspective of the world, and I always will. Perhaps more so as Antony and I build our empire. I do not easily discharge those who hold my trust. In this, I am not like my father." The situation was reminding me of the time my father exiled Charmion over a minor infringement in Ephesus. It had almost cost me one of my dearest friends and even my life. "I do, however, ask that if you sincerely feel you *must* leave my service, you will help me find a suitable tutor for my children," I added.

"That I can do," Olympos replied.

The summer in Alexandria proved even hotter than in Rome, and as often as I could, I spent the hottest part of the days walking the cool halls of my revered Library and Museion. The sea breezes, high ceilings and marble floors together offered a welcome respite. I even took to wearing Roman chitons made of the lightest of Egyptian linen. Traditionally, silk was more suited to royalty, but I found my new line of clothes substantially cooler. Soon, many of the upper class wives in Alexandria were copying my style. I also found the linen chiton more accommodating when my belly began swelling.

I soon found myself craving figs, especially *Dulcis coccora* as I had when pregnant with Caesarion. But I also craved Gallic acorns, which Antony had introduced me to at Philippi, and upon which we had feasted at our triumph. I had a shipload brought in that summer from

Gaul at great expense, making me wish Egypt truly *did* border Gaul.

In any case, around the beginning of Sextilus, the eighth month of the Roman Julian Calendar introduced by my late husband, Julius Caesar—*Pharmuthi,* the Fourth Month of Growth by our Egyptian calendar, and the hottest part of the year—I came upon my new tutor. We met perchance in the Library. I was surprised when talking with him, how closely he shared my philosophy on raising royal children.

His name was David ben Aziz. An Alexandrian Jew, he was eminently knowledgeable in the Scriptures of Judea, yet cosmopolitan in experience, having lived in Greece, Rome and now Egypt. As a result, he was multi-lingual as well. It was clear to me that he greatly enjoyed Egypt, especially the freedom we accorded visiting scholars. David was a treasure trove of knowledge. As our discussions progressed, it seemed he had read every one of the tens of thousands of scrolls in our library! Tall, swarthy, with a long, black, neatly trimmed beard, dressed in blue and black robes, he was pleasant to the eye as well. I soon took great delight in conversing with him.

Initially, we talked in Hebrew, later adding Greek, Egyptian, Latin and even Akkadian. I queried him about other nations, such as Syria, the land of my stepmother, and Parthia, the land Antony sought next to conquer, and Judea, where David hailed from and which, though I was careful not to admit to him, I had jealous eyes on. To my relief, David eventually revealed that he, too, despised Herod. He said he found my desire to learn about other lands and my ability to speak other languages a mark of the wisest of rulers.

"Why do you dislike Herod?" I eventually asked.

He looked carefully to his left and his right and hesitated; I had to reassure him several times it was safe before he would speak.

"Many of my people resent that he is satisfied being a client king of Rome, Your Majesty," David ventured.

"It is not an uncommon situation. It is my and Antony's hope that those we choose as client kings will prove good leaders of their peoples," I said.

"The truth is, My Queen, we Judeans strongly despise Herod's despotism. He is mad for power, trusts no one and disposes of any who dare disagree with him. At the same time, the non-Jewish world despises him because he is set on rebuilding the temple for his own glory."

I nodded in agreement. Much of what David was objecting to, I'd heard from others. Furthermore, there was something about Herod that left everyone including myself distrusting him. I mentioned this to David.

"Perhaps you mistrust him because you desire Judea for yourself," David delicately suggested.

"That is undoubtedly part of it," I admitted. "But not all."

"Well, my Queen. There is a reason that I am in Egypt and not Judea. Queen Cleopatra's sandal is far more merciful than Herod's boot."

"You flatter me." I retorted, smiling inwardly.

"Perhaps. But perhaps not," David replied enigmatically.

I was coming to like this educated, erudite, discrete yet when called for forthright man. "How exactly did you come to Egypt?" I asked, wanting to be more certain about him before I progressed my hopes further.

"Tell me first what you know of Jews," David said cautiously in return.

"I know of the Queen of Sheba named Makeda. She knew Solomon, your wisest king."

"The wisest or most foolish? Solomon had a harem that would make a Roman Imperator seem monogamous. We believe one wife is quite enough for any man," David stated, in doing so, revealing more of his fundamentally Jewish beliefs.

I laughed at this. My Caesar, like most public Romans, had been a flagrant womanizer. And while womanizing generally ran against Egyptian customs, Queens and Pharaohs were known to keep any number of private consorts. Who would know better of the consequences of having multiple partners than a Queen like Makeda or me? Still, Caesar was not a man like Solomon with a harem of a thousand. There was, therefore, a distinct difference.

"You smile? Then you are not offended, widow of Caesar?" David asked, revealingly.

"I am one of two women who can claim that title," I admitted. Calpurnia, Caesar's declared Roman wife had disappeared after his assassination. My spies had informed me that she had judiciously gone into hiding. Given the circumstances, I assumed she would not live long, which she hadn't. "Tell me of yourself, David ben Aziz," I stated, intent on moving the focus from me back to him.

"I was born in Judea. My father, Aziz bel Abdu-el, was a Persian whose family had for generations served as advisors to the Kings of Urdu. His Persian name was Abdual, meaning powerful and respected—literally, 'he who helps the most needed.' When he met my mother, a Jew, he was fascinated by and soon adopted her religion, changing his name to Abdu-el in honor of the most ancient god of both the Arabs and the Hebrews, El. "

I nodded, giving him permission to continue.

"I was named after a famous King of Israel and Judah, who was said to be beloved of the One God. We moved to Jerusalem when Hyrcanus II, the high priest of Judea who coveted the throne appointed my father as his chief foreign advisor. It was a brief appointment during a particularly turbulent time. My family eventually fled to Egypt when Pompey stormed Jerusalem. I was in the crowd that saw Pompey beheaded on the shores of Egypt because he violated the Holy of Holies," David said, matter of factly.

"The Holy of Holies? What is that?" I asked, intrigued. I knew Egyptian, Roman and Greek priests regularly made sacrifices to their gods and goddesses—Ra and Isis, Jupiter and Juno, Zeus and Hera and the like—and I was curious about the Jews who worshipped a single, enigmatic god with an unspeakable name, YHWH.

"My Queen, the high priest visits the Holy of Holies once a year, and he must be sinless, or he will immediately be stricken him down by God," David said as a beginning.

"Pompey, when he sacked Jerusalem and entered the temple, was not struck down," I noted, recalling as David had said that he had met his end in Alexandria, my brother himself having ordered him beheaded, Pompey's head being presented to Caesar, my first Roman husband, as a gift.

"The One does not forget. Justice may be delayed but is never denied. There was a reason he died in Egypt rather than Jerusalem, though it may remain to us inapparent," David explained.

"And he did die a most unpleasant death." I said, grimacing at the remembrance. Like Ma'at, it seemed this YHWH did not fail in his duties either. Yet I found David's explanation surprisingly obtuse, given his directness up to now. This ability to shift between detail and idea was an attribute of Jews that I told myself I must keep in mind when dealing with Herod.

"And do you like Egypt?" I asked, seeking to elicit his attitude towards Egypt, myself, my dynasty and especially my children.

"I find the Egypt of Cleopatra an agreeable place, especially

Alexandria," he answered, with a sweep of his arm encompassing the library. "The Egypt that Moses fled, not so much,"

"I have heard of your Moses. He was an Egyptian prince. But that was hundreds of years ago, and a people change over time," I said. I was surprised to find myself being overly kind to this man. In fact, the Egyptian prince had defied Pharaoh and abandoned the nation that had succored him to wander the desert with his supposedly "real" people. Allegiance to religion over nation was another attribute of these people of which I was aware. It was one reason why I was interrogating David closely despite my admitted attraction to him.

"One of your other women pharaohs, Hatshepsut, saved Moses when his people later abandoned him. We call her 'righteous among nations'," David said.

I smiled. My intuition about David was proving correct. He was loyal to his religion and people but also to the country he now claimed as his own. Such a man could provide Selene and Helios a balanced view of the world they would someday rule. Also, from his very first statement, I surmised he would not spoil or harm them. Here was the kind of tutor who could impart things of true value to my future royals.

"David, I think you are a natural teacher, and the right man to give both of my children an education," I summarized happily.

"Both?" David asked with surprise, first, I suspect, at my sudden conclusion, second at my directness, and third at my having *two* children, Helios, my son, being the more publicly known.

"Yes. my son, Helios, and his twin, my daughter Selene, who will be my royal heir," I stated proudly.

"Teach a daughter? Surely you know, Great Queen, that we Jews are forbidden to teach women the Torah." David paused a moment in thought. "But I suppose if she is destined to be the next Pharaoh-Queen of Egypt, it would be good if she knew the ways and customs of not only the other nations but also of my people. An ignorant leader is a curse on a nation."

"If you are willing, I am prepared to welcome you into my retinue, David ben Aziz," I stated with finality.

"I thank you, Great Queen. I understand from our conversation *what* you would have me teach them. But if I were to agree to do so, *how* exactly would you have me teach them?" David asked. "The Roman way of your husband, Marcus Antonius, would involve corporal punishment, withholding of privileges, and withholding of food. In my culture, we set down Moses' laws, explain they are from the One God Himself, and that learners by agreement must honor their teachers since it allows the learner to live long and prosper. Is this latter your desire for the Gemini?" David asked.

I thought long about this before replying. "It is." Of everything I could give them, long, prosperous, educated lives would best means of preserving Egypt and my dynasty.

"Truly?" David questioned.

I sighed. I liked David, but his constant questioning could be irksome. Still, I knew from my Greek heritage that this way of constant questioning, called by the great sage, Socrates, "*elenchus,*" was one of the deepest and most respected pathways to wisdom, so I allowed him his vice.

"Your older sisters did not honor, by tradition their greatest teacher, your father. They turned against him. My Queen, this is the history of the house of Ptolemy. What makes you think you *or* I can change this?"

I had to admit that the Hebrew had a point.

"Your honesty is noted," I stated with firm conviction. Unlike my predecessors, I, like David valued honesty above most human traits. A saying was already circulating around the world that, "in the Egypt of Cleopatra, there is no place for deceit." I liked and nurtured this saying. "My sisters did not honor this attribute and were able to rule Egypt only briefly. Moses said it was God's will that mortals honor their parents. My own name, Philopater, means 'lover of her father', an attribution which I have tried to uphold my entire life. Indeed, David, if what you Hebrews say is true, my sisters met a just end for their defiance. Tryphaena was murdered by her lover and Berenice met her end by our father's order. I, the child who honored him, am now Queen of Egypt and am seen by my subjects as having saved the country. Perhaps your One God looks well upon me honoring my father, Pharaoh Auletes," I said, wishing to honor all gods, even one so odd as to have an unspeakable name. This god of the Jews increasingly seemed a god whose favor it would be wise to court.

"Majesty, you have answered most wisely," David replied. "I remember Egypt when your sister Berenice was ruler. And as for your younger sister, Arsinoë—her disregard for her elders and appetite for young men would put the lustful Queen Jezebel to shame."

"Queen Jezebel?" I asked. I'd heard of her, but as she had not been a queen regnant, she had not captured my interest until now. She was obviously a woman who didn't command respect, and I suddenly wished to know why. Though I wanted to know more about this woman, I wisely asked a question that mattered infinitely more. "David," I asked. "I have answered your questions. Now you must answer mine: Will you tutor my children?"

This time, he didn't hesitate. "I would be honored, Your Majesty. You have proven yourself to be intelligent and wise. And I have seen you dispense mercy more than once," David said, as if justifying his commitment.

"On those who deserve it," I added to temper his flattery and convey to him that there were limitations to our agreement.

"Indeed," David acknowledged. I knew from this moment on that I could rely on him to conscientiously fulfill my request.

I inhaled through my teeth, remembering my sister, Berenice. I still thought fondly of her, though I spoke to none but Isis of this. Neither Antony nor even my trusted maids, Charmion and Iras, knew of my longing for the only one of my siblings I had ever really loved. Berenice had shown me kindness when we were young princesses, unlike Tryphaena, who had mostly ignored me or Arsinoë who had constantly tormented me. I hoped Ma'at and Isis had heard my silent pleas for mercy on Berenice's behalf when she passed.

"Great One?" David interrupted.

"I was thinking of my siblings. But no more of that. Be welcome as the tutor to my two beloved children," I stated.

Thus it was that David became tutor to Helios and Selene and a member of the new Ptolemaic dynasty.

Helen R. Davis

Chapter Ten

Philadelphos
Year 16 of Cleopatra's Reign
Autumn 36 B.C.
The Portico of Nut

The Great Goddess Isis; Queen Cleopatra V, devoted sister and wife to Pharaoh Ptolemy XII "Auletes" Neos Dionysos; Pharaoh Ptolemy XII and his favorite concubine Tryphosa who he called Astraia meaning "the star," all turned away from the edge of the heavenly portico of Nut to welcome an eighth personage. Berenice, sister of Cleopatra, known as Berenice IV during her short reign as Queen of Egypt, had just emerged after her long sojourn in the land of the dead. Berenice had wandered the underworld for nineteen years, for her soul, though tarnished by her unseeming behavior as Queen, had still been found lighter than the Feather of Truth, so she had been allowed to work her way into the presence of the goddess Isis. Isis anticipated an awkward reunion, for in truth, Berenice had been granted this privilege more because of Cleopatra's pleas for mercy then Berenice's final actions in life. Auletes had had his ungrateful daughter beheaded before Cleopatra's eyes. Her mother, referred to as the Royal Mother by everyone present, had never cared for her second eldest daughter, Berenice being less intelligent—some would say outright stupid. In fact, her stupidity was the only thing the Royal Mother and Roxane, Auletes's wicked foreign wife after the Royal Mother's passing, agreed upon. Yet, despite all that had happened, Isis spread out her robe to welcome Berenice and there was a sense of peace in the heavens, or at the very least, a much appreciated, momentary absence of quarrelling.

Auletes alone did not welcome the daughter who had in life spurned him. He and the Royal Mother were busy talking about their favored daughter, Cleopatra, as she gave birth to their fourth grandchild, a third son. Cleopatra had named this one Ptolemy Philadelphos. Unlike her first three births, this fourth one was difficult, and there were times that Auletes and the Royal Mother feared for Cleopatra's life. Much as when Roxane had, with fear, labored to give birth to Ptolemy XIV, Cleopatra was fearing not only for the child within but also that this child might be the death of her. Unlike Roxane, Cleopatra did not announce her fears to those assisting her, nor curse the child within. Berenice looked down on her sister, now a grown woman laboring with great difficulty, and saw that, while Cleopatra was struggling, the shadow of Anubis, god of the dead which hovered over herm, had departed from her sister, Cleopatra. Cleopatr was now pleading to Isis for the life of her child.

"I wonder which Marc Antony, were he here, would choose over the other, or would he gamble everything on the hope of having both wife and child?" Auletes mused watching Cleopatra struggle, her Roman husband conspicuously absent.

"Marc Antony is a man of honor," the Royal Mother stated. "I would like to think his choice would be the same as yours was." She had seen her husband order the royal physicians to save both Roxane and Ptolemy XIV on pain of death, even knowing Roxane was not worthy of the kindness.

"He is a man of honor, but he is also a Roman." Berenice stated. Auletes and the Royal Mother turned their eyes from their living daughter to the one who had just joined them.

"I fear your trials in the underworld have not really changed you," Auletes said harshly. While Berenice had lived, she had despised all Romans.

"Not much, husband, but perhaps a little," the Royal Mother added. "At least she sees Antony as a man of honor. She must have worked out some of her folly."

"Hmph," Auletes replied, removing himself from the portico.

A moment later, a weak half-scream was followed by a loud cry below. The Royal Mother and Berenice looked down anxiously. Cleopatra had collapsed in exhaustion but was still breathing. The infant, at last free of the womb, was being taken away by Charmion and Iras who were together cleaning it and cooing happily.

The next three days, Cleopatra fell in and out of fever. Olympos, her childhood tutor, and David of Judea, his replacement, offered the royal physicians a variety of remedies, some of which by the end of the second day, the physicians out of frustration allowed. At the end of the third day, David alone pronounced that Cleopatra and her son, though weak, would live, insisting she rest for at least a week and be fed only Kosher food until she regained her strength.

The week passed slowly for Cleopatra, but quickly for the observers in Heaven for Heaven's time ran different from that on earth.

"Like our Egyptian priests, the Jews seem to have a gift for healing," the Royal Mother pronounced when Cleopatra at last sat up and demand food.

"Indeed." Isis stated proudly. "The Jews once lived in Egypt and many became Egyptians. By the time they were called out of Egypt by

Prince Moses, we had enlightened them as a people, sharing with them many of our cultural blessings."

During the conversation, Isis retreated from the balcony only to return and stand alone at its far edge, her thoughts and eyes turning to Judea, the land of the Canaanites, a land promised to the Hebrews by their One God as their future world of "milk and honey," now coveted by Cleopatra and the Ptolemies.

"Great Goddess?" the Royal Mother asked. "Why are you looking towards Judea? I've heard it said your magic doesn't work there."

"I cannot use my magic in Judea; that is correct. A power greater even than even than Amon-Ra dwells there and forbids it. The land puzzles and at the same time attracts me. Judea is a lovely land. I can see why you Ptolemies have always coveted it. But this land has a destiny of its own, a destiny beyond the power of even us gods to change. We give mortals gifts of land to cherish and care for, not to covet," Isis said petulantly.

"Are you saying we are *wrong* to desire that land?" Berenice asked in shock, still believing a royal could have whatever he or she desired, one reason why her reign had been a short one. It was also clear that she believed Egypt to be superior to Judea or indeed, any other country.

"Who are *you* to argue with a goddess?" Isis asked, appalled at the hubris of the woman who, for Cleopatra's sake, she'd shown mercy.

"Great One!" Berenice replied, suddenly aware of the precariousness of her position. "I...I am merely curious. Please forgive me if I've offended you." Berenice bowed low, hiding her weasel-like eyes from the goddess.

"You are forgiven. But you would do well to spend time with Athena and learn the art of wisdom. I will nonetheless answer your question, curious princess." Isis said.

88

Berenice continued bowing low and averting her eyes, having noted that Isis had not addressed her as a queen, even former Queen of Egypt, and suddenly wondered what Isis, the protector of pharaohs, and Athena, the Greek goddess of wisdom, had thought of her brief two years on Egypt's throne.

"Egypt will always belong to the Ptolemys. But I want Cleopatra to be content with Egypt and the lands she acquires while rebuilding of her family's lost empire. Governing beside Antony, I will give her many nations," Isis pronounced with finality, "but Judea she can never have." As Isis finished her prophesy, Cleopatra arose, refreshed from her extended rest, hungering for news from Rome about the result of her husband's most recent expedition.

Chapter Eleven

Allies in Rome
Autumn 36. B.C
Year 16 of Cleopatra's Reign
The Portico of Heaven at the Vault of Nut

After a time, Venus and Caesar joined the ladies at the railing of the portico of heaven. With Cleopatra's recovery, everyone's attention shifted to Marc Antony in Rome. He was wearing the laurel wreath the young Roman boy had presented him, although it had long since withered. Caesar voiced his marvel at how long it had lasted, then wondered aloud at Antony's purpose in continuing to wear it. "Does this man dream of becoming a king?" Caesar asked of no one in particular.

Caesar had descended into the Roman underworld without judgement immediately upon his death, as was appropriate to mortals who rightly claimed divinity. Their trials were assumed to be infinitely harsher than those aware of their mortality. There, he was neither wanted by Tartarus, nor celebrated in the Elysian Fields. Designated neither good nor bad but simply dead, and, having died as a consequence of being brutally stabbed by each of Rome's senators, he was allowed to rest and sleep. It was upon hearing Cleopatra's repeated heart-wrenching pleas that Isis reluctantly descended into the Roman Underworld to request Caesar's presence in Nut. After some negotiation, Pluto, the

Roman god of the dead, granted her request, and Caesar was now standing with the heavenly ladies, permitted to visit Cleopatra in dreams, but restrained from intervening in her fate, Pluto's condition for Caesar's release. A great chasm had always existed between the living and the dead, and, as Athena repeatedly reminded, always should.

"I do not know," Isis stated as Antony ordered his slave, Eros, to dispose of the crumbling laurel crown, "but overall, he is acting wisely. Cicero Minor continues speaking in favor of his Cleopatra, and his decision to marry her in Rome by Egyptian rites appears to have largely placated the Roman mob."

"Perhaps. While he is officially her husband in Egypt, Romans still see her as a foreign consort, an ally at best, and, at worst, an Oriental sorceress greedy for power at the expense of the Republic of Rome. And there are also those who claim that the sorceress plans to rule the world alongside Antony, the two as Empress and Emperor," Caesar said.

"You were absolute dictator of Rome for a while," Athena retorted icily.

"I was," Caesar acknowledged. "And that honor is about be bestowed upon Antony. Rome desperately needs a dictator, at least for the present."

Antony had, indeed, just been declared Dictator for the next six months, a position given him to help him consolidate power and revitalize the Republic. War had plagued Rome for too long and moving from a war economy to a domestic economy was one of the greatest challenges any ruler faced. There was also the question of Juba, a prince of the nation of Mauritania, who had come to Rome after the defeat of his father by Julius Caesar ten years prior. Initially a slave, the boy worked tirelessly and eventually was granted citizenship, in the process growing into a strapping lad. Recently, he'd tried on more than one occasion to enter Antony's circle, and, though generally accepted, he remained on the periphery, having before been a vocal supporter of Octavian. Caesar could clearly remember Juba's Berber father, also named Juba. In Caesar's opinion, there remained much of the father in the son.

"Juba the Elder was a worthy opponent," murmured Caesar. "Juba the Younger appears to have been smart enough to switch sides." As Caesar spoke, Antony, below, unfurled a scroll from Juba the Younger, praising Antony as Dictator of Rome, rightful ruler of the Roman Empire and honorable Triumvir of the East. Antony smiled obliquely as he read the young man's request to serve as Antony's Master of Horse. *This man has not acquired the gift of subtilty*, Antony thought. *I held the same position under Caesar.*

Caesar watched as Antony penned a response to the younger Juba, accepting him instead as a soldier under his command, reserving the title of Master of Horse for his trusted servant, Eros. What Caesar saw as pure hubris, Antony had accepted, at least in part, as an offer of friendship.

Caesar frowned.

"What?" Isis asked.

"Juba the Younger switches sides too easily. For the moment, he claims allegiance to Antony, and Antony has accepted his claim. But what of the future?" Caesar questioned. "I fear Antony will pay dearly for admitting his type into his world."

"Insincerity, or just survival?" Athena noted. "The man's father lost his kingdom and his land. If the son is to have any inheritance, his only hope is to pledge allegiance to the winner. You, yourself, have claimed that you often did what you did 'simply to survive'. Is he then to experience your displeasure for simply trying as you did to survive?"

Athena did not like Caesar, although being the goddess of wisdom, she took great care to veil her dislike of a man she believed to be at heart a ruthless tyrant.

Caesar, for his part, had noted Athena's coldness towards him since his arrival but chose to acknowledge Athena's observation. "Indeed. Men will do all they can to avert death. But there remains the question of the unspoken word for 'ally'."

"And what word is that, Great Caesar?" Venus asked, moving beside him.

While buxom Venus and muscled Caesar pleasured themselves in each other's sight – Venus was, after all, Caesar's declared Goddess throughout his life—Isis and Athena once again made it clear that was all they would enjoy. Besides, being descended from Venus, even Caesar dare not act out his carnal desires on a relative. Caesar's next words nonetheless deeply pleased the goddess of love and beauty: "It was Cleopatra who taught me that the eternal, unspoken word for ally is 'husband'." What Caesar carefully avoided saying was that he envied Antony being alive, sleeping in Caesar's wife's arms, teaching Caesarion how to fight as a Roman soldier and rule Rome. Nonetheless, Caesar felt pleased to know that Caesarion would be the next leader of Rome, even if Antony, not he, was to prove his *de facto* father.

"I tell you truthfully," Caesar said, looking mystically from one to another of the goddesses on the portico, "in the end it will be Cleopatra Selene, daughter of the moon, offspring of Cleopatra and my dear friend Antony, who will prove to be not only the staunchest friend and ally of Rome, but the mother of a New Empire."

"I see," Athena said with raised eyebrows, taking Caesar's prediction to imply the eventual joining of Selene and Juba. Venus, for her part, immediately began showering rose petals on the two from heaven.

Isis blanched. "Selene is far too young, and Juba must prove his worth if Antony and Cleopatra are even to *consider* him as a possible future husband for her. And as for the so-called 'New Empire' you speak of..."

"So-called?" Caesar responded angrily. "Rome is now the greatest military force the world has ever known! Joined with Egypt..."

"The only thing your people have ever really worshiped is victory. Do you recall the great Roman general Crassus who lost Rome's eagles to the Parthians?" Athena reminded.

"There were three things Crassus excelled at: making money, bribing politicians, and eating," Caesar snorted.

"That may be, but how did Crassus lose to the Parthians if Rome is so all-powerful?" Athena continued.

"A Roman army is like all armies—no matter how powerful and well-trained, if a fool is in charge, disaster inevitably follows," Caesar spat out, adding as his anger abetted, "as I learned during the Servile Wars," referring to the successful slave uprising by Spartacus. "However, once I got to know my opponent better, I crushed him and the revolt, as was proper. Crassus, on the other hand, continued to underestimate his opponent and thus was himself crushed."

Athena opened her mouth to challenge his opinion, but Caesar interrupted. "He fell for one of the oldest tricks that exists—the Parthians pretended to retreat, he followed, and by overreaching, was destroyed by arrows. Too many leaders think the only way to get ahead is by direct onslaught. More can often be achieved through judicious retreat, diplomacy and intermarriage than attack."

"As when you married Cleopatra?" Athena, bristling at having been interrupted and co-opted, asked. "I say there was another reason

Crassus had trouble with the Parthians!"

"Perhaps—just *perhaps*—he wandered too far from Rome's center of power," Caesar offered. "I pray Antony and Caesarion do not rush headlong into conquest, in the process overextending the very New World Antony and Cleopatra are planning, but instead, expand it slowly by all means possible, as I did when conquering Gaul."

"So, you would have Antony and Caesarion repeat your 'conquest' of Gaul?" Athena poked, holding as some mortals as well as some immortals did that Caesar had been victorious in Gaul despite himself.

"It will be easier with the help of Cleopatra and Egypt to conquer the world than it was for me to conquer Germania and Gaul," Caesar mused. "Played well, they will not have a Pompey Maximus and jealous senators constantly interrupting."

Athena chose her next words carefully. "If you knew the senators hated you, Caesar, then why did you dismiss your bodyguard that fateful night?"

Caesar waved his hand. "I wrongfully assumed that all they would do was complain. They had done so. Day after day. Seemingly endlessly. Without effect, I might add. It never occurred to me that they would take up weapons and murder me. I was, after all, divine!" Caesar stopped waving his hands as the realization of what he was saying struck him. His body abruptly slumped and he looked away. "I *was* divine," he repeated morosely, realizing the mistake he'd made first in having believed it, and second in having stated this blasphemy in the presence of heavenly goddesses. "In fact," he continued at last, "it was my self-righteousness that killed me rather than their stabs. *Et tu, Athena?* On the other hand, perhaps my death was necessary in order for my son to rise to power." Caesar paused and rubbed his forehead thoughtfully. "Sometimes, the manner in which a man dies has more impact on the future than the manner in which he lives."

"At last you begin to think more like a true god and less like a mortal futilely reaching to attain godhood," Athena stated. The point made, the heavenly narrators turned their attentions back toward Antony, Cicero Minor and Caesarion. The three, surrounded by Antony's generals, were discussing over a large map the very points of which Caesar had spoken. The map contained within it the world as known to humans at the time.

Antony was the first to speak. "The completion of our conquest of Germania should be easier than subduing Gaul as the tribes of Germania have no history of unification. We need a new source of slaves to continue rebuilding Rome from a city of brick to one of marble."

General Dolabella protested. "What of the Parthians' insult to us when they took the eagles?"

"I understand and acknowledge your desire to avenge the slight," Antony replied, "but for the time being, that border is stable. Germania is a hotbed of barbarian tribes, each slavering over the riches of what they perceive to be an exhausted and disorganized Rome. Thanks to Caesar, close-by Gaul and our legions there remain firmly in our hand. It would take long marches and thrice as many legions to conquer far off Parthia as nearby Germania."

Caesarion nodded in partial assent. "All that you say is true, Imperator, but there are far more riches in Parthia than there will ever be in Germania. Besides, will not Parthia become wary if we invade Germania? And if so, would this not allow the Parthians time to amass their considerable forces? Father, we will have to deal with the Parthians eventually. Is it wise to delay the inevitable?"

"Well spoken," praised Antony. "But your mother is working on a solution that may not require military might to conquer Parthia."

"And that is?" Dolabella asked, taken aback by Antony's claim and the thought of Egypt doing what Rome was hesitating to do. Dolabella's voice made it clear that he still wasn't certain that Antony's trust was well placed in his Egyptian wife.

"Cleopatra is working on a solution with Parthia similar to the solution we reached with Armenia," Antony stated.

"You mean letting the Parthians pick their king and administer themselves, paying only a minimal tribute, while we retain final veto power in matters of state?" Dolabella asked.

Antony nodded his assent, then returned his focus on the map.

"It would keep Parthia at bay for the present," Dolabella acknowledged.

"Cleopatra is most clever and, as I said, she is working this problem. Remember, Dolabella, Egypt and Rome are now joined in interests. For the present, Egypt will focus on Parthia while we conquer Germania, each for the collective good."

Chapter 12

Cleopatra Diplomat
Late Winter 36. B.C. – Early Spring 35 B.C.
Years 16 and 17 of Cleopatra's Reign
Alexandria, Egypt

I had not seen Antony since the triumph in Rome, and we were approaching the first anniversary of our wedding by Isian rites. I felt Antony's absence ever more keenly since I bore our son, Philadelphos, and nearly died in doing so. One never forgets the feel of death's shadow.

Now fully recovered, I sat in the throne room on low floor pillows with my four children about me, listening to David tell a story.

"A Hebrew man named Jacob had two great desires: One was to have a male heir; the other was to have Rachel, his favorite companion, as his sole wife," David stated. "I thought of her, My Queen, while trying to save your life."

"Why is that?" I asked, secretly wanting to avoid further discussion about the precariousness of my life.

"She once stated that if she could not grant him his greatest desire, she would surely die. The problem was that despite all attempts, she remained childless."

"So, of course, he took another wife," I concluded. In Egypt, while men typically took only one wife, Pharaohs were the exception. Thinking again of my recent brush with death, I shuddered and breathed a prayer to Isis that I could continue to bear Antony children and be his one true wife.

"In fact, he took her sister to bed," David continued, "not because he wished to, but because his uncle tricked him into bedding Leah in order to produce an heir, and selfishly to advance the uncle's family. Leah bore him six sons and a daughter, but Jacob never stopped desiring Rachel."

"How fitting that Jacob, in fulfilling one desire was tricked into losing what proved to be his greatest," I replied, adjusting sleeping Philadelphos on my lap.

"Yes, but the story is not yet finished, My Queen."

"What happen to Rachel?" asked little Selene, who was totally engrossed in the story. Helios looked bored and was ignoring us, playing instead some distance away with a toy chariot. Still, David and I both sensed his interest. While boys played, they often listened and learned.

"Rachel eventually became pregnant by Jacob and bore him two sons, but she died bearing the second," David said. "The second was well known and loved in Egypt. His name was Joseph."

"Like my stepmother," I mused. In labor, she had prayed heartily for the life of my littlest brother, and Anubis, hearing her, moved his shadow from the unborn and spread it over her while she bore the child. Unlike the wise Joseph, though, Stepmother's second son proved to be the least of Egypt's kings.

"In some ways, perhaps," David admitted. "Rachel said she would die unless she had children, but then died because of having one."

"She was a fool," I stated. "She cursed herself by being unclear and tempting the gods. I cannot pity such a person. What happened to Leah, her sister?" I sensed an allegory in the making.

"Leah remained Jacob's wife, and it is she, not Rachel, who is buried at his side."

"So, Rachel lost more than her life," I observed, "and the undeserving won everything." *The gods often act in strange ways*, I mused.

David nodded his assent. "She did, and Queen Cleopatra, while I have to agree with your opinion of Rachel, she didn't lose everything entirely. It is to her barren women today cry, while Leah is all but forgotten. The lesson for today is done."

"No, it's not, David," I replied, much to his surprise. "As I said, Rachel's story reminds me of my stepmother, Roxane. She was a second wife as well, and she died bearing a second son. But there is, like Rachel, more to her story."

Selene sat up, wide-eyed, waiting eagerly to hear about her step-grandmother. David stiffened and stared at me only slightly less wide-eyed. I finished the story for both of them: "With her last words she cursed my brother, stating that for killing her, he would become the least of Egypt's kings, and his name would be altogether forgotten. Rachel's second son is remembered even today."

"So, you purposefully didn't repeat the sins of your forebearers during your time of crisis, Cleopatra. Instead, you begged your goddess for life for yourself and your son. Instead of cursing, you clearly blessed yourselves. It seems your stepmother spoke a curse on your brother and a blessing on you," David summed. "Ironic, for I have not infrequently heard in the streets of Alexandria tales of the cruelty of Queen Roxane especially toward the young Princess Cleopatra. Her curse may have been honored, but what of her unintended blessings?"

"An excellent question, David, and one that can't as yet be

answered. But I like to think I will continue to be a blessing to Egypt, and so will each of my children."

"You saved your land from Octavian, Great One, and that is already a blessing beyond imagination. But if there is anything one can be certain of, it is that you, your children and Egypt will face more challenges, hopefully always under you and your goddess' beneficent eyes."

I smiled. I was liking David more and more. I knew he did not believe in Isis, or that she was even real, but he did not disdain me for my beliefs.

Suddenly, Olympos burst into the throne room, exhausted from running, sweat dripping his face and body. He bowed breathlessly and handed me a scroll. "From Marc Antony, now *Dictator in Perpetua* of Rome," he stated, panting to get out Antony's newest title.

"Go and rest," I ordered him, for he looked ready to collapse. *Dictator in Perpetua?* That alone was news worthy of Olympos' effort. My concern abruptly shifted back to Olympos, for he had never looked so pale. Was he ill? Without a word on behalf of himself, Olympos bowed and headed for the palace quarters he and Mardian, along with David and some of my other most trusted soldiers, shared.

I opened the scroll and what I read frightened rather than pleased me. Marc Antony was planning to invade Germania on the Ides of Aprilus and would take Caesarion with him onto the battlefield! My son! In battle! I had to force myself to acknowledge that Caesarion was not a child any longer —he was eleven years old and about to enter manhood. Then, as I continued reading, I breathed a sigh of relief. It was not as bad I was imagining.

Antony was bringing him not to fight, but to *learn* to fight and lead others. Germania, Antony stated would provide unlimited timber and slaves to our empire. But that was not all. I was to begin diplomatic relations with Parthia, which controlled the Silk Road trade with the Far East.

Diplomatic relations? I had assumed when Antony asked me to address Parthia, it would be to revenge the Parthian's defeat of Crassus, one of Rome's most humiliating defeats and still an open sore on the flanks of the Roman senate. Antony, however, in his wisdom, decided that could continue to wait. For now, he wrote, I should engage Parthia in parlay. History, he said, had repeatedly demonstrated the inanity of a two-front war. The importance of delaying a war with Parthia was of utmost importance, and, given Parthia's propensity for deceit, he could only feel assurance entrusting this task to me.

Diplomatic parlay? I could not deny I was pleased with my current status as Queen-Pharaoh of Egypt, and my unofficial future as Empress of the World. Still, while I liked the idea, the thought of negotiating with Parthians left me feeling apprehensive. Old Persia, now called Parthia, had conquered Egypt some five hundred years ago, its stranglehold ending only with the arrival of Alexander the Great. But while Alexander broke Parthia's grip on Egypt, he allowed the nation of Aryan warriors to continue to exist, leaving them with a taste for the riches of Egypt and the bitterness of being denied them. Parthia had spent the centuries licking its wounds, rebuilding its wealth and amassing and training filial armies, slowly but continuously expanding its borders. At present, it had economic and military alliances with vast regions to the East. My husband was correct in his belief that Parthia, like a snake, would coil and attack Rome, Egypt or even both at the slightest sign of weakness or distraction. My part, then, would be doubly important: First to hold Parthia at bay, while second, providing Antony time to consolidate the northwestern lands, familiarize his soldiers to his and

Caesarion's command and temper his legions in war, all in preparation for eventually invading and taking Parthia. What Antony proposed, I agreed, but I also knew that the Parthians would consider any diplomatic attempts on my part as a likely prelude to a later sneak attack. Although the Macedonian Greeks through Alexander the Great, from whom the Ptolemy's were descended, had beaten Persia—now called Parthia—it had been a close victory. The Persian king, Darius, hadn't so much lost as he had been unable to win, leaving Parthia's control of its vast population in limbo. Parthia nonetheless remained a huge and powerful if loosely knit proto-empire.

Then, I recalled the Parthian trader couple, Miradates and Narezduct, who had sheltered me when my sister, Arsinoë, who, during one of my brief absences, had proclaimed herself Queen of Egypt and sought to depose me. Without their help, I would undoubtedly have been killed. It was during the time they were sheltering me that I learned from them what it was that bound the Parthians together. It was trade. With this in mind, I took quill to scroll to reply:

To Marc Antony, Dictator in Perpetua of Rome,

I send congratulations on your new title. It is yet another small but important step toward the achievement of our dreams, a step which makes our dreams ever more real.

I will do as you request, gladly performing my duties in regard to Parthia in the short term. I do not know if you know, dear husband, but before our victory at Actium, Arsinoë, who seized my place as Queen of Egypt in my absence, attempted to overthrow me. Upon my return, a Parthian trader couple hid me while my men fought Arsinoë. I plan to make use of this couple's friendship and the Parthian people's love of trade in my diplomacy.

As for Germania, it brings to mind Caesar, and now you, my love, as Conqueror. But please, dear Antony, I beg you, protect Caesarion! He may now be your son, but he is not your equal. Only life can provide the experience necessary for him to rise to manhood.

You will be pleased to know that you are once again a father—your new son I have named Ptolemy Antonius Philadelphos after you, husband, and Ptolemy II, the son of the founder of the Ptolemaic dynasty. Given our dreams, I thought the name fitting.

I send this letter with my signature.

Genethso—let it be so.

Cleopatra VII Philopater, Queen-Pharaoh of Egypt, Your Wife and Co-Ruler

I sent the missive and immediately tasked Mardian with locating the Parthian couple, Miratades and Narezduct, whom, for their service, I had granted especially favorable trading rights. They had been known since to divide their time between Parthia and Egypt. Mardian located the two the next day in the Alexandrian market and brought them directly to me.

Like the first time, they appeared apprehensive at being summoned before me. They wore the same style of flowing Parthian robes I had seen them in before, but the cloth was considerably finer while they were considerably older. Narezduct's black beard was streaked with white, and his wife's hair was completely grey. They appeared dazzled as they looked about my restored throne room. With the economic blessings Antony's victory had bestowed upon Egypt, I had had had all the furnishings in my palace covered in gold leaf and inlaid with precious gems. The couple brought with them a young lad, about Selene's age, whom Miratades introduced as their son.

"Great Pharaoh-Queen, how may we be of assistance?" Miradates, asked in all sincerity, prostrating himself and his family before me as was the custom of the Parthians. Seeing him and his wife trembling with fear, I made a sign for them to rise and approach, hopefully lessening their apprehension. The boy, as with most boys his age, showed no fear, only curiosity and astonishment.

"I wish to create a formal trade alliance between Egypt and Parthia. Such an alliance would greatly benefit Parthia, Egypt, Rome and the rest of the world, as well as the future of my dynasty," I stated.

"You are, then," Miradates asked cautiously, "as people say, truly the wife of Dictator Antony and your newest son is the offspring of that union?"

"We were quietly wed in Rome in the Temple of Isis by Egyptian rites last spring. And, yes, my new son, Ptolemy Antonius Philadelphos, is truly our child."

With my answer, their anxiety visibly diminished, and they congratulated me, showing their pleasure in learning of my good fortune and intent.

"Great One," Miradates said with typical Parthian directness, "it is a bold gesture indeed to suggest a formal alliance, given our nations' past conflicts, but nonetheless, we would be honored to convey your desires to King Phraates."

"Carry not only my desires, Miradates, but also this gift in good faith." I waved, and a servant produced four alabaster pint jars, one each containing natron salt, coniferous resin, bitumen and beeswax, the essential embalming ingredients used to assure a king's eternal afterlife.

"Each is worth a fortune!" Miradates said, inhaling in amazement, his eyes wide in wonder as the four jars were placed before him, his wife and their son.

106

"This is but a token of what I wish Egypt and the Ptolemies to share," I stated.

"A trade in such products would be in value beyond imagination," Narezduct mused.

"I expect King Phraates will be pleased. And your family will be my exclusive trade emissaries."

The couple looked stunned. "Great Pharaoh-Queen. We will be privileged to present your offer to our Parthian king," Miradates said.

"Take also this letter containing my offer of friendship, Miradates," I added, rising and placing it myself into his hands. "Have your workers come by this afternoon to pick up these gifts after I have them packed for travel." As Miradates and Narezduct departed, I breathed a prayer to Isis that the letter and gifts would begin a friendship with Parthia that would preclude any need for us to invade and conquer Parthia. That is, after all, what governing is really about.

Chapter Thirteen

Pharaoh-Queen

35 B.C

Year 17 of Cleopatra's Reign

Alexandria, Egypt

Autumn turned to winter and winter into spring. Antony wrote to me regularly as Caesar had; in terms of content, there was little difference between their letters: they were filled with descriptions of combat. Only the names and places differed. In my letters to him, I was careful to always be positive and supportive, no matter how gruesome the battles sounded, only occasionally mentioning my love and caring, knowing it might seem importune on the battlefield, and it would remain some time before we saw each other. For myself, I loved Antony dearly and missed him more than ever, but I had my own challenges, one of which was ruling alone.

Though many now called me such, I was not yet ready to formally declare myself Pharaoh-Queen, as Nefertiti and Hatshepsut had done, knowing well the difficulties such a declaration had brought them. As Queen, by Egyptian tradition, it was assumed that my husband, Antony, would become Pharaoh; however, our plans were so much bigger and the time was not yet ripe to publicly advance them. The issue of my consort and heir therefore remained unsettled, and with it, the minds of my subjects. There was as much talk of the consequences of a Roman Dictator assuming the Pharaohship in Egypt as there was in Rome of the possibility of my asserting Queenship there.

To placate our subjects' fears, Antony and I had decided I would initially declare Caesarion my consort, Pharaoh and heir; however, being a son rather than a sibling, and being constantly away with Antony in Germania, it ended up creating even more questions and uncertainty.

I therefore decided to declare my second son, Alexander Helios, as Regent-in-Name, ostensibly training him for a future of leadership as Antony was doing with Caesarion. On the other hand, I was having qualms about Helios. Though already five, and in spite of being named for the sun, he was not proving as bright as Caesarion at that age, or even his twin sister, Selene. So, in fact, I continued for the moment ruling alone.

So, what of Helios and Selene? My plan was to encourage Helios to become the warrior he loved playing at while teaching him the art of rulership by having him at my side and observing me. As for Selene, my sole intent was for her to rule Egypt after me. But how to best present these ambitions to my people? In order to maintain order, I needed for now to let the people think that my twins, as tradition dictated, would wed and rule Egypt together after me.

After much thought and several discussions by letter with Antony, I issued a royal decree:

Let it be known to all that Cleopatra VII Thea Philopater, Queen of Egypt, blessed of the goddess Isis, decrees that her current Regent-in-Name, Alexander Helios, having completed his term, shall now become heir with his sister, Selene. Upon ascending the throne he will be known as Pharaoh Ptolemy Helios XVI, and his sister, Cleopatra

Selene, as Cleopatra VIII, together as The Gemini.

Let it further be known that the reign of Ptolemy Caesar, heretofore known as Ptolemy XV or Caesarion by the many, has ended. Caesarion, shall retain his title of Ptolemy XV and the right to be known as the Son of the Queen. When in Egypt, he shall receive the respect due a Pharaoh, though he will no longer hold the title.

Let it also be known that from this day, Marc Antony, Dictator in Perpetua of Rome, the sole husband of Cleopatra VII, shall be the Queen's official Consort, and together they shall serve as Co-Regents for the Gemini.

It is further declared that the years of the Gemini shall be counted beginning now, Year 1, to honor their imminent ascendancy.

Furthermore, the Queen's youngest child, Ptolemy Antonius Philadelphos, shall come in line of succession after the Gemini and any heirs of their body.

Lastly, Egypt shall remain a true friend and ally of Rome.

This decree shall be copied and announced to the public.

Genethso—let it be so.

Cleopatra VII Theo Philopater, Daughter of Isis and by Her will, Queen of Egypt.

My advisors gathered about me in the throne room to hear me read the decree, and, as always, they had questions.

"You are already Pharaoh-Queen to everyone. Why make it public?" Mardian asked when the reading was over. He pretend to be shocked by what I did, but knowing his as I did, it was more admiration than shock.

"I can't afford to make the mistake Caesar did of having secret wills or documents," I stated.

"But declaring your *daughter* our future queen so soon? You are reversing the natural order of things!" Olympos added. Olympos was truly shocked.

"I had my hesitations," I admitted, "but between us, Antony had already decided on an Arabian wife for Helios, and that Caesarion would rule Rome with either a Roman or Egyptian wife at his side."

"There is always Philadelphos," Olympos offered. "And he would buy more time."

I smiled at that. I was blessed with no shortage of sons. That meant that Caesarion's future in Egypt would have depended on whether I had more male children. Besides, it was clear to me that Selene deserved and could best serve Egypt.

"Philadelphos…" I left the phrase unspoken. Though I loved my youngest, he had nearly cost me my life. The love of a mother is unselfish, but I could not forget this fact. Furthermore, his health since birth remained marginal. No one outside of Iras and Charmion knew this, but they were often having to tend to him, for the child became ill easily. Selene, along with Caesarion, were my healthiest. Though but five, Selene impressed all with her desire to learn history and languages, and her burgeoning knowledge of all things Egyptian. She was bright and sturdy. I had no doubt that had the situation at Actium been reversed—Isis forbid—of my four, Selene alone would have fought for Egypt, and of this I did speak openly.

"Lord forbid, Cleopatra," David, dignified, standing next to Olympos, pronounced. "Yet what you say is true. Of your children, Selene is most like you."

I smiled. David was not like Olympos or Mardian. They would require further convincing, and I began immediately.

"Even as a girl, Selene showed a warrior's spirit," I stated.

"Oh?" Olympos ventured, arching an eyebrow.

I nodded affirmatively. "Yes. Once Helios stole the Isis doll I had given her just after she was born, for as my mother had passed it to me, I sought to pass it and Isis' blessings to my daughter. Selene never cried, nor did she tattle to me or my ladies. She went directly to Helios and took the doll back. This I believe an omen that Selene will fight for Isis and Egypt," I said. The story always re-convinced me, but I wondered what Olympos, Mardian and David would think, and waited for a response.

"Her determination and devotion are to be commended," David stated. "If she will fight for a small thing, she will fight for the larger."

Olympos scoffed. "It was just a doll. You both read too much into such things. She's a little girl who directly confronted her brother and won. A tale as old as time."

I turned to Mardian. He could be unpredictable in his reactions, but he sided with David and me, adding, "My only concern is whether she will guard and fight for Egypt as fervently as her doll."

"With the proper training, I believe she will," I assured.

"Proper training is necessary for any avocation, but especially leadership," David added.

The conversation was interrupted by a blast of trumpets, signaling the arrival of a messenger. David, Mardian, Olympos and I turned our eyes to the entrance of the golden palace. Coming up the marble steps was Rufio, the man left by Caesar to guard Egypt when I had been summoned to Rome to become Caesar's wife. Now a trusted member of my entourage, Rufio served many purposes. While I had been fighting to claim my throne, he governed Egypt. Each time I was in Rome, he did the same. Of late, I had dispatched him to Judea to inspect the palms around Jericho, my newly acquired territory, to assess the political climate in Judea, and secretly begin negotiating a marriage for Helios among the Nabataean Arabs around the Dead Sea. Unlike Olympos, who had exhausted himself running to me with Antony's news, Rufio arrived composed and calm, although his face wore a grave expression.

"Rufio! *Wy em hotep*—Welcome in peace!" I called, and walking to my throne and sitting, signaling him to approach.

"I will speak plainly, Queen. I do not have good news, and I know no best way to tell you this," he offered, so concerned he didn't even take time to return my greeting.

"Then tell me quickly," I replied, my heart pounding rapidly, fearing the worst for Antony.

"King Herod of Judea refuses to acknowledge your marriage to Antony, and therefore denies any claim you might feel you have to Jericho. While he continues to pledge loyalty to Rome and Antony, he says he cannot do the same to Egypt, Rome's vassal, and therefore to you, because, he says, you have no authority in this matter. He says further that to be Antony's legitimate wife and be able to speak on his behalf, you must be wed by Roman rites. Until then, he says, you are simply a client queen, even as he is a client king." In spite of the insult, the situation was not as dire as I imagined. I maintained my dignity, reminding Rubio that our wedding, though by Isian rites, had occurred *in Rome* before the Roman citizenry.

"*I* acknowledge you as Antony's wife, Great Queen. Of that there can be no question. But client kings like Herod may not. In the eyes of those still sympathetic to Octavian, you could be held obligated to marry Antony in Rome *in a Roman ceremony*," Rufio reminded.

"Of this, I know," I said, irritated not with Rufio but with Herod's double insult. "Antony and I will marry by Roman rites after he and our son, Caesarion, conquer Germania." While not biologically Antony's son, I seized the opportunity to reinforce both my and my son's positions.

"My Queen, I am not finished. Herod says that since you are not Antony's wife, the only way you can ever have any part of Judea is to become Herod's wife,"

The audacity of this man! Herod was known to have scores of wives, putting even Solomon to shame! I was *Antony's,* regardless of Herod's personal wiles, desires or opinion. Capturing a slave girl in war was one thing; publicly declaring one's intent to have another's royal wife was something else entirely! I turned to David, seeking a way to counter such insolence. "I thought Jews didn't allow polygamy," I said, desperate for any way to counter Herod's triple insult.

David responded, though his response brought me no reassurance: "*Legally,* no. But as in any nation, there is one rule for a king and another for commoners. I fear that you, for the moment, you will have to accept Herod's nonsense without a counterfoil. Herod, you see, is an Edomite and in the eyes of many Judeans, Queen Cleopatra, not truly a Jew."

"Meaning?" Olympos asked, once again raising an eyebrow, this time with irritation.

"Meaning we Jews only tolerate him," David stated. "He does keep our dietary laws but neglects the laws of justice."

"David speaks true, Queen," Rufio said. "I met Herod personally. It is said it is safer to be his pig than his wife or associate, and he knows this. He is, I believe, attempting to goad Antony into warring in the East by insulting you, his true wife. If Antony were to split his legions, assigning your son, Caesarion to lead a contingency to the East, Parthia and perhaps even some of Rome's vassal states might seize the opportunity to war against Rome. In the end, only Herod would win. He could take advantage of the confusion, and, should Parthia and the East prove victorious…" After a brief pause, Rufio asked, "What, if anything, would you have me answer?"

Dealing with trickery and innuendo requires a clear, rational mind. I sat forward, fist to chin, elbow to knee, considering, and my thoughts returned to the Battle of Philippi some years prior. I remembered Herod's hubris and his coarse attempts at flirtation with me. Hubris from a king I could disregard, but his lame attempts at verbally subjugating me, I could not. They filled me with disgust, bordering on hatred. With a sinking heart, I realized that such a man, in declaring his intent, might, if confronted, attempt to kidnap me by force. If he did and was somehow successful, all of my efforts for Egypt would go to waste.

O Isis! How have I escaped Octavian only to fall afoul of a worse man? I wondered.

Rufio replied, as if reading my mind, "Great One, I do not believe Herod so bold as to openly anger Antony by trying to secret you away by force. It is one thing to insult you by not accepting you as Antony's wife. It would be quite another to directly insult Antony. I believe he is bluffing, hoping to elicit from you a response he might use to drive a wedge between you and Antony, in the process weakening Antony's control over him and giving him leave to elevate himself in the eyes of other disfavored leaders who supported the losing side. That said, however, he told me to tell you to prepare for his arrival in Egypt."

"His arrival in Egypt?" I stated, mortified. "As what? Friend or foe?" while wondering, *Does It matter?*

"As whichever *you* decide, My Queen," Rufio stated, abruptly ending the conversation.

Chapter Fourteen

Herod

35 B.C.

Year 17 of Cleopatra's Dynasty; Year 2 of Antony and Cleopatra's Reign

Alexandria, Egypt

I decided to not allow my fear to control me, and instead transform it into strategic and tactical plans. Herod's boldness was scandalous. It should have been I, Cleopatra, Queen of Egypt and wife of Antony, who summoned him, not Herod boldly marching to meet me! By custom, the greater royal always summons the lesser. But didn't Antony and my plans for the future include breaking old customs and replacing them with new ones that would work better for us? With that thought in mind, what I was seeking was something that would cause Herod's boldness to play into my hands and foil any immediate plans he might have against my husband or son.

Herod was, like Antony and me, intent on challenging the world, so using that approach on him seemed the most promising. First and foremost, I wanted to impress upon him and the world that Egypt was superior by showing which had the superior ruler. I decided therefore that I would receive Herod as King of Judea, even if, by his own admission, he was only a vassal king. Isis, whom I personally served and publicly embodied, was a goddess of mercy and forgiveness. I would thus display this to the man whom people were already mockingly calling the "King of the Jews."

I spent as much time as I could discussing Jewish laws and customs with David, in the process perfecting my already extensive knowledge of the Hebrew language. "I will honor this undeserving man of who it was just said, it is 'better to be his pig than his wife or associate' by having no pork present during his visit. That is a shame, since my cooks can prepare an outstanding wild boar for state events." I said.

"My Queen, what is the purpose of showing any respect to a man who is intent on denigrating you and Antony? He should instead fear poison in his kosher meal!" David stated.

"There is always that concern when one is a ruler. 'Uneasy lies the head that wears a crown'," I quoted saucily, returning to the subject of food.

"Cook will prepare many dishes: pomegranates soaked in honey, spiced figs, stuffed dates, various fish and fowl, mainly trout and minnow, along with wild hens imported from Gaul," I said.

"But for what purpose?" David asked again.

"Men may rule nations, but by nature, it is women who rule men. I want to honor Herod beyond his expectations. I want him and his entourage to see placed before them a panoply of delights, never knowing which, if any, might be his death. I want him to be overwhelmed by my generosity while constantly distrusting me, and thereby experience the discomfort I feel around him. When his visit is over, I want his entire court to see his vulgarity, vile snake that he is. As a result, I hope to enlist the friendship and support of his court, especially his wife, Queen Marianme."

David stared at me in disbelief, then awe. I think this was the first time he saw the full measure of my diplomatic abilities.

Three weeks after Rufio informed me, Herod approached Alexandria and my court amidst great fanfare, to the delight of my people arriving with pageantry and parade worthy of a Roman triumph. *Clever man*, I had to admit. *He knows how to put on a good show.*

He was brought to my palace on a royal litter, his body hidden behind plush purple curtains. After him came Marianme's litter followed by that of his mother-in-law, Alexandra, whom I had been informed he had recently appointed to a high-ranking Judean government position, though I knew not which.

Bringing two women, a wife and mother-in-law, to further counter me. The man is even cleverer than I imagined, I had to admit.

I dressed in a sheer gold chiton with gold bracelets in the shape of snakes with eyes of blood red rubies coiling about my arms and wore the crown and uraeus of Egypt. I would not let the man forget that I was Queen of Egypt. Out of respect for Jewish customs, I wore a veil over my hair, but an elaborate one spun of fine gold that did not hide my kohled eyes and crown.

I had the entire court stand for my entrance and again as I welcomed him. Selene walked on my right, holding my hand, and Helios my left. I had Selene dressed in a manner duplicating mine, only without the crown or head covering. The message, I hoped, was clear: I wanted to show Herod that I was Pharaoh-Queen and Selene would follow. Helios I dressed as an Arabian prince. Philadelphos I dressed as a Prince of Egypt. Too young to even crawl, I had him carried in the arms of Iras who wore a fine blue Roman *stola* and *palla*. Charmion, dressed in the white Egyptian flax-linen *kalasiris* of a royal attendant, walked beside Iras, Both of my attendants wore gold-gilt sandals.

Olympos, Mardian and David appeared next, all three wearing

119

swords, indicating their determination to protect me. In addition, I carried a small golden dagger hidden within a secret compartment of my jeweled belt. If needed, I had no qualms about using it. It was a gift from Antony, as practical as it was elegant and deadly. For this occasion, I had Charmion and Iras carry similar daggers hidden on their bodies.

After formally acknowledging Herod's presence, I led my entourage to the dais on which sat my throne, and took my seat surrounded by those in whom I must now place all my trust. Herod's procession continued until, after some time, the long train ended, and his pallet bearers lifted and deposited him at the foot of the dais. Four Judean trumpets blared pompously. *So much of ruling is tedious*, I thought.

"Herod the Great, King of Judea! All Hail!" cried out a Judean messenger.

"Hail," everyone in my court returned in unison as I instructed, leaving out his epitaphs.

I stood, waiting at the top of my dais as the purple curtains of his pallet opened, and he planted himself awkwardly on the marble floor. After surveying the throne room with mild disdain, he approached the throne. I took the moment to carefully study him.

He was dressed in a purple toga and cape, and wore an inexpertly gilded crown on his head. He had aged since the Battle of Philippi. Although his clothing and features made him appear ruggedly handsome, his beady eyes made him look small and brutish. Caesar may not have been the most handsome of men based on looks alone, but his strong personality, his intelligence and conquests made him unquestioningly manly and attractive. Herod, while still outwardly handsome—I could not deny it—had a perpetual sneer and swagger that made him inwardly hideous.

I looked behind him at Marianme, his wife. It was known that he adored her and she loathed him. Marianme was wearing a simple pink chiton, her sad eyes framed by a flood of brown curls. *Any woman married to Herod would eventually have sad eyes*, I thought. I would remember those sad eyes when told of her murder at his hand six years hence.

My attention then turned to Alexandra. While old, she displayed a radiance and pride that could only emanate from a woman of strong character. I sent a smile to this woman, and we momentarily exchanged friendly glances. Herod stopped approaching at the foot of the dais and spoke, ending both my study of him and my inner monologue.

"Cleopatra, Queen of Egypt and supposed wife of Marcus Antonius, Dictator of Rome, I am pleased to visit, albeit disrespectfully on your part, being uninvited, to, among other things, address the claim you make over some of my land. You steal Jericho, the land of the Balm of Gilead, from me and call yourself Queen of the Arabs in the Dead Sea region. By what right do you do this?" he demanded.

This situation concerned him more than I'd thought. He'd thrust a verbal sword blade in front of everyone. Interestingly, while his words and demeanor were menacing, his tone was honeyed. He was clearly provoking me. I inhaled through my teeth, a gesture that gave me extra time to think before uttering anything I would regret.

"Herod, King of Judea, I am pleased you have traveled here to pay me your respects. Come. We are both friends of Antony, whether you believe me to be his wife or not. I would, however, remind you that though Judea was once a possession of the Ptolemies, when meeting with Antony in Rome and being offered Judea as a wedding gift, I told him I would be satisfied with Jericho alone. I could have just as easily taken all from you. Antony remains gracious to us both. Irrespective of your immediate purposes, I will not quarrel or dispute this with you," I stated flatly, hoping he'd noticed I'd refrained from calling him Client King of Judea.

"Very well, Cleopatra," Herod stated, impudently avoiding my title. "I smell a feast. I assume it is for me?" Herod waved a hand and one of the most beautiful and frightened young girls I'd ever seen approached him, head bent down, to kneel before him. "A favorite concubine," he stated matter of factly. "My taster for this visit," adding as insultingly as possible, "An Egyptian."

Herod's wife, Marianme, looked mortified and squeezed her fists in anger at his behavior. Alexandra, his mother-in-law, remained aloof, though I could tell from her body language, she, too, was ashamed of Herod's behavior. The "taster" rose, eyes cast down, her face betraying her fear of imminent death. I felt sorry for her, I suspect, exactly as Herod meant me to.

"It is indeed a feast," I replied, purposefully avoiding both his title and his name while ignoring the implications of his bringing with him an Egyptian as his food taster. "It is ready, and in your honor. Come and dine." I gestured at the doors opposite the room from my throne and they immediately opened to reveal a large room decorated to look like an Egyptian temple dedicated to Isis. The gesture was not entirely lost on the Jewish claimant before me.

Mistrusting and disliking Herod even more than last time we met, throughout the meal I kept my own eyes alert for poison as did my compatriots who, begging bits and tastes of food off my plate, acted as tasters. Having no official tasters gave an appearance of trust that sharply countered Herod's obvious arrogance, distrust and mendacity.

Little was meant to be accomplished at the dinner except feasting and pageantry. I stuck to my plan of impressing our Judean guests while constantly humiliating Herod before them through apparent kindness; I did not, however, allow any further discussion about Judea. The first part of my plan worked well. Marianme and Alexandra and I creating brief opportunities to get to know each other and bond. To my surprise, the second part worked equally well, Marianme and Alexandra finding excuse after excuse to keep Herod off balance and away from me. The result was better than I'd hoped, with Herod becoming more furious with each passing hour.

When Herod and his party finally departed Alexandria and Egypt, I tried to show despair as Herod parted with words of mock friendship and understanding, inviting me to visit Jerusalem. While outwardly I officially entertained his invitation, never for a moment did I intend to accept. I had known the perfidy of counterfeit men like Octavian, and now this particularly loathsome vassal king. Nonetheless, in the days that followed, I found myself thinking, *What if I did accept his invitation? Could anything to my advantage be further accomplished? And, even if so, would it truly be wise for me, a married Queen to visit him in Jerusalem?* I eventually engaged David to explore this odd thought that kept nagging at my mind.

"You are Queen of a great gentile nation and your visit would be looked upon with suspicion by all. Furthermore, as the undeniable wife of the Roman Dictator Antony, the Zealots would likely take advantage of your visit," he said in shock.

"Who are these Zealots?" I asked. "Tell me more of them." If I was to be fully cognizant of the politics of this nation with which I shared a border, I would need to know such. If Herod would not tell me, and I knew he never would, it being not to his advantage, at least David would, and honestly. He responded with a worrisome glance and a long, drawn-out sigh.

"They are a mixed political-religious sect that believes a strong military leader—a Jewish messiah—will be born and free Judeans from Rome. Their battle cry is 'Death to Rome and Egypt', but of the two, they especially despise Rome and whoever leads Rome, namely Marcus Antonius at present. As a group, they are no friend of Herod's," David related.

Now *this* interested me. "Tell me more," I commanded. "I need to know more of Judean politics."

David arched an eyebrow like he'd apparently seen Olympos do. "There are three other major political-religious sects in Judea," he began. "They are the Pharisees, the Sadducees, and the Essenes. The Pharisees are making the lives of many Jews miserable by their rigid insistence on following every scriptural rule in the literal sense. They are righteous and holy men, or so they claim. They believe in a national resurrection of all Jews and the return of a Jewish empire with Jerusalem as its capital. The Sadducees, many being Greek and well educated in the Greek style of inquiry, are quite different in their beliefs. They hold, for example, there is no resurrection..."

"Isis forbid! "I interrupted. This was unthinkable for an Egyptian, especially royalty already preparing a monumental tomb in preparation for resurrection and an afterlife.

David paused to allow each of us time to recollect our thoughts, then continued. "The Essenes are an odd sect, living separate from other Jews in order to 'prepare for those who would make the way for the messiah'. A reclusive sect, they live communally in two major places: the mountains north of the Sea of Galilee which they call Nazareth, and in the stark desert along the sea's eastern shore which they call Qumran. I do not think you will have the opportunity to interact with the Essenes, but since you wished to know..."

Again, I felt compelled to interrupt. I had, in fact, heard of the Essenes, but by a different name. Said to have originated in Egypt, myself being of Macedonian Greek extraction, Greeks and Egyptians knew of them as 'Pythagorean Jews'. "They are the children of Ra, the One God," I said.

"They claim descendance millennia ago from the seventh son of Adam, Enoch, who was said to have been taken bodily to heaven without dying," David embellished. "In Judea, their men and women live ascetic lives in Nazareth and Qumran. Both communities have a strong belief in individual resurrection that is supposed to begin with the appearance of an enlightened religious rather than a strong military messiah."

This concept of a messiah intrigued me. What was this messiah exactly? Would he be like a God-Pharaoh of old Egypt, or a Greek hero? Would he be male or might he be female? My mind was bursting with questions, and they flowed from me like a waterfall.

"Your questions, My Queen, are fitting, but I cannot answer them all, for even we Jews ourselves do not know, it being said that Essenes, when accepted into the sect swear a blood oath to never reveal the sect's innermost secrets," David stated.

"Well, then, I will ask no further questions. It is not unlike the gods to withhold answers from us until the appropriate time." Nonetheless, David's various descriptions of the messiah intrigued me greatly, and now I definitely wanted to visit Judea sooner than later. "I think that I shall accept Herod's invitation. After all, the land around Jericho and the Dead Sea *is* mine and Herod's arguments during his visit here imply he realizes this. David, would you like to return with me?"

David was silent at first. He seemed stunned by both my statement and question. Then tears began to form at the corners of his weathered eyes, tears not of sadness or loss, but of joy. "My Queen, it has been more than twenty years since I have seen Judea. You do me a great honor."

"I ask not just for you, but for my own safety as well," I said, although in fact I was delighted to be able to bring my new sage such joy.

"Indeed." David said, although he was so overwhelmed by the promise of seeing his home, he could converse no further in the moment.

"I will leave Rufio as regent," I stated, for I had done this in the past whenever leaving Egypt was necessary, and Rufio had always proved a trustworthy, loyal leader, "and, like Herod, I will bring an entourage with me."

"Your children?" David asked in disbelief, his tears of joy instantly gone, his expression replaced with one of concern and caution.

"If Helios is to marry an Arab princess, what better place to begin the search than Jericho, a favored destination of the eastern land and sea trade routes? Antony spoke to me once of a princess named Iotape of a nearby coastal city of the same name. He said it is one of the loveliest city-states in the East, having an evenly mixed population of Arabs, Armenians, Greeks, Romans and Medes as well as its own mint and an imposing Acropolis. Iotape is the daughter of Gaius Julius Antiochus IV Epiphanes, who rules the Roman vassal state formerly of the Seleucid Empire, located at the very heart of the Middle East. Without a living male heir, whoever marries Iotape will inherit the kingship. I will bring Selene with me, too. The experience will enrich her education. Philadelphos, however..." I trailed off.

"The nearby Dead Sea offers healing to many of those who bathe in it, its name being truly ironic," David suggested.

Perhaps if I bathe Philadelphos there, he would become stronger?

I immediately thought.

"The Dead Sea is so salty, one does not have to swim to stay afloat," David continued. "The salts there are highly prized. I've heard of many miracles happening there."

"Then Philadelphos will accompany us to Jericho and Jerusalem," I said, already formulating a plan in my mind.

As if on command, Mardian appeared and approached. "So, when do we leave for the so-called Promised Land?" he asked, having conveniently overheard my last statement.

"In two weeks' time," I stated as my plan continued to develop in my mind as if the Goddess were whispering it to me. I called for Olympos and Rufio, who joined us in record time, aware that something major was in the making.

"May Isis protect you," Olympos said, after hearing the outline of my plan.

"And I will ask Minerva to protect you," Rufio stated.

With so many of the gods and goddesses' blessings, including Antony's Bacchus and Mars, and Caesar's Venus, I felt my journey to this land that so many claimed and desired—including, if I were honest, myself—was not just blessed but ordained. I had only to advise Antony of my plan while I finished making the necessary preparations.

Chapter Fifteen

The Plan Unfolds

35- 34 B.C.

Years 2 to 3 of Antony and Cleopatra's Reign

The Vault of Heaven overlooking Germania and Judea

Caesar, considering himself the heavenly guardian of Queen Cleopatra VII Thea Philopater and Dictator Marcus Antonius, looked down with Isis from the portico of the Vault of Nut, to watch Antony fight his way through Germania, a land of wild pines, harsh winters, and seemingly endless Teutonic barbarians. As the months passed, Caesar grew increasingly proud of Antony and his conquests. Antony's emulation of his own Gallic conquests made him feel proud; doubly so to see his book in Antony's hands every evening after the Imperator retired for the night. Still, it worried him that Antony was neglecting matters in Rome.

Cicero Minor continued proving a persuasive orator, a capable general and popular leader. *Perhaps too persuasive, capable and popular*, Caesar mused, for the citizens and senators of Rome were tiring of hearing about the absentee Dictator's conquests. There remained only a small section of Germania near the Elbe River as yet unconquered, and Caesar watched nervously as Antony and Dolabella along with their legions returned to Rome to reconsolidate. Caesar

129

would have stayed in Germania and finished the conquest, but Antony felt compelled to return Rome for the New Year celebrations and to travel to Alexandria in the spring to reunite with his co-ruler and Egyptian wife, Cleopatra.

Caesar's feelings for Cleopatra, his former wife, warmed seeing Antony's eagerness to rejoin her. He felt an equally increasing concern, however, for a Dictator who split his passion between ruling Rome and being with a woman. Caesar, noticing Isis at the other end of the portico looking down on Cleopatra and smiling fondly in anticipation of Antony and Cleopatra's reunion, nonetheless kept his concerns to himself.

Watching Cleopatra, Isis mused about how well her favorite had handled Herod, successfully soliciting the support and even help of his court. She was less certain about Cleopatra's upcoming trip to Jerusalem with her children and her servants. Overhearing Cleopatra's thoughts about the trip, which smacked more of self-justification than rationality, she stepped back from the balcony, pursed her lips, and knitted her brows. After several moments, hours, days or weeks—who could tell in the realm of heaven—she relaxed, re-approached the balcony rim and continued watching her charge, albeit more closely than before.

Cleopatra's journey to Jericho and on to Jerusalem proved educationally valuable for both the queen and her daughter, but was otherwise uneventful. Once in Jerusalem, however, Isis watched in horror as Herod repeatedly attempted to seduce Cleopatra in public, and wondered if because of the long separation from Antony, the beautiful queen would succumb. It was no secret to Isis that her favorite found Herod attractive, love and hate being different names the common point where hearts and bodies often melded. To Isis' relief, Cleopatra openly resisted all Herod's advances, reminding him that, even if not the fully acknowledged wife of Antony, she was not and would never become one of Herod's wives or concubines. Besides, she reminded him, under the laws of his own nation, he would be committing adultery, which, whether commoner or king, was a mortal offense. Isis' pride welled when Cleopatra also reminded him that as the incarnation of Isis, she could never betray her Osiris.

Herod, upon hearing of the queen's imminent arrival in Judea, had spread rumors that Antony had taken a Germanian concubine: a large blonde beauty with overflowing breasts and enveloping hips. Cleopatra, at first mortified, immediately ordered Olympos to determine the source of the information, and, finding it to be Herod, flippantly replied when she confronted Herod later that such was the prerogative of men at war and of "real" kings.

Over the next several days, Cleopatra's repeated spurns, fueled by Marianme's incessant taunts at the husband she hated but to whom she inevitably bowed, infuriated Herod to the point where he secretly plotted to have Cleopatra killed. Isis immediately tickled the ear of Marianme's mother, Alexandra, who, abjectly hating her son-in-law for his abominable behavior towards her daughter, warned Cleopatra.

Prior to the third evening's strained feast, tensions within the palace reached an all-time high. Frightened of what Herod might be plotting, Cleopatra assigned Iras and Charmion along with four of her most trusted bodyguards to watch over her children while she attended yet another state dinner, according to Herod, "in her honor." She also ordered Egyptian guards in full dress to stand alongside the Judean guards, "to honor Herod," and, with her host's permission, additional pairs at the entrance and, as an afterthought, in every corner of the room. After a formal entrance procession, Marianme joined her mother at Cleopatra's side, but not Herod, who sat alone, announcing cryptically that, as host, it would be his responsibility that night to continue the festivities irrespective of whatever might happen. Cleopatra, unnerved by Herod's statement, ordered everyone except David from her *mensam*—the table about which she was to recline—and commanded David to personally tend her.

Despite her deepening concern, Cleopatra's thoughts turned briefly to earlier that day, when she had bathed with her two-year-old son, Philadelphos, in the Dead Sea. Hearing the queen's fervent and selfless prayers, not for herself but only for the health of her son, Isis granted her wish for his recovery. So unselfish had Cleopatra proven, that, anticipating a critical moment later that evening, Isis had whispered to David the description of an herbal remedy she urged him to carry with him to the feast. That night, it was clear to all when Cleopatra rose, dropped her wine goblet and fell to the floor that she had been poisoned, an idea Herod instantly fueled, pointing at David.

David, who was administering the antidote he had brought, looked up to see Herod smugly signal Marianme, who joined her husband in pointing at David and screamed, "Guards! Kill the murderer!" As pairs of guards, swords drawn, ran from every point in the room towards him, he dropped the vial, and fearing for his life, rose and braced for the blow. However, Alexandra at the last moment, interrupted the public execution, instead ordering the guards to remove and imprison him, leaving David to spend an anguished night in prison, awaiting his fate and wondering if his return to his home country had, from the start, been his death warrant.

The next morning, David, filthy, disheveled and distraught, was hauled before not Herod, but his mother-in-law, Alexandra, who, she had argued was responsible for his fate as she had been the one to order his imprisonment. Sitting on her right was a strikingly alive and very concerned looking Cleopatra, and on the left, an openly disgruntled

Herod and Marianme. They were flanked by several members of the inner court and two rows of soldiers, one row Judean, the other Egyptian. David noted with increasing trepidation the guards were all armed.

"As you can see," Alexandra announced to David and loud enough for all present to hear, "the Egyptian Queen you serve is alive and recovering. You are therefore exonerated of the charge of murder. Furthermore, as it was your ministrations that may have saved her, you are declared without blame." Herod stared at Alexandra, eyes wide, teeth barred. Marianme, on the other hand, appeared deathly fearful.

David, flanked by the guards who brought him, shook with relief, unable still to fully accept that, first someone had attempted to poison Cleopatra, and second that someone had tried to place the blame on him. "I…" he began.

Alexandra interrupted with a wave of her hand, and the two guards released the disheveled man. "Your Egyptian Queen, and at her request, this assembly have determined your blamelessness. You are free to go," Alexandra stated, smiling with satisfaction. Herod looked furious. Marianme averted her face from her husband as he stormed out, and then from David as he shuffled out.

Later that day, after bathing and changing his clothes, David cautiously approached Alexandra's room where he'd been told Cleopatra was resting. In the doorway, Cleopatra signaled, and he entered but stopped when her paired Judean and Egyptian guards shifted as one to attention, placing sword hands on hilts. To David, Cleopatra looked no worse off than having overeaten as was socially required at any state feast. Cleopatra signaled again for him to approach and ordered the guards at ease.

"David," she began, drawing him closer by lowering her voice to a whisper, "I am truly sorry for what happened last night."

"My only concern is always for…" David began in earnest.

"Hush and listen. I fainted from the strain of the constant battle of wits with Herod and of not knowing what, given his manner, he planned to attempt that night. In fact, though I hadn't yet sipped from the goblet I dropped, the wine *was* poisoned. It was apparently a slow but deadly poison that allowed it to get past my taster, who later together with me would have suffered a slow death. Had you not dropped the half-full vial, which I later administered to her, she would surely have died."

"But who…?" David asked, astounded.

"I suspect Marianme at Herod's behest. I had hoped beyond reason that Marianme's loathing of her husband would drive her to become my friend, but I was wrong. It appears she is every inch as dangerous as Herod."

David looked astounded.

"It is Alexandra," Cleopatra continued, "who has proven a friend and ally. She intervened at just the right moment, deflecting Herod and Marianme's plot to have me murdered and you killed as my murderer. It would have left Charmion, Iras and my children, and thereby Egypt, completely in his power. In any case, it was your quick wit and action that saved my and my taster's life."

Above, in the Vault of Nut, Isis breathed a long sigh of relief and turned to Caesar. Three months passed in the moment of her sigh.

"Antony's conquest of Germania still remains incomplete," Caesar stated with concern.

"Indeed. And Cleopatra, despite her experience in Jerusalem, still does not fully appreciate the extent of Herod's hatred and anger, or Marianme's true feelings. While Marianme hates her husband for all he has done to her, it was she who administered the poison, though it was on threat of her own death," Isis said.

"Why can Cleopatra not see Herod as he truly is: a monster and her mortal enemy?" Caesar asked. "Herod didn't succeed in gaining control over her, or, in gaining control over her and Antony's offspring. That would suggest Herod is even now plotting something worse. Now that she is safely back in Egypt, I suspect his next move will be more character assassination. It wouldn't take much on his part to reverse all the work Cicero Minor has been doing on Cleopatra's behalf."

"Antony has repeatedly warned her about him," Isis agreed.

"Antony knows he can warn, but, though Roman Imperator and husband, not order her. Not in good conscience. Not if they are to rule the world together," Caesar mused.

"He cannot, because he truly loves her," Venus interjected, walking onto the balcony and standing next to Isis.

"Besides," added Athena, following in Venus' footsteps, "he is busy publicly completing his conquest of Germania." As Vercingtorix, the leader of the Gallic tribes had stood, naked, hands tied, before Caesar fourteen years ago, so the Germanian leader, naked, hands tied, now stood before Antony in the Circus Maximus in Rome to a tumult of jeers. Antony rose and, silencing the crowd, proclaimed before the thousands that those before him who remained loyal to Germania were about to perish. When the barbarian leader boldly refused to submit, Antony announced to the crowds delight that they would be crucified and left to drown in the slowly rising, freezing water with which he would flood the arena. Their leader would be last to die, so Rome could watch the leader look helplessly on as his crucified men and family died slowly throughout the afternoon. The frightened leader eyed his wife and children crying before him and he publicly acquiesced. Those like him who surrendered were led in humiliation into the stands to watch those who refused to surrender suffer crucifixion and suffocate slowly in the tons of ice water directed into the arena, the water eventually engulfing their blue faces and silencing their anguished cries forever.

"Did they drown or freeze to death?" Athena asked.

"The cold water creeping up their crucified bodies killed them before the water could suffocate them," Caesar stated, having witnessed the same punishment in Gaul when he and his troops forced the retreating enemy into the freezing cold northern rivers. "In any case, Antony has at last completed his conquest of Germania and added it to his empire. Cleopatra awaits him now in Alexandria."

"While I care little for Germania, a barren, frozen land, and it's barbarous people, who are the so much the opposite of Egypt," Isis replied, "I care greatly for my favorite, Cleopatra. My fear remains, however, that she does not fully comprehend the danger that the troublesome King Herod represents."

"It doesn't matter for the moment if she does or doesn't," Venus stated. "Antony will soon be sailing to Alexandria. It is time for a lovers' reunion the like of which the world has never witnessed."

Chapter Sixteen

Alliances and Dalliances

29 B.C.

Year 8 of Antony and Cleopatra's Reign

Alexandria

Five years have passed since Antony's return to me and our children in Alexandra, and so much has happened. As I sit in my lamp lit chamber, for it is nearing dusk, I wish to record all I can remember of those years, so I will never forget. Antony sits next to me, penning his memoirs, which will complement mine. A baby leopard I have acquired and named Alexander in honor of the great conqueror, lies curled at my feet, purring loudly.

First and foremost, during and immediately after Germania's conquest, Caesarion rose rapidly in experience, ability and political power—what Romans call *cursus honormum*—from military Tribune to Quaestor, exchanging his military armor for a white *toga praetexta* with a Tyrian purple border. As the son and now acknowledged heir of dead Caesar, whose popularity as a god has continued rising, he is now a patrician. His rise to power continues unabated, from Quaestor to Praetor (skipping entirely the usual Aedile, or supervisor of public works level, which, while not common, was not unheard of) to Consul, responsible for the city's political agenda, and finally Princeps

Senatus—leader of the Roman Senate. Antony through Cicero Minor and Caesarion's efforts has been declared Imperator, the new Caesar of Rome, which was celebrated in Rome and Egypt with a week of state holidays including games, prizes and food. The effect was to become in effect, Emperor, but under a less assuming title that was both more familiar and less offensive to Romans. Ostentatiously, this new title was said to have been chosen to honor Julius Caesar, but everyone knew what it meant in terms of his and Caesarion's power. All the males in our family would henceforth possess the title by inheritance.

Caesarion, at Antony's request, had the eighth month renamed Sextilus Antonicus, for that was the month he had defeated Octavian at Actium and he and I had emerged victorious. We were now laying plans for alliances that would lead to the eventual conquest of Persian Parthia. While discussing the merits of mercy to those Parthians who would support our troops, Philadelphos, now eight years of age, looking over my shoulder, shifted his weight from one foot to the other, a sign, I knew, that he had something he wanted to say.

I paused my writing and signaled for him to speak.

"What is 'mercy'?" Philadelphos asked.

"Mercy is a privilege given to those who deserve it," Antony replied for me, rising from his chair and stretching languidly. "Men, being human, from time to time make mistakes which can be forgiven by the application of mercy."

"Do all men deserve mercy?" our son asked in innocence.

"Some, but not all. Outright rebellion must always be quashed without mercy," Antony explained. "It was, for example, necessary for Cleopatra and I to show no mercy to Octavian and his immediate supporters, else they would have led Rome into civil war."

Philadelphos appeared unsure. He had not yet visited Rome,

which, as a result, was a concept that existed mainly in his imagination.

Antony smiled and turned the focus to Egypt. "Your mother had no qualms about killing her brothers and sisters when they threatened her authority."

"Ptolemy died a quick death by poison and, in the end, Arsinoë got what she deserved," I affirmed.

Our answers seemed seem to satisfy him and he ran off to play.

"Octavian's faction would have sought to have me, you, our children and all those close to us killed, then likely would have broken off all relations between Rome and Egypt," Antony stated, as if needing to justify our actions. "It is for the best of Rome and Egypt. Neither would have survived Octavian or his supporter's rule. What else could we have done?"

As Antony spoke, I recalled the deaths of Octavian's family members immediately after the Triumph. "I would..." I stopped in thought. This "Roman way" of resolving crises was not unreasonable. Irrespective of one's personal feelings, some enemies needed to be disposed of. Arsinoë, the gods curse her, had been one. "I would have humiliated them publicly with words, not chains," I stated, adding, "and then, have them choose how they would die—by sword or poison—reserving inhumane deaths like crucifixion for only the most heinous of criminals."

"Hmmm," Antony replied. "Romans, too, prefer to first humiliate enemies and criminals with words as they deserve. It is in the mode of their death that our national approaches differ. Enemies are typically granted the mercy of choosing the mode of their death, while criminals are not."

For some reason, I felt compelled to continue. "Say an enemy or criminal somehow escapes punishment. This leaves the person free to repeat his or her crimes, deeds which will eventually lead to their death. False words, however, live on long after." My reason for continuing suddenly became clear to me: Though most of Rome now swore loyalty to Antony as my people did to me, and most were coming around to the eventuality of a Egypto-Roman Empire, Octavian's reference to me as "an Egyptian harlot" continued to live in the minds of some. Of these people, many ended up rising against me or Antony.

"You do speak truth, as I know well: '…the evil men do lives after them. The good is oft interred with their bones'—my own words over Caesar's lifeless body," said Antony soberly.

"Yet, I think the opposite *could* be true," I replied. "As Plato said, in an empire with an enlightened and beneficent philosopher king and queen, a perfected male and female ruling together with reason and law, the *evil* men do should be interred with their bones."

"Well, sweet Cleopatra, my enlightened and beneficent Philosopher-Queen-Pharaoh, perfected female to my male, now that all major rebellion has been largely squashed, let us speak of reason, law and the conquest of Parthia."

"Agreed," I said, placing down my stylus and turning to face my lover. "Our recent actions make us sufficiently feared, and Parthia's people, if only out of that fear, have begun to clamor for Roman rule. Besides, I am yet again pregnant," patting my already greatly enlarged belly.

Antony and I had remarried a year earlier, this time under Roman rites, and I expected our undisputed Egypto-Roman baby to be born any day soon. "If the child I carry is a girl, we can marry her to a prince of Parthia or even China," I said. I had a feeling it was a girl and I wanted to name her Arsinoë, not for my hateful sister, but for Arsinoë II, the first of the great Ptolemaic queens who, though she had married her brother, had greatly expanded the role of the queen. In spite of my sister's reign of shame, I wanted the name Arsinoë to forever remain a proud one.

"How can you be so certain it's a girl?" Antony asked, out of curiosity. These last few years, he had more than once stated that I'd done my maternal duty bearing him two sons and giving him Caesarion as a stepson. He was always curious about my thoughts in a way Caesar had never been.

"It is not for a man to ask a woman how she knows these things," I said, smiling at him mysteriously.

"I would prefer a son, of course, but if you present me another daughter, I will not be disappointed," Antony said, knowing full well the value of princesses in empire building. "As you said, a girl now could prove a distinct advantage. There is nothing like a princess to bring peace between present or future warring nations."

I smiled. I knew that Antony, despite being Rome's new Caesar, did not think of his daughters only in terms of alliances. I knew, for example, that of all my children, Selene was secretly his favorite, as Caesarion was mine.

"We can create alliances and avoid war either way much like we did with Armenia," I reminded him.

Antony nodded in agreement. His daughter by his first wife was now Queen to the King of Armenia. Around the time I had been pregnant with Helios, she had been wed to the Prince of Armenia, and the couple now ruled as King and Queen under the combined guidance and protection of Rome and Egypt. She and I had become close friends these past years. Technically I was her stepmother, but she was so close to my age that I thought of her more as a companion than a daughter.

"You asked me five years ago to apply my arts of diplomacy to building our empire. I have plans to build an alliance with Kush," I said, changing the subject to one I had been wanting to discuss with my husband and co-ruler.

"That kingdom on your far southern border?" Antony asked.

"Yes. Though technically I am Queen of both Upper and Lower Egypt, which includes Kush, there are three cataracts that obstruct free southward passage of my ships, making the southern kingdoms wont to forget that I—we—rule them, making them prone to revolt. There are riches beyond description in Kush and southern Africa. King Solomon's mines, for example. As promised, I will apply all my diplomatic skills to bring them under our control. But I must ask you a favor, Antony: Please allow Egypt to have and administer all the parts of Africa that Rome does not already control."

Antony scowled first, but then changed his expression. Rome held Numidia and Mauretania, locales in Northern Africa that were lush and verdant. Numidia was known for its beauty and Mauretania for the open richness of the Berbers who lived there. Both considered Egypt a friend. Farther south, Roman soldiers scorched their white skins in the hot African sun, while my Egyptian soldiers basked in it. More importantly, The Candace, as the powerful, ebony black Queen of Kush was called, would never consider an alliance with Rome, but had continued to talk with me of one, off and on over the years.

Antony wisely saw my point. "Yes. We Romans may freeze up north, but freezing is, for us, far preferable to mummification."

"Thank you for agreeing with me, Antony," I replied. "Indeed, The Candace and I are already more than acquaintances. She visited me last year while you were away. She is a large woman of great stature and girth whose size is seen by her people as a measure of her power. I believe Egypt and Kush can become good friends and, in the future, much more."

"Friends?" Antony asked, eyeing me askance.

"Friends," I replied. "Why do you ask?"

"I am thinking of your 'friend', Herod, who recently had Marianme killed over some imagined affair," Antony said.

I nodded. Infidelity in a man or woman always carried with it horrid consequences. Marianme had been no fool, though her hatred of Herod and his vice-like grip over her had eventually led her to find solace in the arms of another. Even I had known of her supposedly secretive but in fact all-to-public "affair." Though she and I were not friends—she had tried to poison me on threat of her husband—Alexandra, her mother, had proven, as I suspected, a trustworthy friend and ally. Since Marianme's murder, Alexandra's distrust of Herod turned to venomous hatred. I showed Antony a letter Alexandra had written me, describing Marianme being chopped into pieces before her eyes. "That same night, Selene had a vision," I said. "She awoke in great distress over a death she had dreamed. She often has such visions on nights with full moons," I stated.

"She is, I suspect, a seer," Antony admitted. "Even so, some of her visions remain girlish fancies."

"Like the one in which she dreamed of hundreds of men paying her tribute?" I asked, winking sardonically. "Her visions can be quite dramatic. I've begged Isis to remove this gift from her, as it sometimes causes her great emotional pain," I said.

"On the other hand," Antony added, "I believe this tribute dream to be a divine sign that your naming her to succeed you as the next ruler of Egypt has been received by the gods with favor. Caesar is said to have suffered from a peculiar affliction, somewhat like hers. He regarded it as a sign of divinity. It was one of the reasons he eventually declared himself a god."

I nodded in affirmation, then, disliking the implications, changed the subject. "'I'd rather be Herod's pig than his wife'," I quoted.

"Indeed. I am well aware that Herod has proposed to you on multiple occasions," Antony stated blandly. "Too much so for my liking."

Gathering my ire, I replied, "He first said you had taken a Germanian mistress. Then he tried to convince me you were dead." There had indeed been a false rumor of Antony's death two years prior. "Herod proposed I become one of his wives. Not chief wife, but simply another member of his harem, and that I leave Egypt to Helios," I said. "He claimed he would anoint me 'Cleopatra of Jerusalem'."

"Herod's proposal spread all the way to Rome," Antony said.

"Why do we not rid ourselves of him?" I asked in disgust.

"Patience. He is rebuilding his temple, and while he is a despicable man, he controls the argumentative people of Judea for Rome, including, as I'm sure you've heard, a growing number of Zealots. Even I, Imperator of Rome, could not oversee things in Judea better than he does," Antony admitted with more than a trace of envy.

While Antony spoke, I felt my labor pains begin. I called for Iras and Charmion, excused myself from Antony's presence after assuring him I was laboring "in a good way," and removed to my room which had been set up in readiness. Selene, being eleven, was old enough to understand birth and death, and I believed that as my heiress and the future Queen Mother, she should witness what happens when a reigning queen gives birth.

In contrast to Philadelphos, who had been an easy pregnancy but hard labor, this, my fourth child, proved a difficult pregnancy but an easy labor. No labor is truly 'easy', but this child gave me minimal discomfort and no trouble. I labored for less than two hours before delivering, as I suspected, a beautiful girl. I announced to Selene as I had prior to Antony, who had joined me and stayed at my side during the final stage of labor, that I would name her Arsinoë. I explained to Selene that I named her after "brave Arsinoë II, wife of Ptolemy II, who was responsible for creating the Museion, the great library of Alexandria, and a queen whose image I often emulate in my own statues. "

"Enough history, dearest Cleopatra. It's time for you to rest," Antony ordered.

"Yes, get some rest, Mother," Selene repeated, "so the children of Cleopatra can rule the world."

I slept deeply, awakening the next day. Selene, dressed in her favorite red chiton draped with green, was sitting on my bed, watching my eyelids intently. She was lovely, being just one year shy of becoming a woman. After much discussion, Antony and I had decided that she would marry Juba, after going first to Rome to learn the duties of a Roman wife, returning to Egypt after she had born Juba a son.

The moment my eyelids fluttered, she burst out, "Soon *I* will marry and have children!" She'd said it so joyfully, I was pleased I'd decided to have her at my side during birth. In truth, Selene had been smitten with Juba since a young age, hoping for a love match like her parents had. Caesarion had, just before Antony returned to Alexandria, married a woman named Tullia, who had not, as of yet, produced an heir, but was currently pregnant. In my mother mind, Caesarion was still my child, but he was now entirely Romanized. Indeed, not long after Antony and I had staged our Roman wedding, Antony had formally adopted Caesarion as his son. Selene, on the other hand, would be a Roman wife but remain an Egyptian Queen-Pharaoh.

I quickly recovered, and soon Antony and I were discussing Parthia again—and the stolen Roman eagles.

"King Phraates has a son, Phraataces, and we now have a second daughter," I said, determined to avoid future bloodshed.

"Indeed. But I want those eagles. It is about the honor of Rome," Antony stated.

"Do you not think he knows that, too?" I questioned. This was a delicate matter, one that if not attended correctly could easily upset all my future plans.

Antony humpfed, indicating he did not wish to pursue the topic further at this time.

That evening, the two of us played a game of Senet, an ancient Egyptian game of strategy I was slowly teaching Antony. Of course, I often would have won, but was careful to let Antony think he had won on sufficient occasions to keep his interest. This time, though, I did not hold back.

"What is it, Cleopatra?" he asked. Even privately he rarely if ever conceded defeat to me.

"I was thinking of Parthia, again," I said, standing before the stone Senet table and dusting off my yellow chiton. Antony followed, gazing at me intently. "Rome wants the eagles back," he said without emotion, "and war is the only…"

"As you constantly remind everyone, including me," I replied, folding my arms not so much to signify defiance, but just enough to convey a sense of understanding tinged with stoicism.

Once again, Antony humpfed and changed the subject. "For the moment, I am done in Germania, but I believe I will soon be called there, again," Antony said.

"Yes. Keep Germania. Forget about Parthia for the moment. At least, as a conquest," I said.

"And what exactly do you mean by that?" Antony asked, raising an eyebrow. In the moonlight, I could not tell if he was amused or irritated, but as soon as I lit an oil lamp, I could tell to my relief that it was amusement. Antony secretly adored me when I confronted him—in private, of course. He was irritated principally only if and when I woke him from sleep.

"We have a new daughter. Arsinöe. Arsinöe Five," I repeated, hoping he would this time catch my implication regarding the use of marriage rather than war, as the best way to conquer Parthia and bring back the eagles.

"Our dear little Arsinöe," Antony stated, at last, I felt, catching my drift.

"Yes. And as I said, Phraates has a son. A son who will be the next king of Parthia."

"Ah, you think to make her queen of Parthia, as we made my Antonia Queen of Armenia?"

I smiled, knowing that, at last, Antony, thinking it his idea, understood and approved.

"Yes. You negotiated the alliance with Armenia whereby Rome chooses the king and Armenia the queen, as long as it promises that together they will rule on behalf of Rome and Egypt and send regular tribute. Perhaps when Arsinöe marries, the Parthians could be moved to give you the eagles as a wedding present."

Antony laughed at that. "*Give* them to me, Cleopatra? Just like that?" he asked incredulously.

"A victory without bloodshed," I said. "One could hardly ask for more."

Antony frowned. "But the glory of recapturing the eagles..." Though determined, he graciously allowed me to continue speaking.

"Antony, dear. I concede that glory is often bought in blood and war. But, husband, if we remain always at war, our peoples will eventually weary of it and resent us." I had just appealed to one of Antony's strongest points. Unlike Caesar and my father, Auletes, Antony knew the importance of the opinion of the masses. During the past five years, he had had Cicero Minor vigorously working wonders with the populace to shift their opinion and get them to approve of our union. Taking advantage of Antony's willingness to listen, I continued pressing. "Think, dearest: You and I could bring peace to both our territories for the first time in centuries. A grand Pax Romana. And with it, a flowering of commerce and civilization as never before."

Antony's eyes brightened. "It is important to honor glory in blood and war, but, as you say, both our nations' citizens tolerate war mainly as a means to peace and prosperity. With the military might of Rome and the wealth of Egypt, Cleopatra, we could indeed make and enforce a great Pax Romana."

"Yes!" I replied with enthusiasm. "With you ruling the Northwest, and me the Southeast, together we rule the world." I used the royal 'we', of course, as I sensed Antony did not yet fully share my interest in expanding Egypt southward or making an alliance with The Candace. However, he would, he promised, permit *me* to do so. In anticipation, I had already begun planning an expedition to meet The Candace. She had recently buried a statue of Octavian on her territory in an act of public desecration, for it was known that there were still those in the world, even in distant Africa, who wished he had won. By such a small but overtly public act, The Candace had endeared herself to me, and I had immediately invited her to Egypt.

Of course, the matter of Herod still remained, and Herod had not lessened his determination to have me as one his conquests. In consolation, I had leased Herod the territories around Jericho and the

Dead Sea, primarily to ward off his advances, though, in the end, this did not make our relationship any more agreeable. Antony, to sweeten things, granted Herod the title and privileges of a full client king, so there was, for now, relative peace between the three of us, though it was a fragile and clearly transitory peace. In the meantime, Herod kept adding to his grand harem in Jerusalem, much to the disgust of his people. My quote that, "I would rather be Herod's pig than his wife" was being increasingly repeated by one after another of the women of Judea, especially after the unseeming death of Marianme.

The Candace arrived in Alexandria that Junius. She was a commanding, midnight-ebony-colored woman of proud stature. She arrived with a train of eunuchs and her equally commanding daughters, the line of rulership in Kush being passed through women. Dressed as a warrior in a leopard-skin skirt and sash that left her ample left breast bare, and carrying a large ebony colored bow and quiver in one hand and a gemstone studded mace in the other, she pledged eternal friendship to me, Egypt and, because of my husband's presence, Rome. Her gifts included thirty-six similarly dressed women warriors, as well as two elephants and several giraffes. The female elephant, bedecked in bright colored cloth sparkling with diamonds and edged with gold fringe, was given to me personally. To Antony she presented the fully armored male war elephant, the mate to mine, as well as the couple's trainer. To Selene she gifted the best young giraffe, and to baby Arsinoë she presented a pair of trained chattering baboons from the Ethiopian jungles. The Candace even honored Helios and Philadelphos each with a small horse. But what I found most interesting was that she had only one eye.

"I lost my right eye in battle," she said proudly, describing in detail to Antony how she and her army of women had fended off several armies of male invaders from lands to the South. "As ruler, I've learned

149

to see just as well with my remaining one!" Antony joined her, laughing loudly at the *double entendre*, as she winked at him. From that moment on, I felt assured both Antony and I commanded her respect, though in different ways—Antony as her gentleman military leader and I as a strategist.

I treated The Candace to the grandest banquet Alexandria had ever seen, attended by Antony and his Roman commanders in full military regalia. There was much dancing and feasting, but not so much as to stop The Candace and I from, in between, quietly discussing our nations' futures. Selene being engaged to Juba, Arsinoë being saved for Parthia and the boys being considered for other nations—Helios for Iotape, a Median princess, to rule Arabia and Nabataea, Philadelphos to rule Numidia, and Caesarion Rome—I had no more children to marry off to cement this new alliance.

"All your children are promised to others," The Candace acknowledged, and with a nod she slowly rose, looked about the banquet room then back to me. "But, Cleopatra, you and I, we are women. Let the men war and marry off their children. Instead, let us forge an everlasting agreement of filial friendship."

"'An everlasting agreement of filial friendship'," I reiterated. "I like that idea. But what exactly shall we agree upon?"

At that moment, Antony made brief eye contact with me and I smiled in a way to warn him not to intrude.

"On husbands, of course," The Candace said with a sad but coquettish smile. "My latest and most beloved perished beside me in battle."

At first, I was unsure what she meant. Was she asking for an Egyptian husband? A Roman one? Or was she perhaps, based on what I knew of her customs, inviting me to share Antony with her? The thought struck me like a sword through the heart. I could never…

"But let us discuss, as you said, what we will agree on, and leave the past, the dead and men to their own devices," The Candace said to my immediate relief.

Taking the lead, I said, "I suggest we begin our friendship by forming a security alliance. Antony and I will defend your western and eastern borders against all enemies and send sufficient troops to you, whenever requested, to avert any internal situation that might demand of you another husband or eye. In return, Kush can provide Egypt with the necessary gold and gems to help rebuild our treasury," I said, pleased to divert the discussion away from even the slightest hint of sharing my husband.

"Oh, ho, ho, ho!" The Candace laughed. "I see! You want *us* to finish paying off your father's seemingly everlasting debt to Rome!"

"Yes," I admitted in a hushed voice. This was still an aspect of shame for me.

"Well, I certainly have enough to spare and share. And it would please me to know that my existing eye and any future husband would be safe. Based on our agreement, you can call me Candace, but unlike your father, you must keep your word, " she warned.

"Of course," I replied. Candace in her language meant "Great Woman" and was her informal courtly name. "Let's, as you said, discuss the living, not the dead. To address your concern, I suggest we write and sign an agreement of friendship in each of our respective languages. As sisters in Isis?" It was common knowledge that Kush, known as Lower Egypt in my country, shared Upper Egypt's gods and goddesses.

"Sisters in Isis," The Candace reiterated. "I like that! And now, my friend and sister, after our banquet is over, will your husband begin preparations to conquer Parthia? I ask this because Parthia has long lusted for Kush and, my spies tell me, is once again considering a war to conquer us and encircle Egypt."

This news was not entirely new to me. I had heard the same from Antony, but more in terms of a nationalistic desire than an actual campaign plan. Still, I appreciated her forthrightness.

The more we talked, the more I liked this bold woman warrior-ruler. She easily saw my strategies within strategies, and I could tell she liked me, too. I think we reminded each of the other. "No, Candace," I replied. "We plan to invite Phraates here to see and experience the might of Egypt, Rome and our new ally, Kush, quietly introducing to him the idea of his son marrying our Arsinoë," I said.

"A very wise course, Sister," The Candace, smiling, replied with the slightest glimmer of sadness in her wide smile, but whether the sadness was over the memory of the loss of her husband and eye in war, or at my not having suggested sharing Antony with her, I would never know.

Chapter Seventeen

Diplomacy

28 B.C.

Year 23 of Cleopatra's Reign

Vault of Nut

After sending off The Candace, Cleopatra had couriers sent to Parthia with a personal invitation for Phraates to visit Alexandria. As Phraates' visit drew closer and Alexandria prepared to receive him, Caesarion's Roman wife, Tullia, went into labor, and the moment she did, a shimmering, translucent veil appeared about Julius Caesar, blocking his curious, inquisitive eyes. Males, even those in Heaven, were forbidden to watch the actual childbirth. To Caesar's indignation, Athena, on the other side of the portico began teasing, saying she would watch for him; Venus and Isis, in turn, promised to reveal the outcome of Tullia's labor. Caesar, blocked from further view of his grandchild, turned his attention to Cleopatra's preparations to meet with King Phraates.

"Antony did not remain in Egypt to assist," Caesar stated gruffly to no one in particular.

"But Mardian, her faithful soldier, remains at her side," Athena replied, though icily. Athena and Caesar's relationship was one of strained civility. Athena still objected to Caesar's heavenly presence and rued Isis's mercy in allowing him there. Caesar, for his part, was developing a distinct dislike of Athena. Her arrogance chafed him, yet he knew better than to argue openly with Isis' friend, the goddess of wisdom and battle. Besides, Isis had just blessed his last wife, Cleopatra, with another child.

"Mardian is a capable soldier," Caesar acknowledged.

"Yes, he is," Athena replied, snarling her words to remind him that, having died, he, at least, was no longer such.

"He *is* a capable soldier," Caesar repeated, once more swallowing his pride, this time with hurt in his voice. "But I would feel easier if Antony were with Cleopatra, as he was during their visit with The Candace. The Candace was generous and actively sought friendship. Phraates…well, Phraates is Persian, and Persians are known to be difficult to discern. He may, in the end, prove friend or foe. It is Antony's duty to protect Cleopatra and our children! He *is* her husband, after all!" Caesar called out begrudgingly.

Athena chuckled. "*Our* children?" she asked smugly, satisfied that Caesar had finally begun to feel at least some remorse for the pain he had caused the many women in his life.

"What is so funny?" Caesar demanded.

Venus approached Caesar and placed an arm about his shoulder. "I know of what she smiles," Venus offered.

"How *dare* you presume…?" Athena demanded.

"Lay aside your anger, Athena," Venus replied, "for I think this once you and I are in full agreement. You are thinking Caesar is finally coming to realize how Cleopatra, as well as his other wives and concubines actually felt," Venus stated.

Athena paused and pouted, her expression slowly warming, but towards Venus, not Caesar. And though Athena refused to confirm

Venus' statement, she and the goddess of love were momentarily in accord. The dialog between Caesar, Athena and Venus was interrupted by Isis's announcement that Tullia had just borne a son. With a wave of her hand, the veil was lifted and Caesar saw the healthy boy cradled in the arms of his mother.

"A son! A son for Caesarion and a grandson for Cleopatra and me!" Caesar yelled. Athena, Isis, the Royal Mother, Auletes, and Berenice joined Caesar his side of the portico, and all six rejoiced together as they looked down on mother and child.

After their celebration, attention returned to Cleopatra.

"Why is Cleopatra preparing such a warm welcome for this upstart 'king' of Parthia?" Athena asked rhetorically. "Has she forgotten that while she may be Egyptian by right, by family she is Greek, and Macedonian Greek at that? Has she forgotten that the Parthians, who had called themselves Persians under Darius and later Xerxes, were sworn enemies of Greece?"

Unable to resist goading her rival, Venus asked, "And what do you make of her preparing to welcome him as Artemisia, the Greek Queen who fought alongside Xerxes *against* Greece. Against your own city, Athena?"

"Artemisia was a traitor..." hissed Athena.

"So, which disgusts you more, her attempting to make an alliance with Parthia, or her dressing as Artemisia?" Isis asked.

"I am a goddess of war, as is Antony's god Mars. War clarifies. Politics obfuscate."

"Initially, perhaps, but many senselessly lose their lives in a war, and sometimes, afterwards, it is politics that ultimately clarifies..." began Venus.

"I admit that politically, this appears a wise move," Athena interrupted grudgingly. "But as a Greek goddess, her ploy pains my heart."

"So, you *do* have a heart?" Venus asked cattily.

"Of course I do! Even as you appear this moment to have a brain of sorts," Athena retorted.

Isis laughed at the squabble between the Greek goddess of wisdom and the Roman goddess of beauty. Peering over the portico ledge, Isis announced: "I see Phraates accepting her dressed in the image of Artemisia as a sign of friendship." The heavenly retinue one by one joined Isis to see for him and herself.

Below, Cleopatra directed Phraates, a man tall in stature, dressed in purple robes studded with purple gemstones, the whole bordered in traditional Persian designs woven in pure gold thread, into her palace overlooking the whitewashed city of Alexandra, with its magnificent harbor and lapis blue sea in the distance. Beneath a tall, circular gold crown carved with images of the king atop his legendary flying chariot, a cluster of tightly curled jet-black hair framed a heavily weathered face complimented by a full beard of similar character. Barely discernable flecks of white along his temples made King Phraates appear distinguished, venerable and wise. His queen, walking to his right and slightly behind, appeared amused by Cleopatra's dress, but in a jocular way. To either side of Cleopatra, her children, dressed in the costumes of the lands they were poised to rule, made a similarly strong positive impression on Phraates.

After court formalities, the entire party retired to a banquet hall made to appear like the front of the Taq Kasra, an over one hundred twenty-foot-high wall consisting of five levels of consecutive stone arches, each level decreasing approximately two-thirds in size, the center dominated by a massive arch reaching to almost the top of the wall. In front of the *faux* archway Cleopatra had constructed rows of low dining tables at the opposite end terminating in a large artificial lake.

"How very like my favorite palace along the Tigris River in the center of Parthia," Phraates commented, nodding his approval.

The outdoor banquet lasted until moonrise with course after exquisitely prepared course of alternating Persian and Egyptian delicacies. Towards the end of the banquet, fully sated, Phraates ventured to ask Cleopatra if she would grant him Selene as his daughter-in-law, rather than the newborn girl Cleopatra cradled in her arms. Selene, like her mother, had that evening been charming everyone present with her sharp wit and youthful beauty. Dressed in chiffon-like robes of sheer, see-through pink, her hair combed into the domed shape of the hedjet—the crown of upper Egypt—Selene appeared in every way an Egyptian queen. When Phraates addressed her as Queen Nefertiti, Selene blushed and explained to Phraates that she was already promised to Juba, Prince of the Berbers, as a means to make peace between one of the oldest and staunchest supporters of Octavian and now of Antony's new Roman empire.

Phraates smiled, laughing openly with the mirth common to those of Parthia. "I see in you a magnificent Queen of Egypt. You are truly your mother's daughter." Turning back to his hostess, he continued, "So, Cleopatra, I will in deference agree to the marriage of Princess Arsinoë to my son. I do, however, have conditions."

"And those being?" Cleopatra asked.

"I know well of Antony's pride and…interest…in Parthia. In honor of the pending marriage, I will return to Antony the eagles," Phraates explained, continuing, "but not quite yet. The eagles will be my wedding gift, the day Arsinoë actually marries my son, Phraataces, but not before."

Cleopatra pursed her lips. Antony had expressed his strong desire that she have them sent to him when this meeting concluded. "I therefore also have a condition," Cleopatra answered. "Antony and I cannot build a *Pax Romana* on a spoken future understanding. However, I believe Antony would accept your *written* agreement. Will you, before leaving Egypt, have your royal scribe write a letter to my husband detailing and guaranteeing what you have just said, knowing as you obviously do that should the written promise not be honored, Rome would be forced to appear in front of your favorite palace with its legions?" Cleopatra carefully asked.

"I shall do so," Phraates agreed. "Now that we've met, I feel I can trust you, Cleopatra, my loyal servants and traders with Egypt, Miradates and Narezduct, having already advised me that I can stake my kingdom and life on your trustworthiness."

It was left unspoken but apparent that Phraates, despite his stated trust in me, was still uncertain about Antony. Later that night, he, as promised, dictated the requested letter to his scribe, addressing it personally to Marc Antony while I and my children watched:

To The Honorable Marcus Antonius, Imperator of Rome
From Phraates IV, Honorable High King of Parthia

Greetings! I have enjoyed meeting your wife, Cleopatra, Queen-Pharaoh of Egypt, and your delightful children. Juba is a blessed man to have your eldest daughter, as is my son to have your youngest. I trust and pray to Ahura Mazda, our god of fire, that Arsinoë will grow into a strong and wise woman, capable of bearing sons and serving as our Parthian Queen when I pass the kingship to my son, Phraataces. As for the matter of the captured eagles, it will be my pleasure to present them to you as a surety of our peace when Arsinoë arrives at Taq Kasra, my favored palace, to marry my son. You have my solemn, written, unbreakable word on this. As a further gesture of immediate goodwill, I have presented to Queen Cleopatra gifts of gold, frankincense and myrrh to honor you…

"Gold, frankincense and myrrh—gifts fit for the greatest of kings and pharaohs," Caesar mused as he watched Phraates sign, roll and place upon it his seal with a flourish.

"Antony is not yet either king or pharaoh," Athena stated.

"Rome does not have kings," Caesar reminded, recalling his assassination over just such an issue.

"As I said," Athena replied, "He is not *yet* a king or pharaoh. He is already Dictator for Life and uses the title Imperator freely and with impunity. Theoretically, an Imperator has the power to pass the title to his male offspring, the first being your and Cleopatra's son, Caesarion. In essence, he is king in all but name…"

"The implications of his Imperatorship have not yet been publicly spoken of," Caesar interrupted.

"Some things are better left unsaid," Isis mused, choosing that moment to close the discussion.

Cleopatra returned to Parthia with King Phraates and remained at Taq Kasra for a month to meet Prince Phraataces and learn the customs of the land her youngest daughter would one day co-rule.

Chapter Eighteen

Problem Child

Years 23-24 of Cleopatra's Reign

28-27 B.C.

Parthia and Alexandria

Though words of friendship and written promises of peace had been honestly exchanged, while visiting Parthia, I had taken time to learn everything I could about the land from which my husband wished to reclaim his eagles. It slowly became apparent to me that it was much more than a land that needed conquest. Parthia, like Egypt, was ruled by a single king, but unlike Egypt, the Parthians, in order to effectively administer and coordinate governance, employed a network of satraps, or governors, much like the Romans employed client kings and Roman-appointed governors. A satrap's role was between that of a vizier of old Egypt and a modern Roman governor. I also met the Magi, the wise men who had the power to consult stars and planets, and in doing so, predict future events. There were three prominent Parthian Magi: Belshazzar, Melchior, and Gaspar, and I came to know and like each of them.

"How can you dedicate your entire life to studying the heavens at the expense of the world?" I asked one day. One thing Egyptians and Hebrews held in common was that neither believed wholeheartedly in astrology.

"Egyptians put some, but less stock into the study of the stars. We Babylonians, however, once the world's mightiest empire, always have. We are descended from the Chaldean star-gazers. Did you know that your own Greek ancestors studied the stars, Great Queen? If you would allow, we could speak for you a prophecy. Perhaps over your youngest daughter?"

At the time, I saw no harm in this, and I knew much good could come from prophecies. Still, I caught myself momentarily praying to Isis it would not be a negative or ill-fated one, as with poor Oedipus.

It was Gaspar who spoke over Arsinoë.

"The world is changing. Our greatest prophet, Zarathustra, in primordial form established our world as a reflection of the *dwazdah-an*, the stars that divide the heavens into twelve natural sections, each of which inexorably influences our mortal lives be we slaves or kings. We are moving from the Age of Varak, the ram, to the Age of Mahik, the twin fish, and this moment in time exists on the cusp of that change. The Age of Mahik will be a time of peace and love. However, to mortals, the details of that future are veiled as if by a sandstorm. Nonetheless, the stars and planets surrounding Arsinoë imply that she is pre-destined to play a major role in both the change and the coming new age, *should she choose to*. The land of Judea will be at the center of the change and, while her role may be initially perceived by her and others as minor, even insignificant, shockwaves from her mere presence during the waning moments of the time of change will reverberate throughout the world and continue to do so for centuries to come. In part because of her, Egypt and Rome will grow in power and influence for many years, but Egypt will eventually dominate after Rome ruins herself," Gaspar stated as if in a trance, and with that, his prophecy ended.

At first, I knew not what to say, then, still in shock, stated without comment, "Thank you, Gaspar. You are dismissed."

"Great Queen?" Gaspar asked, struggling to shift back into the present moment and surprised by the brevity of my response.

Focusing totally on the present, I replied, "It is good to have a vision of the future, but I know from experience that I dare not let it interfere with my present decisions. I say again, 'Thank you, Magi Gaspar', for your prophesy and that vision. You may now take your leave." In truth, I wanted this exchange to end. This was a strange prophecy, and one must always remember that prophesies are given from the perspective of the prophet, his nation, his culture. I needed time to process what he'd said from an Egyptian perspective, then from Arsinoë's point-of-view, in both cases with Isis' guidance. Yet later, pray as I might, Isis did not grant me the insight I sought, and I was left to ponder alone what I'd heard.

Not long after returning to Alexandria, the first part of the prophesy came to pass. It began with a riot. There had been a rumor circulating that my younger brother, Ptolemy XIV, had not truly died but was hiding in Kush, waiting for an opportunity to seize the throne and re-establish the tradition of a ruling male Pharaoh. In fact, a young man who looked much like him appeared in Alexandria, claiming he was Ptolemy. I immediately ordered him arrested and questioned, to discover he was neither Egyptian nor Kushite, but rather had come from Mauretania, the land once governed by Juba's father. The man, whose true name was Aetius, had been a fervent supporter of Octavian. There is, of course, only one remedy for sedition.

Uncovered, Aetius immediately begged for mercy.

"Being from Mauritania, a country soon to be ruled by Juba and my daughter Selene, I will show you mercy, but only in the manner of your execution. I will grant you a quick death," I proclaimed coldly, "by public beheading," adding as an afterthought, "on the day of my choosing."

"So, it shall be," my scribe behind me answered, writing Aetius' sentence to be posted city-wide.

Aetius paled and was taken to prison to await execution.

When the determined day came, I decided to have Selene and Helios at my side to witness justice, but not Philadelphos or Arsinoë. True, the traitor would die by a merciful beheading rather than a barbaric crucifixion as many nations, including Rome, would have had it, but a beheading could still frighten a child. Although I had to admit that Philadelphos was not truly a child anymore—he was approaching eight—still, I felt him too young to experience a beheading, though he begged to go.

"I want to see the man die!" Philadelphos said to me with a strange glee in his voice.

To be completely honest, I did not know what to make of my son's attitude toward Aetius's imminent death and execution. I was not happy to see Philadelphos delight in this man's sad fate. Such might be a mark of an unjust future ruler. It all troubled me, and I worried repeatedly of Gaspar's prophesy. "He is to forfeit his life and have all public memory of his existence erased because he is a traitor. He deserves to die," I stated, "but I don't want you or Arsinoë watching."

"Selene and Helios are going to watch! It's NOT FAIR!" Philadelphos yelled back at me, crossing his arms in anger.

At that moment, my son reminded me of my younger brothers, Ptolemy XIII and Ptolemy XIV, both spoiled boys who threw temper tantrums whenever they didn't get what they wanted, and who later forfeited their own lives and had their images struck down throughout

Egypt. Perhaps if their nurses had disciplined them better, they would have lived their lives as co-rulers of mine. "Selene and Helios are eleven. They are old enough to understand what is happening. For now, Philadelphos, it is enough to understand that life sometimes is not fair," I said firmly. Caesarion and Helios, under my firm hand, had come to balance their ruler's need for violence with justice. Philadelphos had clearly not yet learned this. I had been late to turn my attention to him compared to my older children, something I was trying to remedy with baby Arsinoë. "You are *not* watching! Not at this time!" I said, adding, "Next year, *maybe*," and that ended it, although it did not end Philadelphos' tantrum. During his outcry, I gave strict instructions to Iras and Charmion to let him rant and rave, and whenever he acted this way again to not give in to any of his demands.

Mardian and Olympos ignored him; eventually he became exhausted and threw himself face down onto his bed.

David suggested that the boy was still not completely healed. "He soaked in the Dead Sea, which rid him of his physical ailments. But something seems to be troubling his mind."

"Indeed," I acknowledged. Inbreeding, the rule among Egyptian royalty, had in the past caused madness, which was one of many reasons I had sought to end the custom. But Philadelphos was the offspring of Antony, not the son of one of my brothers. What could have gone wrong? I didn't know, but I blamed myself. Queen or commoner, every mother does.

Just before sunrise, I exited the palace and stood on the top steps of the grand palace entrance, bedecked in a sheer golden chiton, wearing a gold-gilt band-crown with rearing cobra or *uraeus*. The view of the sunrise was breathtaking. Below, the brilliant white marble stone courtyard where Aetius would meet his end glistened in the rising sun.

The courtyard was quickly filling with people intent on viewing the execution. Beyond that, the whitewashed buildings of Alexandria stretched out, flowing around the busy marketplace to the wharf dotted with innumerable white ship sails.

It was going to be a hot day, even for Egypt, and the quickly rising heat made many milling about wish for the event to occur as quickly as possible. Still, I waited. I needed a public display of the justice, power and mercy of the Queen-Pharaoh of Egypt, especially now that people were calling me Empress of the East. The sun's rays spotlighted me and the ruby eyes in the *uraeus* suddenly flashed red. I signaled the trumpets to sound, and walked over to and sat on my portable gold throne. Selene dressed identical to me to display to all Egypt their future queen, the eighth Cleopatra of the Royal House of Ptolemy, stood at my right hand, and Helios, dressed as a Medean Arab to indicate to all present the lands he would soon be ruling by right and marriage.

Aetius was brought out, bound and forced to kneel in the middle of the courtyard far below me by two heavily muscled, bare-chested prison guards. Aetius, sweating profusely was crying for his life. Everyone took the hot sun of that day as a clear indication of Ra's displeasure at this man's lying and subterfuge.

"This one dared to claim he was your brother and the rightful Pharaoh of Egypt," the larger of the two, bare-chested men called up to me. "What is his punishment to be?"

"This one, like all such traitors, must die," I called out loudly.

This was the signal for Mardian to emerge from behind my throne. Always my defender, he descended the steps slowly, one by one, until he reached the shaking victim, then lifted his sword high to let the sunlight and retributive blessing of Ra fall upon it. I despised Aetius for what he had done, but seeing him shaking pitifully, I immediately raised my hand, partly to take his mind off the sword that glinted above him and at the same time to order Mardian's sword down onto the man's neck. It was quick; so much so that Aetius' severed head lived on for several seconds wide-eyed and disbelieving after the decapitation.

A loud shout, almost a cheer, rose from the crowd.

"Justice has been done," I announced, rising from my throne and stretching out my hands before the distant crowd. "Ra, God of the Sun, by the heat he is raining down, has shown his displeasure towards the dead lying before you. I pray Ra will be satisfied and no further persons die this day."

Back inside the palace, my attentions returned to Philadelphos. *How to remedy his strangeness?* I wondered? Praying fervently to Isis, it came to me that the best way to teach was to do so by demonstration. I decided to have Philadelphos begin formally accompanying me to observe me as I ruled. *What better way to model the proper actions of a strong but fair ruler than to show him?* I was glad now I had not allowed him to witness the execution of the man who had attempted to foment an uprising against me. After further thought on this issue, I explained to Philadelphos that though his father was Imperator and Caesar of Rome where the punishment for breaking the Pax Romana was death by slow crucifixion; however, in Egypt, we allow ourselves more flexibility, and could, by royal decree, allow prisoners to meet their deaths quickly. Sometime later, another opportunity presented to model self-restraint before Philadelphos.

Antony had recently returned to Alexandria. Thanks to our joint rule—some had now taken to calling our joint rule "Mercy and the Fist"—caravans were now coming regularly from Nabataea, the land Helios would one day rule. As always, I loved to visit the market *incognito* to see the bright colors, smell the exotic smells and listen to the sounds of the caravan bells. One day, one of the Nabataean caravan leaders brought a camel into my palace to present to me—one of the highest gestures of honor the desert-folk can bestow.

Antony thought it a magnificent creature; his only complaint was he could not easily take it back to Rome.

Selene thought it looked "very sturdy" and asked to ride it.

"Princesses are more suited to horses, Selene, but, if we ever have to travel the desert, you will ride one," I said, recalling the time when, fleeing Egypt for my life, I was forced to live among Arabs, as a member of a desert tribe.

Philadelphos, curious, walked closer to examine the animal, and bumped into it. The creature reacted by spitting at him.

"It spat on a Prince of Egypt!" Philadelphos screamed. "Kill it!"

The caravan leader and his assistant fell to their knees, horrified.

"Why did the creature spit on Philadelphos?" Helios asked me. In fact, the camel's spit had also landed upon me, and though like my two male children I was surprised and irritated, I knew from its eyes that the animal had simply acted by reflex and without ill intent.

"Great Antony! Great Cleopatra! Mercy!" the leader cried out without lifting his head from the floor.

"Kill the beast! Kill the beast!" Philadelphos chanted, attempting with poor result to wipe the foul-smelling liquid from his face and clothes.

I turned to the merchant, ignoring my son's rant. "Arise," I commanded, "and be not afraid."

The man, trembling uncontrollably, attempted to stand and in doing so, stumbled, paling as if he would faint.

I looked at Antony, who spoke next. "We appreciate your introducing us to this fine animal. Our son can be..." Antony said nothing further. He shared my concerns about Philadelphos' troubling nature, and, while we couldn't agree about how to best help him, we did agree to not speak of it in front of the world. As such, I turned the conversation back to the camel.

"The animal is forgiven, as are you. But tell us why the creature spat," I said.

Antony, pleased with the demonstration of my diplomatic abilities, whispered to me, "We have the opportunity to show Philadelphos the difference between a crime and an inconvenience."

"The beast, Great Ones, was surprised by the Prince's touch. They do it automatically, without malice, as a means of self-defense," The leader explained shakily, slowly regaining his color.

Antony nodded, winked at me, then turned to Philadelphos. "A lesson, my son. The camel is but an animal. When you ride a horse, you will be thrown if the horse is frightened. This man sought to honor us. Do not dishonor him and us by ordering his camel slaughtered. One day, if you are in the desert, such a creature may save your life," Antony stated, adding, "besides, with incidents like this, it is rarely about the animal and more about the man. Men can be far more dangerous. This one is clearly not."

Philadelphos said nothing, but he did not pout or cross his arms as was his habit when admonished.

"Does the creature have a name?" I asked, seeking to restore equanimity.

"Indeed, Great Queen. The camel is named Aladdin. It was named after a famous Persian who was a personal friend of mine. This camel is my most precious possession and was meant to be an honored gift to you."

I had heard tales about a famous Persian named Aladdin during my visit to Parthia. The man was portrayed in the tales as an attractive, though roguish thief, and my understanding was the tales dated back hundreds of years, so I did not believe the man's claim of being Aladdin's friend. It was my knowledge that the tale, in fact, had originated far to the East of Persia. Men often lied to impress women. Nonetheless, I used this as an opportunity for further demonstrating diplomacy and accepted the gift, mentioning quietly to Antony, "This camel is an omen from Isis, who is smiling on my plan to make Arsinoë queen of Parthia." I dismissed the Nabatean warmly and with a gift, if not my most treasured possession like the camel was for him, one sufficient to widen his eyes, and ordered Aladdin be taken to the palace stables.

During the next months, I returned my attention to my children's education. Selene, like me, learned languages quickly and I ordered her taught to speak and write Egyptian and Latin for the next four years, after which she would go to Rome and become Juba's wife. I kept David in my service, being pleased with the job he had done educating Selene and Helios and teaching them rudimentary Hebrew. I asked him to continue teaching them Hebrew history and language, but I wanted to further expand their history and language lessons, so I found an additional tutor to teach Helios Aramaic and Medean.

Helios learned Aramaic quickly, but unfortunately despised Medean. He said he had seen his intended wife, Iotape, and dreaded marrying her or speaking her language. *Strange*, I thought of my son's reluctance to become the husband of Iotape. It is often the wives who dread their future husbands, not the other way around. But male or female, as royalty, duty counted above all, and it was my responsibility to effectively convey this to him.

"It is your royal duty to marry Iotape, Helios, and rule her lands for your parents," I explained succinctly.

Given what he'd said about Iotape, I was surprised by his answer. "Very well, Mother," he stated equally succinctly. Unlike Caesarion, my eldest son, who often insisted on his own way, Helios wanted mainly to please. Nonetheless, he continued to begrudge Iotape at every opportunity, and this worried me.

Philadelphos was now old enough to join in the classroom. After the incident with Aladdin the camel, Antony and I thought long and hard, and finally decided to give Philadelphos Numidia, the land next to Juba's country of Mauretania. Philadelphos would rule Numidia in his own right while Selene would be Queen of Egypt and consort of Mauretania. Collectively, our children would rule Northern Africa and the former Persian Empire, along with any additional territories each through their rule could obtain.

In the meantime, Antony and I came to an agreement. As he was now Caesar, he could no longer easily leave Rome for Alexandria, even briefly in the spring, summer or fall. However, he could, he felt, trust Dolabella to serve as a capable regent during the winters, which he would spend with me. I, in turn, would join him in Rome as needed. In fact, I had come to like springtime in Rome, though summers were uncomfortable and autumns were always iffy. This way, we could effectively govern our respective realms—he the North and West, I the South and East—while liaising. There remained one problem, however. My former husband, Julius Caesar had given Cyprus to Arsinoë IV, my hateful sister, though she had lost it in her foolish attempt to wrestle the Queenship of Egypt from me. I wanted to have it, as a prize at having survived, unfortunately both Rome and Egypt had become thoroughly entangled in the incident and I knew any resolution, especially giving it to me to rule, would be complicated. Nonetheless, I inquired of Antony that winter.

"I would *like* to give it to you, Dearest, but because the Senate approved Julius Caesar's initial request to give it to your sister, even though I am Dictator for Life, Imperator *and* Caesar, I would still need first to consult the Senate. As I consolidate my power, the Senate becomes more difficult to predict and control."

"Then this spring I shall return with you to Rome. I want to regain Cyprus and, if possible, its twin, Crete. They are what's left of the great Phoenician League that formerly provided shipping and trade to all nations within Mare Nostrum. As I foresee Egypt supplanting this role..." I began.

"I will do what I can," Antony interrupted, his thoughts having turned from politics to me.

Chapter Nineteen

Empress

28 B.C

Year 23 of Cleopatra's Reign

Rome

Antony and I arrived at the Port of Ostia and made our way to Rome. I would be staying at Antony's villa, which he had rearranged to look much like Julius Caesar's old home. Memories of my times at Caesar's villa returned as I entered and we walked through and inspected it. I recalled with fondness Julius Caesar coming in to ask of Caesarion; the times I had spent preparing for dinners and banquets; my early meetings with Cicero Minor.

"You will like this even better, I think," Antony stated that afternoon after ushering me outside onto the portico, where, surrounded by rows of swaying cypress trees, we dined.

"I will like what?" I asked, as several slaves cleared the low tables and another refilled our wine goblets.

"I have had this, Caesar's villa, turned into a shrine to his memory and have added a library," Antony said.

"Oh," I replied simply. True, I was glad to hear that, but I had hoped Antony was going to speak to me of regaining Cyprus and Crete.

Antony read my face. "Patience, Cleopatra. You Easterners can be

173

so impatient."

I declined more wine and rose, wanting to settle into the rooms prepared for me at the villa and, yes, explore the library. Accompanying me were Charmion, Iras, Mardian, Selene, Helios, Philadelphos, and baby Arsinoë. Arsinoë was small, but no longer an infant. She was now three—the same age Caesarion had been when Julius Caesar, his father, had been assassinated. Although sixteen years separated me from that horrendous moment, my heart raced at the memory, made no less acute by the fact that Antony and I had arrived at Ostia on the Ides of Martius, which throughout Rome was now a time of public veneration in honor of Julius Caesar. I was to participate in the festival later in the evening.

The idea of the festival was Cicero Minor's. He had suggested after Antony's victory at Actium that Antony take the title of Antonius Caesar, to honor his friendship with Julius Caesar, which he eventually did. The festival was created so that the people of Rome could honor Julius Caesar, my former husband, and thereby Antonius Caesar, my current husband, doubly elevating me. It was now universally held that Julius Caesar, a self-proclaimed god, had joined the other gods and goddesses on Mount Olympus (if one was Roman) or in the Vault of Nut (if one was Egyptian), the implication being that Antony would one day similarly proclaim himself a god, and, with him, me a goddess. The expectation helped blunt fears of Antony becoming a Roman king or emperor and me his empress, though this was exactly what we were planning.

This festival is interesting, I thought reviewing the list of events. A young man was chosen to read the speech that Antony had given at Caesar's funeral: "Friends, Romans, countrymen, lend me your ears..." This would be followed by various oral tributes paid to Caesar, first as a General, then Dictator, then Imperator and finally as Caesar, a god, all of which Antony would oversee. This year, Antony would also declare that not only would I be honored as Julius Caesar's widow and the wife of his successor, but towards the end of the week-long holiday, a Roman girl of marriageable age would dress as "Cleopatra, the truest and the most loyal of his wives'" leaving the audience to guess to which of the Caesars or both reference was being made. The exact words had been carefully chosen by Cicero Minor for this express purpose.

I beamed as I took in the evening's eulogies, enjoying in my heart my own moment of glory, and even a moment of genuine applause at my presence from those senators who favored Antony. That night, I asked Antony if he was jealous of the Roman girl who would be imitating me at my festival wedding to Julius Caesar, not him.

As always, he was honest and forthright. "As a man, I would lie if I said no," Antony admitted. "As the new Caesar, being celebrated indirectly by this festival, there can be no more brilliant a gesture than this. I need to silence those few who continue to oppose my ascendency and decry my alliance with you. As leaders, we are required to make certain personal sacrifices." He smiled at me as if I were the Roman girl chosen.

I agreed and kissed him dearly, while Philadelphos bullied little Arsinoë and snatched her Isis doll from her. To my surprise, Arsinoë, like Selene when Helios had done the same, neither fought for the doll or nor cried. In fact, she didn't seem to care at all that Philadelphos had taken it. Antony and I separated from our embrace to watch this interaction between our two youngest.

"That doll has been in your family for years," Antony observed.

"It was made for me by my mother," I stated. "I liked it very much. When I was young, my sister Arsinoë took it and ripped its head off."

Philadelphos had already lost all interest in the doll and dropped it.

"Selene was much more attached to that doll than Arsinoë is," I replied, the event making me think of Cyprus being wrested from me by my sister of the same name. "Antony, what of Cyprus?" I asked bluntly.

He inhaled through his teeth, then spoke. "I will appear before the Senate tomorrow and announce my intention to give you Cyprus, as they have recently taken up debating whether or not to give it to Herod," Antony admitted. I knew instantly why he had not wanted to speak of it. He *had* been hiding something from me and now I knew what!

"Herod?" I gasped.

"Herod has been a good client king. I need to let the Senate debate before pressing upon them my desire. Coming as it is during the festival, it will be hard for them to argue against me," Antony stated.

Nothing more was said of Cyprus or Crete that night. We made passionate love, pleasing each other to exhaustion though the time for me to bear children had since passed.

The next day, the Senate gave me Cyprus and, to my added delight, Crete. In return, they gave Herod permanent control over Jericho and the Dead Sea. To make up for this slight, I was given the territories of Phoenicia and Cilicia, as well as the parts of Nabataea not ruled over by Herod, so I could prepare for Helios's eventual kingship there. Satisfied with the outcome of the Senate meeting my husband had so efficiently directed, I vowed to relax and enjoy the rest of my time in Rome.

As Antony's at least titularly acknowledged wife, I had become, in fact, not only queen over many lands, but also the ruler of what was the beginning of a true empire. My popular title throughout the world was now "Queen of Queens;" however, I took care not to use it in Rome. In Roman eyes, I was Antony's wife first, and an Egyptian Queen-Pharaoh second, reserving the title of Empress, should it arise, for my rule in Egypt.

My time in Rome had been productive to say the least. Romans were fast becoming used to seeing Antony and me together. Our strategic plan, with Cicero Minor's continued help, was on schedule. My only disappointment was that Antony would not be coming back to Alexandria with me, as he had to squelch a rebellion in Germania, that troublesome new province he had himself added.

Before leaving, I spoke to my future son-in-law, Juba, who had joined us in Rome about Germania.

"Germania is strange, dark, cold and filled with barbarians," he informed. "Even the summers are chilly, Great Queen. But the trees are interesting. They are..."

"Please tell me of the people," I asked, interrupting. Men often thought of the land and its resources, while women of the people.

"The Teutons are fierce warriors. Their women sometimes fight beside them," Juba said.

"And their way of fighting?" I asked.

"Their tactics and methods of war have shocked even the Roman veterans who served under Julius Caesar. They show no mercy, gladly sacrifice prisoners, slaves and even their own girls to their gods."

"Have they a chief god?" I pressed.

"Their chief god is a falcon."

"Ah, so they worship Horus then," I replied, wondering if, with this information, I might be able to open diplomatic relations with Germania on behalf of my husband and Rome.

Hearing my reply, Juba second-guessed my thoughts and cautioned me. "It is true that their chief god is a falcon, as is Egypt's Horus. But their falcon is a god of prey. He does not watch over Germania, as Horus does Egypt. He seeks to devour it."

This last information troubled me. "O Isis! What horrible gods these Germanians serve!" Was my Antony aware that he had to conquer this merciless land once and for all or Germania would seek to prey upon the world?

For now, I would have to put Germania out of my mind. Germania was Antony's responsibility. Having now given up the idea of offering him my diplomatic assistance in this endeavor, I needed to refocus on my own responsibilities. Upon my return to Egypt, I needed to finish instilling in my children a ruler's wisdom and display them before the public as future kings and queens. As such, I began planning to have Selene appear more and more as Isis. As my future successor, she would one day embody the goddess even as I did now.

In the aftermath of Philadelphos snatching Arsinoë's Isis doll, Selene ended up repossessing it. She did not play with it now, but displayed it proudly in her chambers over her dressing table. The doll had been repaired many times by Charmion. Being made of sturdy Egyptian linen, with her help, it would likely be passed onto my granddaughters, perhaps even my great-granddaughters as well. But an Isis doll is one thing. Displaying Selene as an incarnate Isis would require considerably more thought and effort.

"A miniature Isis, ladies, what do you think?" I asked Iras and Charmion.

"She's about to marry Juba," Iras said. "Isn't she a bit old to be made up like a doll, even an Isis doll?"

"Indeed," Charmion agreed, adding, "however, she's still twelve, and I believe it is never too late to enjoy a bit more of one's childhood."

Charmion was, of course, correct. But this posed a problem. Though I was proud of Selene's intellectual growth, in my heart, I, too, still thought of her as a little girl. Iras, however, could always be counted upon to resolve matters. "Why don't we have a celebration and make her to look like an adult Isis. Show her standing. Arms open wide, embracing the world?"

"Iras, that's a great idea!" I said, clapping my hands. "Now, what about my sons?"

"Helios should be shown as Horus," Iras said.

"In Rome, Horus is linked with Apollo," Charmion noted.

I frowned.

"My Queen?" Charmion asked.

"Apollo was Octavian's god," I explained.

"My Queen, may I speak frankly?" Charmion asked boldly.

"Yes," I answered, though with some trepidation.

"Iras and I have been thinking..." Charmion hesitated, leaving Iras to complete her thought. "You favor Selene too much over Helios, Great Queen."

My mind began spinning, but I thought it best to let Charmion and Iras explain.

"While it is important to present Selene as Isis, Queen of Egypt, Helios' should be presented in the strongest way possible. Nabataea is a wild, dangerous land, full of treachery," Charmion completed.

"Helios is not as natural in royal demeanor as Selene. He has always looked to his sister; he needs to experience himself as being more powerful and separate from Selene. Perhaps even more so now as Selene approaches womanhood," Iras said.

I didn't have to think further about this. "You are both right. Thank you," I said. They *were* correct. And I suddenly knew exactly how to present Helios to his own best advantage. "Horus is our falcon-faced god. I don't want Helios associated in any way with the bloodthirsty falcon god of the Germanians. I shall present him as Ra, the Sun. Ra has no Roman link, and is above all the gods."

Both ladies expressed delight with this solution.

"And Philadelphos?" asked Iras.

"Now that is a question without an immediate answer. I must pray to Isis for her guidance," I replied.

As summer continued, I began to further investigate the Kushites and Ethiopians, as well as the rumors I'd heard of Solomon's extensive gold and gem mines even further south in Africa. What stood at the moment between Egypt and the wealth of Kush was a splinter kingdom called Nubia.

Situated within Kush in the area of the third cataract, beyond which Egyptian boats couldn't pass, Nubia was forever a goad in both Egypt and Kush's sides. The Candace had shared with me her desire to crush the Nubians and end the constant internal fighting. I wanted the same, not only for the resulting Nubian slaves, who were known to be strong and intelligent, but also for better access through Kush to Nubia's renown farmlands and rumored hordes of gold, gemstones, copper, slate and faience. The Candace had secretly agreed at our previous meeting to aid me in attacking Nubia, which, because of its formidable archers and spear welders was rapidly becoming an outright threat. She would add her knowledge of the land and her fierce women warriors, and we would divide Nubia and its wealth between ourselves. My military generals, as so often, thought it "overly ambitious."

"You cannot march down there without Antony," Rufio stated.

"Yes, it would be best to have Antony by my side. Or perhaps The Candace," I tested.

The men ignored my suggestion, so I continued to press: "She and her legions of women warriors are strong, valiant and know both the land and the enemy."

The men continued as though I had not spoken. "Perhaps if we simply announced our *intent* to war with them, our world-renown militarily superiority would force them to strike a deal," Mardian suggested, knowing my bias towards diplomacy over overt war.

I sipped at my wine. My generals were trying my patience! "Gentlemen? Did you not hear me mention my alliance with The Candace? Why is it that you will not even consider military action by the two of us a possibility? She is a strong leader of powerful women warriors, and we are already allied as if blood kin," I argued.

Everyone stopped. Olympos turned to me while the others looked away.

"Oh, well, ahhhh, Great Queen, but of that, how one can be absolutely certain? We have only seen a *display* of her alleged might, clearly meant to impress," he offered. "And all her warriors are f... f..." he began, stumbling.

When I clenched my fists and started to frown, Mardian judiciously cut in. "What Olympos is trying to say, Great One, is that we've never fought side-by-side with the Kushites in battle. Wouldn't it be best to wait for Antony, with whom you've fought and won perhaps the greatest of battles?"

"Very well," I replied. "You may not be certain, even though I am. I will not march down to her yet, but instead will summon her for 'more talks' while I write a letter to consult with Antony," I announced, knowing that their objections were not really about what they were sharing, but about warring alongside women, more specifically, massive, bare-breasted women warriors.

The Candace arrived a month later, dressed not as warrior this time, but as a Kushite queen, wearing billowing robes of fine white cotton studded like brilliant stars in a daylight sky with rare, multicolored gems. Her crown, collar, arm bands and wristlets were made of solid, reddish-hued gold. She brought with her a hundred chests of ivory, gold and gemstones. When I informed her of my intention to assist her in ridding Kush of the irritating Nubians, we came to an immediate deal—she would provide me with Nubian slaves as well as access to the resources of Nubia in return for Egypt's military assistance. I then relayed my Roman general's reservations.

"I want to hear from whom *you* believe we Kushites need protection: the Nubians or your male soldiers? I need to hear it from your own lips," the Candace asked with a tone of amusement, referring indirectly to her previous comment about her blinded eye. "Or from Rome, perhaps?"

"No," I replied. "With me and Egypt beside you, my husband and Rome will never pose a threat to Kush. Rome is only interested in responding as promised to aid me in helping you solidify Kush by defeating the Nubians." After a moment's thought, I added, "And any other African invaders."

"Can you give me further assurance that, when Nubia is defeated, all your soldiers will return to Egypt?"

This was an interesting question, and my solution, I feared, might be difficult for my generals to accept. Nonetheless, I offered this assurance: "First, your generals will command alongside mine. Second, it will be your choice as to whether all the Egyptian and Roman troops return or whether some who wish to create Egyptian- or Roman-Kushite families may stay, furthering both friendship and trade relations.

"Very well, that's fair." The Candace agreed. Our trust was indeed absolute and she knew I spoke the truth. "I will send to you my best generals and their staff members to meet with yours. You can expect them in the winter." Several of my generals, standing about us, scowled, but all in all seemed sufficiently assuaged as to not openly revolt. There was, of course, much more to what The Candace was saying than what was being stated. I assumed, and my generals obviously also did, that the Kushite envoy of women would be looking with their "second eye" for suitable Egyptian and Roman mates, as well as *vice versa. Good,* I thought. *What better way to advance our countries relationship than this?* Besides, despite sending the missive to Antony as I promised, I already had his permission to do what I thought necessary to expand Egypt's influence and hopefully its borders south.

With this taken care of, I settled down to what I hoped would be a pleasant summer with my children. I knew that like Caesarion, Selene and Helios, too, would all too soon be gone from me.

Helen R. Davis

Chapter Twenty

The Pact
Year 23 of Cleopatra's Reign
28 BC
Kush

Despite my generals' and, to be completely honest, The Candace's generals' misgivings, our alliance proved strong. She had visited me, as was proper, and now my curiosity about her country fully piqued, and I decided to return her visit. I wanted to irrevocably seal the alliance upon which we had agreed. Antony would definitely not be traveling with me. I liked The Candace but remained wary of what I increasingly perceived to be her constant insinuations to share Antony as a husband! I left Rufio behind as Regent, glad that he was supportive of my alliance with Kush.

"I will guard Egypt on your behalf, My Queen," Rufio said as I prepared to leave. I would be travelling with Mardian and Olympos, David, Charmion, Iras, and my four remaining children. David, too, saw the wisdom in cementing the alliance, mentioning he had heard that the legendary Hebrew King Solomon's phenomenally rich gold mines were located in the far South of Africa. Charmion and Iras were amused to travel south, but Olympos and Mardian, being northerners, felt otherwise. Nonetheless, they all agreed to accompany me.

We had a pleasant voyage up the Nile as far as Aswan, Kush's capital. Aswan was no Alexandria; still, it bustled with dark-skinned people, many of whom cheered as we were escorted though the city to The Candice's palace. Most looked like my Nubian companion, Charmion. Iras and Olympos, being particularly fair-skinned, were viewed with awe and wonder. The male Kushite warriors, many having fought at one time or another against lighter-skinned "Northerners" as they tended to refer to us, seemed mostly indifferent. Iras said she enjoyed the fact that the young men of Kush did not ogle her. At first, I wondered, but then understood: Having once been a slave in Egypt and constantly ogled by men of the North, this was a refreshing contrast. Yet, I also sensed an uneasy reticence. This was no longer her home or country.

Aswan was a wonderful place. The buildings, for example, while built lower and made mostly of red mud and straw, emulated Egypt's in style. The interior walls of The Candice's palace were, again like Egypt, decorated, but mostly with cut outlines of plants, animals, historical figures and a panoply of sacred gods and goddesses, all accented in soft, natural earth tones. I was pleasantly surprised to see that the city had a library. I was more surprised when The Candace, personally escorting us into a massive open courtyard, that quickly filled with both court and commoners. I noticed with some trepidation that many of the men pouring into the wings of the courtyard were dressed in leopard skins and carried short spears and small shields decorated with various family designs and colors. Though I was solidly ensconced in Egypt, this was something I would never allow there. It was meant, I assumed, to be a show of her popularity and the strength of her support. The women, on the other hand, were bare breasted, wearing brightly colored woolen skirts, decorating themselves with gold rings about their wrists, ankles and necks. The courtyard was soon packed along three of the walls for our reception.

The autumn weather proved cooler here, and for it, we had unfortunately come ill prepared. The Candace kindly supplied us with wool undergarments and leopard skins to fend off the chill, making us appear like smaller, bleached versions of our hosts. Mardian alone remained dressed in scarlet-robed Roman battle dress, presenting a particularly formidable figure. So formidable did he appear that many onlookers took him for one of our gods. The illusion was sufficient to cast a hushed awe over the packed crowd.

The welcome celebration began immediately after The Candace sat us about a long table. While food and wine were served, the people began buzzing, eventually breaking into groups that, one by one, danced for us while we ate and discussed the details of our alliance to defeat Nubia. As the night wore on, fires were lit in various places within the huge courtyard and people began dancing about them, singing songs of joy and victory. After our talks, The Candace invited us to join with her in a circle dance about a particularly large bonfire that had been constructed while we dined. Under a black, star-studded sky, to the combined singing of her people, shadows of our dancing figures projected onto the walls of the court, creating an otherworldly scene I would treasure the rest of my life. The next morning, the Candace woke us early to finish solidifying our battle plans, after which my retinue and I returned to Egypt.

Chapter Twenty-One

Dispersal

25 B.C

Year 26 of Cleopatra's Reign

Alexandria

The next three years passed all too quickly. My alliance with The Candace remained strong and with the assistance of Egyptian and Roman soldiers, Nubia fell quickly. Afterwards. every six months without fail, I received a caravan from Kush loaded with food, gold and Nubian slaves. The Candace and I at times visited one another, our nations being not far from the other, but politics and marriages were now clamoring for attention. Unbeknownst to us, our treaty of friendship would last a hundred years. I had now to turn all my attention to Selene and Helios' weddings and the politics of bringing into being an Egypto-Roman empire.

Selene was now fifteen, and ready to become Juba's bride. Though she had been legally marriageable at twelve, both Antony and I decided to wait until she was fifteen. Young brides sometimes died in childbirth and Selene was too precious to take any chances. Still, I could not delay any further: Antony had written to me that Juba was impatient for Selene to join him and become his wife.

"Dearest," Antony wrote me, "I understand your love for Selene, but you must let her go."

The time, too, had come for Helios to wed Iotape, the Medean princess he so dreaded, and begin his rule as King of Nabataea. Preparations for both weddings had begun several months prior, and, as my husband reminded me, it was time to let go and allow them to find their own places in history.

Selene and I sat together while Charmion and Iras hurriedly packed the remainder of Selene's trunks with extra clothing, jewelry, Egyptian cosmetics and her favorite perfumes. Selene, eyes averted, was gently combing the Isis doll's hair.

"I am excited to become Juba's wife," she said as Charmion closed the last of the trunks.

"You have long been smitten with him," I said. Since she had been a girl, she had spoken of no man other than Juba.

"I have been blessed by Isis," Selene said, fingering the doll lovingly. "Mother, my doll? Should I burn it like I did my others?"

"No!" I exclaimed in horror, for though it was the custom for a Ptolemaic bride to sacrifice her dolls to Artemis before marrying, one should never burn a goddess!

"Arsinoë doesn't want her," Selene said.

"Well, then, you keep her," I said softly.

"I could never forsake Isis' favor for Artemis'," Selene replied, showing the kind of wisdom I had sought to instill in her. To burn that doll would be a sign of disrespect for all I had worked. I had not burned her when I married Caesar or Antony.

"Pass it down, instead, as my mother did to me," I advised.

"I must bear sons," Selene said distractedly. "What should I say to Juba about the doll?"

"All royal women are expected to bear sons, that is true. But should you bear a daughter, she will become Queen of Egypt after you," I stated. "And queens can rule in Egypt either with a consort or alone as Queen-Pharaoh. As for the doll, if Juba asks, explain simply that it is a family heirloom."

Selene smiled. My daughter well knew how free Egyptian women were compared to their Roman or Athenian Greek counterparts. When it was time for Arsinoë to leave, she, too, would be blessed, going to Parthia, a land that also granted women considerable freedom.

"Selene, my dear, I must see to your brother," I stated, feeling a pull at my heart. "He dreads Iotape."

"As would I, Great Mother. She is ugly, and her personality is as ugly as her face," Selene said. Selene, like me, believed that power often made princes and princesses attractive when they were truly not, but we both also knew that, on occasion, a rulers' heart could match his or her ill continence. "Is there no way out for him?" Selene had always been quite close to Helios, her twin. She had once confided that she considered him a part of her soul. It was once whispered widely that Selene and Helios would marry, but I had ended that custom, hopefully forever.

"None, but I believe his fears unfounded," I replied, although my own maternal instincts made me share Selene's fears. "Iotape admires Helios greatly, and that admiration will turn to love, and love will enhance her beauty.

"I don't know, Mother. Iotape can be wicked," Selene stated.

"And what do you know of wickedness?" I asked as Selene handed Charmion her Isis doll to pack with her traveling clothes.

"I know that Herod and you have been bitter rivals since Helios was declared the next king of Nabataea. And you yourself have often said that he is a wicked man."

Sighing, I nodded in resignation. In spite of, or perhaps because of the Roman legalization of my marriage to Antony, Herod's hatred of me had only grown. When the Roman Senate announced its decision, he began to rule Jericho and the Dead Sea without asking my permission. This had led to a bitter dispute, and almost outright war. It ended instead in an icy stalemate—I relinquished Jericho and the Dead Sea to him but retained control over the trade of the Balm of Gilead. Herod immediately denied Egyptians access to the Dead Sea and its healing powers. He and I had come to barely tolerate the other, and then, only as long as Antony lived and intervened.

"You are a good actor, Great Mother, and you are a much better person than Herod," Selene stated.

"I have to be," I said, "for myself, you, Egypt and the world."

Selene stood, gave me a long hug, and turned her attention to final preparations, leaving me time to think for the umpteenth time about the details for both weddings. Selene would be marrying Juba; it would be a large, but relatively simple Roman wedding. Helios' wedding was more complex—Iotape would travel to Rome, they would wed at the Temple of Isis, then Helios would return with her to Nabataea, where they would have a second wedding following the local Arabic customs of that land. Several months ago, I suggested a double wedding for Selene and Helios. Antony loved the idea—he loved all my new ideas, and the way I challenged customs without actually breaking them. "A double wedding for the Gemini," he'd said with a genuine smile. In the end, however, diplomatic, national and religious concerns required they marry at different locations, creating a logistical challenge for which I was truly in my element. Antony and I eventually decided that I would attend our daughter's wedding and he our son's. I would not be able to attend Helios' second wedding, so for him, all of my attention was on making his first wedding an outstanding one.

The weddings took place in June, for the augers had stated that June was the most auspicious month for both. Although they were married in separate parts of the city, all of Rome appeared for the wedding of the Gemini. Being privy only to Selene's wedding, I can supply only those details, but oh, what details! Selene was made up Egyptian style and wore the same kind of gown I had worn at my wedding with Julius Caesar: a simple, but sheer white *stola* and *palla*. If her gown was simple, her jewelry was anything but! She wore a golden double crown of Egypt encrusted emeralds, rubies, and peridots, and a lapis lazuli and gold neck collar. On her wrists were coiled snakes of gold with ruby eyes; on her feet she wore sandals of woven gold thread. In addition, she would add a ring to her third left finger, as Roman brides did, though in her case it would also be her royal signet. This was a custom I had chosen not to adopt, but Selene did.

Juba wore a scarlet toga, one of sturdy build that accentuated his trimmed and curled Berber beard. Berber men native to Mauretania liked to wear jewelry, and Juba honored this aspect of his heritage at the wedding. He was covered in jewels similar to Selene: He wore a matching lapis lazuli sunburst necklace with matching earrings and peridot rings on all ten fingers. He had had small diamonds woven into his toga so it sparkled brilliantly like the sun. I smiled to myself and exchanged a knowing glance with Charmion. "Is it she or Juba who is the bride?" I whispered, and we giggled together like young girls. This custom of men wearing jewelry which the Berbers enjoyed was not unknown to Egypt, but I had not expected so magnificent a display!

And his display was not wasted. Many of the Roman elite as well as the all of the most influential people from Juba's homeland attended. Though Juba had, over the course of time, become fully Romanized in his demeanor, his people who attended were less so and proved an interesting lot. They were not as fair-skinned as Romans but neither as dark as The Candace and her people. I found them an interesting contrast to both extremes. The Berber women smelled of lavender and wore it so heavily, I became drowsy and had to leave to sit with the Roman women. The one I sat next to was Cicero Minor's wife, Terentia. She was always pleasant company and I could sense she liked me.

The ceremony finally began. Selene said her vows to Juba —"Where you are Gaius, therein I am Gaia," and, as he untied the knot of Hercules, it was clear that he was as smitten with Selene as she was with him. The marriage ceremony completed, he paused to take in her beautiful black hair, her dark eyes, and kissed her long and sweetly on the lips. As they kissed her, I turned to Charmion and grinned. "She will be a good wife to him," I said.

"Indeed," Charmion replied, more as a sigh.

Then Juba spoke. "I am now truly King Juba II of Mauretania," to which Selene replied loudly, "And I am the eighth Cleopatra of the Royal House of Ptolemy!"

Selene placed her hand in Juba's and together they walked down the aisle under showers of rice and flower petals to the cheers of everyone.

"He adores her," Charmion summarized.

"Much as Antony does me," I agreed.

Antony, however, was not by my side at this wedding. He was busy attending Helios' wedding.

The events of this and the next day kept me completely occupied, and I was only able to speak with Antony the second evening, after both twins were gone. When we did speak, to my surprise, he was reluctant to say anything. I assumed it was a combination of his masculine reluctance to let go of his son and the overwhelmingness of hosting a royal wedding, but as I probed him beneath the evening lamps, he finally relented and spoke.

"Fine, I will tell you, as all of Rome and the world will know soon enough. "Antony said. "Helios' wedding was a disaster. Despite being a bride, Iotape was not at all beautiful, and the exquisiteness of her wedding apparel only made her look more common. She was as ugly as a horse, Cleopatra! In fact, I do not wish to insult my horses by comparing them to her!"

I inhaled slowly to allow Antony time to continued speaking. My heart went out to Helios, who when he first saw her, kept saying over and over to me that he wished he could have married Selene, for he was a Prince of Egypt not a keeper of dogs. Worse, his comments had not gone unnoticed. Caesarion and Tullia were, at first, as mortified by his statement as was I. After a brief pause to calm his anger, Antony continued: "And Iotape was no more pleased with Helios. She insulted him during the binding, turning her face away when he attempted to kiss her, and as the wedding ended, it was thought by some that she invoked some sort of curse of her Nabataean gods over Philadelphos, whom she had been told had once called her people desert monkeys."

I inhaled slowly and deeply once again, holding my tongue. Despite all our efforts, Philadelphos had, if it was possible, become more indiscrete. He was now eleven, an age at which admittedly many youths seemed to delight in defying customs and conventions, delighting in a constant stream of irresponsible and demeaning antics. Recently, however, he exceeded the norm by stating before Antony and I that he did not need to study to learn to be a king, he was a king by right, and was ready to begin his reign as King of Numidia. Where responsible Caesarion had studied and learned the customs of Romans, at times practicing ruling as Antony's regent when Antony was away, Philadelphos was the exact opposite.

"At the wedding party," Antony continued, "Iotape announced that if Helios ever took a mistress, concubine or second wife, she would kill him! And I believe she would, and dare I say it, eventually will. She knows he loves Selene and, I think, is insanely jealous of her husband's continued bond with his sister."

"How does Iotape truly look in appearance?" I asked, wondering at her jealousy of Selene.

"She has long black hair and a fair face but has become fat and waddles when she walks. I am told she has been seen evoking Medusa while wearing a crown of snakes on her head like Medusa," Antony replied with exasperation.

Medusa, I thought. *It was said that any man who looked on Medusa's face, which was nonetheless beautiful, would be instantly turned to stone.*

"I'm told that, as her marriage to Helios approached, the woman secretly nurtured her devotion to Medusa," Antony continued, "and at the wedding feast, she thrice spoke as if this abomination were her goddess. I personally overheard her say that Medusa had given her the power to curse and destroy anyone she doesn't like."

I shuddered. O' Isis! Why had I not recognized of the depth of each's displeasure with the other? *Please protect my Helios*, I begged Isis, but said to Antony, "Snakes are sacred to Apollo. They need not be harbingers of death but can be a conduit for recovery and new life." I hoped that, in making the statement, I might to ward off any evil Iotape might have already called up in her rage.

"Indeed. Well, Cleopatra, I am exhausted and need to sleep." Antony, as if in a daze, proceeded to snuff the lamps and undress before me. The events of the past two days should have left me just as dazed, but seeing his muscular body displayed naked before me, I couldn't help but reach out to him, assist him in undressing me, and lead him into my arms and our bed. Antony, my dearest, slowly cast off his melancholy, replacing it with joyful ardor and rose more than sufficiently to the occasion.

I slept physically satisfied but mentally conflicted, having had recurring nightmares of the death of one of my sons. I could tell it was not Caesarion, thank the gods, but it was unclear whether it was Helios or Philadelphos. Drenched in sweat, I struggled as if fighting Antony. More disquieting, when I shared my dreams with Antony, he admitted to having dreamed the same.

"The gods are warning us," Antony said, clearly shaken. "Helios and Iotape left this morning for Nabataea. Cleopatra, we must send spies to there at once to keep a close eye on Iotape."

"I was thinking the same thing," I said, equally shaken. "But Selene..."

"Selene will be safe in Rome. Caesarion and I will see that Juba honors her," Antony said with authority, allowing me to believe in my mother's heart that Selene, at least, would truly be safe. Both Antony and Caesarion were widely respected and feared there.

To take my mind off of Helios, I spent the next day with Caesarion's wife, Tullia. Tullia typically spent her days weaving clothing for Caesarion. Antonia, Antony's daughter by his first wife, was sitting with us, for the king of Armenia had attended the double wedding. It was a blazing hot day, and on such days, it had become my custom to bathe in the *frigidarum*, the cold bath, in the privacy of Caesarion's villa located not far from Antony's villa. Tullia had been at Helios' wedding, and Antonia had been at Selene's with me. Together, Antonia and I picked Tullia's mind for details.

"Iotape looked truly hideous," Tullia confirmed as she loosened her clothes and prepared to enter the cold bath water. "Uglier even than most barbarians."

"Some barbarian women can be surprisingly attractive," Antonia said, carefully not mentioning the Germanian woman, who had, it turned out, served briefly as Caesarion's rather than as Antony's mistress as Herod had told me.

Antonia and I joined Tullia in the cool, refreshing water.

"I have been told so, too," Tullia said. "But trust me, Iotape is *not* among them." As she chatted on, a young girl-child entered. Tullia's youngest, she was but two. The slave accompanying Tullia's daughter brought with her wine as well as figs for me and pomegranates for Tullia and Antonia.

"At the wedding, did she truly threaten to kill Helios if he were ever unfaithful?" I asked.

"Oh, yes," Tullia answered with a sardonic laugh. "And in no uncertain terms. She hates his sister with a passion, sincerely believing their bond will eventually lead him to incest."

I listened and thought while the two others chatted on. I had broken the custom of royal incest, but it could not be denied that Selene and Helios were close. Their separation had drawn tears from both. I suddenly feared not only for Helios but also for Selene, but before I could express my fears, Antonia spoke again.

"Why must it be scandalous for a brother to love his sister, even erotically, as long as it is not enacted?" Antonia asked.

"Do tell us more of Iotape," I said, wanting to skirt the issue altogether.

"Well, she's recently become noticeably fat. It took *six* men to carry her litter from the wedding to the festival," Tullia stated.

"Some plumpness is necessary in order for a wife to more easily bear healthy children," I said, realizing my mistake even before the words left my mouth. I had always been careful to not carry any excess fat. My husbands, Julius and Antony had both told me they hated bony women, though, in truth, I think they both found excitement in a woman's youthful litheness.

"Indeed, what man wants a woman with *no* fat? She would then be a man!" Antonia agreed and we all laughed

"Unattractive as she has made herself, she will face much competition for Helios' bed. He is dashingly handsome. She can never kill all his admirers," Tullia said cattily.

"And did she really curse Philadelphos?" I asked. This was what I truly wanted to know. If she cursed my son, I would need to ask Isis to remove the curse.

"Yes, but in Medusa's name, and Medusa is no goddess, therefore the curse cannot be truly evoked," Tullia explained.

"Even so, spoken words can sometimes be a curse with or without the intervention of a god or goddess," I said, though inwardly relieved.

As we finished bathing, Antonia sampled her pomegranates and me my figs.

"Tell us more of Selene's wedding," Tullia asked, graciously changing the subject.

Antonia and I described the marriage ceremony and festival, explaining that by now Selene and Juba were on their way to Mauretania for their own second wedding. Selene was now publicly in direct line on ascension to become the next Queen or Queen-Pharaoh of Egypt and would soon be Queen of Mauretania.

"Selene will be fine. She and Juba are lovely people and clearly in love," Tullia said, as if personally feeling my unspoken sense of loss at the two leaving at once. "And I believe Iotape's hatred cannot last indefinitely, Domina Cleopatra."

Tullia's remark, meant in consolation, caused a shudder in my heart.

"Soon it will be dinner," I said, and, as we dressed, I prayed the shudder I felt was from the cold bath rather than hidden fear. Each of us was to dine with her husband that night.

"Nonetheless, the thought of Iotape makes my stomach turn," Tullia said.

"It's good we don't have to see her tonight," Antonia said, but my heart sank as I thought of my Helios dining together with someone who neither loved nor respected him.

"The gods and goddesses willing, none of us will ever have to," Tullia stated to my added consternation.

Chapter Twenty-Two

Dynasty

25-24 B.C.

Years 26-27, which are also Years 12-13, of Cleopatra's Reign

The Vault of Nut

Isis, Berenice, Auletes, and the Royal Mother looked down in horror at Helios, who, despite his name, was fast becoming the least publicly favored of Cleopatra's three married children. He was King of Nabataea and Medea, but the marriage had begun poorly and Iotape remained barren. This only added to her hatred, pushing her closer in devotion to the monster, Medusa, whom she now openly idealized, pushing her ever further from Helios. Snakes were a blessing of the god Apollo and the goddess Athena, and, they had been known to save entire cities by eating plague-infested mice, but they were *not* a blessing the strange way Iotape worshipped them. In the days that followed their Nabataean wedding, Iotape's ill mind and jealous disposition led her to repeatedly plot against her husband, who she was constantly accusing of adultery. High above, on the portico of Nut, Auletes was reminded of his second wife, Roxane, who, upon her death, had had her soul devoured for her wickedness. Even so, Roxane had never truly desired Auletes' death and certainly not the number of times and in the many wicked manners Iotape did Helios.

"Ma'at's scales will weigh heavily against her if she does not change her ways," Isis observed. "Auletes: She is your grandson's daughter-in-law. Looking back on your life, what do *you* see for her future?" Isis was clearly using the moment to aid Caesar in his own self-evaluation, something every immortal who was initially mortal was required to eventually undergo.

"In many ways, I see my grandchildren reliving the life of my own family," Auletes stated. "Philadelphos is spoiled like his uncles were. Helios has a jealous wife, as I did."

"Auletes, my dear husband. Roxane was not the wife of your youth," the Royal Mother said graciously, reminding the introspective Auletes of the devotion and kindness she had borne him all their years together. The two exchanged a moment of poignant eye contact, while Astraia, the concubine who had so pleasured Auletes during the reign of both of his queens, looked away.

"It seems to me that the women in this family receive all of Fortuna's blessings and the men, save Caesarion, are at best left empty-handed and at worst cursed," Berenice said.

"Are they truly cursed, and if so, forever? Can a curse not be broken?" Astraia wondered aloud as she strummed her lyre.

"Of that, I do not know," Berenice stated, looking at Isis, who was watching below while listening above. "Great Mother Isis, what of my male grandchildren, Helios and Philadelphos?" Cleopatra V ventured, but Isis did not reply. "Will they be spared the fates of their uncles?" Berenice asked, having herself had to work her way slowly through the Underworld to purify her tainted soul before being allowed to join Isis in the Vault of Nut. Both of Cleopatra's brothers had had their souls devoured by Ammut for their overarching selfishness, insolence and lack of respect for the gods and goddesses.

"Why must you ask?" Isis replied with noticeable sadness. "Sometimes it is not better to not know, and thereby avoid tempting the Fates."

"I ask because, Great Isis, being in your presence has changed me. I have come to care for others more deeply than my heart can contain," Berenice replied.

"Well, the fact is, child, though I know and see all, I know also that of the past, present, and future, the past alone cannot be changed. If the shadows of the present remain unchanged, former Princess of Egypt, I see an empty throne where Helios once reigned."

Berenice noted tears wetting the goddess' averted eyes.

"O' Isis! Please tell me my nephew can be saved!" Berenice begged. Isis said nothing, but her tears continued, swelling the Nile and granting the prayers of Egypt's farmers for the end to a month-long drought.

"Great One, what of my granddaughter, Arsinoë?" asked Auletes, his face reflecting his concern at Isis pronouncement and continued tears. "Isn't it sometimes better to know one's fate so that action can be taken?"

Auletes' concern for Arsinoë appeared sudden but was actually long founded. Growing up, the child Arsinoë had proven as strong-minded as Arsinoë II, wife of Ptolemy II, the queen after which she had been named. In truth, Auletes' granddaughter did not share Selene's devotion to Isis. Recently titled Arsinoë V to distinguish her from the four previous Ptolemaic queens of that name, she prayed on occasion to the goddess—and Isis welcomed the girl's prayers—but it was clear from the beginning that Arsinoë V's heart was divided between thoughts Egyptian, Parthian and Jewish, and of the three, she was particularly enamored with Judaism, having formed a close bond over the years with her Hebrew tutor, David. Interestingly, Isis, too, liked David. She relished the kindness and attentiveness he freely gave to all of Cleopatra's children, and caught herself several times wishing to appear before him. Knowing David was a strict devotee of the singular desert god with the unspeakable name, a rule of respect among the gods and goddesses prohibited her from directly interfering in the relationship between a devotee and his or her primarily heavenly benefactor.

Unlike her mother, Cleopatra VII, who was able to embrace different languages and cultures without losing her identity, Arsinoë V felt increasingly torn to choose between the three different peoples and cultures. In Arsinoë's mind, the many cultures her mother had always so successfully navigated, seemed to her to share little but enmity and long histories of wars.

All-knowing Isis, aware of young Arsinoë's distress long before the child was born, had quietly sent an idea to her mother. From the Jews had sprung great prophets and from them would spring many more. Isis had reminded the little girl Cleopatra of the story of Pharaoh Thutmose I, who had been unkind to the Jewish people at a particularly vulnerable period in their history. When Thutmose I later called upon Isis for help, she had refused to answer the Pharaoh's plea. While it was true that the Jews of that time had been little more than desert savages, that did not mean in her mind that Pharaoh had been right to enslave them purely for his own purposes.

"Be kind to the Jews, Cleopatra. You and your children," Isis had whispered in her beloved adherent's mind—and she now placed this idea in the mind of Cleopatra's child, Arsinoë—for Isis knew that Arsinoë V held the key to resolving a great dilemma. Five hundred years ago, a particularly wicked Persian named Haman had tried to annihilate the Jews and it was to be Arsinoë V's fate to resolve and ultimately determine the fate of these people. Future wars might be inevitable, but it was often wars or rumors of wars that drew out not only the worst but also the best of cultures and civilizations, and with that, honorable people and customs worth preserving. It would be up to the future Queen Arsinoë V whether the worst or the best would seize headship within Parthia, and whether these leaders would answer their call with clarity and positive sincerity to the Hebrews. *Woe to the human,* Isis silently decreed, *who desires the utter destruction of another country or people.*

Helen R. Davis

Chapter Twenty-Three

Philadelphos

24 B.C.

Year 27 of Cleopatras Reign

Alexandria

I awoke the next morning to news that the Nile had flooded its banks and the month-long drought during our long, hot summer had ended. Dressed in my red linen sleeping chiton, I arose to light a lamp to thank Isis. Antony rose as well, and we lit the lamp together and thanked Isis. Though it was public knowledge that we had been married by Isian rites, it was not known to anyone except me that he worshipped Isis alongside me in private.

Antony joined me in Egypt throughout the summer to assist me in preparing Philadelphos and Arsinoë for their roles as King of Numidia and Queen of Parthia. Caesarion was now experienced enough to govern in his stepfather's stead, and, in fact, had encouraged Antony to remain longer with me in Alexandria.

Antony and I had little concern that morning about our youngest daughter, but every concern about our youngest son. Philadelphos was now twelve and had taken to wearing a Roman toga at public appearances, Antony and I assumed in emulation of his father. When interacting with others, however, he continued to act quite childishly. He was not worrisome in the way that Iotape, Helios' wife, was, but neither of us had any idea how to aid him towards maturity, or if such an expectation was even reasonable. At the moment, he remained wedded to his toy soldiers, spending hours every day manipulating them, recreating past as well as imagined future battles.

"It's not that he lacks intelligence," Antony said with frustration. "It's more that he acts like a girl, favoring toys over actual experience. He seems more satisfied *playing* at than actually being a warrior and leader of men."

Ignoring my spouse's slur against women, I mused aloud, "Perhaps if I took his toys from him?" and that afternoon hid them. Philadelphos, who had inherited the Ptolemaic wit along with Antony's cleverness, located them almost as quickly as I hid them, and then roundly scolded Antony and me for hiding them from him. The only "lesson" learned was the futility of our trying to remove his toys from him. He was still the rude boy to whom we'd promised Numidia, though it was increasingly clear that he was unfit to rule. *Or must he?* I began to wonder.

That evening after our dinner, Antony remarked, "Juba has been governing Mauretania as a client king quite well."

I nodded my assent, adding, "And Selene has become as much the Royal Wife as any. Juba has even minted a coin with his image on the front and hers on the back. Why don't we give Numidia to Selene? We could say it is a reward for her good work. That might motivate Philadelphos and help draw him out."

Antony pondered this for a moment. "I agree with giving his realm away, Cleopatra, but not to his sister. It might create enmity between them. We have another child, Helios."

"Helios is already king of Nabataea."

Antony nodded. "Indeed, but he could also be King of Numidia."

Numidia was some distance from Nabataea and Medea—and Helios' jealous, dangerous wife. "Have him go to Numidia and let Dolabella govern Nabataea in his stead?" I half-asked, half-stated, admiring my husband's increasing command of diplomacy over force. *I must be doing something right*, I thought. *My husband is taking after me.*

"And perhaps," Antony added, equally proud of his display of diplomatic acumen, "if Philadelphos learns from this, I can honor him with a governorship. I will talk to Philadelphos if you will write Helios."

I inhaled deeply. Antony had just addressed my second great concern: what Philadelphos would think of me if, after taking his toy soldiers away, I now took away what might seem to him his birthright. "Thank you, dearest Antony," I began, but was interrupted by a grin on Antony's handsome face.

"You are indeed the great Caesar I married, dearest Antony," I said, causing his grin to extend boyishly from ear-to-ear.

Antony and I left immediately for Philadelphos' chamber. It had been previously occupied by both of his uncles, Ptolemy XIII and Ptolemy XIV. A young Numidian Dinka boy who had been gifted to Philadelphos to help him learn more about the Numidians and their ways shared his chamber. He and Philadelphos had become fast playmates. When Antony kicked at the door, it was the Dinka boy who greeted us with a bow. The Dinka were an exceptionally tall and graceful people. This one was still Philadelphos' height, but about to enter what would inevitably prove an awkward adolescence. In anticipation, Philadelphos had named his playmate Titan. Of course, Titan had a name in his own tongue, but being Philadelphos, my son refused to use it. As we entered, Titan down-everted his eyes and backed away. My son, standing to his side, did not.

"Philadelphos," I said in greeting.

He said nothing.

"Philadelphos!" commanded Antony firmly. "Your mother, Queen-Pharaoh Cleopatra VII Thea Philopater, Empress of the East, wife of Julius and Antonius Caesar, the divine incarnation of the goddess Isis has spoken to you!"

"Mother," Philadelphos insolently replied. "Soon you, Mother, and you, Father, as well as the rest of the world will address *me* as King of Numidia!"

"No, my son," Antony replied. "You have just lost that privilege. Simply by your statement, you have shown to me that you are not fit to be a king. Not yet. I have decided to give Numidia to your brother, Helios."

Titan's eyes darted nervously from Antony stern eyes to Philadelphos shocked face, and he backed away when Philadelphos' face turned red with rage. Philadelphos impulsively scooped up a handful of toy soldiers and threw them at Titan, whom I granted permission to leave the room. My son responded by seething even more, abruptly lurching at me and attempting to tear my gown. Antony intervened and called for Mardian who lifted the screaming and kicking young boy by the waist and held him firmly. To his credit, Philadelphos did not swear or curse, though he screamed so loudly and so angrily that Herod and his infamous harem in Jerusalem should have heard his tantrum. Herod would have laughed.

"In Rome, I would have you beaten for acting this way," Antony stated icily.

"In Egypt, you can shriek and pound the air all you wish," I corrected.

Antony sent me a horrified look.

"Dear husband, is it not better to let him to rant and rave? Eventually he will expend all this excess energy," I said, "and we can talk like parents should to their child."

"Is this behavior unstoppable?" Mardian asked, a look of disgust on his face as he carefully placed the screaming, kicking child on the bed.

"Not by anything we seem to do," I admitted. "I have learned to let him scream but not give in to his childish reactions. Eventually he will sleep and afterwards, his reason will return."

Philadelphos continued screaming, pounding his bed with his hands and feet. Antony, finally able no longer to accept the boy's behavior, walked over to the bed and slapped him hard across the face. "How dare you act this way? How dare you attack your mother, my wife and Queen-Pharaoh of Egypt!" he said, his hand reaching for his Roman *puglio*, a short killing dagger he always kept strapped at his side.

"Antony!" I begged. Antony held up his hand, signaling that at this moment, Philadelphos' life was in danger. What happened next would determine whether the boy lived or died.

"You two have taken away my kingdom!" Philadelphos whined, trembling beneath Antony's raised fist.

"We have every right to do so. Numidia was a *privilege* given you, boy, not a right. And you alone have forfeited that privilege," Antony said angrily, slowly releasing his grip on the haft of the gold and ivory inlaid *puglio*.

"I didn't intend to hurt Mother," he explained, turning aside his deep crimson face, his reason returning at last.

"If you would threaten your own mother, what would you do to another nation's envoys?" Antony asked, slapping his son hard again. I had never before seen Antony this angry, but I had seen him like this whenever anyone threatened me. I stood, subdued, not knowing how or if I should intervene.

"I am a Prince of Egypt!" Philadelphos screamed, then, trembling as Antony again raised his right hand and gripped his *puglio* in his left, fell silent. I think it was at this point that my son realized his life depended on his next words and actions.

"Indeed. That is what you are and what you will remain for now. Be grateful, young man. For your mother's sake, I will spare your life!" Antony yelled, turning on his heel and leaving, stating forcefully as he exited the room, "This time!"

Titan, in the meantime, had cautiously slipped back into the room. Eyes wide as saucers, I could sense that he didn't know whether when he entered the room it would be to see Philadelphos alive or dead. I liked Titan, at times, I'm sad to say, even more than my own son. Despite Antony's rage, this sweet Dinka boy showed his continued concern for Philadelphos clearly on his face.

Mardian was silent, as was I.

"Your Majesty," Titan quivered. "Let me try to calm him."

"You are his friend, so I leave him to you. But I warn you: Fear for both your lives."

Titan appeared strong, but I did not know if Antony would return to vent further rage on both, or if Titan could withstand a similar rage from my son. Still, with Isis' help and Antony's intervention, I felt satisfied that Philadelphos had learned his limits this time. Isis was a goddess who kept her word. But I still did not know who or what, as David had so wisely stated, might be possessing my son, though possession it increasingly seemed.

Chapter Twenty-Four

Daughters

24 B.C.

Year 27 of Cleopatras Reign

Alexandria

The next day, the entire palace was abuzz. Philadelphos continued to be treated as a Prince of Egypt, but his tantrums were now known to everyone inside the palace. After his father's intervention, he seemed to accept that he would not be king of Numidia. Overall, he seemed calmer; he resumed attending David's teaching sessions, and appeared to listen more attentively alongside his sister, Arsinoë.

In contrast to Philadelphos, Arsinoë was a delight. I found it hard to believe that she and he were siblings, and, equally, that she so easily accepted sharing the royal name of her wicked aunt. Lamentably, she and her aunt looked similar, with the black hair, dark tanned skin and almond-shaped eyes, but the name and appearance were the beginning and the end of the similarities. Whereas my sister Arsinoë had ripped my Isis doll from me and torn off its head before my tearful eyes, my daughter, ever since Philadelphos had taken the doll from her, showed no enmity to her brother at all. My sister had hated the Jews and the Medes; my daughter seemed the opposite, being deeply intrigued by David's telling of the history and legends of the Hebrews. My sister cared nothing for learning except how it might be used as a weapon; my daughter was as much a linguist as myself, already writing to her sister, Selene, in Mauretania in Latin, Egyptian, and sometimes, for practice, in Parthian. Arsinoë also wrote regularly to her intended husband, Phraataces, in his native tongue. Being fluent in Parthian, I marveled at the poems she read to me, written by Phraataces back to her. The Persians of Parthia were renowned for their love poems, and her prince of that nation and future husband did not disappoint. He even sent her a gold Persian eagle brooch which Arsinoë wore proudly everywhere.

"Can I send him a gift in return?" Arsinoë asked me one day while stroking the brooch lovingly. I laughed and shook my head in the negative.

"No, dearest. That is not done," I said. "It is for the man to gift the woman."

"But I love what he writes to me," Arsinoë said. "And Selene often shares with me some of the pleasures of being the wife of a loving husband."

I sighed. Selene indeed enjoyed being a wife, but she had not yet experienced the joys of motherhood. She had written to me after miscarrying. Thankfully, the pregnancy had not been far enough along to identify the sex. Equally thankfully, Juba had not held it against her. Instead they both looked forward to her conceiving again and had already made plans to come to Egypt to seek Isis and Hathor's blessing on her womb. I had not told this to Arsinoë.

"Your sister is a great wife and queen. Like you, one day her offspring will rule many lands," I said sadly, in the saying, hoping it would prove true.

Arsinoë immediately noticed the change in my demeanor. "What could possibly be sad in light of such a destiny, Mother?" Arsinoë asked.

I thought for a moment, and decided to redirect the topic of our conversation. "Philadelphos," I suggested.

"Well, he wasn't behaving like a future king, so it is right he lost his kingdom," Arsinoë said, adding judiciously, "for now." Arsinoë might be only eight, but like her sister and I at the same age, she spoke with wisdom far beyond her years.

"Mother, look what Selene sent me along with her letter," Arsinoë continued, unrolling a short scroll containing a drawing of a Temple to Isis that Selene had proposed to build in her adopted homeland. The drawing displayed excellent perspective and detail. Selene had quite a talent for drawing and even had even included plans for smaller versions of the temple to be built in neighboring Numidia. Written beneath the drawing was a note in Egyptian to her sister:

"Do not neglect your prayers to the goddess, Sister. Isis will be pleased to bestow on you the richest of blessings even as she is upon me, should you choose hold her tightly in your heart and to accept them."

Yet again I sighed. I could understand Arsinoë's lack of interest in the goddess-doll, but not the goddess herself. In fact, she did little beyond occasionally honoring Isis with incense. *Who does she truly worship?* I wondered.

"This looks like a great temple to Isis," I said, pleased at the designs Selene had done and shared. In each case, four great steps led to an elaborately frescoed altar to the goddess that was surrounded and protected by Ionic Greek columns. The design was Greek with nods to Rome, but the interior entirely Egyptian.

"I respect Isis, Mother, but I find the stories of Ahura Mazda and the Jewish god with the unpronounceable name interesting, too," Arsinoë said. "I make my petitions to all three."

"Why would a god who cannot be called upon by name listen to a woman's petitions?" I asked.

"I think the strange Jewish god does listen, despite what some say. David told me that he listened to a woman named Deborah."

I nodded my assent. Deborah was the woman Herod had had the effrontery with whom to compare me by way of flattery. When later, I asked David about Deborah, he elaborated that Deborah had been a warrior, seer, prophetess, and, as I understood the story, like myself, had deeply loved and saved her people, leaving me to treasure the compliment, almost as much as I disliked the flatterer. "Herod once asked if I fancied myself a Deborah," I told my daughter.

"Well, Mother, you're smart and brave like her. And you have saved Egypt, like she saved Israel," Arsinoë stated.

I smiled and took Arsinoë in my arms. She was still young enough to accept hugs from her mother. "Bravery is a true virtue when needed. And remember that feeling fear does not mean you are not brave," I sermonized, kissing her on the forehead.

"I'm going to be a great Queen of Parthia," Arsinoë said in perfect Parthian, "and like you and my sister, a great wife to my husband."

"Of that I am certain," I replied in Parthian, hugging her tightly. Arsinoë had not only mastered the language but spoke it with its attendant innuendo quite well. She and I continued to converse in Parthian, for it was among the tongues I particularly enjoyed. As we talked, shared and laughed together, I realized that soon Arsinoë, too, would be leaving me—much sooner than my heart at this moment wished. Then I thought of Philadelphos. Would my problem child end up remaining with me? I did not know, but I hoped not.

I had to admit that since Antony's admonition, Philadelphos had begun progressing and his tantrums, while still occasional, were fewer, shorter and less intense. Antony and I had, as of yet, been unsuccessful in finding a princess for him. My nemesis, Herod, it seems, had missed no opportunity to spread rumors about Philadelphos, claiming that our youngest was mad. I remained hopeful that eventually Philadelphos would altogether shake off his fits of possession. At least Philadelphos and my other children held no ill will against each other, as my brothers and sisters and I always had. My break with Egyptian tradition regarding royal incest along with Antony and my careful planning for the future of each of our children had been for the best. Still, my Egyptian blood kept me wondering how Isis and Ma'at would judge me when my time came to leave this world. That was one thing of which I never spoke, not even to Antony. There were priests who claimed that, in changing the tradition and marrying not one, but two Roman Caesars, I had violated the laws of Ma'at. I knew of these priests. They were the same priests of Ra who had maligned my father. It was true a Pharaoh could do as he—or in my case, she—wished. Still, I tried not to be careless with that power intending to offend as few as possible. That was what I held at the core of my strategic diplomacy that had successfully advanced Egypt and my alliance with Rome so far without resorting to war. I believed my people appreciated this, and that Isis would continue to bless me in spite of the continuous gossip. I had no desire to squander or abuse the goddess' blessings. In any case, I had committed myself to this approach to rulership, and it was too late to change now. What would be, would be.

Chapter Twenty-Five

The Priests of Ra

23 B.C.

Year 28 of Cleopatra's reign

Alexandria

The priests of Ra, who troubled me from the first day by addressing me merely as "Princess" and not as "Queen," continued to prove a difficult lot. Until now, they had been content to lie in wait while I governed Egypt, celebrating me on occasion as having saved Egypt from Octavian some thirteen years past. But as I grew older, they began whispering against me.

Thankfully, I learned from Rufio Minor, Rufio's observant son, that not all the priests and dedicands of Ra were against me. In fact, most of the priests were from Alexandria and supportive of me. A few, notably the chief priest and some of the temple dancers, who had come to Alexandria from Heliopolis immediately after my victory over Octavian, were the ones constantly stirring up trouble. The cult of Ra had its origins in Heliopolis, an ancient city roughly five to ten days by boat up the Nile. The chief priest and some of the temple dancers were busy spreading a rumor that I had insulted Ma'at. They said that in proclaiming myself Empress—which technically I had not; it was the people who had, quite on their own, taken to calling me thus—I had invoked Roman, Greek and other foreign gods and goddesses, mentioning Isis only after-the-fact or when I sought to legitimize an action. This was, of course, not true, but my husband and I, in the process of joining our two empires together and expanding our conjoint rule, when viewed from the isolated halls of the Heliopolis temple of Ra, could seem that way. The lesser priests being mostly Alexandrian argued against this position. If I were really so wicked as to turn away from Egypt's gods and goddesses, why would Ra have given his blessing to my victory over Octavian, my alliance with Antony, my current reign and the ever-successful expansion of our joined, or if you wished to view it so, conjoined empires through our children? No, rather Ra had through me and with the benefit of his multiple blessings poised Egypt to attain a prominence in the world as never before.

But there was more. There always is.

Millennia ago, Isis was said to be the daughter of Ra; however, more recently, with the rise of Alexandria, it was being said that Isis had tricked an aging Ra into revealing his heavenly name, and thereby usurped his power. Those who held to such a belief also held that in doing so, Ra had had to take a new name, Osiris, and through nefarious means, had been compelled by Isis to become her mate.

While I was not personally interested in the cult's internal schism, Selene would be arriving in Egypt soon to seek the blessings of Hathor and Isis to open her womb and was concerned that this might afford an opportunity for these dissenters to act. Why might they act at this particular time against me? It was known throughout Egypt that Arsinoë had asked not only Ra/Osiris, but also the Jewish male god with the unpronounceable name, as well as Ahura Mazda, the Parthian god of good, and Isis together to open her sister's womb.

"You are a good younger sister," I had assured Arsinoë,

nonetheless wishing her prayers had been more private and less public. "My sisters were never as kind to me as you and Selene are to each other."

Suddenly, a distant bevy of trumpets sounded, announcing the arrival in Alexandria of my daughter and son-in-law. I stood, smoothed my new, long, white, see-through chiton, and prepared to greet them.

I received the King and Queen of Mauretania in the throne room with Antony standing at my side. He was dressed in a red toga as Caesar of Rome. He held my left hand, signifying his other role as my Divine consort, my Osiris. Together we warmly greeted Juba and Selene.

I had chosen a long chiton that veiled my feet, the newest fashion in Parthia, which Arsinoë had discovered in preparation for her future betrothal. It made walking a challenge, so, descending the steps from the throne to our guests, I lifted the chiton a bit, allowing my sandals to show. A personal gift from Antony, the sandals were studded with emeralds, amethysts, sapphires and rubies from Kush. My hair, done by Iras in a melon coiffure, was woven with pearls and diamonds, upon which I balanced the serpent crown of Egypt while holding in my right hand both crook and flail.

Antony guided me down the steps. Once on the bottom step, Selene approached with her husband, and I studied the couple. Mother and daughter looked longingly in each other's kohl-rimmed eyes. She was dressed in a deep purple chiton, in the same new fashion as I. She wore golden snake bracelets on each arm and golden rope bracelets about each wrist. Juba was as magnificently dressed as she, and although he wore a Roman toga, it was colored the same purple as my daughter's chiton. Selene was, in every possible sense, a consort queen, but as a client to her father, she was of lesser rank than me. Still, neither Antony nor I indicated to her or her husband to kneel before us. One day, all I commanded would be theirs through her.

"Welcome to Egypt, King Juba, Queen Selene," I said in stately fashion.

Antony spoke next, praising Juba aloud as a true friend of Rome. Antony then quieted for Juba to speak.

"Pharaoh-Queen Cleopatra, goddess who loves her father, wife of Antony Imperator and Caesar of Rome, I, Juba II, king of Mauretania, come to Egypt with my wife to seek the blessings of Isis and Hathor, your Egyptian goddesses who have the power to open wombs. I come on behalf of my wife. Our marriage, though blessed in so many ways, has remained barren, and we need the goddesses' blessings."

I listened as Juba recounted first of the Berbers of Mauretania, the native people, and then of his allegiance to Antony and finally of the great mercy of Cleopatra's first husband, Julius Caesar, who had granted him life when he deserved death. Much of it was a carefully rehearsed public political speech, as one would expect whenever kings met. He praised Antony for his mercy in granting him pardon after siding with the deceased Octavian and thanked me effusively for granting him a wife who would one day be Queen of Egypt.

When he finished, I motioned everyone to a less public set of four gilded settees located about a golden table laden with drink, fruit and light delicacies. When everyone had comfortably taken their places, I spoke: "You are here, Juba and Selene, to seek the favor of Isis and Hathor, and it shall be so. But Juba, I have a request for *you*. I have an ongoing dispute with the high priest of Ra, our supreme sun god, before whom we must present ourselves to seek Isis and Hathor's blessings. Under duress by and clearly in association with the dancer-priestesses, the high priest has dared to continue claiming my rule illegitimate, for though I as queen married Antony, I rule Egypt on my own and now dare to bestow the kingdom upon my daughter, your wife, when it is my turn to be judged by Ma'at."

At this point, Antony intervened: "The traditions of Ra and Ma'at state that Cleopatra should have married a brother, though, as you can see, there are none left." Antony's situation in Rome was not dissimilar. There remained senators who challenged Antony, saying that though Caesar had claimed Caesarion as his son, Antony was breaking the laws of Rome by taking me as his wife and spending winters in Egypt. "We desire your consent," he continued, "to challenge the high priest immediately prior to our asking for permission to seek Isis and Hathor's support in your favor. The high priest, feeling compelled to bless your request, will also feel hard pressed to answer my challenge publicly, knowing that the favors of Egypt, Rome and Mauritania all depend on his acquiescence."

Juba and Selene understood and agreed immediately, displaying bold, confederate smiles.

"So, dearest daughter and son-in-law, let us go," I announced, rising and gathering my chiton. With us would come Philadelphos, Arsinoë, Charmion, Iras, Olympos, and Mardian commanding three armed Roman and three armed Egyptian guards. We left the Palace and walked as a group to the temple of Isis-Hathor currently being serviced by the priests and dancers of Ra.

I had been careful to deny the high priest any indication of when we would be arriving, but his priests and dancer-priestesses were nonetheless ready, being charged to receive the Pharaoh on any day at any time. *What a surprise the high priest will have*, I thought, *when he deigns to welcome not just me and Selene, but a bevy of kings, queens, princes and princesses along with armed guards!*

It was a chilly day, but the promise of spring was in the air and I could smell the first blooms of jasmine as we walked past the outer pillars and into the temple. The smell of jasmine brought back memories of Julius Caesar, and our unfulfilled dreams. Selene, noticing the sweet smell, stopped momentarily to inhale deeply and sigh. As we walked directly into the inner temple, Antony and I saw Juba stop Selene momentarily to give her a jasmine flower, which he had picked himself. I smiled at the vivacity of their romance in face of the gravity of the situation we were about to face.

A ceremony to Ra was just ending, and, as was proper, we waited for it to finish completely and for the high priest, Amon-Ra, whose name embodied that of the sun deity, Ra, to join us. He was a tall, stern looking man, whose skin was of the blackest ebony. As a mark of austerity, he wore only a kilt and modest headdress. Both were decorated with black and gold stripes.

I spoke first. "Great Priest of Ra," I said loudly. He reacted with a twitch of his eye, the slightest acknowledgement possible.

"I am the Seventh Cleopatra of the Royal Dynasty of Ptolemy, Queen-Pharaoh of Egypt, Blessed of Isis." The vaguest hint of a sneer swept briefly across his otherwise stony face.

"I have come to settle a dispute." This time, I saw not only surprise on his face, but a flicker of fear in his abruptly widening eyes.

"High Priest of Ra," I announced, again, for all to hear. "Why do you allow rumors to spread that Ra has cursed me when it is I who saved the nation, rule Egypt in prosperity, and have done my duty to continue the line of Ptolemy?"

The priest, clearly shaken, did not speak, so I continued. "Pharaonic lines have always passed through women to their men or women. Why then do you and your followers question my authority? Are you intent on tempting the gods?"

"The rules of Ma'at do not favor a woman pharaoh," he stated carefully but strongly, though his voice waivered.

"Our proud history," I stated, "has seen several Queen-Pharaohs, some within my own dynasty. My grandmother, Cleopatra III, honored the laws of Ma'at though she ruled Egypt alone, and did so for decades. I wonder if part of the insidious rumor going around is based on my choice of Antony as mate. As Queen, one of my roles is also that of a wife in order to produce heirs. In good times when there are brothers to marry, the queen often remains in the background. But these have been turbulent times, and Ma'at has historically acknowledged that in such times the queen may take independent action in rulership and mate, which I have," I said.

The priest appeared speechless, and a hush fell over the chamber. Finally, he broke the silence with but one sentence: "You have no brothers to marry because you killed them."

"Of course I killed Ptolemy XIV," I admitted for all to hear, realizing fully that one day I would have to answer to Ma'at for it. "At the time, it was him or me. The death of my other brother, Ptolemy XIII, however, can be attributed only to his own folly. If you will recall, twenty-three years ago there was a war over the throne of Egypt. It was Caesar and I against my brother and sister. Were I wrong in my actions, Ra would have killed me that day. Instead, my brother drowned that very day in the Nile. The gods know and see all, and Hapi, the river god, is no exception. Gods do not make errors," I argued.

I silently called on Isis before continuing: "The Pharaoh, whether man, woman or child, must do what is right for Egypt. Ptolemy XIV, whom I admittedly 'murdered,' was concerned not with Egypt but with his toy chariots, and my sister…" I paused, reluctant to address her as Arsinoë IV which might lend legitimacy to her horrific reign over

Cyprus and Egypt as Queen. Still, I did not want to treat my sister, Arsinoë, as spitefully as she had me. She had refused to acknowledge my reign, but posthumously out of familial respect, I would acknowledge hers. "...my sister, Arsinoë IV, if you recall was a disastrous queen. In fact, all of my sisters were disastrous queens. And as for my marriages to Julius and Antony..." I looked at Antony out of the corner of my eye. "...I freely chose to marry both. I chose my husbands, the way a strong Queen should when looking out for her country. I chose these two men because they are brave, bold, worthy representatives of Osiris, my heavenly consort, as well as the gods of Rome whom they serve."

Antony cleared his throat, a look of admiration shining on his face, and continued for me: "High Priest of Ra, I, too, am a devotee of Isis. As a Roman, I am required to honor my Roman gods above others, but Isis is the goddess who brought to me Cleopatra, and who together with me defeated Octavian. You would be foolish to challenge both my wife, your ruler by the will of her father, Pharaoh Ptolemy XII Auletes, and myself, Imperator and Caesar of Rome. You would also do well to remember that it was my wife who granted you the right to retain Heliopolis and your temple though Heliopolis favored Octavian over me."

Antony's right hand touched his sword hilt and the three Roman guards followed suit.

A ripple coursed through the priest and he visibly blanched. The word 'Rome' always struck a note of terror in human hearts. Yet still he would not budge.

"I also know of your use of Ra's priestess-dancers as prostitutes for your own monetary gain," I added, quietly this time.

This time, the priest audibly gasped.

The priestess-dancers had sided with him, I felt, out of fear rather than devotion. If word escaped of his use of them for public prostitution, the people might rise against him and in an instant, his hold on Heliopolis and the temples of Ra could disappear.

I watched his stone face melt. The priestess-dancers represented Ra himself. If Amon-Ra's secret got out, it would completely destroy him.

Seizing the advantage, I continued, "Good Priest, perhaps it is *you* who, through your actions, are inadvertently questioning the gods. How can I be judged merely for doing what was needed to save and rebuild the nation? Surely the gods care more for Egypt than under which formal title Egypt's leader governs. I will always honor Ra, as is proper, but I seek to resolve this dispute here and now so I can call on she of whom I am the divine representative, the goddess Isis herself. Would you choose to question the Goddess on Earth?"

The high priest, to everyone's surprise, shuddered violently and collapsed. My party and the priests and priestess-dancers stared agape at the pitiful heap lying at my feet. Inspecting him, Olympos declared for all to hear that the man had died of fear. Interestingly, none of the priests or priestesses challenged Olympos. Instead, they sighed, as I had suspected they would, in collective relief. His "death" was, of course, not my intention. I had sought merely to publicly bind him to me, but that had not worked. At my signal, everyone, murmuring, left, while Mardian knelt next to the man and, talking his head in his hands, with an imperceptible jerk, made certain his "death" was a reality. Standing, Mardian whispered that the man had obviously not been favored by the gods or Ra, having, like Icarus, held himself above them. Mardian would later explain to me that he had felt it his duty to assist the deluded man on his inevitable journey towards judgement. In my mind, if it was true the man had felt himself above the gods—and I more than strongly suspected such—then death was a just punishment. More important, however, was that everyone including those who'd served him, saw that neither Antony nor I had touched him. Whatever his fate, it was not of either of our doing.

Still, I was uncertain what to do, and waited in silence until the temple attendants removed the body. As they did, one of the priests came forward and spoke directly to me.

"Great One, everything said about Amon-Ra was true." This priest was one who had known me since well before I became heir apparent. Rahotep by name, he was, in fact, the eldest son of the dead high priest. I waited patiently to hear where he stood.

"You are Egypt's greatest blessing," he said with sincerity, kneeling before me.

"Speak truthfully, Rahotep. I desire truth, not honey. Whatever is said between us here and now, I will spare your life," I said, recalling my fondness for this man who had briefly captured my heart while I was still a young princess.

"The truth you spoke struck the High Priest, my father, dead. I had warned him not to be so arrogant."

"More likely, his heart stopped of old age," Olympos said, seeing my sorrow for the death of this young man's father, sensing my hope that his son would prove more worthy.

The young priest nodded. "He was old in body and demented in mind, and it is likely he would have died soon anyway. Truth can be an explosive shock when brought into the light. It is for the gods to decide when and how we die. He was not wise to anger Ra, Isis and Isis incarnate."

It seemed to me that he was coming to a decision, so I continued

228

waiting and listening.

"The timing of his passing, My Queen, cannot be coincidence," he said at last. "There has been, as you pointed out, a division in this temple over your reign. Though Ra gives us the ability and responsibility to interpret the signs and omens, we cannot ever ultimately know the will of the gods. In truth, your reign *has* been good for Egypt. I and most of Ra's adherents here in Alexandria believe you are loved by both Isis and Ra, and that he guards you as if you were his daughter and consort. Despite what my father said, I believe that the Ptolemies are the legitimate rulers of Egypt. It was primarily because of your Greek stock that he vowed not to bow before and support you, Great One."

"So. it was my Macedonian Greek blood and not my Pharaohship or womanhood he disdained? How interesting," I said soberly, while inside, smiling at Rahotep's ingenuity.

"As the new High Priest, I say the gods will do as Ra truly wishes. And I see, Great Queen-Pharaoh and Empress, that your serving Egypt is favored by them. But, with your permission, I ask one favor before assuming my duties."

"Yes?" I asked, increasingly impressed with this young man's excellent diplomacy, sincerely interested in what his request would be.

"Permit me to honor my mistaken father with mummification, Generous One," he answered.

About that, I would have to consider carefully. This young man was requesting more than an undeserved honor for his father. Mummification was an assurance that the person would bodily reappear in an afterlife and that would I meet him at some future time. There was no reassurance that I would prove as blessed in the future as I just been. On the other hand, propriety demanded that his body be preserved as I needed this new High Priest's dedication to me to be assured, even if his father at the end had proven a man of dishonor.

"You may do so," I replied after a long pause, adding, "and may Ma'at judge him rightly," adding after a second pause, "In return, however, I must now ask a favor of you: I wish the blessing of Ra's new High Priest as I proceed to ask Isis and Hathor to open my daughter's womb."

"My father informed me this was the reason you were coming to visit, and, while he was undecided as to his response, we Alexandrian priests prepared ahead to assist, should his answer be in the affirmative. Please proceed whenever you are ready and do so with the blessing of Ra."

As Antony and I ushered our entourage on to Isis/Hathor's alter, Antony looked about, and discerning that we were at last alone, whispered to our two youngest, "And that, children, is how a great ruler rules."

Chapter Twenty-Six

Republicans

23-21 B.C.

Years 28-30 of Cleopatra's Reign

Rome

Not long after the new priest took charge of the Temple of Ra, Antony and I, satisfied we had resolved the crisis, set sail for Rome with the same entourage minus Juba and Selene, who left for Mauritania at the same time with Ra, Isis and Hathor's blessings of fecundity along with a potion for conception that I had uncovered several years back. Our purpose for visiting Rome was twofold: Philadelphos was to observe his brother, Caesarion, and hopefully learn from his example proper behavior for a royal son as well as how to govern, and Arsinoë to further her general education of the world, this time from a Roman perspective. It would be my first visit to Rome in several years. It was my plan to stay for the spring and return to Alexandria in the summer. At the time, I had no idea that, like when I visited my former husband, Julius Caesar, nearly twenty years ago, this visit would also prove far longer and more eventful than anticipated.

Trouble began the moment my flagship left port. It proved a long and exhausting journey, fraught with rough weather, causing Arsinoë to be continuously seasick, but to which Philadelphos proved surprisingly immune. I had not noticed until this voyage how the sea seemed to soothe the boy's mind and moderate his thoughts and actions. I mentioned this to Antony, who agreed.

"The sea has strange powers," he noted. "Perhaps we should seek the blessing of Neptune when he is in Rome."

I nodded my agreement, recalling that bathing in the salt sea of Judea had seemed to strengthen Philadephos's disposition. Perhaps the *Mare Nostrum* was the cure for which we'd been praying for his disturbed mind. "What else is there left?" I asked, raising my hands in despair and wrapping my woolen cape more tightly about me. Evenings, when the harsh sea calmed for a moment, an ominous mist would invariably gather about our ship, and Antony and I would head into our cabin, leaving the captain to navigate the fierce storm that always followed. That evening, we sat below in our luxurious cedar wood quarters, lying about a large golden bed and plush recliners located about a large table where we often played chess or dice, sometimes alone and other times with the children. Neither game would have finished before the ship began its violent nightly tossing and turning.

"It is April. The sea gods should have been done fighting for the year," Antony said with irritation.

"One cannot manipulate the gods," I reminded him. Indeed, I wondered if petitioning the gods and goddesses for Juba and Selene's wish might not have incurred a debt.

"Not even Antony and Cleopatra can," Antony admitted glumly.

I looked at Antony. He was still admirably handsome, though like me, he was getting older and beginning to show it. Fine wrinkles had begun to appear at the corners of the eyes of his manly face, reminding me that I, the younger of us two, would soon be turning forty-seven, reflecting a surprisingly long life. After placing the children into the care of Iras and Charmion and kissing them goodnight, Antony and I retired with difficulty to our bed. There, as the ship rose and fell in increasing heaves, I took Antony's hand in mine.

"Octavian lies dead at the bottom of the sea," Antony stated. What was unspoken was *Will we meet the same fate?*

I, too, worried similarly. Had we defeated Octavian at sea only to be snatched by Poseidon and Neptune fourteen years later?

The storm continued in this manner for days. At its end, Philadelphos had become completely calm. Titan, his Dinka playmate who had accompanied our retinue, remarked to me that he had never seen Philadelphos so at peace.

What could this mean? I wondered, but instead asked Titan, "Do you think it will last?" I knew that as a result of their frequent playing together at sea, Titan had come to know my son better than anyone.

"My people believe in a god who sometimes takes temporary possession of people in order to speak his will through them," Titan offered.

Oh Isis! I knew demons sometimes came from the Underworld and tormented people! *My little boy!* "Do you believe my son to be..." I began in horror, wondering how Antony and I could not have seen it. One is often blind to the most obvious.

"I do not know, Great One," Titan replied. "I am but a commoner. But Philadelphos is now in his right mind. Perhaps the unknown god has finished speaking through him at last."

That night, we approached Ostia on a calm sea, and I prayed fervently to Isis that Philadelphos' change would prove permanent, though I couldn't help wondering that if what Titan had said was true, exactly what it was the god had spoken through him. And to whom.

Arsinoë's seasickness ebbed at this time. Though both our

youngest arrived in Italy healthy and eager, their health problems were the only things that ended upon our arrival. Antony and I were greeted by Cicero Minor with "bad news, more bad news, and horrid news."

"The bad news first," Antony ordered, as yesterday's squall and storm clouds rolled inland from the sea.

"I can tell *you*, Great Caesar, but first, would not your wife and children like to rest in the tent we've constructed, while we await the palanquins? What I have to say is…"

"My hearing has not lessened over the years, Cicero Minor," I said. "I am Antony's wife and I deserve to know," I stated in irritation that Cicero Minor would even *think* of hiding anything from me. Accepting my rebuke, we all took shelter in the tent.

"The bad news, Cicero Minor," Antony demanded, the moment we settled inside.

"The bad news is that some Republican senators are claiming that Julius Caesar's will stating that Caesarion is Caesar's son was a forgery and you are not rightful ruler of Rome. There are also reports that Octavian is alive in Greece."

"Impossible! "Antony bellowed.

Cicero Minor paused a moment before continuing.

"We all know, Imperator, that he died at sea, but there are those who desire to see their lost power return again and are quick to put their hope in anything that might do so. I sent trusted men to look personally into both claims. Regarding the first, no 'proof' whatsoever has surfaced to support the claim, and regarding the second, a man about Octavian's age, calling himself the true heir of Caesar has indeed arisen. But now, more bad news: Caesarion has fled the city."

"What?" Antony, incredulous, bellowed even louder than before. "And what of him?"

"He lives, Great Caesar. We have that assurance. But, the truly horrid news is of Helios, your middle son."

I braced myself for the worst and received it.

"Helios is dead," Cicero Minor stated flatly.

Antony was dumbfounded. Though I fully expected to lose my composure and begin wailing as any grieving mother would, I did not. I felt numb, as if another person were speaking my words when I asked, "What happened?"

"I am as of yet uncertain," Cicero Minor stated, explaining, "Iotape, his wife, is believed involved and likely responsible. It is said an asp was found in his bed next to his and an Arabian mistress' body. Iotape claims he committed suicide upon hearing of the death of Selene, his sister."

"Selene is...?" I screamed, awakening from the shock of hearing that my son, Helios, was dead.

"...alive and well, Great Queen!" Cicero Minor stated emphatically.

"One asp..." I began, abandoning my emotions momentarily to pure logic, "while sufficiently venomous to kill one person, has never been known to kill two. If what you say is true, Cicero Minor..." I stated emotionlessly, "If what you say is true, this cannot possibly have been suicide. It could only be murder!"

"How can you know for certain his death was from asp venom?" Cicero Minor asked skeptically

"Because I know poisons as well as I know cosmetics and perfumes," I stated. "I believe this is a story likely made up to cover Iotape's guilt. Were there other findings?"

"The bed was said to be soaked with blood, My Queen," Cicero Minor offered reluctantly.

"Blood-soaked?" I echoed. "Asp bites cause minimal to no bleeding. Were the bodies inspected by an Egyptian physician? Were any snakebite marks found on the bodies, and, if so, was there discoloration about the bites?" I questioned.

Cicero Minor shook his head, first yes, then no in uncertainty.

"Everyone who knew her said Iotape was evil, but..." I summarized, still in shock.

"I agree," echoed Antony blankly, also in shock.

"And what of Medea, Numidia and Nabataea?" I asked. "Helios ruled these nations for three years."

"We believe Caesarion is traveling to Nabataea to avenge his brother while hiding from those who claim he is not Caesar's son and are demanding his death. However, this again I do not know for certain."

"It is his duty to avenge his brother, as it is mine to crush dissidents and murderers, and reassert control before Rome falls into civil war," Antony stated, shaking off the worst of his shock.

"Will my children and I be safe in Rome?" I asked.

Antony looked at Cicero Minor.

"With your permission, Great Caesar," Cicero Minor replied, "I believe it best to house the Queen and children in one of my villas with my wife, Terentia. I have already ordered guards discretely posted at my least-known urban holiday villa in the Carinae district. While little known to the public, it is but minutes from the Forum Romanum. Anyone wanting to find your wife and children would not think to look there," Cicero Minor explained.

"Yes, thank you," Antony replied, his color returning more with each second. "I need some time to assess the political situation in Rome, which I can best do from the Forum."

Mardian, it was agreed, would accompany Antony, as he had

Caesar in the Battle of Alexandria. Olympos would wander Rome in disguise, observing the city's mood, reporting back regularly to Cicero Minor.

"It is settled then," Antony announced, seizing command. "Cleopatra, you and our two children will be Terentia's guest. I must leave soon to quash this uprising."

Antony left within the hour, after the palanquins arrived filled with a handful of armed Roman soldiers who would accompany him. My children and I would replace the soldiers in the palanquins and travel in in curtained secrecy to Cicero Minor's urban holiday villa. Just in case, we would travel at his suggestion disguised as a Roman family returning from holiday.

"This is for your safety," Cicero Minor explained. "Those opposed to Antony will likely seek to capture his wife and children." Charmion and Iras, it was decided, would walk behind our litters, dressed as household slaves to alert us to any dangers.

I listened carefully to the chattering of wives as we passed the various public wells located throughout the city. None of the gossip was directed at Antony or me. Mostly they complained of the city's year-long draught. One woman said her husband had taken to wearing trousers, a barbaric custom from Germania, and loudly cursed the "son of that Egyptian who first introduced trousers to Rome!" At least she called me "that Egyptian" and not "that Egyptian whore."

We arrived at the villa that Cicero Minor had volunteered, where Terentia awaited us, at nightfall. Our anxiety had made it another exhausting day. In spite of, or perhaps because of our exhaustion and worries, everyone proceeded immediately to bed. I slept deeply with my children in my arms, but when I awoke next morning, I surrendered myself to the storm of grief that overnight had welled from deep inside of me. "Helios is gone! My son Helios is dead! Oh, Isis, I feel his earthly absence in my heart of hearts!" I screamed, beating my chest between sobs and tears.

Charmion called my children aside, then held me in her arms and rocked me like she did when I was hurting as a child.

"Helios is dead, dead, dead, and nothing I can do or say will bring him back!" I wailed. "I am Pharaoh-Queen of Egypt and Isis incarnate! I am the most powerful woman in the world, yet I cannot bring back my son!" My sobs woke everyone in the villa. Terentia came immediately to me accompanied by several house guards, swords drawn, ready to give their lives in my and my children's defense.

"What is happening? Are you alright?" Terentia asked with great trepidation, shooing Iras, Charmion and my children out of the room.

"I am *not* alright!" I managed to scream between sobs. "Helios is dead and my grief has overtaken me!"

Terentia proved a great comfort to me then and later. She was a woman of noble grace and beauty, younger than me, close to Selene's age. When I had cried myself out, she told me knowingly that as the relative of a prominent politician, she heard much, but was careful to not let the men know all that she knew.

"That seems always the case between men and women," I said, between sniffles, momentarily calmed. Isis had blessed me with Antony, but I, too, knew much more than I could ever tell him. The difference was that Antony *knew* I knew much and was both kind and clever enough to discretely build on what he and I collectively knew. He was an extraordinary man. Few men listened to a wife as he did.

"Queen Cleopatra, may I speak freely?" Terentia asked.

Craving any distraction that would avert another outburst of grief, I nodded my assent, and washed my face with cool water from a basin

Terentia's slave provided.

"I promised my husband to keep your presence a secret, but I do not know how long this will be possible. Everyone in Rome knows of Antony and your visit, and eyes everywhere are seeking your whereabouts. My slaves, while sworn to silence, may wag their tongues in a moment of weakness or gossip. You are the royal wife of Antony and your loyalty to him and Rome are increasingly well known, thanks to my husband who has been working hard to move public opinion in your favor. But this moment in time could also be your undoing."

"Is it then your or Cicero Minor's opinion that I ought to return to Egypt forthright with my children?" I asked as a slave arrived, offering us a breakfast tray of figs, wild honey and thick, tart, creamy goat *labnah*, it's delightful consistency somewhere between yogurt and cheese beckoning me.

"That I cannot say," Terentia answered while we sampled the treats together. "If you are as clever as you are beautiful and knowledgeable, I believe you and your retinue will survive. But as long as the rebellion exists, and Antony and Caesarion live, you and yours will be mercilessly hunted. If something should happen to either your husband or your eldest son, Caesarion, I can guarantee nothing. You may, however, count upon me as a friend. That much I can promise."

"Friends are precious," I stated, recalling the kindness that many, like Julia, Caesar's daughter, had shown me in times of trouble.

"Precious, and *rare*," Terentia added in agreement.

It was May, and despite the political turmoil, the days at the villa passed lazily. I spent the hottest part of each either napping in my room with my children about me or relaxing in the cool baths with Terentia. I could do little else and took advantage of our meetings to gather from Terentia any news.

"What of the situation?" I asked Cicero Minor directly on a rare occasion when he personally visited. The evening was pleasantly cool. I felt hopeful, seeing him projecting a particularly calm demeanor.

"Dolabella has ridden to join Antony in the North," he replied. "That is where the 'Republicans' are assembling. Caesarion is believed to be in Nabataea avenging Helios, but I am still unable to confirm this for certain."

"Did Caesarion convey anything I should know before he left?" I asked.

At my question, Cicero Minor produced a letter from inside his toga. Helios, I was told, had written it the night before his death, and Caesarion, having acquired it forthwith, had passed it to Cicero Minor to pass to me.

I extended a trembling hand and reluctantly unrolled it.

It was addressed to me.

I read, then reread the strange letter several times, checking to make certain that the handwriting was, in fact, Helios', for I had encouraged all of my children in times of crisis to write and sign their letters to me in their own hand. It was indeed Helios' handwriting.

"...I curse the sun god, Apollyon, the name of Ra in Nabataea, for laying upon me so dark a destiny. I have called upon him again and again to deliver me from my wicked wife, who I am now certain is resorting to sorcery to end my life. I have petitioned Apollyon, the sun god, but he refuses to answer! Abandoned, I curse him and curse him yet again!

"I have recently learned that, in the apex of battle, Octavian called upon the same god for victory. Could it be that this accursed god destroys all who call upon him?

"I wish I had never been born. I write, alone in my bedchamber, every night awaiting death. Tonight, I am told, the moon will eclipse the sun.

"Please know that whatever Iotape says about me is false. Despite her ravings, I have sought neither mistress nor concubine, for, as you know, I have never found such behavior becoming. It is my last request that you give my kingdoms to my brother, Philadelphos. A mad man could do better to rule them than a cursed one."

The letter was deeply disturbing. "The moon will eclipse the sun..." I mused.

"Sounds like the ramblings of a man who, despairing of life, desires death. Perhaps to him, death was a blessing," Cicero Minor said awkwardly.

I ignored his comment and reread the letter where Helios cried out to Ra—or had he meant Apollo by mention of Apollyon—and receiving no answer and called down a curse on the god whom he felt had deserted both him and Octavian.

"Did Caesarion convey anything further to you before he left?" I asked.

"Only that he would see to it that Helios would be avenged," Cicero Minor stated.

I sighed. Then there was nothing I could to do but wait. *O Isis! How I hate waiting!*

"Cleopatra?" Cicero Minor asked, interrupting my thought.

"There is nothing I can do but wait," I said, stating my thought aloud, "which is something a woman of my personality and royal stature does not do well!"

Cicero Minor seemed genuinely sympathetic. "I understand. Women, though thought to be more contemplative, seem to me no more patient than men, and, in situations like this one, even less so. Men are simply more impulsive." After that, Cicero Minor respectfully took leave of me. Terentia entered the room as he left. At least life was not boring with Terentia about me. She was good company and an excellent conversationalist. And, when I tired of politics, we could speak of cosmetics and fashion.

"What kind of perfumes do you use? To attract Antony?" Terentia asked. "I should like to attract Cicero Minor."

"Attract him?" I asked.

"These days, he is too busy to speak with me," Terentia said.

"Rose and neroli, I think, are best for that," I replied, being an expert in perfumes, cosmetics, pharmaceuticals, and, yes, poisons.

"And can you recommend something for pests?" she asked, swatting the air with her hand as a mosquito buzzed by.

"Try burning citronella," I suggested.

"For mosquitoes, yes. But what of larger pests?" she asked obliquely.

"I burn sage to keep away troublesome spirits," I replied with the barest of smiles.

"From where does citronella come?" Terentia asked.

"Africa," I said with a smile, thinking momentarily of the wealth I could accrue simply by bringing citronella to Rome.

The next several weeks were hell in slow motion. *Never has time creeped so slowly!* I thought, tossing some weaving I had been doing aside. It is much like when I was hiding in the desert awaiting the appearance of Julius Caesar. Fearful boredom is often worse than outright war.

While waiting impatiently for news of my husband and Caesarion, Philadelphos and Arsinoë amused themselves with children's games: dice, chess and Senet. I focused my attention on rereading scrolls written by my former and present husbands, and began recording recipes for perfumes and medicines, including a cure for baldness, which I had procured while Julius Caesar's wife. It was also during this time that I began to pen these memoirs, which you hold in your hands. I was also able to watch Philadelphos change for the better.

It seemed that the news of Helios' death had struck Philadelphos hard, causing within him a sense of guilt that his past behaviors had somehow caused his brother's death. I felt compelled as his mother to explain that this was not the case, and then, at the advice of Titan, realized this was the opportunity I'd prayed for to lead my youngest son towards a path of responsible kingship. I needed to help him to balance his newfound sense of responsibility without allowing him to wallow in false guilt. *This will not be easy*, I thought, as I walked to Philadelphos' room.

I kicked at the door out of respect. Philadelphos opened it and invited me to enter in a polite and cordial manner I didn't know he had within him.

"You did not kill Helios, Philadelphos," I told him, seizing the moment, remembering my own destructive feelings of guilt after murdering my brother, Ptolemy XIV, of which I had come to think increasingly often in this decade of my life.

Philadelphos said nothing.

"You did not kill him. His actions did," Titan affirmed.

I smiled. This was exactly what was Philadelphos needed to hear. "Titan is correct. You did not kill him. By your actions, you forfeited your kingdom to him. Perhaps this contributed indirectly to the acuteness of his situation. Perhaps. But not necessarily so. My son, because you are royal, your actions will always have consequences. But you did not cause Helios' death," I repeated gently but firmly, taking

Antony's approach which was always firm. I found firmness best mixed with gentleness, especially with my children, my people, royalty and rulers, especially young future rulers.

Philadelphos sighed. "So, in the end, it *was* my fault."

"The fault, sin, and crime were of his wicked wife's. Your actions may have contributed, but only indirectly," I stated.

"I know, and I'm sorry for it," Philadelphos said, sounding truly remorseful. "If only there was something I could do…"

"Why don't you petition Apollyon, Helios' god and ask him to forgive Helios for cursing him. Ask that, as Helios requested, he transfer his kingdoms to you. Promise you will be the king Helios was not able to be," I said. "The gods regard justice favorably, and your petition could do much to rectify several injustices. I will accompany you, if you wish."

"Mother, I would do this with your company," Philadelphos replied, much to my relief and Titan's joy.

In fact, as a woman, I was not permitted in the Temple of Apollo, and I knew from what Cicero Minor reported that even if I were, it would be dangerous for me to travel the streets of Rome at this time, and worse yet for me appear before a god whom my son had cursed. It was never good to tempt fate. True, Antony had won several skirmishes against the Republican forces, but victory was not yet his and Rome was still in chaos. There was, however, a statue of Apollo in Cicero Minor's main villa, and my plan was to accompany Philadelphos there to pray to the god. It was my belief that as Queen-Pharaoh, even if our prayers didn't reach the ears and heart of Apollyon, *my* prayers at least would reach Isis and Ra. What I didn't know was if, given his deaf ears to my son, Helios, the same god under his Roman name would listen to an Egyptian woman.

Our trip to Cicero Minor's main house and back was thankfully uneventful. We traveled in separate covered palanquins, each with only two armed guards to lessen attention. During our transits, I once again paid particularly close attention to everything I could hear outside, and what I heard was not good. Rome was in the clutches of an impending civil war. What was good, was that most sided directly with Antony and his cause, and thereby indirectly with me.

Once there, while Philadelphos prayed to Apollo, I petitioned Isis and Ra for mercy towards my two younger sons. "Ra," I pleaded, "I ask that Helios, whose life on Earth has ended, be forgiven his worldly sins, and, after the weighing of his heart before Ma'at, have what blessings he has accrued in your and Isis' service transferred to his brother, my son, Philadelphos. Also, please, I beg you, consider finding Philadelphos a wife as loyal to him as I have been to Antony," appending in a whisper, "and as loving as Selene is to Juba, and Tullia is to Caesarion."

Satisfied my plan had worked based on Philadelphos' sustained change in demeanor, I turned my attention to Arsinoë, whose devotion to the gods of Persia and interest in Jewish history and their mysterious god without a name had only continued to grow. She, like me, spent much of her time reading during these frightful years in Rome. And, as she did, she grew into a highly educated, stunningly beautiful woman.

In continence, she looked much like her father, although she held onto some of my most outstanding Greco-Egyptian features: Her hair was jet black like mine, though curly like her father's. She wore the kohl of Egypt as if it were natural, though her eyes were admittedly Antony's. Unlike me, her build was stocky, making it likely that she would mother many children.

Autumn dragged uneventfully on towards winter. On the last day of autumn, I received a missive from Caesarion and immediately afterwards, another from Antony. To my relief, Caesarion had successfully avenged Helios' assassination, for that was what it had proved to be. Iotape still lived in hunted exile, but those who had supported her in Helios' murder were no more. Caesarion didn't provide details and I didn't want to hear them. He then stated that he was returning to Rome, which meant that by the time I received this letter, he would be at Rome's doorstep, which he was.

Antony wrote that he had succeeded in removing the last of the Republican opposition, mostly hangovers from the days of Octavian, thereby permanently securing his and my position in Rome. He also stated that he was returning to Rome, which meant that I would very soon be welcoming both Antony and Caesarion. It was therefore no surprise to me when, that same day, Cicero Minor visited and told me he and Antony had just met and decided that they'd been too merciful to Octavian's memory. As winter began and Proserpina descended to Pluto, Antony, now back at my side, declared that all mention of Octavian's honors be stripped from public memory, and all were forbidden henceforth to name their sons Octavius. I was surprised when he further declared that, though a woman, I was to be allowed to enter the Senate at any time and I was to be regarded as if I were Antony. I was therefore present that night at a ceremony in the Senate in which Antony, dressed in a red toga, the color of triumph, and wearing a golden laurel wreath, ordered a pyre built in its center where, before all the assembled Senators, he spoke:

"Friends, Romans, countrymen, lend me your ears."

Antony opened all of his most important speeches in this manner ever since he'd given the public eulogy for Julius Caesar.

"Tonight, we celebrate my final victory over those who followed the vile rebel Octavian. These past seventeen years, I have proven to you time and again that I am Caesar's true successor, and I have shown due mercy to his line. However, Julius Caesar, may the gods preserve him, held that mercy should be reserved for those who deserve it. Those who tried again and again to rid Rome of me have shown they do not. These men who called themselves Republicans, were the same men who publicly denied my victory over Octavian and lied to you, recently stating that Octavian still lived. He did not live, as everyone here knows, and, I assume, based on his actions prior to his death, his soul also no longer exists. Tonight, therefore, I burn before you the last of his supporters' armor, biographies, clothing of office and family signets, to once and finally release Rome from his and his supporters' grip. Octavian died seventeen years ago at Actium, drowned in the ocean, swallowed by the sea. Those who continued to support him have all now met their fate." Cicero Minor passed Antony a flaming torch and Antony lit the pyre, reducing all reminders of those who had fought against him to grayish ash.

That night, for the first time in months, I slept soundly. My dreams were of a moon eclipsing the sun, which I believed to be a sign from the gods that I should continue to direct my attention to the education of my two daughters. Caesarion, although of my womb, was now more Antony's son than mine. Helios was dead. Philadelphos, my last remaining son, I hoped would show Antony that his transformation into that of a true king was truly now in progress.

Chapter Twenty-Seven

Revenge

Years 30-32 of Cleopatra's Reign

21-19 B.C.

The Portico of The Vault of Nut

Isis, Caesar and Athena looked down on the vast panoply that was Rome, Nabataea, Mauretania and Egypt. Isis' prophecy of Helios' empty throne had come true, and, new intelligence in hand, Caesarion had re-ridden to Nabataea to finish avenging his brother's death. There, he located Iotape and her remaining Arab defenders, exacting final vengeance in what would one day be called The December Revenge.

Iotape, though generally held to be insane, had become a rogue warrior made ever bitterer and angrier by the sting of Helios' bond to his sister. In Iotape's jealous mind, Helios and Selene shared a love she could never have or comprehend.

When Caesarion had entered her desert tent, he found her dressed like Selene in a purple *stola* and *palla*, her eyes painted inexpertly with Egyptian kohl, her hair arranged roughly in black braids similar to the style Selene wore in Mauretania.

"It is not enough to murder my brother; you must also mock my sister!" Caesarion yelled, as he charged at Iotape.

"You will never take me to Rome," Iotape hissed and she drank deeply from a goblet of red wine into which she had poured a vial of cobra venom. Caesarion frowned as Iotape, startled, dropped the goblet, struggled briefly and gasped her last breath. He had hoped to return her to Rome and march her in triumph, for he hoped to declare Nabataea, Medea, and Arabia to be Roman provinces in revenge for the death of his brother.

"Was this done with your help, woman?" Caesarion asked Iotape's Medean servant standing in the tent's entrance, eyes wide, watching Iotape momentarily writhe and gag. "Shall I take you for my triumph in her stead?" In abject fear, the servant flew to her master's side, lifted the goblet and drank the rest of the wine, falling next to her mistress.

"Good riddance," Caesarion mumbled, and Athena, above, echoed his statement.

"As I believe you said about me when I died," Caesar said to the goddess of wisdom.

"Indeed," said Athena. "I am the one who punished Medusa for her transgressions, and those two worshipped Medusa. And trust me, Julius, it is for the best your son seeks to make Nabataea and Arabia part of a greater empire. It will open a door for Philadelphos."

"A greater empire? Don't you mean the Roman Republic?" Caesar asked.

"Caesar, haven't you of all people noticed how Rome and Egypt increasingly behave more like a single empire with each passing day?" Athena asked.

"Goddess of wisdom, what would have happened had Helios not died and my son had not gone there to exact revenge?" Caesar asked, speaking to Athena this time with respect rather than disdain.

"A greater disaster than you could ever imagine would have overtaken Greece, Egypt, and Rome," Athena stated.

"All of the West, and much of the East," Isis reiterated. "It is for the best that Helios died, although I dislike it having to be that way."

"As Goddess of Battle, it is now become my duty to protect Caesarion," Athena stated.

In fact, Caesarion's conquest of the three lands would take some time. Antony would bring several legions of veteran warriors later in spring, only to find his son already victorious. And Caesarion would soon realize to his surprise that the three nations—Numidia in particular—while in theory had been ruled over by Helios, because of the constant interference of Iotape they had been ruled by his sister, Selene, in all but name.

"I wonder what Alexander would have said," Caesar brooded, thinking of his wife, Cleopatra, and her second husband, Antony, dividing their inheritance up among their children. In the end, it was decided that Arabia would be ruled by Roman-appointed governors and Nabataea by a client king, namely Philadelphos. Numidia would be ceded to Juba—Antony and Cleopatra knew now that they'd been unwise to allow Helios to be king of that nation, even if it had taught Philadelphos rulership.

"Philadelphos has awoken since his brother's death," Isis noted. "He is displaying the rudiments of a decent king."

"Tragedy often incites mortals to awake and do their duty."

In truth, the change in Philadelphos was enormous. Philadelphos effortlessly shouldered the burden of governance. In Rome, this fourth of Cleopatra's children to reach adulthood stood tall and proud, dressed in a toga, the mark of Roman manhood. He remained for several months in Rome with Cleopatra, judiciously studying the art of leadership, developing a close bond with Arsinoë, a bond he was would be reluctant to break when it became time for him to fully assume his role as client king of Nabataea.

Soon, he would be leaving with a legion of Roman soldiers hand-picked by Antony, at which time I and Arsinoë would return to Egypt. Upon our return, only one year would separate Arsinoë from womanhood, and her becoming the wife of Phraataces and Queen of Parthia. In the future, though Arsinoë and Philadelphos would rule separate nations, the two, like Selene and Helios, would never be far from each other in thought or spirit.

"I am proud that Philadelphos at last accepts his duty and fate, but I still feel sad for Cleopatra and her loss of Helios," Caesar stated.

Isis nodded her approval. "Helios' death was tragic, but necessary."

As Isis spoke, Helios stood before Ma'at. Trembling, he thought of how ineffectual a husband and king he had been during his mortal life, and watched with trepidation as Ma'at carefully weighted his heart. To his surprise and relief, it weighed lighter than the Feather of Truth, for in so many ways, Helios had been more a victim of others' wrongdoings than his own, and he was allowed to begin his journey through the Underworld.

"I am surprised he was allowed past the Keeper. In many ways, Helios was a misfit. In spite of being named for the sun, he was always too passive for my liking," Caesar stated as Helios disappeared into the maze of the Underworld to work off his transgressions. While he spoke, Caesar smiled slyly to himself, thinking, *Helios was Antony's son, not mine.* Although Caesar considered Helios weak, he was proud of Caesarion for avenging his half-brother. He also had no further doubts that his half-grandson, Philadelphos, would make a fine king of Nabataea.

"Helios' life was not wasted, Caesar," Athena said, echoing Isis words, interpreting Caesar's quiet for concern.

"Is any life ever truly wasted?" asked Isis rhetorically. "His example horrified his brother into becoming a man worthy of kingship."

"A man, yes. But whether he is worthy of kingship remains to be seen," retorted Athena. "All kings are men, but not all men are kings." At that moment, Athena felt she alone of the heavenly group could fully visualize the complex events that were playing out as a result of Octavian's death. Octavian's death, going against the Fates, had led to Antony and Cleopatra's triumph, and had planted the seeds for their joint empire, which Cleopatra, as her famous ancestor, Alexander, was already attempting to accomplish by simultaneously dividing and at the same time enlarging it. The potential for greatness in Caesarion, Selene and Arsinoë blazed before Cleopatra like a shining beacon. When Athena looked over the portico rail at Judea, Isis followed. Both knew how strongly Cleopatra craved this land. But what they saw was Herod rebuilding a gigantic Hebrew structure he was calling the "Second Temple," proclaiming it a sacred place where Jews could sacrifice directly to their powerful one god with the unspeakable name. A place *he* had built. A place where Jews, in thanks, would immortalize his name.

"Sacrifices..." Athena murmured as the structure slowly rose in Jerusalem. Even as Herod was building his temple, a greater Isian temple was rising in Mauretania under the direction of Selene.

"Was Helios, then, little more than a precursor of the future?" Caesar asked reflectively to the assemblage.

It was for Athena to answer simply, "Perhaps." Then, not wishing to disclose the countless others who had been sacrificed in Iotape's bring down of the young king originally named for the Sun, or the countless many who were yet to be sacrificed in the building of Antony and Cleopatra's joint empire, she turned away in silence.

Chapter Twenty-Eight
Of Kings and Queens
19-18 B.C.
Years 32-33 of Cleopatra's Reign
Egypt and Rome

Much changed the next two years. In Egypt, I had to put down another rebellion by the priests of Ra in Heliopolis, this time at the request of new High Priest. The young man whom I had given permission to mummify his father had remained loyal to me, but that had not stopped others secretly dedicated to his father from attempting to incite crowds in all the greater cities including Alexandria by resurrecting the belief that I had defiled the laws of Ma'at, and as such, that either I needed to pay or ultimately Egypt would.

During this wretched time, Rufio's control over the Egyptian mob was shaken and he died by their hand, leaving his son, Rufio Minor, to take over his duties. Although Rufio Minor had been well trained by his father and repeatedly proved a capable politician and regent, he was, nonetheless related to Rufio, and the mob's appetite for his family's blood had been whetted. Not just his family's, but because of his father's longstanding association with me, my family's also. The loss of Rufio the Elder was so devastating, I was forced once again to leave Egypt and hide in Gaza with Azor, returning to Egypt and Alexandria this time with

Caesarion at my side to defend my dynasty. Caesarion had remained in Nabataea in case anything untoward should surface with Philadelphos' reign. At my request, he marched his personal legion out of Nabataea through Judea and into Gaza, transporting me back to Alexandria. Together with my son, Rufio Minor and I easily crushed the rebellion – it had remained leaderless—and reinstated me yet again, much to most of my people's delight.

As if that alone weren't enough, I faced further losses. Of my children, only Arsinoë remained with me in my palace, though that summer she, too, would leave when Phraataces came to Alexandria to claim her as his wife, which he did, and all too soon for me.

While I prepared for the loss of Arsinoë, I continued a lively correspondence with Selene. She was becoming increasingly astute in the ways of the world.

"Juba says he will never forsake me, yet I know he has had children by a concubine. He does not speak of her or them, but he no longer comes exclusively to my bed, and I am not blind," Selene wrote.

Men will always be men, I thought, suddenly wondering if the rumor that Antony had bedded a Germanian woman during his conquest there might not have been true after all, and if so, whether any children had come of it. I doubted either, but, if true, I knew they would haunt the both of us to our last days, and eventually become a stumbling block to Antony and my dream of a single unified empire.

"Even so, I have missed my courses this month," Selene's letter continued. "I am praying to Heket to shape a baby in my womb. Juba keeps saying he wants first a son and then a daughter. I simply want to conceive." The rest of her letter was a series of requests for advice on cosmetics, perfumes, potions, and any tips I might have on how to increase Juba's interest in her and her chances of future conceptions.

"Seek Isis' blessing above all else," I wrote in return. "Though you do not write of it, the death of someone dear like your brother can delay conception. His murder is a sobering reminder that we are here on this Earth for only a while and always at the whim of the gods. You must move past your grieving. Don't allow it to come between you and your husband.

"Please do not take this, my child, to mean that I disdain your grief. As your twin, he was and will probably always be a part of your soul. You may even feel his absence, at times the void being filled with sadness, as I do your half-grandfather. For me, Julius Caesar's death has never gone away completely. Like your brother, his death was horrid, but one must let go and continue accomplishing those things fate lays before us. His son, Caesarion, has avenged both losses in this world, and Ma'at will revenge their spirits in the next," I wrote to her.

As for Caesarion and Philadelphos, Caesarion was now Antony's co-ruler in all but name. In fact, though Antony had been proclaimed Caesar Imperator for life he had not yet publicly declared Caesarion his "official" heir, in spite of the fact that Tullia had borne Caesarion as requested many fine children. Yet again, the Republic, simply by its tenacious existence, was still blocking Antony and me from achieving our and our progenies' dreams.

That summer, Phraataces did travel to Alexandria to retrieve Arsinoë. The night before his arrival, Arsinoë and I spent the evening under a full moon to receive its blessing, for it was now firmly acknowledged the world over that Selene would eventually command Egypt and the world.

Phraataces had grown extraordinarily handsome, though being not much older than Arsinoë, I remained secretly concerned that he was too close to her in age. I found it better for the husband to be older than the wife, as Caesar and Antony had both been to me. Maturity causes a man to more strongly protect his wife, and Arsinoë, in spite of being the youngest of my children—or perhaps because of it—was the boldest of the lot, an incredible feat considering the accomplishments of Caesarion and Selene. I tried repeatedly to place my trust entirely in Isis, but like most mothers, I worried, too. Arsinoë, however, found the lack of age difference a relief.

"I don't *want* him to be older than me," she said with a blush.

"Why not?" I asked, curious about her thoughts beyond the moment about the man to whom she was about to link her life. "Marriage is more than laying together and raising children. Even as a queen, Arsinoë, you are not invincible. We may be the goddess incarnate, but we are still mortal," I explained.

Arsinoë sniffed. I knew she did not like to be reminded of these things, but she did know of them.

"Look at Helios. He was near the same age as Iotape…" I left the sentence drift off into nothingness. Bringing up Helios' sad fate was my newest way of admonishing my children how to behave.

"I still want my husband and I to be close to the same age. I believe a husband and wife should *love* each other, and act on the basis of that love. It is better that way, I think," Arsinoë stated emphatically.

"You have never been a wife," I reminded her, thinking to myself, *What is this 'love' nonsense? Love comes of a good marriage over time; it is not a wedding gift.*

"As you did with your first husband, I, too, must learn by experience," Arsinoë concluded, and with that, I wisely ended the conversation.

With my admittedly romanticized memories of Julius Caesar fresh in mind, when King Phraates's court arrived, I was unpleasantly surprised. The queen of Parthia, Musa, had for a time been a mistress of my first husband. She was now the favored wife of Phraates IV and had accompanied him and their son to Egypt. The meeting between Phraates IV and myself was cordial and without problems. The meeting between Musa and myself, however, proved awkward and unsettling. It began when, by Parthian custom, Musa asked to "inspect" Arsinoë.

Affronted, I replied, "My daughter is not a slave requiring inspection." I was curt, but careful to not be impolite, looking squarely into the face of this woman as I replied. She was actually quite pretty. Her hair was drawn back into a bun and she wore flowing white robes. Her face showed no sign of ill intent. Musa continued as though I had not spoken.

"Good child-bearing requires the right hips," Musa stated equally curtly, making her comment sting with its slight edge of disrespect.

Still, it was I who had initiated the curtness. "Arsinoë easily meets this requirement," I assured the woman. "She gets them from her mother."

Musa gave me an odd look. "Great Queen Cleopatra…" she began, stopping as if unsure what she wanted to say.

"Queen Musa," I replied, nodding politely, still not certain what to make of her.

"From the start," she continued, "it is you who captivated two Caesars, and thereby saved Egypt and our worlds as we know them from destruction."

Her words were flattering, but their intent was still unclear, and I remained on my guard. *Honeyed words spoken to me in my kingdom,* I thought and decided to resort to humor as I often did in odd or unclear situations.

"Indeed," I replied. "And I believe we two of all women shared one." I waited to see if my humor would loosen her stiffness a bit and provide more clarity, but sadly, it did the reverse.

Musa laughed, but not kindly. "You had a choice. I did not. I will never forget my days as his sexual slave, Cleopatra," Musa said darkly.

I tried hard to envision this woman standing before me as Caesar's mere "sex slave" and even harder to fix the diplomatic damage I had inadvertently done. "A 'slave' rising to become a queen. You must have the favor of the gods," I said.

"The gods?" Musa asked. "I produced for my current husband a son and therefore have his favor. That is all. I only seek to insure the same for your daughter and my son," Musa explained.

I found her perception of queenship surprisingly simplistic, but finally understanding her concern, I replied, "My line have always produced offspring. Your son and my daughter have been writing each other regularly, and I believe they are sufficiently eager to enter into the joys that produce children."

"Perhaps," Musa acquiesced. "But your daughter, Selene..."

Suddenly I saw her point and decided to end this farce. Either she and I would become close friends or bitter rivals. Clinging to the fragile hope of a close friendship, I asked her, "Musa, please speak freely with me. Do you consider me a friend and ally, or an enemy and rival?"

She seemed taken by my forthrightness.

Good, I thought.

"The truth is, Great Queen-Pharaoh, I do not yet know. That is up to both you and me, is it not?"

I nodded, acknowledging the wisdom of her answer. "True," I agreed, adding, "but I prefer friendship."

"As do I," Musa agreed. "But as you more than any would know, friends can become enemies in the blink of an eye. Also, those you may *think* of as enemies may actually be the staunchest of friends."

Musa departed with those words, which, though leaving me undecided, I knew to be true. Perhaps I had misjudged this woman, and her apparent simplicity was simply a cover for her own insecurities and for her love of and concern for her son. Perhaps. In any case, I decided for now to give her the benefit of the doubt.

Arsinoë would depart with them in two weeks, but before she did, there would be great feasting and banqueting, as there always was when a royal couple were formally presented for marriage. The actual wedding would not take place until my daughter arrived in Parthia and they were married by the customs of the future husband's land. Only our families and retinues were present at the welcoming feast. Dressed in long, flowing, white Parthian robes, her hair arranged down loosely in the style of Persian women, Arsinoë, flanked by High Priest Rahotep and my trusted regent, Rufio Minor, and led by Philadelphos, was presented to Phraataces, who, young, swarthy, handsome and eager, was dressed in purple robes depicting his royalty. Many gems were woven into his beard and hair to additionally indicate his personal wealth and status.

Over three hundred courtly people were present in my grand hall for the final banquet. Alternating dishes of Egyptian and Parthian food were brought out on great golden trays. We feasted upon hen, duck, lamb, trout, stuffed figs, grapes, olives, and my own favorite, *dulcis coccora*. As Antony was not present, I sat next to Musa, watchfully attended by Charmion and Iras. For me, the evening proved a particular delight in that it was focused not on me but my daughter. This also gave Musa and me the opportunity to talk more intimately, as one mother to another.

"Our children seem quite taken by one another," Musa said, as Arsinoë and Phraataces feasted upon honey-soaked pomegranates, which, I hoped, was a positive omen of Arsinoë being able to bear children. As Musa spoke, Arsinoë picked a slice of pomegranate and playfully offered it to Phraataces' lips. He accepted with a mischievous smile, then did the same for her. To my surprise, Musa seemed annoyed by this.

"They do appear to be so," I replied as a slave presented me a tray of candied figs. I took one, but it felt sticky to the touch, so I returned it.

This did not go unnoticed by a now frowning Musa. "The figs do not please you, Queen Cleopatra? I thought you had a taste for them. Julius Caesar knew that quite well," Musa said with what seemed a forced, too-sweet smile.

I still could not decide whether to trust Musa, but for Arsinoë's sake, I continued to try for friendship and trust. "I am merely full from so much feasting. I am quite pleased with what my cooks have done, and the gifts you brought from Parthia," I said. She had as of yet done nothing to praise my hospitality, although she had provided me with a gift of a matched pair of pigeons in a gilded cage that I kept in my private chambers. I secretly planned to free the pigeons after she left. I do not like to see birds caged when meant to fly.

"I would have thought the great Queen Cleopatra would always like figs," Musa said, selecting the one I replaced and eating it.

The feasting continued well past midnight. Arsinoë and Phraataces, along with Musa, thank the gods, departed the next day, and as they did, I felt a heaviness in my heart. Not only were all my children gone, Arsinoë's future felt to me less than certain given Musa's cryptic words at the feast. I did not know if Arsinoë was headed towards a marital victory or defeat. To remove my mind from this, I examined the two pigeons in their golden cage. Each was grooming the other's feathers, seemingly content. As I opened their cage door, the pair immediately flew out of the cage and towards the harbor of Alexandria, leaving me a profound sense of peace. I took their side-by-side escape towards the open sea as a sign that Arsinoë and Phraataces would have a blessed union and great future.

"My queen?" came a voice from the doorway. It was Iras.

"Hello, Iras," I said. In Iras' hand was a pet monkey she had acquired in the market during the spring.

"My queen, did the birds Musa gave you somehow escape?" she asked.

"No, Iras. I let them go," I said, my prior sense of loss and sadness returning.

"I understand. You have had to let the last of your children go," Iras replied. She and I embraced, while Iras' little pet monkey grabbed hold of my chiton and squealed loudly. I looked again at the empty cage, then at the lively monkey.

"What is the creature's name?" I asked Iras.

"His name, My Queen? His name is Hercules," she answered.

"Such a big name for such a small monkey," I said.

I now felt truly alone. My children were all either dead, or married and living elsewhere, and I would have no more in this lifetime. My heart ached, and, for the first time, I felt the weight of mortality, but, as I had often advised others, I made a conscious decision not to dwell on such things and instead silently rededicated myself to pursuing that which fate placed before me and I had yet to accomplish. Soon afterwards, I received a summons from Antony to come to Rome. He needed me, he said, and it was urgent.

I arrived in Ostia three weeks later, to be greeted by Dolabella, who told me I was to be carried into Rome, this time, not in secrecy, but openly, to be welcomed as Queen-Pharaoh of Egypt, wife of the

Imperator, Antonius Caesar, as a staunch friend and ally of Rome. For the occasion, I chose a special ensemble of spun gold I had had made for exactly this occasion when it should arise—a golden, see-through *stola* and *palla*. I would show my deference to Roman customs in the style of my dress, and my pride in and command of Egypt by wearing the double crown and carrying my crook and flail. This time, the Roman crowd welcomed me, cheering loudly, "Cleopatra! Cleopatra!" as I rode through the streets resting on my side, peering at them from the open litter. I was welcomed by Antony in the Palatine. It was the first of Romanus, the month during which we had triumphed over Octavian.

After a lengthy ceremony in which I was honored as Queen of the East, Queen of Kings, Mother of Kings and Wife of the Great Imperator, Antony and I took our leave for a long, luxurious night of lovemaking in his feather bed at his villa. We slept in each other's arms and awoke late. It was then he told me of the changes in Rome since the events in Nabataea.

"Caesarion and I having successfully quashed the Republican Rebellion—that was what it is now being called—restored order in the city and provinces and brought peace and prosperity back to Rome. Cicero Minor even convinced the Senate to declare me Imperator for Life," Antony recounted as we soaked together later that morning in the *tepidarium* in his villa, a welcome refreshment on a morning already hotter than the day before.

"That's almost a king!" I exclaimed in delight. We eventually exited the water, dried and retired to our spacious bedroom with its expansive view of the hills of Rome. A slave brought bread, olives, figs, diluted wine, and we reclined together for breakfast.

"Except that, without an official son, I cannot pass on the title," Antony said, teasingly.

"Yes, that's a problem," I agreed, smiling and playing his game.

"Ah, but not anymore, "Antony said, and I knew at last that it was time for one of my greatest wishes to come true.

"Caesarion has at last proven himself a Roman to the people. He's giving speeches in the Senate and Forum in flawless Latin."

I smiled at that. "Under Cicero Minor's continuous tutelage, no doubt," I said.

"Exactly," Antony replied. "And I have good news about Nabataea and Arabia."

"Yes?" I asked, barely able to hold my excitement in check.

"I have decided to make Philadelphos governor of Arabia instead of a client king of Nabataea, to which he has agreed. Malchius, the native ruler of Nabataea, will become client king. Arabia has just been declared a Roman province. Philadelphos can govern it while keeping a close eye on Malchius."

This is truly good news, I thought, waiting for Antony to tell me when he planned to publicly announce Caesarion as his and thereby our son and heir to his title. Hearing no such announcement, I said, "And what of Herod?" I was still resentful over not being given Judea.

"Herod is busy rebuilding his 'Second Temple'," Antony stated. "There are several religious groups in Judea which Herod closely governs…"

I recounted to Antony what David had told me of them and of my later meeting with several representatives of one of the more powerful groups—the Pharisees—Jewish scholars who interpret the laws and rules of the Jews 'one god' down to the smallest letter. "Much like the Roman Senate used to do to you," I joked.

Antony chuckled with me, but only momentarily. "We must be careful to never tell the Pharisees that. They believe that a military leader will soon arise and deliver them from Herod...and Rome," Antony stated.

It was my turn to laugh. Antony was a good and just ruler. No nation or group needed to be 'saved' from him.

"The Sadducees are the second major religious group," I offered, "with whom Herod will have to work closely." When Antony didn't answer, I continued. "They are a group of educated, Hellenized Jews who also look to the appearance of a national savior. However, their interpretation is that this 'messiah' as they call him will herald a new era in which good Jews and non-Jews alike will become equal members of a future nation-religion." Antony seemed piqued at this, so I continued. "A third, but much smaller group, the Essenes, keep largely to themselves. They live in closed communes in the Nazarene hills and in Qumran alongside the Dead Sea, studying and preparing themselves for the coming not of a military or national but rather a spiritual leader. Then there are the Mystics and the Zealots..."

At my mention of the Zealots, Antony's brows knitted. "The Zealots openly work to overthrow Rome, may Mars curse them all," he stated angrily.

We spoke no more of politics that day. Instead, I sought to share with Antony a tome I was writing on cosmetics, and, listening intently, he turned from the angry statesman to the love-struck boy I had first met at Tarsus, twenty-one years ago.

"Cosmetics?" he asked, in a teasing tone. "From the woman who through her knowledge of astronomy caused Caesar to change our calendar?"

"I am a woman of many talents," I said, coquettishly. "I wrote this as a guide for women to use throughout the various parts of our fledgling empire, advising them what and what not to wear if they are privileged to travel under Egypto-Roman protection."

Antony, for a moment, seemed in awe. "An ingenious way to begin uniting the world..." he began thoughtfully.

"Antony..." I said, then stopped. This was not all I wanted him to see. I had a faint notion that had been growing in my mind for months that I wanted to somehow share with him. "Antony, what if there are more lands located beyond the great Eastern and Western oceans?" I asked, not sure where the idea would take us.

"Another interesting idea," Antony said respectfully. "You are full of deep ideas today, but then, you have always been the far-seeing strategist. However, even if such lands exist, we would never be able find them, unless Neptune suddenly allowed mortal men to traverse the great oceans, something he has never shown any inclination of doing."

We spoke no more of it throughout the rest of the day, but that night, I dreamed of strange new lands, exotic yet oddly familiar. Lands with pyramids much like Egypt's, but with gods and goddesses who were frighteningly cruel, even more so than Roman soldiers at war. In my dream, I saw a woman and a man being led up the steps of the tallest of the pyramids, for what purpose, I did not know. My dream ended with Antony gently shaking me awake, stating that today he was planning to pass his title to Caesarion.

I awoke, my mind still on the couple walking up a thousand steps towards the top of the gigantic pyramid. It took me some moments to remember where I was. I was not in the land of strange plants and vaguely familiar pyramids, but in our bed in our bedroom in Antony's villa. I sat up on the bed and pulled the top of my red night shift about my throat. Antony and Caesarion were standing at either bedside, smiling warmly. A Germanian slave on Caesarion's left was holding a tray with wine and figs.

"Mother," Caesarion said. "You called out in your sleep for Antony Minor and Cassandra."

"Oh?" I replied, gathering my wits about me and thinking again of the couple ascending the strange pyramid. "It was just a dream," I ended up saying, though I very much hoped to speak more of it with my husband when we had a moment alone. And possibly David, too. Yes, definitely David.

"Then let us speak no more of it. The gods reveal what they will in their own time. We have only the present in which to live," Antony stated.

"Indeed," I agreed, relaxing my grip on my night shift. "The past we cannot change and the future we do not know. The Fates give us only the present."

"Dearest Mother. I must leave to make my speeches in the Forum about the recent addition of Arabia to our empire," Caesarion said.

I liked how he emphasized the words "our" and "empire."

"But you cannot call it that," Antony reminded Caesarion.

"No, though Egypt and Rome have become functionally one," Caesarion stated, smiling as he looked from me to Antony and back to me.

"I would hear your speeches," I said, rising behind a curtain held by my trusted companion Iras. I was truly curious as to what my son would say.

"Can she come?" Caesarion asked Antony. We both knew that by Antony's recent decree, Roman women were now permitted to appear without escort in the public square. Even so, I quickly realized he asked over concern for my safety.

"Yes," Antony said to Caesarion; then to me, he said, "but take Olympos," adding as an afterthought, "and Mardian, too."

Antony and Caesarion left the bedroom arm-in-arm deep in discussion while I finished dressing and attended to my makeup. I had Iras dress me sparingly in the Roman style and, calling for Charmion, deferred to Roman makeup to provide nothing that might incite the crowds against me. I was still flush with my Roman greeting as "Queen-Pharaoh of Egypt, wife of Imperator Antonius Caesar, staunch friend and ally of Rome."

By the time Olympos, Mardian and I arrived, a large crowd of men had gathered at the Forum, and were listening, spellbound, to Caesarion. Being dressed as a Roman woman, I was relegated to the sidelines, and it was hard to hear Caesarion. When I finally found a place where I could hear him clearly, I could barely see him.

"It is for the good of Rome that the caravans must be assisted and protected!" Caesarion cried. "They will bring gold, slaves, food, goods, frankincense, myrrh...and gold!"

The men in the crowd began to shout, cheering, clapping, trilling and stamping their feet at the second mention of gold. Some displayed the traditional Roman thumb up sign.

"My son," I said softly to myself, drawing the attention of a man standing nearby.

"You are his mother?" the man asked looking first at me, then at Olympos and Mardian beside me. "You are the Great Queen-Pharaoh Cleopatra?"

"I am," I said warily, ruing having let my mother's pride get the best of me.

At first, the man seemed stunned, then amused, leaving me unable to discern if he was a friend or foe. Olympos stepped forward, and Mardian's hand went for the hilt of his sword.

The man instantly fell to knee and bowed. "Cicero Minor often

269

spoke of your brilliance," the man said, adding awkwardly, "and your son is a bright man, too. A brave one. Both Caesars must be proud. Of both Caesarion and you."

I sighed at the mention of my beloved first Caesar and, his kneeling attracting attention, gestured for him to rise.

"Your son is even now speaking of giving Arabia to you," the man said.

"Egypt is Rome's greatest friend and ally!" Caesarion continued. "By giving Arabia and select other territories to Egypt, she will seize control of the southern and eastern trade routes for Rome. With Egypt policing the routes *without charge to Rome*, we can rest assured that these goods will arrive safely here where they belong!"

A hush came over the crowd. Then some of the men began to click their mouths, a Roman sign of understanding.

"Listen! Friends!" Caesarion continued, and the crowd again quieted. "Egypt is the bread basket of the civilized world, and since the days of Pompey has never faltered in her promise to provide grain to Rome, irrespective of flood or drought. As an ally to Rome, she willingly provided us with food, ships, sailors and soldiers when needed. If Rome enlists her to govern Arabia as a province of Rome, we must provide the necessary legions to assist her and guard against rebellion as we do with Hispania and Gaul! Our leader, Antony, wants a Roman world held together by trade and citizenship. Some will tell you each province must be subdued, enslaved and taxed. But I ask you: Would you rather have a friend you can always rely on and for which you don't have to pay, or multiple surly slave provinces for which you will have to constantly guard against with hired soldiers paid for with money from your pockets?"

"He makes good sense, your son," murmured the man standing

next to me.

"LONG LIVE ANTONY! LONG LIVE CAESARION!" came the cries of the crowd, the man standing next to me adding, "and long live the Great Queen Cleopatra, Wife of Antony and Mother of Caesarion!"

I never saw that man again, but I will always be grateful for his positive comments. It was exactly what I needed to hear.

The next week, I decided my work in Rome was done, and it was time for me to return to Egypt. I needed to talk directly with Rufio Minor, who I'd made regent during my absence. He was young and, while well-schooled by his father, still largely untested. All the reports I'd received from him while I was in Rome were positive, but it was time to see for myself.

After an uneventful three-week return voyage, I called on Rufio Minor.

"Queen-Pharaoh," Rufio Minor said as he entered the administrative room of my palace where I'd been pouring over scroll after scroll detailing the everyday doings of a true empire in its own right. He was a young, wildly handsome man, bearing both the features of his warrior father, and a youthfulness that reminded me of Antony in his younger days. Aesthetically, he pleased me greatly, and I was reminded of the time in Rome when, as Julius Caesar's wife, I had discussed Antony with Charmion and Iras, saying in summary, "Looking at another is not infidelity."

I was suddenly stung by thoughts of lust and desire, but quickly reminded myself that while Antony lived, my relationship with Rufio Minor have to remain completely political. But what stung me even more than my lust and desire was my own self-declaration, "while Antony lived." I shook my head to clear it of all such ruminations.

"Update me," I ordered rather unkindly to further quiet my

emotions.

Rufio Minor said nothing, though I felt his eyes inspecting me like one might a horse about to be purchased. *Or a lover*, my mind offered as a quick afterthought. I wondered what he was thinking and became irritated with his silence.

"Well?" I demanded.

"Much has happened in your absence, Majesty. Some good and some not so good," the very words his father had once spoken.

I looked him directly in the eyes, trying to ascertain how, if at all, his heart and demeanor actually resembled that of his father's. Rufio Major had been a close confidante of Caesar's. His words and voice had always instilled strong confidence. However, his son, standing before me, did not instill that same confidence. Instead, Rufio Minor's voice seemed too silky smooth, which made me cautious, though at the same time, making him seem even more overwhelmingly enticing.

"I expected such," was all I chose to reveal of my thoughts.

"Which would you hear first, Great One?" he replied quietly, though I felt as if he were teasing, even taunting me.

"Whichever you decide, so long as it is truthful," I said with a hardness I had never before heard in my voice.

"Very well. There was a rebellion in Sabaste that we had to bring down with force," Rufio Minor stated bluntly.

"We? Sabaste?" I asked, raising my eyebrows suspiciously. I hadn't heard of this city.

"During your absence, the name of the ancient city of Samaria," he explained, "was changed to Sabaste." I recalled from my discussions with David that Samaria was the ancient name of the former capital city of Israel, a nation that had comprised the northern ten original Jewish tribes. Israel had been absorbed by the Persians, and was now part of

Parthia, the nation my daughter Arsinoë now ruled alongside her husband, King Phraataces. The southern two tribes had formed a smaller nation that existed to this day named Judah, a nation currently ruled by my nemesis, Herod.

"An insurrection arose in Samaria, incited by whom we still do not know. Herod renamed the insurgent city Sabaste 'in honor of their courage'," Rufio Minor further explained. "I received a request for assistance from your daughter to help crush the rebellion before it spread throughout Parthia. The Sabasteans are a strange people. I lost many men accomplishing their downfall."

I was irate. This so smacked of Herod. It was just the kind of thing he would do, fomenting revolution in Egypt while using Sabaste as an excuse to assemble a host and "defend" Egypt in my absence.

"And you left Egypt to quell this uprising?" I demanded, inhaling deeply. If he had indeed done so, while not a crime, his leaving Egypt unattended was more than disconcerting. I began to wonder if my trust in Rufio's son was misplaced.

"No, Your Majesty. Well, I mean, yes," Rufio Minor waffled.

"Which is it?" I demanded suspiciously.

"Great One. I am not a soldier, but I couldn't ignore your daughter's request. It would have taken too long to send a message to you in Rome and receive your reply, so I rallied support for the fight, and I saw our solders off as far as the border," adding, "Sabaste is close enough to our northeastern border, that I could direct things from there. I never actually left Egypt proper."

"So, you left Alexandria, but not Egypt," I confirmed.

"Great Queen-Pharaoh, did I do wrong?" Rufio Minor asked, not daring to breathe while awaiting my reply, this time with a genuine display of contriteness.

"No," I replied. "You exercised good judgment. I'm glad to know you did not leave Egypt and appoint someone to rule in your stead. The principal mistake of my dynasty has been ignoring Egypt for Alexandria. I have vowed never to repeat that mistake."

Rufio Minor slowly let out his breath. "There is good news, also."

"Good news often more than suffices to balance the bad."

"While you were in Rome, there was a rash of piracy incidents on the Red Sea. As you know, we share that border with Herod."

I listened, thinking, *Herod again!* this second mention of his name angering me. "And?" I asked. "What is the good news?"

"The Egypto-Roman navy has ended almost all piracy on the Red Sea."

"Almost?" I asked.

"Yes. It should entirely vanish soon. We've established new naval bases at all major ports on the Red Sea and from there, all the way down the western coast to the tip of Africa."

"Excellent! What else?"

"Herod has delivered a significant amount of taxes and Hebrew slaves from Judea, and we've received quite a few Syrian as well as South African Pygmy and Dinka slaves." Rufio Minor paused to take another breath before continuing. "And we've had a very good harvest this year. There is an abundance of grain for both Egypt and Rome."

"And is there more?" I asked, seeing his growing smile.

"Yes," Rufio Minor replied. I was feeling better and better about our relationship as it shifted to one of pure politics. It was exactly what I hoped.

"While you were away, letters arrived from both of your daughters."

"Then you were right: The good far outweighs the bad. The gods have blessed us while I've been away," I said.

I returned his smile as he handed the scrolls to me and took his leave. These letters were truly precious to me.

I first read Selene's. She had conceived and given birth in spring to a daughter, whom she had named Cleopatra, in honor of the line of Ptolemaic queens who had long borne that name. Juba had wanted a son, but the couple at least now knew Selene was not barren. Furthermore, their daughter had been born, like Caesarion, on the Feast of Isis, which I took to be an omen that Selene, like me, was being strongly favored by the goddess and that the newest Cleopatra, like her mother, would eventually become an outstanding queen of Egypt.

Arsinoë's letters, on the other hand, dealt more with the gods of Parthia, or rather, the Zoroastrian religion to which she had converted in order to better fulfil her role as the wife of Phraataces. She was now Queen of Parthia, but because Musa and the court of Parthia was so different in almost every way from Egypt's, though she was treated respectfully, she found herself in a state of constant confusion. She had, however, found three close confidantes in the court—Magi named Gaspar, Balthasar, and Melchior—all adept astronomer/astrologers. In fact, I knew and trusted all three, the first having prophesied correctly regarding Arsinoë when she was still a small child. These three men who took an instant liking to Arsinoë were also close confidantes of Queen Musa. It was through Musa and Arsinoë's mutual interest in astrology that the two at last found a commonality upon which to build a true friendship.

"Musa appears to like me," Arsinoë wrote. "She has become a mentor to me and is teaching me Parthian ways and customs. Did you know, Mother, that she was once a Roman slave? She recently confided that, like you, she knows what it is like to often be far from her husband or homeland, speaking of the irony that she was once Julius Caesar's concubine, and is now mother-in-law to the child of his favorite wife.

"I am learning much about Parthia, but also of Achaemenian Baharata and Zhonggua, two lands far east of Parthia. Musa says they're great empires in their own right, larger than Rome and Egypt combined!

"I continue to adapt to Parthian dress and food, but Musa recently ordered the cook to regularly prepare for me foods from Egypt that I especially like.

"I rarely see my new father-in-law. Musa tells me that in Parthia the duties of a queen are to hunt with her husband and govern while he is away fighting, much like the Royal Wives of Old Egypt.

"I find solace in the local religion. It is said that the Great God of Fire, Ahura Mazda, values all life as does our goddess, Isis. As such, one of my duties as a queen is to oversee tax tables and ration scales used in administering to the commoners of Parthia. I am learning to manage these quite well.

"Musa is a good though strict teacher. While I have become Phraataces' wife, Musa says I am still too young to safely bear children and has advised me to wait a year or so before I try to conceive."

Arsinoë's letter was of particular interest, especially her mention of Achaemenian Bharata and Zhonggua, great lands farther to the West than even our best Alexandrian cartographers have imagined. Consulting the best scholars in Alexandria's Museion, I learned that the vast land beyond the Indus Valley that called itself Bharata—linguistically Hindustan—consists of many nations worshiping a common set of gods and goddesses not unlike Egypt and Rome but far more numerous. The land is known to distant travelers simply as India. Beyond that is said to be a massive desert and endless plains, called by its inhabitants Zhongguo, from which our furthest and most exotic goods come. It is rumored that beyond Zhongguo, which the most distant of world traders call China, is said to be a vast ocean that, if crossed, touches an even more distant land of monstrous trees and exotic game.

While questioning the Museion scholars, I received a scroll from Caesarion. Unlike my daughters who wrote of important details of their lives, Caesarion's letters were short and business-like.

He wrote that Romans were becoming accustomed to regarding Egypt as an ally and not a client kingdom, citing the absence of having to put down costly rebellions in many other client nations as a major perception changer. His wife, Tullia, had died and he was looking to remarry, but would not do so until he returned from aiding Philadelphos in Arabia. With Malchius as client king of Nabataea and Philadelphos as governor of Arabia, it had been decided by my son and supported by my husband that Numidia, in north central Africa would be placed under Juba and Selene's competent command. Philadelphos, having proven himself a competent ruler, wanted to be a king, so he was given Cyprus, resolving his long-standing personal hurt while further consolidating Antony and my ruling of the vast swath of western territories. Of the details, Caesarion only shared that his younger brother, Philadelphos, had changed into a fine statesman and a man of recognized honor. Titan, his loyal Dinka servant, was serving in Philadelphos' Cyprian court as Master of Horse, the office Antony once held when he first served Julius Caesar.

I rerolled the scroll, but as I did, a slip of papyrus dropped out in which Caesarion wrote to me—privately—of his grief over his loss of Tullia. Tullia had died in the streets of Rome shielding him from an assassin's arrow which had cost her life. He wrote that he sought to remarry for the benefit of their three sons, but feared that no woman could ever replace his noble Tullia. I said a prayer to Isis for this brave woman, asking that Ma'at show her mercy and that she quickly find her way through the underworld to heaven.

Chapter Twenty-Nine

The Magi

18 B.C.

Year 33 of Cleopatra's Reign

The Vault of Nut

Isis watched, horrified, as Cleopatra in her reply to Caesarion suggested he consider one of Herod's daughters for a wife. The gesture to make peace with her enemy made perfect sense from a strategic political standpoint. But that didn't make it gall Isis any less. From Isis' perspective, Herod's blatant inhumanity appalled her, more so that he felt no remorse for ordering the murder of anyone unfortunate enough to cross him.

"It's time to present Cleopatra a test," Athena said, shaking her head in disgust.

Isis clucked her tongue angrily at the suggestion. "A test, Athena? Why? And of what?"

"Of her reasoning and devotion. You were incensed a moment ago when she suggested her son marry one of Herod's daughters," Athena noted.

"And I have the perfect test," Caesar interrupted. "Send her to Parthia."

"Why Parthia, Julius?" Isis asked, suddenly more intrigued than incensed.

"The Parthians have troubled Rome's eastern border since Crassus stupidly attacked them and was destroyed. Antony is attempting to recover the eagles lost by Crassus through the marriage of their daughter, Arsinoë, to the Parthian Crown Prince, now the younger King of Parthia. The elder King promised to return the eagles as a wedding gift, and, though the marriage has taken place, the eagles have not yet been returned. Because of this thorn, the empire Antony and Cleopatra seek to create will at some future time likely end in a long and bitter war with Parthia, unless the greater strategist, Cleopatra, can find and implement a solution," Caesar said. "Let us challenge her with this, watching to whom she appeals, seeing if she can get the old king to return the eagles while supporting the new alliance between my family and the new king of Parthia."

"That would indeed test both her devotion and reasoning," Athena agreed. "If she fails, I sense never-ending conflict until an even greater power arises from the South to destroy Egypt, Rome and Parthia together."

"Then go she shall," Isis commanded, and sent Arsinoë a warning dream, in which Caesarion was trampled to death by Parthian horses and buried in pig's blood under a Star of David.

After receiving the dream, Arsinoë immediately sought out Gaspar, considered by many to be the greatest of the Parthian Magi, to interpret the dream, the interpretation of which Arsinoë then conveyed to her mother: "Do not ally with the House of Herod. It is destined for desecration, destruction and desolation. It is still your choice whether this fate extends to Caesarion, your Dynasty and your and Antony's future Empire."

Isis, Athena, and Caesar watched as Cleopatra sent letters

throughout Egypt and Parthia inviting Gaspar to meet her in Alexandria. Within the month, Gaspar was sitting next to Cleopatra, allowing her to question him directly about his reading of her daughter's dream.

"What do you know of Judea and Judeans?" she asked after being satisfied that Gaspar's interpretation was sound. Cleopatra's continued lust for Judea did not go unnoticed by an increasingly troubled Isis, who had previously decreed that the one land Cleopatra desired most she could never have. Worse, her favorite hadn't appealed first to her for help. The test had truly begun.

Gaspar replied. "There are many Judeans, mostly Jews, who live in Parthia, some of whom have become Magi, though they call themselves *chakkiym*. They have different skills, and appeal primarily to their universal 'one god', but all of them believe that a messiah will rescue their nation at the end of a 490-year period as foretold by their prophet, Daniel. By star-reckoning, that is more or less fourteen years from now."

"What exactly are they expecting?" the group high above heard Cleopatra ask.

Gaspar laughed. "Well, their thoughts are not consistent about this, Great Queen. There are many divergent opinions. Some look for a warrior-king like King David; others, a supernatural being who will, with the wave of a ghostly hand, usher in a new era in human history. One *chakkiym* I know expects the messiah to be a great physician who will take onto himself all human pain, suffering their collective pain in order to heal humanity. Yet others believe he will be a wise man, who through the sharing of wisdom thus far denied humanity, will open the door for a new world where rationality reigns."

Several things about Gaspar's information clearly caught Cleopatra's attention. First, in all cases, the messiah was a man. This made a certain sense—heroes were almost always male, regardless of culture. On the other hand, throughout Egypt it was well known that creation, birth, healing, nurturing and rebirth were the domain of women. Second, David had told her the messiah would sojourn for a time in Egypt. The heavenly ensemble watched as Cleopatra asked Gaspar of these.

"One person can be many things to many people, Great One. All I can say with assurance is that there is a strong collective belief among Jews, especially Judean Jews, that *something* is about to happen, though no one knows exactly what or by whom. Where it will begin, however, is a different matter. Most believe it will occur in or around Judah. This agrees with our star charts. You would have to travel to Parthia to learn more."

From above, the host watched Cleopatra consider Gaspar's intriguing suggestion: *I have a new, capable, and trustworthy regent in Rufio Minor who can serve in my absence; all my children now have lives of their own; Antony is busy preparing Rome to evolve into an Egypto-Roman Empire; our most immediate problem remains Parthia's return of the eagles; there is a growing apprehension everywhere that the world is poised for unprecedented change; how and if the coming of the messiah and Antony and my Egypto-Roman Empire are related is yet to be seen.* Cleopatra decided to take the Magi's suggestion on condition that Antony would accompany her.

All watching from the portico of the Vault of Nut stood back in shocked silence. The "test" had gone awry. Cleopatra still hadn't called upon her benefactor, Isis, but instead had shown reasoning which, from Isis' advantage, should she actually travel to Parthia, might rewrite history, though in a new and particularly convoluted way.

"My favorite has begun thinking independently like a god," Isis stated.

"No," replied Caesar. "She is simply becoming the living goddess she has always been destined to be."

Chapter Thirty

The World

18-17 B.C.

Years 33-34 of Cleopatra's Reign

Parthia

I did not enjoy my travel to Parthia. First, Antony was unable to accompany me, agreeing instead to meet me in Parthaunisa, the capital of Parthia, the hub of the East-West trade route. I left Alexandria during the night to cross into Nabataea to, first, avoid broadcasting my absence, second, to avoid the intense heat typical of this time of year, and finally to join an existing caravan continuing its northwest travels. For the next several weeks, I spent my evenings sitting about a fire listening to legends and tales told by the desert caravan drivers. It was a much-needed respite from the pressures of ruling.

This, however, changed when we entered Judea, where several times I came into contact with fanatic Zealots. The tensest was in Jerusalem, where an armed mob surrounded my palanquin, and I heard shouts of, "Death to Rome!" and "If not Antony, Cleopatra!" Ironically, as the mob prepared to take action, it was Herod who extricated me, stating afterwards I was too valuable to him to be murdered by fanatics, though of what purpose in his evil mind, I shuddered to think.

I left Jerusalem in distress, disguised, at Herod's suggestion as one of a number of slaves, walking in single file, bound one to the next, his soldiers marching on either side. Despite my best efforts and the humiliation I suffered, I learned nothing more than what I already knew of the messiah and the future kingdom he was to herald.

Once outside the city, I resumed my palanquin and, carried again on the shoulders of my own soldiers, I continued in relative safety to Syria. There I was afforded protection by the ruling descendants of Queen Roxane, who my father, Pharaoh Ptolemy XII Neos Dionysos had loved, despite her betrayal of both him and me. Their concern was palpable. They knew that as Antony and my empire grew, Syria, being a close physical neighbor, would eventually come under our scrutiny, and, given our past associations, likely be absorbed into our empire, quite possibly ceasing to exist.

In fact, nothing could be further from the truth. What had happened in the past was in the past. All that mattered was how I was treated now, and the Syrians treated me extraordinarily well, providing me with pleasant food as well as support and protection fit for a queen while I crossed through Syria. When I stopped briefly in Syrian Antioch, I was welcomed and celebrated by the entire populace as Aphrodite. To be honest, I felt loathe to leave the safety and warmth of Syria to cross the Euphrates and Tigris Rivers into Parthia.

If I had any concerns about my treatment in Parthia, they were instantly dissipated upon my arrival. Though I knew Antony coveted and even desired revenge for the stolen eagles, I couldn't help but fall in love with Parthia at first sight. The nation was a rich mixture of the ancient and contemporary: ancient Greek and Persian architecture stood side by side and in instances were blended seamlessly together into something entirely new and delightful to the senses. The people reflected this both physically and intellectually, being both beautiful and openly welcoming. I felt so safe that I shopped among in the Parthaunisean marketplace, which the Parthians call The Bazaar, with only a personal bodyguard. There I purchased some beautiful gold lamps, including one the merchant said was enchanted by a spirit that would grant its owner his fondest desires. I thanked him warmly, brushing aside the flowery story, intending this lamp as a gift to the young Parthian king.

I was welcomed into the palace warmly but distantly by one of old King Phraates' ambassadors.

"Your husband awaits you," he said, rather curtly for my liking.

After pleasantries, Antony informed me that Phraates and he had worked out "an agreement" regarding the eagles, but before we could discuss the details, I was led alone into a royal receiving chamber. There I learned I would be meeting with young King Phraataces, husband to Arsinoë, my daughter and recently declared Queen of Parthia.

The youth was even taller, leaner and more handsome than when I met him in Alexandria. He now sported a thick black beard woven into many tight little braids. He was draped in rich purple robes and wore the gold crown of Parthia. As when I first met him, both of his hands were adorned with gold jewelry. Despite his formal appearing exterior, upon seeing me, he smiled and welcomed me graciously. I could see that he respected me, but by the mere fact that he hadn't invited Antony, I could also tell that, for some as yet unspoken reason, he did not respect Antony as much. The thought left me wondering if I was being called upon to untangle some problems resulting from "the agreement" between Antony and King Phraataces' father. I called my forever attendant, Charmion, to my side and ordered her to open the box I brought with me containing the lamp. Here was a man just entering young adulthood, and I decided to tell him the story of the lamp the merchant had told me. Upon hearing it, the young king, enchanted, happily accepted both the story and lamp.

"Welcome to Parthia, Queen Cleopatra, Mother of my Wife and Queen," he said to me in Parthian, meaning, of course, that he did not command fluent Egyptian.

"I am pleased to be here," I replied in perfect Parthian, much to his relief and delight.

"I…I wish to discuss empire with you," the young king blurted out, then blushed at having been too forthright.

"I would be glad to, but where is Antony?" I asked.

"Your husband?" young Phraataces asked in reply. "He is the honored guest of my father. They are meeting in the receiving chamber next to this one." A jeweled finger pointed at the wall next to us.

"I see," I said, wondering, *Why separate us?* replying, "I have the impression Parthia remains at some odds with Rome."

"Ah, yes," the young monarch replied signaling me to sit next to him in on a gilded, two-person couch brought forward by attendants. "After much 'discussion', Antony and my father came to an understanding of sorts. But, as King, I wished to discuss things with you before I sanctioned their agreement. Everyone in Parthia knows you are the one who rules the Empire."

I could not tell if Phraataces was flattering me or speaking his true mind. Such it often is when dealing with inexperienced royal youth. After some thought, I decided to regard it as both, and replied, "Great King, there is nothing that need be said that can't be said before Antony."

It was his turn to stop and ponder, which he did, displaying knitted brows. In fact, I wanted to laugh and then hug this young man, trying his best to discuss royal concerns directly with the 'Ruler of the Empire' as he saw me. After a short pause, he nodded affirmatively, and at his signal we rose and I followed him into the next room where Antony and the Elder King waited. When we entered, both had raised goblets of wine, which they immediately replaced on a large marble table about which they sat.

"Imperator Antony. Queen-Pharaoh Cleopatra," both Phraates and King Phraataces said at the same time in Latin.

"Thank the gods!" muttered Antony in Latin. "A language I can fully understand!"

On the table lay piles of parchment scrolls. Antony spoke first and explained that the two had negotiated and finally agreed that King Phraataces could, when he was older, take additional consorts, as was the way of many past and present kings, but that any resulting offspring could never be high king or queen of Parthia, as that would go solely to Phraataces and Arsinoë's sons and daughters in perpetuity. Phraates had, in response, agreed to acknowledge and respect Philadelphos as the son of Antony and Cleopatra the Great, and would return to Philadelphos the controversial eagles. It seemed a reasonable agreement, though I could tell that the young King was not pleased at having been left out of the negotiations. *Men!* I thought, complimenting Phraataces for his diplomatic astuteness by having his father negotiate this "ancillary" concern separately, leaving us free to negotiate more important matters. That seemed to smooth the young man's ruffled feathers, and, if it further increased his admiration for me, so be it.

As we concluded further diplomatic negotiations, there remained in my mind two burning questions: First, Parthia bordered a land my daughter, Arsinoë, had called in her letters Bharata, and I wanted to know more about this land, also called India, that had eluded the Great Alexander in his attempt to conquer of the world. Second, I wanted to visit Gaspar's colleagues to discuss what, if anything more, their star charts might reveal.

"A land impossible to defeat, as generations of my men well

know," Phraates said. "It is more a collection of kingdoms that ally whenever anyone is attacked. I value the land for its spices—especially curry. Musa is quite fond of this particular mixture of spices and has our cook to put it on everything. It is thought to drive away evil, and, based on the success of our negotiations, I must agree." Phraataces nodded in tacit agreement.

What I really wanted was more details about this land and those beyond, and curry seemed an excellent segue. "You've piqued my interest. I should like to try this 'curry'. Might I also procure a small sample to bring back with me?" I asked.

"Of course," young King Phraataces replied, eager to please. "That I can most certainly do!"

To my disappointment, the opportunity to move the discussion from curry to the details of what lay beyond Parthia's western borders never materialized. Both kings seemed wary of any further inquiries into Bharata or beyond. That night, however, I was afforded the opportunity to reunite with my daughter, Arsinoë. It was arranged for her and I to share a private chamber together overlooking the city of Parthaunisa. I immediately asked her of the lands of Bharata and Zhongguo of which she'd written, and of the whereabouts of the Magi.

Arsinoë seemed willing to talk, but nervous. After dismissing her servants, she spoke to me in Egyptian about the reticence of her husband and father-in-law to talk of either land.

"Both fear Father's attempts at diplomacy with Parthia are a façade," Arsinoë explained. I noticed she had taken on the style of Parthian dress, wearing long robes and adorning herself with golden jewelry, her hair done in a bun in the style of the Parthian court.

"What exactly do they fear?" I asked of her.

"They fear that Antony intends to invade Parthia. Your questions have made them suspicious if this is in order to seize Bharata and Zhongguo for their riches, which are far beyond what they've said," Arsinoë explained. "In Parthia, Zhongguo is sometimes called China. I have learned that it is an immense but isolated land protected from invasion by an impenetrable wall," Arsinoë explained.

"What else do you know of this Zhongguo-China?" I asked.

"The land is ruled by the Han dynasty. Much of Parthia's silk and exotic spices, as well as weaponry come not from Bharata but from Zhongguo. As for the Magi, my husband's father has ordered them to have no contact with you or father while here," Arsinoë stated while we blew out the lamps one-by-one in preparation for sleeping.

The next morning, having done all we could, Antony and I departed Parthaunisa for Rome in an elaborate caravan overflowing with camels, slaves, spices, silks, gold and jewels. Antony and I took our place together at the rear of the caravan surrounded by Egyptian, Roman and Parthian guards. As we plodded along, I shared the discussion I'd had with Arsinoë.

"I know King Phraates and his son do not trust me," he replied. "That is not new information. But that which you are sharing of Bharata and Zhongguo is."

"They say Zhongguo is surrounded by an impenetrable wall," I recounted.

"Whether that is so or not, it is clearly meant to give people the impression that it would be a waste of time, men, money and energy for any invader to even try. The question remains, however, whether this is true, and if so, to what extent. It is hard to imagine a wall thousands of *atur* long that is uniformly impenetrable. Irrespective, it was one thing to conquer Germania; it would be quite another to conquer either Bharata or Zhongguo," Antony said.

"You not envision our Empire expanding East of Parthia, then?" I asked. I was testing him. Rome and Egypt together with Parthia would be formidable.

"No one can rule an entire world," Antony said in a moment of supreme clarity. "Alexander tried and was cut down in his prime. I think it wise for us to forget about Bharata and Zhongguo," Antony said, adding with a wink, "as a conquest, at least. From what I've heard and seen in Parthia, they would make excellent trading partners."

It was a hard time of year to be traveling overland, as we would be ending our journey during winter. Antony and I stayed warm by traveling in carried tents, covering ourselves with layers of warm Parthian blankets as needed. Traveling eastward, we again passed through Syria, turning upwards through Antioch, and then proceeded to Rome by way of Athens. In Athens, Antony and I were welcomed as Aphrodite and Dionysus, and we took a much-appreciated rest until winter turned to spring.

For me, Athens was always a treat. While there, I visited the Parthenon and there, made an offering to Athena, goddess of wisdom. Antony accompanied me everywhere. Unlike Julius Caesar who had tried his best to destroy everything Greek and repaint it Roman, Antony admired Greece and my Macedonian-Greek ancestry. Though the women in Athens were generally not allowed to be seen in public, as Queen-Pharaoh of Egypt, I was exempted from the ban by decree of the Greek *Ecclesia*, the all-male assembly unique to this democratic nation-city. During our walks, I often discussed the Greeks and Alexander with Antony.

"The Greeks made their mark on the world, that is certain," Antony said to me late one night. "But the Golden Age of Greece is a thing of the past."

"The past is always equally before us," I said, examining a small statue of Athena I had purchased at a stall in the *Agora*, Athens' market place.

"It is equally hard to forget our own past," Antony said, kissing me while fondling a lock of my hair in his fingers. Both of us were aging, but our passions remained.

"Do you remember our time in Tarsus, Cleopatra? When you were Aphrodite?" he asked.

"How could I forget?" I said as he and I looked over the city of Athens from the portico of the house where we were staying, a small but lovely place made of white-washed, sun-dried mud. Evening had descended and with it, millions of stars had begun to appear in the darkening sky all about us.

"Who is your favorite Greek?" I asked him, rising on my toes to kiss him.

"Cleopatra," Antony replied. "Always."

We made love together on the portico under the heavens long into the night.

All too soon our time in Athens ended, and we began preparations to continue on to Rome. While we were away, Rome had experienced unprecedented economic growth and Antony's reforms in preparation for our conjoined empire were slowly being passed by the Senate one-at-a-time with constant pressuring by Cicero Minor. Of these reforms, the one that interested me most allowed a Roman citizen to marry a foreigner and, if the Roman had sufficient financial resources, claim the foreigner a citizen of Rome! Of course, I was already Antony's legal wife by Egyptian and Roman marriage as well as by decree, but this reform cracked open the door to Egypto-Roman marriage in general, something we both felt imperative towards building our empire.

Unfortunately, I also heard that Cicero Minor's health was failing. From his letters, I suspected poison, and wrote Dolabella of such including various antidotes I thought might be helpful. Further news would have to await our return.

Upon our arrival, I was greeted with a pleasant surprise: Aprilus was approaching—the ill-fated Ides of Martius had passed—and a grand celebration began the moment Antony and I entered the city! I had suspected something was afoot when Antony repeatedly brushed aside my inquiries about what might await us in Rome. It began with loud blasts of trumpets and a huge mob welcoming us! We were carried along streets filled with revelers tossing petals at us, so many that it gave the normally dour-smelling city air a delight fragrance! Looking out, I noted rose petals everywhere eventually forming a thick carpet. We were greeted in the city center by Dolabella who loudly proclaimed me a Roman citizen as well as wife.

Shouts of "Long live Imperator Antony! Long live Domina Cleopatra!" immediately rose from all about us. News of Cicero Minor' health would have to wait until after this grand day in which I was at last being fully accepted by Rome.

My joy turned to concern that evening when I spoke with Dolabella about pressing matters of state as we three dined privately on a simple meal of bread and fish. "Is Cicero Minor well? Was he indeed poisoned?"

"He may well still be, Domina Cleopatra," Dolabella answered, greeting me as one would a true Roman wife. "There remain senators who secretly—a handful not so secretly—question Antony and your intention to form an ever-stronger bond between Rome and Egypt. Today's celebration for you, though truly heartfelt on the part of the common people, was opposed by certain senators, the same ones questioning whether, like Julius Caesar, your former husband, Antony and even you will demand to be recognized as god and goddess, perhaps even Emperor and Empress. They would see you and Antony destroyed well before anything resembling either takes place. These also see Cicero Minor as your voice and hand."

"Did any of my antidotes work, or do you think he will soon be with the gods?" I asked.

"I cannot answer either of your questions, Domina. I want to believe that Cicero Minor will be all right, but knowing neither the poison nor poisoner, we must not be foolishly optimistic," Dolabella said.

Who could? I thought. *Only the gods and goddesses. All we can know is that Antony and I still walk this Earth and are not one with them, yet.*

Spring and summer brought further challenges. Brigands in Nabataea attacked and burned Antony's ships stationed there to stop piracy. Antony had to return to Parthia to replenish his lumber and supplies. That done, he left for Nabataea to fend off the peninsular Arab-pirates, while I remained in Rome, slowly making my voice his. During this time, Cicero Minor's "illness" became steadily worse, and one day, I was summoned to his side. He appeared much older than his years, but he was not so ill he could not receive me himself.

"Great Queen," a voice called to me as I passed through the vestibulum and entered a beautifully decorated atrium replete with a fountain issuing water, surrounded by a group of intricately carved, life sized animals, a delicate fawn at its center.

"Cicero Minor?" I called, searching the atrium and finding him sitting in a chair in a small study at the opposite side of the room. Olympos and Mardian were already there. Cicero Minor looked well but seemed feeble in his movements. "Tell me. How ill are you, really?" I asked, looking into his glazed eyes and wondering how much longer he had in this world.

"I am being called to the Underworld as we speak," he confirmed in a hushed voice.

I choked back a sob. *What a poor reward to the man most responsible for Antony and my success*, I thought.

Cicero Minor coughed violently, but when I started to approach him, he held up a hand and spoke: "Do not worry, Dear Queen. I have long been grooming my son to take my place," Cicero Minor, ever our staunchest supporter, declared. Later that evening, I wrote Antony, updated him on the seriousness of Cicero Minor's condition and begged him to come quickly.

Cicero Minor held death at bay until Antony returned. He got sicker, then better, then sicker after his initial joy at Antony's return. His wife, Terentia, and ever-close sister told me they wished that if the gods meant to take him, they would quit issuing false hope. Finally, at the start of Junius, a somber looking messenger came to Antony's villa with the news of Cicero Minor's passing.

"Imperator Antony. Queen Cleopatra. He is gone," the messenger said simply.

"Thank you; you may leave us," Antony said, equally curtly, though I saw tears forming in the corners of his increasingly age-lined eyes.

"Yes, leave," I reiterated wanting to save my husband embarrassment. In truth, I had never seen either him or Caesar cry, making me sometimes wonder if Roman men were capable of making tears. But as Antony proceeded to weep bitterly in my arms, I knew they both could and did. Antony said nothing, except that we would host a funeral for Cicero Minor on the Ides of Junius.

When the day came, Antony, myself, Cicero Minor's wife and sister, and what seemed like the whole of Rome gathered around the lifeless body adorned in his best toga and laid atop a huge wooden pyre. His face looked pitifully thin and his body wasted. Antony made a fine speech extolling his virtues and service to Rome, then lit the pyre.

I sighed as the fire crackled and quickly engulfed his mortal remains. Personally, I found Cicero Minor's choice of cremation distasteful. In Egypt, we attempt to preserve rather than destroy. Eventually the roaring fire peaked, then began quickly diminishing, leaving behind little more than a handful of white ash.

With Cicero Minor gone, Antony and I had to shoulder the process of empire-building ourselves. Part of that process was to declare a successor to Antony. Antony, in spite of adopting Caesarion, had still not yet openly declared him his successor, and I was beginning to wonder why. To my satisfaction, Antony told me that this very week he would issue a public proclamation declaring Caesarion his successor. It would consist of a repeat of the adoption ceremony, where Antony would sell Caesarion and buy him, after which Caesarion would publicly accept successorship in exchange for forfeiting his Egyptian rights to the title of pharaoh. While I was widely acknowledged as Queen-Pharaoh of Egypt, Caesarion had been serving in title as Pharaoh Ptolemy XV. That meant I would either need to take another male or openly declare myself Queen-Pharaoh at last. I quickly decided on the latter.

The succession ceremony was attended by everyone in Rome, a display both of Antony's might as Imperator and Caesarion's as Imperator-successor. I attended, dressed as Queen-Pharaoh of Egypt, to reinforce Caesarion's relinquishment of any future claim to Egypt. This solidified Selene's succession to the Egyptian throne as Queen-Pharaoh upon my passing.

"We need more allies if we are to take the final step towards empireship," Antony said abruptly one hot day at the end of Romanus, a month now also known as Antonius for my husband. Although Cicero Minor was gone, he had proven successful at fully restoring my reputation and elevating me to the status of a Roman citizen and wife, making it safe for me to travel freely about Rome.

"Let's begin by visiting Julius Caesar's library," Antony suggested.

"Believe it or not, I've never been there," I replied.

"A library you've never visited?" Antony asked wryly. "Never?"

I shook my head indicating such.

"Well then, you are in for a treat. You shall meet there a gathering of the greatest scholars of Rome. It's a good place to begin researching future allies, and I'm certain you will enjoy it every bit as much as your Alexandrian one."

Of all my days in Rome, our day at my former husband's library will perhaps remain one of my fondest of memories. Antony and I spent a joyous time there, me parsing the hundreds of scrolls collected from everywhere in the world subject to Roman law, meeting and getting to know the brightest minds of the day, while Antony talked and strategized with military and political writers about whose help to forge a "newer, stronger Rome" he should enlist. I once again talked with Virgil, a man who many years ago had befriended me and championed my cause before Rome. I would be remiss if I didn't acknowledge that he had redeemed my reputation among scholars at least as much as Cicero Minor had among the people. Virgil informed me just before we parted that he was writing a history of Rome he called *The Aeneid*.

"What exactly is an *Aeneid*?" I asked.

"It is not so much a thing or place as it is an epic inspirational poem about the ancestors of Rome, much like the Greek *Odyssey*. I hope to do for Rome what Homer did for Greece." Virgil said proudly. "I am also writing a scroll about your husband."

"In a good way, I hope." Antony interjected, turning his attention momentarily away from a retired Roman tribune with whom he'd been talking.

"We must never forget to honor those who win. It is our Roman way, is it not, Imperator?"

Antony nodded his tacit assent, quickly reengaging the tribune in discussion.

"In my own biography, you will, I think, be pleased to know that I praised you as Antony's loyal wife and the devoted mother of Caesarion," Virgil said to me, smiling.

"With your pen, my oldest son will be forever remembered, but don't forget that I have borne five children," I said. History is recorded exactly this way: Hindsight, and through it, our understanding of who we are in the world, would always be subject to serendipity. My comment was more than offhanded. My father had sired six children, all of whom had at one time ruled Egypt, but aside from me, they were all but forgotten.

"All your sons and daughters will be remembered, Great One, immortalized by poets and writers of all the lands which your children now rule," Virgil said.

"May the gods of Rome smile on Antony's favorite wife," a richly sonorous voice interrupted.

"And who might you be?" I asked this brash man, thinking himself an equal of Virgil.

"Quintus Horatius Flaccus. I am but a humble poet struggling in the shadow of Rome's greatest. The mob calls me Horace," The man said.

"He is two books through his quadrilogy, the *Odes*," remarked Virgil, adding in an aside to me, "All hope it will read less odiously than his earlier poetry."

Chapter 31

The Beginning of the End

17 B.C

Year 34 of Cleopatra's reign

The Vault of Nut

Isis, Athena, Venus, the Royal Mother, Auletes, and Berenice were locked in conversation after observing Antony and Cleopatra in Julius Caesar's library attempting to establish their world empire. Each was focused on a different aspect of the future Empire.

Isis focused on Selene, the wife of Juba II and the publicly announced successor to Cleopatra, as she constructed her Temple to Isis. It was progressing well, and Isis was pleased. Selene burned sweet incense daily in the almost complete temple. Even after being barren for so long a time and questioning if and why Isis had abandoned her, Selene had never truly abandoned the goddess. Juba had had children by a concubine but given the circumstances and his enduring love for Selene, she forgave him, and then not long afterwards conceived herself. Their son, Juba III, whom Juba adored, had died a year ago in a chariot accident in which he had been run over by his own horses. Selene subsequently bore twins, Ptolemy Antony and Cleopatra IX.

Athena focused on Caesarion, son of Cleopatra and Julius Caesar. The child of an Egyptian and a Roman, and now an avowed Roman—

Athena still disdained Romans for having "stolen" Greek culture and claimed it as their own—had become an imposing man. Athena looked down with dislike at Virgil and Horace, but despite her feelings for them and Romans in general, watched Caesarion give speech after speech in support of his future position as Roman Imperator and possibly eventual Emperor of Antony and Cleopatra's emerging empire. His father's son, Caesarion was thinking that a campaign might be necessary to fully exercise his right. There had been a small but violent reaction to Antony's proclamation of Caesarion as his heir. Most accepted it, but a few Senators had openly opposed it. As such, Caesarion thought to silence them by a show of military might. Athena watched anxiously as, a day later, Caesarion prepared to invade and conquer these Senators' stronghold in the Roman cities of Novicum and Raetia located by the Danube. "Caesar, is your son so foolish to risk his life because of a few bickering Senators?" Athena asked irately.

Caesar turned from his own observations of Philadelphos, currently client king of Numidia who was at this moment fleeing for his life. "It appears so," he said, "however, I feel honored that he would use my strategy to meet his ends."

"You men are such fools," Athena, exasperated, stated.

Venus smiled, looking away from her focus, Arsinoë, now a Parthian Queen, making pleasant love to her husband.

"What is so funny?" Athena demanded.

"Arsinoë. She is so in love with Phraataces, she is completely blind to the scheming of his mother, Musa," Venus said. "Musa will not give up Queenship easily."

"That's not at all funny," Caesar remarked. "It's dangerous." Turning toward Athena, he added, "Women and their ways are always dangerous."

"Indeed, Arsinoë is in grave danger in Parthia. But there is a power watching over her. A power that is, as yet, little known to our pantheon," Athena stated.

Caesar returned his gaze to Philadelphos, and Berenice, Cleopatra's only righteous sister, the Royal Mother and Auletes joined him. All looked down upon a frightened and contrite Philadelphos dictating through Titan, his always loyal friend, a desperate missive to his mother.

Mother,

I am alive, thank the gods, but that is all. I have left the palace after a poisoning attempt against both the Numidian noblewoman I married and me. I do not know why they attempted to poison my wife, but the result was that our child which she was carrying was lost. The pregnancy was far enough along to determine it was a boy, adding further to my grief. When I attempted to question my servants as to who was behind this, their tongues had been cut out.

I remain ignorant about who has done this and if whomever it was will attempt to kill us again. I suppose so. I will travel to Egypt as soon as I finish this, hoping that, in my absence, my appeal to King Herod will somehow result in my retaining my throne. By his advice, I trust no one. Burn this letter after you read it.

Your loyal son,

Ptolemy Philadelphos

"Cleopatra only now arrives back in Egypt. What kind of fool is Cleopatra and Antony's son to abandon his throne and seek the aid of Herod of all people?" Caesar asked in disgust, watching Cleopatra being carried along the main causeway to her palace amidst cheering crowds.

"Herod and he have corresponded regularly. What promises of

'help' has that old fox given him?" Auletes asked. Though he had eventually sworn fealty to Antony, Herod was known to regard the children of Antony and Cleopatra as bastards to be treated outside his oath.

"A fox? Herod calls himself a lion," Caesar interjected.

"There is what a man *calls* himself and what a man truly is," Auletes reminded Caesar.

"Foxes are considered deceitful..." Caesar began.

"Exactly," interrupted Auletes.

Caesar then saw his father-in-law's point. "Yes, I must agree. He *is* a fox. A treacherous, lying fox of which one must always be careful,"

"Those in desperation often make unwise decisions," The Royal Mother said, at the same time, quietly praying for her youngest grandson's life. "Will he live, do you think?" she asked the group, recalling with deep sadness the fate of her grandson, Helios.

"Titan is a loyal friend to him," Berenice said. "He has finished penning Philadelphos' letter to Cleopatra. Whichever arrives first, the son or letter, my daughter will intervene," hesitating not to add, "but not so, Antony."

Chapter 32

Triumphs and Tragedies

17-12 B.C

Years 34-39 of Cleopatra's Reign

Alexandria

I arrived in Alexandria in Maius and immediately headed to the Palace, where Rufio Minor anxiously awaited me, several scrolls in hand. To my surprise, Philadelphos was standing next to him. "Hail, Cleopatra!" Rufio Minor cried.

"Hail, Rufio Minor!" I said. "And to my son, Philadelphos, *em hotep nefer weret*. I paused to take a good look at him. The immature boy who had stamped his feet at the idea of ruling Numidia had matured, appearing frightened but more sober from his sojourn in that land.

"In very great peace, Mother!" Standing just behind him was Titan, his strong and loyal friend, his strength now tempered with experience. In my mind, Titan was to Philadelphos what Charmion had always been to me.

"I feel, Titan, that in your being here with him, there is something my son is hiding from me," I said.

"Yes, Great One. His life was nearly forfeit. His son died in his wife's womb, and she on the trip to Alexandria. Both died of poison," Titan confirmed.

Rufio Minor squirmed, dropping some scrolls while gripping one in particular, apparently undecided as to what to do.

"Yes, Mother," Philadelphos said, tears welling. "I am in desperate need of a wife. I need to find one, and soon, to take care of your grandchildren."

"And so you shall," I said, my anger at the injustice of his situation rising. "But first, I must know the details of what happened. Do you know who attempted to poison you?"

Rufio Minor held out the scroll he was clutching, but Philadelphos brushed it away. "No, Mother. All I know at this point is that, regaining what I have lost will not be easy."

"Philadelphos' control over the native Numidians was never secure. It will be quite difficult to reassert his rulership as he says," Titan confirmed.

"I see that," I said, this time with some irritation. Then I noticed Philadelphos' stance. He looked like an old man, exhausted, beaten by life. I saw the look on his face of one who had been robbed of his life's love. Had he truly grown so fond of the Numidian woman he had married in such a short time? I suddenly recalled my feelings when I became aware of Julius Caesar's assassination. My heart gripped my throat, and words would not come.

"Leave this to me, Great Queen," Rufio Minor said matter-of-factly, hiding the scroll he was clutching behind him. "The three of you need to talk and rest."

"Good advice, well taken." I said, excusing myself from Philadelphos and Titan and walking to my chambers. There, exhausted by what I'd heard, I collapsed onto my silken bed and fell into a deep, dark, dreamless sleep.

I received some news the next day that at least partially restored my spirits. It was a communique from Caesarion, informing me that he had returned from Novicum, having destroyed the resources of the errant Senators and seized the territories for himself, which had, in turn, returned the balance of power in his favor in Rome. That meant he was free to avenge his brother and help restore Philadelphos' position in Numidia. I immediately wrote back, congratulating him on his successes, explaining Philadelphos' current situation, and stating I would greatly appreciate his assistance.

Yet, I remained sad. I was in Alexandria, but Antony was in Rome. He and I had lived a full, exciting and fruitful life, but I had noticed before I left Rome he was not just aging, but was doing so far more quickly than I. His once black curly hair had turned snow white, and he had acquired a night cough that wouldn't seem to go away. I worried that my Antony might soon depart this world, leaving me with only my servants and close attendants. Of course, Antony would acknowledge nothing of this and repeatedly sent me away after showing me a display of manly strength.

Unfortunately, back again in my favorite palace overlooking my capital city and the harbor, Charmion, Iras, Mardian, and Olympos were all visibly aging, too. Only for me did time seem to suspend itself, as if some god or goddess, Isis perhaps, were offering me some much needed time to collect and record my thoughts in order to fully appreciate the life I had been given.

Time passed, and my spirits returned. How could they not in glorious Alexandria? In the spring, Caesarion arrived with seven legions—30,000 soldiers—many surprisingly young. I was pleased to see him in his Roman leather breastplate with its two eagles, his gold incised, ivory handled *gladius*, and brilliantly polished electrum shield. He greeted Philadelphos and me warmly, saying he could only remain briefly. "We march to Numidia before the day's end to deal with those who dared rise up against my brother," he said proudly. "Philadelphos, you must come with us."

"As I am?" Philadelphos asked, having brought little with him other than the clothes he had been wearing the day he fled.

"As you are, dear brother," Caesarion replied. "You are a king. We are your soldiers. That is enough."

Mollified, Philadelphos agreed upon Caesarion's promise of suitable Roman military gear.

"Mother?" Caesarion then asked. "You have seen many battles and you are known for your powers of strategy. Will you come with us?"

I hesitated.

"It would give me great assurance to have you at my side," Caesarion said. "Especially since my first father cannot."

"Thank you, dear son, for acknowledging my military and diplomatic contributions. I believe I am still a good strategic planner, having served both your first father and Antony well in this manner," I replied.

"That is exactly why I need you," Caesarion continued. "Numidia is more Egyptian than Roman."

After some thought, I came to my conclusion: "Caesarion...I fear I must decline your offer. You are still young, but I am too old for such ventures."

"Very well," Caesarion replied, but looking into my son's eyes, I could see that, alone, without his father, he was afraid.

"I will send Rufio Minor in my stead," I said.

"Indeed. If I cannot have you or Antony beside me, I will gladly have him," Caesarion replied. His eyes seemed to reawaken, and his stance stiffen.

*My boy. My son...*I thought fondly.

"Mother, Queen-Pharaoh, Great Queen over Queens and Kings, may the gods bless and watch over you," Caesarion said, striking his chest with his fist in the manner of Roman soldiers, departing moments later with Rufio Minor and Philadelphos.

They left Alexandria before midnight. With my husband in Rome and my trusted regent gone, I was once again ruling alone, as the Queen-Pharaohs Hatshepsut and Nefertiti had. I still had Olympos and Mardian with whom I could discuss issues of statecraft, David with whom to talk religion and philosophy, as well as Charmion and Iras as close friends and confidants. Even so, I noticed Olympos, my childhood tutor and life-long advisor, acting as if he were becoming tired of this life, and I feared I might soon lose him. Similarly, David had less and less time to discuss with me the Hebrew Scriptures about which I remained so curious, and when we did meet, he quickly became weary, sometimes recounting differently a previously-told story, although he had, to my delight, recently begun sharing with me King Solomon's Song of Songs, a great Hebrew love poem. Charmion's health concerned me as well, although she seemed to be made of stronger stock than Olympos. Still, Charmion these days often fell asleep in the middle of a discussion. Iras would awaken her, but she would simply doze off again. It was to be expected. We were becoming exhausted by the pace of life, and they were both a decade older than me.

Only Iras, like me, seemed immune to time, and Mardian, being younger, was still strong and healthy. Iras liked to talk with me of the days when I was but a child-princess, remarking over and over how grateful she was for her freedom, which my father, at my request, in gratitude, had purchased for her.

"You have always been kind to me," Iras recounted. "I do wonder about Andromeda, my twin, since she, too, was abandoned by our family, but I'm certain she is dead now..." Iras mused.

"Jewish custom forbids abandoning infants," David, sitting with us, said. "A daughter is not as valued as a son, but she is not denied the privilege of life in Judea."

"Life?" Iras asked, yawning.

David mirrored her yawn. "We Jews are admonished in the Scriptures to always choose life and blessings over death and curses."

"I agree with that philosophy," I said, mirroring David's yawn. "In Egypt we celebrate life, unlike Rome, where they celebrate glory in death. As for Andromeda, Iras, life today is not easy. I suspect you are right and that she has likely long gone to the Underworld."

"I wish I had known her better and shared some of my good fortune with her. I wish I could believe as you do in Ma'at's feather of truth, My Queen, or the God-without-a-name's mercy, David, but I cannot. Worse, I fear my few memories of her will be erased when she stands on the shore of the River Styx," Iras said.

"We Jews say as long as one is remembered, that person lives. You may never have known your sister well, Iras, but she remains as long as long as anyone can recall her name. And what a beautiful name: Andromeda. It means, you know, 'to think of a man'."

"Perseus rescued the Ethiopian princess Andromeda, but my sister will have had no such luck," Iras stated bitterly.

Her words made me think of my own siblings, and the pain quickly became too much to bear. "I have been reading about Zoroastrian beliefs in the afterlife. I am interested in the beliefs of the Jews, too, but, not being a Jew, no Jewish rabbi will speak to me of them. However, from what I gather, your god-without-a-name and Ahura Mazda seem quite similar. Zoroastrians believe in a paradise for the good and torment for the evil." I looked to David to confirm this.

"Similar, Great One, but not identical. We Jews expect when we die to go to Sheol, a sort of waiting area, 'the Pit', to await judgment," he replied.

"As we Egyptians do awaiting the judgement of Ma'at?" I asked David.

"In our case, it is our unspeakable-named God who judges," David said.

"Ah. So only the judge is different," I summarized.

David nodded.

"We also hold that our heroes, Enoch, Abraham, Isiah and the like, live in heaven, while others judged worthy must still await the Messiah. The wicked remain simply dead," David elaborated.

I nodded. This was very close to Egyptian beliefs.

"Eternal life is a gift. The wicked's punishment is the destruction of their eternal soul," David said.

"Octavian?" I asked.

"I am not the God of Israel, but if I had to guess, I would say Octavian's soul vanished like smoke when he died," David offered.

"I do not think anyone would spend the time or effort to judge me good or evil. I fear I will simply be dead," Iras mumbled quietly.

"No, Iras!" I exclaimed. "When my time comes, you can go with me to Ma'at. I have done both good and evil, but I believe that together our hearts would be found lighter than Ma'at's feather and she will allow us to proceed to Isis." In truth, though I was proud of my Macedonian Greek ancestry, I disdained their depressingly horrid afterlife stories, which were held to be a blasphemy in the ears of the gods of Egypt, and I sincerely believed that my heart would be found lighter than the Feather of Truth, and, being beloved of Isis, I would meet her in the

Vault of Nut, where together, we would spend eternity observing the world, seeing the results of all I had done, helping others where possible. My afterlife, and Iras', too, should she choose to accompany me, would be one of neither hedonistic pleasure nor depressing sadness.

"If what you say of Ma'at is true, then surely *you* at least shall, My Queen. You are the best and greatest that Egypt has ever known," Iras said.

"I have tried to be ever faithful to Isis and have followed the laws of Ma'at as best I could," I said. "Even so, at times, Iras, I, too, doubt." Indeed. When younger, I had had no qualms about eliminating my brothers and sisters; now that I was approaching the time of my own judgement, I wondered how Ma'at would judge me.

"Cleopatra, please. I cannot hear my dearest companion and Egypt's Greatest Queen-Pharaoh, the Mother of an Empire that will someday span the world, talk like this," Iras said.

"Think of the good you have done for the people of Egypt and Rome. Think of the good wife you have been to Caesar and Antony. Think of the good mother you've been!"

I chuckled. "My concerns, Iras, are not in those areas. In coming to what I am and all that I've been able to do for Egypt and the world, I was not a good sibling," I confessed. "If I have violated the laws of Ma'at, it is in how I treated my siblings, although I did so not out of malice but to fulfill my and Egypt's destiny." I turned to David for his support, but he was dozing, and I decided not to wake him. But I thought to myself that this god of the Hebrews seemed to wield in combination the might of Ra, the justice of Ma'at, and the kindness of Isis.

Iras continued to reassure me not to fear Ma'at. "Your brothers and sisters were a constant threat. Isis has always favored you and will intercede for you if necessary, of that I am certain," she stated with conviction.

"She will," I reiterated, trying to convince myself. "At least, I hope she will." In my heart of hearts, however, I hoped neither my husband nor I would outlive the other, that we might face Ma'at together. Then I worried about Ma'at's judgement of Antony. Like me, his rise to Imperator had not been without bloodshed. I wondered if both the sins and virtues of one person could be shifted like money to another, affording both whatever necessary advantages presented. I wondered...

I tried after our conversation to be more attentive to Isis, praying and offering her incense on awakening and before retiring for the night, hoping that she would continue to favor me and my children. Even so, the news from Numidia frustrated me. Caesarion's campaign had ended in a stalemate. The barbarians fought fiercely and, while their victories were short-lived, in the end, Caesarion's victory was not absolute. In the end, the barbarians agreed to honor the *Pax Romana*, but warned that if any Ptolemy ever set foot in Numidia, he would quickly find himself dead. Caesarion would be returning soon to Alexandria to rest his legions before returning to Rome. Philadelphos returned to Alexandria in disgrace.

"What now?" I asked when we three were once again face-to-face.

"My Queen, all is not lost. You have other children successfully ruling other parts of the world," Rufio Minor stated. "Your empire continues to grow and will come into itself with or without Numidia. Numidia was simply not the wisest choice for Philadelphos."

"Where would be wiser, I wonder?" I hissed.

"Syria, I think," Rufio Minor ventured, and, to my surprise, Caesarion agreed. So did Philadelphos. "It should have been my kingdom all along," he stated, as if the "problem" had always been one of choice of place and not of himself. "Besides, Syrian women are much prettier than Numidian ones."

I wanted to slap my son, but instead laughed with him. In his travels with Caesarion and Rufio Minor, he had developed a rudimentary sense of humor. An odd one, perhaps, but a sense of humor no less. Being able to laugh at oneself was a giant step towards knowing oneself, something I prayed twice daily that Philadelphos would experience.

"I loved my Numidian wife..." Philadelphos ventured guiltily.

"Of course you did," Caesarion said kindly. "But for royalty, marriage is not for love, though with time, more often than not, husbands grow fond of their wife, and wives of their husband."

I smiled at this fraternal exchange. "Very well. Philadelphos shall go to Syria. The home of my stepmother," I said with reserved trepidation, remembering Roxane with disdain.

"I would like to remain in Alexandria a year before I go to Syria," Philadelphos said. "I want to study Syrian language and culture."

"Of course," I said, thinking, *Perhaps Philadelphos is learning.*

"Father slowly approaches death, Mother," Caesarion said, breeching a subject which all of us had been reticent to bring up. "I heard from Dolabella he calls for you at night."

I knew of this, and in its expression by Caesarion, I knew what I had to do. This year had been extremely trying for me. Antony and I both knew how important my presence in Egypt was to advance our dream of a single empire, but I had by now faithfully discarded my most critical duties, and handing crook and flail to Rufio Minor, I ordered my necessary belongings packed and alerted my navy. "I leave for Rome this night. Caesarion, I place Philadelphos in your hands."

The next month was filled with fear and trepidation. While the passage itself was uneventful, I was so sick with worry I had to drink wine to fall asleep, and my dreams were a recurrent nightmare in which

I got to Rome only to find it in chaos and my husband long dead. I prayed constantly I would not be too late. When at last I disembarked at Ostia, it was to a very grave Dolabella.

"You must come quickly, Great One," Dolabella said helping me into an undecorated palanquin. Two long rows of soldiers accompanied me to Antony's villa.

Disembarking, I asked Dolabella "Is he...?" as I ran alongside him.

"He was alive when I left to get you, but I fear he is very near his end," Dolabella replied.

As with my first husband when I last saw him, my dear Antony was unhealthy, but constantly buried in affairs of state, like me, trying to accomplish everything possible towards the formation of a singular empire. When I entered his room, my heart shattered.

Antony's body was flushed. His white curls were matted to his forehead. He was calling desperately for water, which he refused to drink when offered. He was, as our son had said, calling my name over and over.

"Cleopatra, my love!" Antony called out upon seeing me, and I knew I had made it just in time. "Cleopatra! Oh, my love! Cleopatra! My wife and lover for all eternity!" he exclaimed weakly between fits of coughing. "Now that you are here, I shall be well," he said, attempting to sit, and, in the attempt, falling back exhausted onto the soaked bed.

"Antony! Oh, Antony! Do not go to be with Bacchus. Not yet. Not without me!"

"I shall not. I cannot, now that I know you are here."

I ordered his assistants to prop him up and this seemed to lessen the coughing. "Tell me. What of Philadelphos? What of our Empire?" he asked like the father and Imperator he always was.

"Not now, Antony. Just rest," I begged, holding his fevered hand.

"Stay with me. Please."

And Antony did.

Revived by my presence, he clung stubbornly to life. Dolabella said my arrival had likely saved him, at least for now. "Perhaps it is the goddess in you who saved him," Dolabella offered.

"Antony and my gods and my goddesses have always looked fondly upon the two of us. His recovery is nothing less than a miracle," I said, wondering if it was not also the strength of our love, a blasphemy against Isis perhaps, but I was infinitely grateful for whatever time we still had together.

"Indeed. But for how long, Great Queen?" Dolabella asked. "Imperator Antony remains weak. You alone give him reason to live."

With persistence and love, Antony did finally recover, although not to full health. He would be plagued by the cough and subject to occasional outbursts of uncontrollable anger the remainder of his life. I gauged them a small price to pay for his remaining with me. When I finally spoke to him of Philadelphos' failure, he was at first angry and I saw in his eyes a flash of my young lover and co-ruler, but then he calmed, stating that Syria would indeed be more advantageous to both Philadelphos and the future empire.

"What of Caesarion?" Antony asked.

"In Alexandria, still," I replied, running my fingers lovingly through his white curls. "When I left for Rome, he sent all but one of his legions with me, but remained in Alexandria to assist Rufio Minor in my absence."

"I see. Well…bring him home.

"I do not think, dearest, that his return would be best for us just yet. I have written to him and he plans to arrive in Septembrus," I said, entwining my fingers in his, thinking, *Oh, how thin and frail my dearest has become! Will I someday look as thin…?*

"Good. And have him bring Philadelphos," Antony ordered, interrupting my thought. "Rufio Minor, like his father, is capable of ruling Egypt for a time without us."

I was particularly pleased to hear him say "us." It gave me hope, which I just now desperately needed. "Rest, love," I said. "Rest and gather your strength."

Caesarion arrived as planned in Septembrus with Philadelphos and more sad news. Olympos had died. I grieved privately, for Olympos had been my tutor and friend for as many years as I remembered. Mardian was well, Caesarion said, but no longer able to captain my guard or armies and had, with my leaving and Olympos' death, fallen into sadness, questioning his worth if he couldn't serve me directly anymore.

We had a family meeting the next day: Antony, Caesarion, Philadelphos and myself, to discuss all that had thus far occurred and what we should do with the immediate future. Caesarion's details of his campaign in Numidia were depressing. Antony, however, rose to the occasion, and ordered that Numidia should go to Selene and Juba, and that Philadelphos be sent at once to Syria. To each land, he ordered two legions of his finest. Philadelphos would rule Syria from Damascus, it was decided, not as a king, but as governor. From Syria, he could keep an eye on Herod.

"I will destroy Herod someday," I whispered to Antony.

"I believe you," Antony said. "But you must wait for the right moment."

While we waited to hear of Philadelphos' safe arrival in Damascus, I received news from Arsinoë. Her letters were always joyous and happy. She spoke again of her love for her husband and new homeland, and the fact that her parents-in-law at last adored her. Though things had begun badly with Musa, the two women had smoothed out their differences and were now fast friends.

At least Arsinoë is happy! I thought.

"Cleopatra?" Antony asked, interrupting my reading.

"Her letter contains nothing new of importance to the empire. She says she is happy at last," I said.

"Happy? I am delighted," Antony said, his eyes sparkling momentarily. "Cleopatra, if she is truly happy, would you object to reading me the letter?" he asked. "I would like to hear something truly positive in our daughter's words."

"Not at all," I replied, and began reading, translating the missive from Egyptian to Latin.

Antony listened, looking increasingly satisfied. Then he smiled. "She was destined for Parthia. If Rome cannot own Parthia, it can at least be ruled by our youngest girl." When I finished reading, we embraced warmly, once again counting ourselves among the blessed.

Selene and Juba appeared in Rome for a visit shortly after, and Antony and I got to meet our namesakes, Ptolemy Antony and Cleopatra IX.

Cleopatra IX was a beautiful baby, looking the most like me of any of my descendants. She had my nose, my skin color and my eyes. I was very pleased and so stated.

Amidst these moments of delight, however, there loomed a cloud of darkness. Antony's illness had begun to insidiously reassert itself. The signs were subtle at first: tiring more easily, refusing food, fussing over nonsense. He was nearing sixty, and few men lived that long. He had been blessed with an additional prolongation of life, but I felt he could leave me at any moment, which made every minute we had together precious.

"I am getting old, Cleopatra," Antony, lying beside me, said one night in late summer with a sigh. "And I have melancholy. I have asked the gods over and over to take it or me, but for some reason both remain."

"Antony, you are all but a god. You must believe that you are here for a reason," I said.

"Yes. And I *will* continue to rule together with you, until death finally takes me. I trust that when my soul departs, Caesarion will assume Imperatorship and see to finishing our dream of a single empire with him as Emperor. Cleopatra, let's not lie to each other. I have been given a second life, but it is already fading, and I am soon to die. When I do, I worry about you."

"With Caesarion in Rome, I can rule Egypt and all its possessions. I have done so before. Our dreams will live," I assured him.

"True and good. Now I feel the need to sleep, Cleopatra."

"But Antony, what of tonight's banquet for Juba and Selene?" I asked.

"I cannot be there, my love," Antony said. "You must be both Queen-Pharaoh and Imperator Caesarion's co-ruler tonight. I need to sleep."

Antony passed on that night, while I was at the banquet. I could tell by the look of satisfaction on his face that the gods were merciful and granted him a peaceful death.

I remained in Rome for the funeral, at which I was publicly honored as Antony's widow. But before the funeral pyre had died, I was informed by messenger of an uprising in Egypt and that Rufio Minor's life was in danger.

"Mother, you cannot leave. Not now. And not in winter," Caesarion said. "Neptune curses those who traverse his waters this time of year!"

"My dear son. If that is so, then I curse Neptune back." I had to go or take the risk of losing everything for which Antony and I had dedicated our lives. Antony was dead. Caesarion, Selene and Arsinoë's positions were solid. There was nothing to keep me in Rome any longer.

Chapter Thirty-Three

Cleopatra Defender

12 B.C

Year 39 of Cleopatra's reign

Alexandria

I traveled by the quickest available palanquin to Ostia, the chill Roman winter wind clutching at me through the sheer curtains. Iras shivered next to me. Charmion had died in Rome during Saturnalia and, by her wish, she, too, had been cremated. I left her ashes at the Temple of Isis in Rome. She had died the day after Antony, affording me a double portion of grief, increased by my not being able to be there for her funeral.

The voyage took six weeks instead of the usual three or four. The whole trip, the waves surged heavily back and forth, and the skies were a constant dark grey. Jupiter frequently saw fit to toss lightning bolts at the ship. Several times they struck the mast but didn't shatter it. I took the lightening as an omen of things in Alexandria and the ship's survival as an indication that Isis was and would continue protecting me.

When at last I landed in Alexandria, I decided to travel to my palace anonymously until I could assess the situation. As I was carried in my curtained litter through my city, I heard cries of, "Death to the Roman lapdogs!" and "Kill the killers of Cleopatra!"

'Killers of Cleopatra'? Should I reveal myself? I wondered, fearing if I were to do to so, an angry mob might not recognize me and be my death. The palace was shrouded in ocean mist and hundreds of people were gathered there, Greeks in white chitons, Arabs in flowing robes, Egyptians in short skirts, and Jews in colorful robes were chanting loudly in unison their hatred of Rome and anger at what definitely sounded like my death. Standing on the bottom steps of the palace entrance was a horrified Rufio Minor.

One man surged from the crowd. I could not make out his features, but watched in shock as he drew a knife and lunged at Rufio Minor. "You killed our Queen!" he shouted.

The crowd spurred him on. "Die, you dirty Roman!

I had heard enough to decide that I had to reveal myself. Stepping out of the curtained litter, I cried, "Silence! Your Queen-Pharaoh stands before you!"

Shocked into silence, the mob turned its rabid attention from Rufio Minor to the harried woman dressed as a Roman widow standing before them. Rufio Minor let out an audible gasp. I could sense that many were suspicious of what they were seeing. At last, one man close to me shouted, "It's her! It's Queen Cleopatra!"

I smiled calmly though I feared for my life, given Rufio Minor's narrow escape. "Of course it's me! You! Lay down your weapons. All of you! And let my regent be."

As I walked toward Rufio Minor, I saw a momentary look in his handsome face I had never seen in a Roman before: abject fear. His toga was torn and he had several bleeding cuts, and I felt pity for this young man who had tried to defend my dynasty to the bitter end. My anger immediately welled towards the man standing next to him who had surged forward to slay him.

"What is your name?" I demanded of the would-be assassin.

The man trembled and dropped the knife; it clanked forlornly onto the marble courtyard floor.

"Having just returned from my husband's funeral in Rome, I am feeling merciful today. Perhaps I will let you live, maybe even let you go free *if* you tell me who you are," I stated.

"I…I am Seti, a priest of Amon-Ra," The man blathered. *The same Ra priests who had troubled me in the past,* I thought. "Very well, Seti. You may go. But you are forbidden to return to your temple," I said.

"But I am Chief Priest!" Seti protested.

This was a surprise to me. When I left Alexandria, Rahotep had been Chief Priest and had sworn loyalty to me. "Chief Priest or not, you are a traitor to Egypt, and I forbid you to return to Ra's temple. I am Queen-Pharaoh and I hereby relieve you of your position. You are from this moment on a slave." I called for the palace guards, who suddenly appeared. "Take him away, And, Seti, you would be wise to do better in your job as a slave."

I ordered Iras out of the litter to tend to Rufio Minor's injuries. While I was attending Antony, Charmion had spent her last days imparting to Iras her innermost secrets of both her medicinals and perfumes. Iras would never exceed Charmion in these areas of expertise, but she was already competent enough to treat Rufio Minor, procuring a mixture of animal fat and lint from a medicinal pouch she had carried with her from Rome. Ordering the guards to disperse the crowd, I turned my attention to exploring my palace and assessing the damage. Walking down the lapis and gilt corridors, it seemed nothing was amiss. Sensing that something was, however, not quite right, I scoured my personal library and noticed several scrolls missing. I couldn't be certain exactly which ones, so I resumed walking my inspection, past the nursery, now empty, with its echoes of giggles, laughter and tiny feet long since gone.

My chamber, no longer that of the Queen but of a singular Queen-Pharaoh, was intact. I threw myself on the bed from which I could see my city and its famous harbor and lighthouse. All seemed well enough, and after posting my rooms and corridors with loyal soldiers I'd brought with me from Rome, I fell into a deep and much needed sleep.

At noon the next day, I summoned Iras before me.

"I passed Rufio Minor in the hallway earlier. You saved his beauty," I praised.

"I...I..." Iras stuttered, then I noticed my old friend trembling, in fact, trembling so much that she dropped the jar of animal fat she had been using to heal Rufio Minor's cuts.

I placed a hand on her arm to steady her. "Iras, you have no need to fear me."

"I am not trembling because of *you,* Cleopatra. I am afraid of the men protecting Rufio Minor. All including the captain of his guard were conspicuously absent when the crowd was confronting him. I do not think he is as wise as his father was," she explained.

Iras was quite intuitive. I nodded my interest and encouraged her to continue speaking.

"I especially fear the Roman captain. He did nothing to stop Seti from attacking him."

"From what you've said, I should fear them as well, Iras, but I as they are Roman soldiers under Rome's command. I must consult Mardian and ask him what to do. That is all I can promise for now," I said.

The next day, I spoke in private with Mardian and Rufio Minor. From the look of my regent, he had suffered more from the encounter than I had first guessed. He kept glancing nervously at his bandages.

"Rufio Minor," I said. "I do not like the men who protect you. Especially the captain of your guard."

"Cornelius?" he asked. "To be truthful, My Queen, neither do I. Father cautioned me about him, but I thought he said that to teach me not to be so trusting."

"I will order him sent back to Rome immediately," Mardian cut in.

"And I will replace the rest of my personal guard immediately," Rufio Minor agreed.

Chapter Thirty-Four

Royal Dilemma

11-10 B.C

Years 40-41 of Cleopatra's Reign

Egypt

As a widow and sole ruler of Egypt, I was quickly sought by unwed kings and their representatives from everyone within the known world. I turned them all down, of course. I still loved and missed Antony. Besides, any new alliance might end up a threat or stumbling block to my dream of a unified empire.

The worst proposal came from King Herod. He had finished rebuilding the second temple in Jerusalem, a magnificent building I had to admire from the sketches shown to me by messengers and travelers. When news of Antony's death reached Judea, Herod came directly to Egypt to court me.

"You and I together could make happen that of which you and Antony only dreamed," Herod proposed, purring like a kitten while licking his lips like a fox.

"He is likely not proposing this in truth," Rufio Minor whispered to me from behind the corner of my throne.

"I know that, Rufio Minor! He would prefer to kidnap or kill me, and take Egypt for himself," I whispered back. But, for a brief moment, I must admit I was tempted. If I consented, I would at last have Judea at the cost of everything for which I had worked. *Isis knew what she was doing, not giving me this land,* I thought to myself.

"Leave my court at once!" I ordered Herod.

"I will do so, Cleopatra," he said in Hebrew, bowing only slightly while backing away, "but remember: A woman widowed cannot rule alone for long."

The threat was obvious. If he could not have me now, he would have my kingdom later.

"He sounded sinister," Rufio Minor stated from behind the throne. "I do not think he will honor you as Antony's widow for long."

David agreed. Having gone to Judea to honor his powerful one-god during Passover, he discovered no better place for his talents than my court.

"That is exactly my fear," I replied.

Rufio Minor inhaled through his teeth and an awkward silence ensued, during which I wondered at his thoughts. It had been over a year since Antony had died, and I had been, in fact, ruling successfully alone during my year of mourning. But as Herod pointed out, I could not remain a mourning widow forever. *Oh Isis, deliver me!*

As if reading my mind, Rufio Minor cleared his throat and quietly asked, "Perhaps you should consider marrying *me*?"

"Impossible!" David and I cried simultaneously. So, this is of what the man was thinking while silent! I stared at him, astounded at his gall!

"My Queen?" Rufio Minor asked a second time, changing from the chief advisor's station behind my throne to my left side as my regent.

David said nothing, and though I reflexively declined, I found myself trying to justify my answer. Try though I did, I could only come up with, "You are so much younger than I. It would be a scandal."

"True. But you survived scandals with your first two husbands," Rufio Minor pointed out.

Again, David said nothing, looking inquisitively from Rufio Minor to me.

"You all too boldly assume there will be a third," I said, although my regent and chief advisor were correct.

"I may be young, but consider the alternatives," he insisted, bowing deeply.

"My alternatives appear to be either remaining a seemingly vulnerable, constantly vexed, widowed queen in a world of aggressive self-serving kings, becoming Herod's toy, or..."

"Exactly," Rufio Minor stated. I had not accepted his proposal, not yet, but the current alternatives were, as he had pointed out, decidedly unpleasant. Besides, to be honest, I liked the young man, even if I did not love him as I had Antony and Caesar.

"Exactly?" David echoed.

"No." I replied, and the conversation, at least for now, ended.

After several more weeks of marriage proposals from the world's royalty ranging from invitations for dalliances to outright threats, in all earnest, I called Rufio Minor aside and said simply, "Yes, I'll marry you." It helped Rufio Minor's cause that Herod had renewed his suit, "resting" five legions of armed men outside Alexandria while he pursued another audience with me. If married, I would be unavailable to Herod, and he would be compelled to return with his men to Judea.

"I do not lie when I say you are attractive," Rufio Minor, pleased, stated.

"Like a Fury, perhaps?" I joked. I wanted to hear him flatter me again. It had been so long since a handsome, strong man of my liking had done so.

While Rufio Minor shook his head in the negative, his face lit with a smile. "Your beauty is like Helen of Troy. Age cannot ravage, and time can never destroy such beauty."

I laughed, though I treasured the praise, and when he placed a hand on my shoulder, to my surprise, I felt desire, though not as I had for Caesar or Antony. This was a deeper, fiercer desire born of a mixture of profound loss and fueled by an increasing sense of loneliness.

This will likely be my last marriage in this life, I thought. "For my own safety, we should marry as soon as possible," I ordered. My people would expect me to remain Queen-Pharaoh of Egypt but would welcome my taking on a consort in order to restore the sacred heavenly duo. As far as being Queen Regnant, I saw no barriers. As a Roman widow, I was legally allowed to marry without the consent of a Roman family or the Senate.

The announcement of our intended betrothal was all that was needed to send Herod back to Judea. Rufio Minor and I were officially married early in the autumn by Egyptian rites, and, as anticipated, scandal there was! Some asked how I could remarry so soon after Antony's death. Some questioned my marrying yet another Roman. I had, however, been careful after my husband's death to continue elevating myself in the Roman mob's eyes as the widow of *two* Roman Caesars, both of whom had declared themselves gods in their own right, and, deceased, most likely were now gods. That, along with presenting myself as Isis incarnate, meant my choice to remarry could never be officially questioned. And now that it was done, I could once again turn my energies to consolidating Egypt and Rome into one empire, with a consort-regent at my side. To further accomplish this, I turned to Selene and Juba.

There remained the question of how to fold outlying countries into the titular empire I was now firmly recommitted to building. I had asked Caesarion's opinion awhile back in Rome while Antony was still alive. Caesarion foresaw the adjoining of smaller nations to Egypt and Rome as a prelude to the final consolidation of Rome and Egypt. This had been, in essence, my first husband, his father's approach to building a Roman empire. Having witnessed the result, Antony and I had taken the opposite tack of bringing Egypt and Rome together into one, then adding outlying nations.

"As far as adjoining Egypt and Rome, you have positioned my sister and her daughters to rule Egypt," Caesarion had said, "and Antony has positioned me and my sons to rule Rome. I will *never* deprive Selene or her line of their destiny, but am committed, when the time comes, to rule our joined nations, together. Juba, I believe, will bring Mauretania and Numidia to the empire; their marriage having been the first step, and this will be the foundation upon which the empire later will grow." This was quite a contrast to what I had had to do to seize, retain and prepare Egypt. *O Isis! Forgive me for what I have done to my siblings!*

Juba and Selene arrived in Octobrus, sailing just ahead of the winter storms. I felt ecstatic seeing them again. Selene was dressed Egyptian style in a translucent white chiton and wore a gold cobra coiled about her right forearm. Her eyes were deeply kohled. Juba was dressed Roman style in a purple toga with a gold embroidered border. Together, the two were the re-embodiment of Cleopatra and Caesar. Observing Selene was like watching myself in a mirror. Selene clapped her hands and a servant brought forward a jeweled box, which she opened and presented to me. Inside was the twin to Selene's cobra armlet.

"A gift to you and your daughter, Great One, commissioned by the noble Antonius Caesar on his last visit to Mauretania," Juba explained.

So like Antony, I thought, tears suddenly welling, *gifting me even after death*. Rufio Minor was a much-needed comfort, but he could never be to me what Caesar or Antony had been. While I was admiring the bracelet and reliving my past with my beloved Antony, two giggling children ran from behind Selene and Juba, and stopped abruptly before me, looking up at me with wide eyes in wonder. My twin grandchildren were now almost five.

Selene reached out and nudged them forward into my opening arms, and I felt myself glowing with pride that only a mother can truly understand. I suddenly felt years younger and prolonged the embrace as long as I could.

Ptolemy Antony and Cleopatra IX eventually wriggled their way out and began running after each other as children do. I embraced Selene, then Juba, and noted how fondly he watched his son.

Running after her brother, Cleopatra IX seemed to me the bolder of the two. It was she who broke off the chase to look at the view from my porch. Selene was always bolder than Helios. *O Isis! Please protect my children and grandchildren!* I cried in my heart.

"Where are the dolphins, Mother?" Cleopatra IX asked, scouring the distant harbor.

"There are no dolphins this close to shore, Cleopatra," Selene explained. I turned toward Selene at the sound of my name, then quickly realized she was talking to her daughter and not me.

"I want to see dolphins!" Cleopatra IX said, pouting.

"There were plenty to see on the voyage here, but you were too seasick to care then," Ptolemy Antony said, arms on his hips, to his sister.

"Enough talk of dolphins," Juba said matter-of-factly. "The Great Queen-Pharaoh, your grandmother, brought us here to discuss the fate of nations. Ptolemy, Cleopatra, you have had your amusement for the day.

There is a room next to this one that I believe you will find interesting." He pointed towards the open doorway at the far end of my room that led into the nursery. "You can wander the docks in search of dolphins with your mother and grandmother another time."

Ptolemy Antony and Cleopatra IX ran into the nursery, but after a short while, Selene and Juba insisted they be brought to the throne room so they could listen to our discussions. I approved. Children are never too young to begin learning statecraft.

Mardian joined us, as did Rufio Minor. I sat on my throne, which I noticed Selene eye covetously, while everyone assembled about me.

"Juba," I began. "You are King and ruler of Mauretania. I always thought this would be a strategic advantage for Egypt, and today, I believe, will begin to prove me right. Would you have Selene not just as queen of Mauretania, but as a High Queen?"

"Great One, I do not understand your question. If you are referring to her Egyptian rights, there is no law stating that my wife cannot be both Queen to the King of Mauretania and next Queen-Pharaoh of Egypt," Juba stated, "and I think that the daughter of Cleopatra the Great would accept nothing less. Am I correct, Wife?"

"You are correct, Husband." Selene stated.

I beamed with pride. Caesarion had pleased me greatly when he had joined my and Antony's plan to build a single world empire; now my daughter and her husband were doing the same. "So, now we must discuss this," I replied. "Juba, I wish you and Selene to continue to rule Mauretania. To your kingdom, my son, Caesarion, Imperator of Rome, will add Numidia. Egypt shall remain mine until the day my name is engraved on the pyramids and I go to Isis," I said.

"As it should be," Rufio Minor said with a flirtatious glance in my direction that did not go unnoticed by Juba and Selene.

"And I agree, Cleopatra," Juba said. "This is a good arrangement, one I believe would have pleased Great Antony as well. I thank you on behalf of myself and my Queen."

Having all but built the foundation for the empire, this was the perfect time to bring up my marriage to Rufio Minor, which I did, carefully employing all my diplomatic skills. To my surprise, Selene and Juba accepted the situation without objection. Rufio Minor was not only handsome and loyal, but also very congenial. Having him "officially" at my side not only gave me great pleasure, but it made me feel more complete.

Selene and Juba departed the following week. My two grandchildren had constantly entertained me, further uplifting my spirits, and, as the week progressed, I began to see already in Cleopatra IX the making of a true Egyptian Queen-Pharaoh.

Immediately after they left, I received a scroll from Arsinoë. These days, she and I corresponded often, of which I was particularly grateful. She said she had successfully born twins—the women in my family seem adept at producing twins. Phraataces named the boy Phraates after his father, and Arsinoë named the girl Cleopatra Berenice after me and my sister. She also said that her father-in-law, old King Phraates had taken ill, and that soon she and her husband would alone rule Parthia. On a much graver note, she wrote that Herod was showing signs of madness.

"He is not ill in body, but in mind," Arsinoë wrote. "When Philadelphos passed through Jerusalem on his way to Damascus, Herod toasted him in a banquet held in his honor. Philadelphos was shocked when, touching his goblet to his lips, he tasted raw blood instead of wine. It was, he later learned, the blood of a swine, something absolutely anathema in Judea. I believe that father was unwise to place any trust at all in this man. In fact, I would not call him a man, but neither could I call him an animal, animals being by nature innocent. This man is the embodiment of evil. I believe his treatment of Philadelphos was aimed at you. I remember what you said years ago: 'I'd rather be Herod's pig than his wife'."

Arsinoë's letter made me think of Herod, something I hadn't done since taking Rufio Minor as consort. Herod had written me several times after I announced my plan to marry Rufio Minor, I assume before receiving Philadelphos, asking for an alliance between Egypt and Judea and offering himself as a second consort. I tore the letters into shreds before finishing them. Herod was no friend of mine, nor would he ever be such. I could hide my disgust for this monster no longer, especially after his insult to my son, Philadelphos.

"In his moments of madness, he appears frightened, almost terrified, and actually becomes kind, or so the Judeans say," Rufio Minor said.

"Kind?" I asked, puzzled by Rufio Minor's statement, but he would say nothing more.

Shortly thereafter, I heard that Herod had fallen sick in body as well! But shortly later that he had recovered his physical health and taken it as a sign from the Jewish god with the unspeakable name that he alone was destined to rule the world. *O' Isis, how much better for us all if he had died!* On a whim, I thought to ask his god to strike him down. The gods of Egypt would not care if I prayed to this 'YHWH' and what harm could it do anyway?

God of the Hebrews, strike this man down! I silently begged. I had never prayed to the Hebrew god, but after I made my petition, a strong wind blew through my palace. I took it as a sign that the Hebrew god did not care for Herod, either. I laughed at this and thanked Isis! Even

Herod's own god hated him and preferred Cleopatra!

A month later, I received word that Herod had "pardoned" me, and was offering me forgiveness for all my past transgressions against him. *Him* pardon *me?* I thought in anger, a day later, thinking, *but two can play this game.* I decided to accept his pardon and agreed to forgive him of his sins against me just to see what he would say.

After writing my reply, I asked David to review my Hebrew. "You would dally with Herod?" David asked in horror.

"I haven't implied any form of alliance, have I?" I asked my old friend. "I merely said that I have decided to show him mercy. He is not my enemy, but neither would I ally with that odious creature."

My messenger said when Herod read the letter he first wept, then afterward reviled my name loudly before his court and did not bother me again for several years, thank the gods!

In the spring of the next year, Rufio Minor and I decided to repeat the voyage my former husbands and I had taken up the Nile so long ago. By now my desire for my third husband had awakened to love, and I wanted to re-experience, with him at my side, the Nile and the full glory of Egypt.

When we viewed the pyramids, our heart rejoiced together.

"They will stand until the world ends," I said of them.

"They and Egypt, my Queen-Pharaoh and Wife," Rufio Minor replied.

On this brief but happy voyage what pleased me most was witnessing the priests of Ra carve my name onto each of the three Great Pyramids. "Cleopatra the Great, Lady of the Two Lands, Incarnation of Isis, Queen of the East, Noble wife of Gaius Julius Caesar and Imperator Marcus Antonius. Mother of Kings, beloved of Egypt and the world," Rufio Minor read. It was inscribed in Egyptian, Greek, and Latin.

"You are the greatest queen Egypt and the world will ever know," Rufio Minor said fondly. He truly did adore me, and I would spend these last years of my life as a joyous woman.

Chapter Thirty-Five

Cleopatra Victorious
10-2 B.C
Years 40-48 of Cleopatra's Reign
Egypt and the World

Though I sensed the years of my life coming to an end, the gods were still not done testing me.

First, Mardian died – peacefully, in his sleep – and with his passing, I had to let go of yet another protector, this one, military. Then, Iras passed not even a month after him. Though old, her death was not pleasant. She was bitten in the foot by a snake that had somehow found its way into the palace. Hearing her screams, the palace guards took her to the royal physician, who tried to suck the poison out of the wound, but to no avail. She died in agony in my lap. My oldest and perhaps dearest friend was dead.

As if this were not enough, David, my loyal tutor and intellectual friend, returned to Judea to spend his remaining days among his own, exchanging letters with me until the end.

There were, however, joys among the losses.

Philadelphos, cursed in Egypt and Numidia, proved blessed in Syria. He established good control over his subjects and rebuilt Antioch to be much like Alexandria: a mixture of the best the Syrians, Romans,

Egyptians and Greeks had to offer. Philadelphos had married a Syrian woman named Zaida. She was not overly beautiful, but she loved him dearly and was fertile, eventually bearing him three sons. From what he wrote, I ascertained she was also wise. I was glad that my youngest and most troubled had at last found his place in the world.

Antonia, Antony's only daughter from his marriage to Fulvia, married King Artaxias of Armenia and thereby became a Queen by her own right. Although the king she married was eventually replaced by another of Caesarion's choice, she quickly married the king Caesarion appointed, Tigranes III, and she, like Philadelphos, found her place in history.

In Parthia, Musa now ruled unchallenged, her actions both astonishing and disgusting me. Though Arsinoë had taken her as a friend and confidant, that friendship had soured over Phraataces' adoration of my daughter over her, and Musa suddenly one day, out of pure spite, killed all her grandchildren. Upon discovering Musa's crime, Arsinoë fled the capital, Parthaunisa, for her life. What happened to Phraataces is still anyone's guess. It was as if he disappeared from the face of the Earth.

I still ruled in Alexandria, and increasingly thought of my poor Helios, who I assumed was in the Vault of Heaven in Isis all-encompassing arms and wondered if I would soon be reunited with him.

It was during these twilight years that I realized Antony and my dream of a single empire was not to be, at least not within either of our lifetimes. Like Alexander, the Fates declared it. It was during this time that I noticed from my porch a new star appearing in the heavens. I first saw it twinkling at dusk above and to the right of the Lighthouse while searching the watery horizon for what, I knew not. Initially, I was convinced the star was in my imagination, then maybe that it was Antony's or Helios' soul calling out to me. But Rufio Minor, entering my room, shook his head in the negative. "No, it is not in your imagination, Dear One, for I see it, too," he said lovingly.

"Many years ago, three Parthian Magi prophesied about it." I replied. "They said it would herald a new world. I thought perhaps they meant the empire that Antony and I were planning. Just before Antony left this world, I mentioned their prophesy to David, and he said it would be a sign that a new Jewish king, the long-awaited Messiah, would be born! What a pleasant thought, don't you think, Rufio, that I might finally be rid of Herod and his antics, once and for all?"

Rufio Minor laughed with me, but there was an edge to his laughter.

The star burned brighter for each of several subsequent days, then, visible even in daylight, persisted for weeks. I visited the Museion and spoke with my Egyptian astronomers. They confirmed it was a star being born, but were divided about its further significance.

"The gods are likely angry about something," a well-regarded visiting Chaldean astronomer offered. "The Jews say it means their Messiah is being born, but there has been no word of a royal birth anywhere."

True, I thought, but even so, the Chaldeans were known for their pessimistic outlook on life. In the corner of my eye, I noticed a Hebrew rabbi in conversation with a Greek astronomer and walked over to listen to their debate.

"Over Bethlehem?" the Greek snorted. "Bethlehem isn't even a hamlet. No king would ever come from there…"

"I have heard of this Bethlehem," I interrupted.

"I cannot imagine that, Great One. It is of utter insignificance," the

Greek reaffirmed, bowing before me.

Turning to the Rabbi, I asked, "Was there not a story in your Torah about a woman named Ruth finding shelter and being welcomed among your people in this city of Bethlehem?" I knew well the stories of the Hebrews from my discussions with David, and the tale of Ruth was a particularly beautiful love story. The rabbi ignored my question about Ruth but did answer my question about Bethlehem.

"Its name, Queen of Kings, means 'house of bread.' *Jerusalem* is our city towards which one should direct his or her attention if the star truly foretells the birth of a king," The rabbi explained.

"And what exactly are your people saying about the messiah these days?" the astronomer asked.

"It is said a new King of Kings will arise—pardon me, Great One—to free Judea from Roman rule," the Hebrew replied cautiously. "This king is supposed to herald in an era of universal peace and forgiveness."

"Forgiveness? Forgiveness is a good thing," I said. "Julius Caesar practiced forgiveness throughout his reign. Isis encourages it as well."

"And, forgive me Great Queen, look what it got your beloved first Caesar: Twenty-three knives in the back," the Chaldean astronomer, overhearing our conversation, said sarcastically from a distance. Though the event was now in the distant past, when brought up by this insolent man, I felt as though the knives in Caesar's back were now planted in mine, so deep both his comment and the event pained me. I frowned and practiced with difficulty my royal forgiveness for his ill-worded assertion. We wisely spoke no more of the mysterious King of Kings.

The star continued burning brightly for many months and was eventually accepted as a sign of the gods' universal goodwill. During this time, I received good news from Arsinoë. Musa had died under mysterious circumstances, and Arsinoë and her husband were once again ruling Parthia. Things in general seemed to be getting better, but I was aging fast, so I summoned Juba and Selene back to Alexandria. This time, they would stay.

Selene and Juba arrived at the end of Septembrus. The star was still visible in the sky, but rapidly diminishing in brilliance. Selene and Juba arrived at my palace around dusk. Both their children, Cleopatra IX and Ptolemy Antony—my twin grandchildren—were twelve years old now. Despite his age, Ptolemy Antony was uncommitted in marriage, though his twin sister was already being pursued by suitors from throughout the world. Selene, however, said that, as I had done for her, she would wait an extra year before deciding on a husband for Cleopatra IX, wanting her to, first, have the opportunity of seeing and experiencing her homeland, Egypt, and, second, get to know me better. Thus, she came to Alexandria with her parents, while Ptolemy Antony remained behind in Mauretania.

I stood before my people, Rufio Minor at my side, watching from the wayside as my Egyptian honor guard escorted the first of the three from their ship. Selene was dressed in a sunburst chiton with gold cobra earrings, armlets and bracelets, proud symbols of Egypt. She wore minimal cosmetics, in keeping with Roman custom, but had brilliant white pearls woven into her loose, jet-black hair, which would have been considered scandalous in Rome.

Next came Juba in his usual gold-embroidered, purple toga. I noticed as he exited the gangplank that though his eyes were still young and bright, he was starting to bald. Streaks of grey in his temples and braided beard, however, made him look even more distinguished than last I'd seen him.

My granddaughter, Cleopatra Minor, walked beside him. Dressed

343

in an unadorned white cotton chiton and leather sandals, she resembled more her Romanized Berber father than Selene. Her skin had grown darker than her mother's but was still lighter than her father's, somewhere between a native Egyptian and a Semitic nomad. I found it becoming. She wore golden ankh earrings and had kohled her eyes, as every Egyptian princess should. She was busy taking in all the sights about her as if this was the first time she'd seen Alexandria. Her gangly youthfulness suggested she hadn't yet lost her love of running.

Rufio Minor and I greeted them warmly amidst shouts and cheers from the crowd.

"Mother," Selene said, approaching and hugging me. "You look concerned. Is there something worrying you?"

"You may say it, Selene," I sighed. I have grown old."

"Which means I will soon be required to serve as Queen-Pharaoh of Egypt in your stead. Mother, I am not ready, yet," Selene said. She tried to sound bold, but being her mother, I could tell she was frightened.

"Egypt already belongs to you," I said softly. "Now, come. And you as well, little Cleopatra." Cleopatra IX had left her father's side to play in the water.

We five walked together to the palace down the causeway lined with cheering people, but barely halfway there, I felt exhausted and my bones began aching. I attributed the former to my age, but the latter to the darkening clouds above us signaling the development of an unusually intense summer storm, which began in earnest later that night.

In the palace, after more pleasantries: I invited them to the banquet room where I had had an array of Egyptian and Mauritanian dishes laid out for them. Trusting them into Rufio Minor's care, I went at once to bed, where I had an attendant massage my arms and legs with almond oil, for they ached so. Despite this, I felt eminently satisfied. While

Antony and my dream of a unified empire hadn't come to fruition, my hopes with Julius Caesar had. Egypt was once again a powerful nation, almost an empire in its own right, and was a solid friend and ally of Rome, whose might under my and Julius' son, Caesarion, continued to steadily grow. All of my sweet children were now kings and queens, except for poor dead Helios. I had many grandchildren and the possibility of me living to see a great-grandchild was not entirely out of the question. I slept that night very soundly, to be awaked next morning by my granddaughter.

"Grandmother? Grandmother?" she was saying, shaking my shoulder lightly, her voice betraying concern that I might not awaken.

I opened a sleepy eye.

"Grandmother! Mother wants you in the throne room!"

"My daughter is not *yet* Queen-Pharaoh of Egypt," I murmured, my irritation finally waking me.

It took me longer to bathe and dress now that I was sixty-five and no longer had Charmion or Iras to serve me. Given the urgency in my granddaughter's "command," I decided not to bother with cosmetics. Nonetheless, I arrived in the throne room as dressed as a proper Queen-Pharaoh. Selene and Juba were talking with several ambassadors from Parthia.

"My mother, Queen-Pharaoh of Egypt," Selene announced as I entered.

I yawned sleepily, then forced myself to focus, and immediately recognized one of the men. It was Melchior the Magi.

He bowed low. "Queen of Queens, Great Cleopatra," he said.

"To which Cleopatra are you referring?" I joked, for there were indeed three women there who could answer to that name.

"The great woman who still rules Egypt and commands the world, of course," Melchior replied, visibly shaken by my humor. "Great One, I come with news from your beloved daughter in Parthia."

"A letter?" I asked.

"Queen Arsinoë does not wish to send letters at this time, and instead sent me with a message for her mother."

"Speak, Melchior," I ordered.

"Arsinoë wishes her beloved mother to know that all is well in Parthia, and that she has been researching the star in the sky."

With that, I became completely awake and alert. "Has she? I have been as well," I said.

"Yes. A male infant was born in Bethlehem, directly under the star, and is being hailed there as the future King of the Jews. He was overlooked entirely, being born in a cave used to stable animals."

"Kings are not born in caves, Melchior. Surely you must be mistaken," I said, though I knew as a mother that babies came when they came, and a royal baby was no different.

"I do not believe so. My two colleagues and I traveled there and saw him with our own eyes," Melchior said.

"So, this new King of the Jews, will he overthrow my nemesis, King Herod?" I asked.

"I believe so, Your Majesty," Melchior replied. "More important many Judeans as well as the Queen of Parthia, your daughter, believe so. Thus, she summoned me to personally convey this news."

"Interesting," I said. "Have you more to share?"

"Merely, Great One, that at hearing of the infant-king's birth, Herod went raving mad. As bizarre as it may sound, he's blaming the child's appearance on you and is threatening to kill you and all your offspring," Melchior said.

O Isis? Would Herod's madness never end? "It does not matter,

Melchior, if he kills *me*," I said. "I'm old; I've lived most of my destiny. But Selene is the future of Egypt and along with my other children, the future of the world. They must be protected at all costs."

"Indeed, Honorable Queen-Pharaoh. When Herod threatened death to your family, our Parthian King and Queen immediately sent me along with a contingent of our fiercest and most loyal Parthian guards here to protect you."

Rufio Minor frowned.

"In addition to your Egyptian and Roman legions, of course," Melschior immediately appended.

"Herod is even now being punished by the Furies," I said matter-of-factly.

"Yet madmen often prove the most dangerous, Mother," Selene added soberly.

"Will you accept Parthia's gift?" Melchior asked, looking from me to Rufio Minor and back.

"The Parthians are fierce warriors, and if, as you say, these are the fiercest and most loyal of all, I would be a fool not to accept them," I mused.

Rufio Minor nodded his agreement. "I will personally check out each guardsman. They can form a first barrier to any unauthorized intruders, with my Romans forming a second and your Egyptians an innermost. Anything else?"

"That is all," Melchior replied. "May the light of Ahura Mazda shine upon you and yours forever."

Two months passed without incident, months which I savored together with my daughter, granddaughter and my daughter's husband-in-law. I once again had a family about me, though I knew my end was near.

I was growing weaker every day, feeling in my bones the creeping shadow of Anubis, so I officially delegated the government to Selene to rule as regent until my death. Then, sensing the end of my life fast approaching, I asked for one last tour of my beloved Alexandria. I would travel in a litter, with the curtains open. I especially wanted to see the harbor, the Museion, Alexanders' tomb, the Lighthouse and Antony's monument.

I was carried by four Egyptian slaves flanked by four Roman centurions surrounded by two columns of Parthians in full military dress. I dressed as Isis this one last time, wearing the golden double-crown of Egypt, carrying the crook and flail in my hands.

It was an unusually cool day and the sea breezes felt brisk. I first passed by my completed tomb where my loyalist of servants, Charmion and Iras, lay awaiting me. I got out and prayed briefly before their sarcophagi, and ordered incense burnt to Isis for their souls. Then I shuddered, remembering my murder of my siblings, and I asked Isis to allow me to pass the feather test and that Ma'at would judge me to have been a merciful and just ruler in spite of my mistakes. If not...well, I tried not to think of that. I still had some time left, and I wanted savor the sweetness of life to the end.

Climbing back into my litter, I was carried through the Library and Museion. I tried to get out of the litter, but my joints ached so much that when Rufio Minor tried to help me out, I had to refuse.

"Perhaps it is time to return to the Palace," Rufio Minor suggested out of concern.

I shook my head in the negative. "No, dear Rufio. My time is close but there is more to see before I am satisfied to leave this world."

Just before I left the Library, I was given the Egyptian Book of the Dead by the conservator, a native Egyptian who wept openly as he presented it to me. "What will Egypt do without you? I fear the gods may abandon us!"

I turned to him, still aching, whether from bodily pain or heartache, I didn't know and said for all to hear, "You need have no fear. My daughter Selene will rule. You may trust in my choice."

Extremely tired from even so little exertion, I asked to be taken by the Lighthouse and Harbor on my way back to the palace. I could feel Isis whispering to me, as she had when I was a young queen. She was saying I would miss something particularly important if I returned home before sunset.

It was already late afternoon and the sun, the body of Ra, was resting blood-red on the horizon before completing its descent into the underworld for the night. There he would board his *Mesketet*—his evening barge—to journey through the *Duat*—the dark underworld—to the other side of the world, to rise again the next day. The lighthouse flame was already burning brightly, and the harbor, despite the lateness, was lively. Continuing along the pier, I noticed an odd sight. A husband and wife, by their dress Judean Jews, talking openly with a small boy, who I assumed, was their son.

The boy could not have been more than two years old, but carried himself with the air of someone considerably older. He reminded me of Caesarion at the age when Caesar had been cruelly taken from me. This boy, though, held a dead dove in his hand. *Why would anyone wish to touch a dead bird?* I wondered.

"Stop," I ordered, tired to the point that my voice was barely a whisper. "I wish to observe this boy." Rufio Minor, who was walking beside my litter, repeated my order to the litter bearers. As I watched, an interesting thing happened. The boy stroked the dove gently and it shuddered, then flew into the sky, far away, seemingly into the last rays of the setting sun.

"He healed it!" I said.

Rufio Minor, too, was impressed. "If I hadn't seen it with my own eyes, I would not believe it. Such power in but a small boy. Who is he, I wonder?"

"A boy with, as you said, great power," I stated. Then in a voice surprisingly strong, I recited, *"And by his age, he has yet to ascend to his full power, which he will wield for only a short time before joining the gods."* As I spoke, a vision was given me by Isis of the boy as a young man. He looked strong, though his body was bloody and beaten and his countenance sad, being abandoned by all except the boy's mysterious father and mother who were suddenly holding him, dying, in their arms. *O' Isis! Have mercy!* I my heart cried. Then the vision vanished.

The boy's parents, noticing the royal litter and myself watching them from inside, turned and bowed deeply, while the man said in Hebrew, "She is righteous among nations to allow us and our son refuge here in Alexandria."

I looked from him into the eyes of the woman, and I thought to myself that although this woman was wearing the garb of a peasant, her face was of that of a goddess. It seemed to me to be glowing even brighter than Isis. *Oh Isis, is this blasphemy to see such in the face of a mere mortal?* The woman bowed again before me and I ordered her to speak.

"Your Majesty. Thank you for granting me, my husband and my son refuge from Herod here in Alexandria. You are more than merciful; may our god abundantly bless you, yours and Egypt as well, " she stated.

"I do not know you, but I am glad Egypt can be a land of safety for you and yours, " I said, adding, "and for your god with the unpronounceable name as well. Please tell me how you came to be here."

The man, her husband, shook his head back and forth, as if warning her not to answer, but, looking steadily in my eyes, she did anyway. "We fled our home when Herod ordered all male children in the province of Judea under the age of two slaughtered."

"I had not heard of this, but it does not surprise me." I said, anger seizing me. I took a closer good look at the boy that the woman now held tightly in her arms.

"I would speak for a moment with your son," I said.

Both parents hesitated, but then she pushed the young boy towards my litter.

"What is your name?" I asked the boy in Hebrew.

"Yeshua," he replied, curtly but courteously, approaching me without fear. The boy who had healed the dove, reached forward and began playing with the string of pearls I was wearing about my neck. I smiled, reminded of young Caesarion having once done the same, now the absolute ruler of Rome.

"He reminds me of my Caesarion at that age." I said, my eyes tearing at the memories of the past. The woman smiled, and I knew we had bonded for just a moment. A messenger appeared, and I passed Yeshua back to his parents so that I alone would hear what the messenger had to say.

"Great Queen. Good news. Herod is dead."

"Thank the gods!" I shouted. "I have outlived the sly fox after all!"

Rufio and the family I had just been talking with couldn't help but overhear my exclamation. "Thank the Lord," the woman said. "Husband, we can return home now."

"If that is your desire, I wish you blessings and a safe journey," I said, "but if you should decide to stay in Egypt like your prophet Moses did, you and your family will also have my blessings and protection," I said, signaling to Rufio Minor to provide them with enough money to make either happen, as my litter bearers lifted me and I began my own journey home.

Epilogue

Cleopatra Victorious

2 B.C.

Year 48 of Cleopatra VII's Reign, which is also Year 1 of Cleopatra
VIII's Reign

The Vault of Nut

Queen-Pharaoh Cleopatra VII Thea Philopater, Empress of the
South and East, wife of Julius and Antonius Caesar, the divine
incarnation of the goddess Isis, who had saved Egypt and elevated it
above all other nations on the earth, clung to life for yet another month
after her memorable last tour of Alexandria.

On the Ides of Antonius, Isis looked down from the Vault of Nut as
Cleopatra breathed her last. Athena, beside Isis, looked down in with a
mixture of pride and sadness. The two of them, different as they had
been, had grown to love the now dead Queen during the years of their
guidance. Isis watched Cleopatra's body being prepared for embalming
in the memorial the Queen had prepared for herself, while her spirit
went before Ma'at, the stern goddess of justice. Would she pass the
feather test? Isis held no doubts in her heart, but it was Ma'at alone who
would judge her, and Isis was powerless while she watched and waited
for Ma'at to decide.

The situation did not look good. In spite of the fact that this seventh Cleopatra had elevated Egypt to its greatest, Ma'at scowled at the former Queen's murders of her siblings. Isis watched in trepidation as Cleopatra's heart was placed on one side of the scale, and a single, pure white feather on the other.

Ma'at finally spoke. "Cleopatra VII Thea Philopater, beloved daughter of Pharaoh Ptolemy XII 'Auletes' Neos Dionysos, as the fated Queen-Pharaoh of Egypt, you did what was necessary to fulfill your destiny. And while you did wrong, the right you did for all far outweighs the wrong. You were a loyal and loving wife to three husbands, even though at times your husbands did not repay that loyalty. You were a devoted mother and strove to make certain your children as well as your spiritual children, Egyptians everywhere in the world, prospered and were safe. You watched over them like no other monarch in your dynasty. Cleopatra VII Thea Philopater, I admit you directly to the heavenly host to join those who love you."

Isis smiled and spread out her winged robe to welcome her.

Cleopatra arrived at the Vault of Nut in the midst of a celebration of joy. *Is that not Julius Caesar talking with Venus, his goddess, in the far corner? And on the portico, is that not my dear Marcus Antonius squatting and talking with Helios? And is that not the goddess Athena smiling protectively at both?* Cleopatra wondered as she ran across the portico to embrace her parents. As she approached them, Berenice, the one sister who she'd truly loved, caught her in her arms and hugged her lovingly.

"Mother!" Helios cried, suddenly seeing her.

"Dear Sister," Berenice cried, tears of joy streaming from her face.

"Cleopatra!" Julius Caesar and Marc Antony both exclaimed warmly.

"My Lady!" Charmion, Iras, Mardian, and Olympos exclaimed,

appearing from the far corner of the portico.

Cleopatra looked on all the people standing before her whom she had adored and lost. Then all bowed as one before Isis, as she approached in all her resplendent glory. "Salutations, Dearest Cleopatra," she beamed, holding her arms out and receiving her favored devotee. "Indeed, child. Welcome home at last," she murmured, encompassing all there under her protective wings. "Welcome home at last."

If you enjoyed CLEOPATRA VICTORIOUS, consider the Helen R. Davis' prequel, CLEOPATRA UNCONQUERED:

The first book of three in a richly imagined ancient world where the course of history is altered by one battle. In this world, Antony and Cleopatra triumph at the Battle of Actium, and Cleopatra emerges as a queen, stateswoman, and politician. Those around her come to life as the reader returns to those days to live them with her.

About the Author

Multi-award-winning author, editor and poet **Helen R. Davis** has a long interest in history, religion, politics, and all nations. She has studied the ancient world through the gift of books since a very young age, her passion for this era kindled long ago. She has also researched and studied many other times and eras and has a passion for strong women who have governed nations from the past to the present.

Author website at http://HelenDavisBooks.com

Helen R. Davis

If you enjoyed *Cleopatra Victorious*, consider these other fine books from Savant Books:

Essay, Essay, Essay by Yasuo Kobachi
Aloha from Coffee Island by Walter Miyanari
Footprints, Smiles and Little White Lies by Daniel S. Janik
The Illustrated Middle Earth by Daniel S. Janik
Last and Final Harvest by Daniel S. Janik
A Whale's Tale by Daniel S. Janik
Tropic of California by R. Page Kaufman
Tropic of California (the companion music CD) by R. Page Kaufman
The Village Curtain by Tony Tame
Dare to Love in Oz by William Maltese
The Interzone by Tatsuyuki Kobayashi
Today I Am a Man by Larry Rodness
The Bahrain Conspiracy by Bentley Gates
Called Home by Gloria Schumann
Kanaka Blues by Mike Farris
First Breath edited by Z. M. Oliver
Poor Rich by Jean Blasiar
The Jumper Chronicles by W. C. Peever
William Maltese's Flicker by William Maltese
My Unborn Child by Orest Stocco
Last Song of the Whales by Four Arrows
Perilous Panacea by Ronald Klueh
Falling but Fulfilled by Zachary M. Oliver
Mythical Voyage by Robin Ymer
Hello, Norma Jean by Sue Dolleris
Richer by Jean Blasiar
Manifest Intent by Mike Farris
Charlie No Face by David B. Seaburn
Number One Bestseller by Brian Morley
My Two Wives and Three Husbands by S. Stanley Gordon
In Dire Straits by Jim Currie
Wretched Land by Mila Komarnisky
Chan Kim by Ilan Herman
Who's Killing All the Lawyers? by A. G. Hayes
Ammon's Horn by G. Amati
Wavelengths edited by Zachary M. Oliver
Almost Paradise by Laurie Hanan
Communion by Jean Blasiar and Jonathan Marcantoni
The Oil Man by Leon Puissegur
Random Views of Asia from the Mid-Pacific by William E. Sharp
The Isla Vista Crucible by Reilly Ridgell
Blood Money by Scott Mastro
In the Himalayan Nights by Anoop Chandola
On My Behalf by Helen Doan
Traveler's Rest by Jonathan Marcantoni
Keys in the River by Tendai Mwanaka
Chimney Bluffs by David B. Seaburn

Cleopatra Victorious

The Loons by Sue Dolleris
Light Surfer by David Allan Williams
The Judas List by A. G. Hayes
Path of the Templar—Book 2 of The Jumper Chronicles by W. C. Peever
The Desperate Cycle by Tony Tame
Shutterbug by Buz Sawyer
Blessed are the Peacekeepers by Tom Donnelly and Mike Munger
The Bellwether Messages edited by D. S. Janik
The Turtle Dances by Daniel S. Janik
The Lazarus Conspiracies by Richard Rose
Purple Haze by George B. Hudson
Imminent Danger by A. G. Hayes
Lullaby Moon (CD) by Malia Elliott of Leon & Malia
Volutions edited by Suzanne Langford
In the Eyes of the Son by Hans Brinckmann
The Hanging of Dr. Hanson by Bentley Gates
Flight of Destiny by Francis Powell
Elaine of Corbenic by Tima Z. Newman
Ballerina Birdies by Marina Yamamoto
More More Time by David B. Seabird
Crazy Like Me by Erin Lee
Cleopatra Unconquered by Helen R. Davis
Valedictory by Daniel Scott
The Chemical Factor by A. G. Hayes
Quantum Death by A. G. Hayes and Raymond Gaynor
Big Heaven by Charlotte Hebert
Captain Riddle's Treasure by GV Rama Rao
All Things Await by Seth Clabough
Tsunami Libido by Cate Burns
Finding Kate by A. G. Hayes
The Adventures of Purple Head, Buddha Monkey and Sticky Feet by Erik and Forest Bracht
In the Shadows of My Mind by Andrew Massie
The Gumshoe by Richard Rose
In Search of Somatic Therapy by Setsuko Tsuchiya
Cereus by Z. Roux
The Solar Triangle by A. G. Hayes
Shadow and Light edited by Helen R. Davis
A Real Daughter by Lynne McKelvey
StoryTeller by Nicholas Bylotas
Bo Henry at Three Forks by Daniel Bradford
One Night in Bangkok by Keith Rees
Kindred edited by Gary "Doc" Krinberg

Coming Soon
Navel of the Sea by Elizabeth McKague
Talking Story: Storytelling Meets Phenomenology by Jamie Dela Cruz
68 Via Ccondotti: Book 1 - Eternity Ltd by A. G. Hayes
Crowned Rose of York by Carolina Casas

Helen R. Davis

and from our *avant garde* imprint, Aignos Publishing:

The Dark Side of Sunshine by Paul Guzzo
Happy that it's Not True by Carlos Aleman
Cazadores de Libros Perdidos by German William Cabasssa Barber [Spanish]
The Desert and the City by Derek Bickerton
The Overnight Family Man by Paul Guzzo
There is No Cholera in Zimbabwe by Zachary M. Oliver
John Doe by Buz Sawyers
The Piano Tuner's Wife by Jean Yamasaki Toyama
Nuno by Carlos Aleman
An Aura of Greatness by Brendan P. Burns
Polonio Pass by Doc Krinberg
Iwana by Alvaro Leiva
University and King by Jeffrey Ryan Long
The Surreal Adventures of Dr. Mingus by Jesus Richard Felix Rodriguez
Letters by Buz Sawyers
In the Heart of the Country by Derek Bickerton
El Camino De Regreso by Maricruz Acuna [Spanish]
Diego in Two Places by Carlos Aleman
Prepositions by Jean Yamasaki Toyama
Deep Slumber of Dogs by Doc Krinberg
Saddam's Parrot by Jim Currie
Beneath Them by Natalie Roers
Chang the Magic Cat by A. G. Hayes
Illegal by E. M. Duesel
Island Wildlife: Exiles, Expats and Exotic Others by Robert Friedman
The Winter Spider by Doc Krinberg
The Princess in My Head by J. G. Matheny

Coming Soon:
Comic Crusaders by Richard Rose